Catrin Morgan was born an[...] she has drawn on her ow[...] LILY OF THE VALLE[...] THORNS. She has written several contemporary nov[...] under her real name, **Merle Jones**. Her home is now in Anglesey, North Wales.

Also by Catrin Morgan in Futura:

LILY OF THE VALLEYS

CATRIN MORGAN

Lily Among Thorns

Futura

A Futura Book

First published in Great Britain in 1990 by
Macdonald & Co (Publishers) Ltd
London & Sydney
This edition published by Futura Publications in 1991

Printed in Great Britain by
BPCC Hazell Books
Aylesbury, Bucks, England
Member of BPCC Ltd.

ISBN 0 7088 4838 9

Futura Publications
A Division of
Macdonald & Co (Publishers) Ltd
Orbit House
1 New Fetter Lane
London EC4A 1AR

A member of Maxwell Macmillan Pergamon Publishing Corporation

For Joy Hill
The best of friends at
the worst of times

As the lily among thorns, so
is my love among the daughters

Song of Songs
Ch. II v. 2

PART ONE

Take us the foxes, the little foxes,
that spoil the vines;
for our vines have tender grapes.

Song of Songs
Ch. II v. 15

CHAPTER ONE

Abercarn, Monmouthshire
Summer 1920

From the overgrown lane Trwyn Farm looked deceptively well occupied. Orange-gold sunbeams had coaxed some colour back into rain-bleached window frames, and lengthening shadows from the conifer plantation masked the tangle of weeds that had once been a front garden. Closer inspection revealed the extent of the neglect. The old house had been unoccupied for years.

The land agent's yawn was exaggerated. 'I'm sure there are far more profitable investments available to you, Dr Henderson,' he said. 'It's true that we're asking a derisory price, but no one who's looked at current farm incomes would dream of taking on a place like this. It's not worth tying up even such a small capital sum.'

'I'm not particularly interested in immediate returns,' Charles Henderson told him. 'There are other considerations.'

Edward Brunton uttered the mirthless wheeze that was his best attempt at a laugh. 'If you're day-dreaming about a gentleman's retreat for your eventual retirement, old boy, you're really wasting your money. At today's prices you can snap up a house on the Test, with first-class fishing, for half as much again as we're asking for this, and when values recover you'll be sitting on a gold mine in Hampshire.'

Henderson sighed. 'Brunton, are you working for the Llanover Estate, or against it? I want a small farm within easy reach of Abercarn, with plenty of peace and quiet. Neither a portfolio of shares nor a place in Hampshire will be a sensible alternative.'

'It's your money. Three hundred's the lowest we'll go, and that's only because it's been empty for . . . er . . . three years.'

'Now that's a good joke! Look at those window frames, and the cowshed. If this place has been tenanted since well before the war I'll eat my hat.'

Brunton shifted uneasily. 'No, no – I'm not deceiving you. Stretching the truth in the interests of good business, perhaps, nothing worse. It was last tenanted in 1918, but very briefly, I confess. Before that, the place had been empty throughout the war – lack of manpower, you know. We ran sheep on the land, but the house was unused and the outbuildings were only back-up accommodation for livestock in winter.'

'And before that? It looks as if it's been neglected for a couple of decades.'

'It has, in a way. It was a family farm, you see, for genera-tions – literally a couple of hundred years or more. The line died out at the turn of the century, and nobody ever seemed to settle in after that. Too lonely, I suppose. You need family roots in a place like this if you're not going to feel cut off from the world. There must have been at least half-a-dozen tenants since the Jobs. Two winters was the longest anyone ever stayed. That's another thing you should bear in mind. If you're putting in a tenant, make sure he's got a big family to keep him interested. Otherwise he'll be gone in ten minutes.'

Henderson shook his head. 'Man's a bachelor, but take my word, he'll welcome the solitude. He hasn't been happy with his fellow men for some time.' He took another look at the dilapidated building. 'If you've finished trying to talk me out of it, you've made a sale. My solicitor will be in touch within a few days. Now, if you'll drive me back to the Swan, there's some respectable brandy waiting for us.'

Brunton shook his head in resignation. 'Well, at least you'll never be able to say I pulled the wool over your eyes. Come along, then; I need a drink after going over this old ruin.'

As soon as he had got rid of the land agent, Charles Henderson pushed open the door which connected his house with the surgery. The practice's receptionist, Lily Walters, was already in the outer office, sorting patients' records in prepara-tion for the evening session. As usual, her welcoming smile snatched at his heart. No fool like an old fool, he told himself.

But that was nonsense. Who could fail to love Lily? She was a lovely and a most unusual young woman. But remember the word 'young', he thought. Get the romantic notions out of your head and concentrate on just making her happy.

In fact Henderson was fifteen years older than Lily – scarcely an unbridgeable gap, he told himself in optimistic moments. But years of medical practice in the slums of Camden Town, followed by the horrors of being a front-line surgeon in Flanders during the war had aged him before his time, and too often he felt closer to a hundred. Never mind; at least he was in a position to solve the odd problem for her.

'How's brother Billie today?' he asked.

Her smile wavered. 'Oh, all right, I suppose. We mustn't expect too much at first; they said that at the – the hospital. But Mam don't help much.'

'Hmm . . . it had to be the son she'd rejected who turned out to need help. Trust Lady Luck to come up with a twist like that.'

'Mam wouldn't agree she'd rejected him. The way she sees it, he was the one who did the rejecting.'

'As in any human relationship, my Lily, it takes two. What exactly did happen?'

The girl made a dismissive gesture. 'Too long ago now. A lot of water have flowed under the bridge since then . . . wasn't just Billie. Him and John Dan, my eldest brother. Mam haven't got time for either of them no more, not since years before the war.' She contemplated the past for a moment and then seemed to jerk herself out of it. 'Good God, you can tell it's getting at me, can't you? I sound like a proper little *Sioni oi* the way I'm talking.'

Henderson smiled. 'I had noticed you were becoming a little . . . er . . . colloquial. It's quite charming, though. Don't let it worry you.'

'I shan't always be tucked away in the Valleys, and if I ever get out I want to sound like a lady, not a kitchen maid. That means never forgetting.'

'And when were you planning to forsake us?' He hoped his flippant tone concealed the real alarm her remark had generated.

'Oh, this year, next year, some time, never, I suppose!

13

Don't get me wrong, I love this job. But it's a bit different from when I lived in, isn't it? I know I had to go back and stay with Mam once Dad was killed, but I always meant it to be just for a little bit. Now our Billie's home, I can't see me ever getting out. There's too much between them and they'll always need a referee to keep them apart. Sometimes I do think that getting right away from Abercarn will be my only chance.'

'But where would you go?'

'A good question! Nothing for me in Cardiff now our Lexie have gone. That's all changed for the worse an' all. Doesn't seem to be any other possibilities.'

'Then I have a chance of holding on to you?'

She dimpled prettily. 'There was never much of a chance of your getting rid of me, except inside my silly head.'

'In that case we must see what we can do to solve at least some of your problems.'

'That'll be the day! To do that you'd have to bring back our Dad and get rid of Billie – not too likely, is it?' There was no self-pity in her tone. For her, that ended the discussion. She turned back to the tall oak filing cabinet.

Finding nothing to say, Henderson went into his consulting room. Poor Lily! To be offered prospects which seldom arose for girls of her background, then have them dissolve overnight . . . it must be so much harder to adjust to the plough once you'd glimpsed the stars . . .

The doctor had first encountered the Walters family more than nine years before, when he was a young locum in the Abercarn practice and Lily was still a child. Her drunken father had half-killed Lily's eldest sister and Henderson had performed an operation on the kitchen table in the Walters' house to save the girl's life. After that, the family's fate seemed to interweave with his own. He had left Abercarn briefly before joining the RAMC on the outbreak of war in 1914, then had found himself back in the village, this time as a partner in the practice, when he was invalided out by a severe leg wound. Meanwhile Lily had been spirited out of the claustrophobic life of the mining community to her uncle's pub in the brawling depths of Cardiff's Tiger Bay, spending five years there while her sister Rose recovered her shattered health and her parents their shattered marriage.

She had returned, transformed, during the war, and had gone to work as Henderson's receptionist-driver when his wound prevented him using the car. Inevitably, he had fallen in love with her, while she met and became engaged to a young miner who worked alongside her father. At the time Henderson had even managed to get her a little flat of her own, over the garage at the surgery. But within months of the Armistice, her father and fiancé had both been killed in the same pit accident, and after escaping briefly again to Cardiff, Lily had returned to the family home to keep her mother company. She had resumed her job at the surgery, but there was no longer any question of her living away from home, and she had once more been drawn into the web of her mother's smothering domesticity. Just when it looked as if her independent streak would rescue her, Lily's brother Billie, a wartime shell-shock victim, had been released from the local mental hospital and was back in their over-crowded little terraced house with the mother he detested. Now Lily seemed doomed to stay at home for ever, acting as reluctant buffer between mother and brother. Henderson hoped his solution would work. He could think of nothing else which would restore Lily's good spirits.

A week later, as his last patient left, Henderson joined Lily in the office. 'I hope you've nothing planned after the calls,' he said, 'because I shall need you to drive me to Newport and we shall be away at least three or four hours.'

Pleasure leaped in her eyes at the prospect of an unexpected outing. 'Nothing that can't be unplanned,' she said. 'Just got to make sure Mam and Billie promise not to kill each other over dinner. I'll call in there while you're seeing Mrs Yearsley. She's down for a visit today, isn't she?'

He had planned the trip with the care of a lover arranging to surprise his girl with an engagement ring; but his love token was more valuable than any piece of jewellery Lily was ever likely to acquire. Their first stop was the Llanover Estate offices. He sent Lily off to look at the shops for half an hour while he finalized the farm purchase, then moved on to his solicitor's office to make out the lease to William Walters, of the Ranks, Abercarn. After that, he took Lily to lunch at the

15

Westgate Hotel, intending to surprise her afterwards with the solution to her more pressing problem.

The hotel alone was enough to keep her happy for weeks. Henderson had just been about to criticize its provincial standards and general ambience, when he caught sight of her face and held his tongue. She was enraptured.

She leaned across the table and whispered: 'D'you know, this is the first time I've ever been inside a proper hotel – for anything, mind, let alone to have a meal.'

Momentarily he was incredulous. 'But your years in Cardiff . . . surely – I mean, I thought your uncle was prosperous and pretty generous with his money too. It never occurred to me . . . ' Realizing he sounded feeble, he tailed off into silence.

Lily laughed, but for the first time he heard bitterness in her tone. 'Oh, Uncle Rhys would have been happy enough for us to go up the Angel or the Royal and enjoy the bright lights. But I couldn't have gone without Lexie, and Lexie . . . well, she couldn't, that's all.'

'Why on earth not? You'd pass muster with the best for good manners, dress and everything else. I can't believe it was any different for a girl you practically grew up with.'

'You never saw Lexie. She had a mother as well as a father, you know.'

'I had assumed she did. What about it?'

'Her mother was black.' Lily's expression was truculent. The normal relaxed friendliness between them had disappeared. Now she was a wary stranger, watching him for any sign of disgust or disapproval, ready for immediate flight if he said or did anything to insult her cousin.

Henderson let his breath escape in a long sigh. 'So that's it! That's why she never came to see your mother! Poor child. She must have learned early and hard who her real friends were.'

Lily relaxed visibly, and astonished him by reaching out to clasp his arm. 'You are a nice man,' she said. 'I don't think there's anybody else I'd have dared tell and have them stay just the way they were before.'

'Why on earth not? The colour of your cousin's skin is nothing to do with you.'

'Yes, but it is. She's more a sister to me than any of my real sisters, and anyone who do hurt her does the same to me.

16

That's why we never went to restaurants or anything down Cardiff. We never needed to talk it over, it just happened, after Lex had people say rotten things to her in the smart streets up town.'

'But as I said, she must have been used to it from an early age.'

'Not down the Bay. There's always been more colours than a packet of Liquorice Allsorts down there and when the first big trouble started between black and white, she was already grown up. That's what drove her away, I think. Her story is that she got a chance to go into films, but if she have, there's no sign of it yet.'

Henderson was fascinated. For the first time he realized how remote he had held himself from Lily and her day-to-day concerns, and felt faintly guilty. He had spent a couple of years locked into a dream of loving her, but in reality he had never involved himself in anything below the surface of her life. Well, at least that was about to change. He smiled at her. 'Come on, now that we're here, I'm going to abet you in becoming a fast woman. What'll you have to drink while we look at the menu?'

She startled him again by saying: 'Well, whisky's my tipple, but I do always think it's a bit heavy before food . . .' He had a momentary vision of the scene in *Pygmalion* where the partially gentrified Eliza Doolittle riveted her respectable female audience with a pithy exposition of her aunt's addiction to gin, and almost collapsed with laughter. If ever he nerved himself to propose to Lily, it was conceivable he would witness a real-life version of the drama when he introduced her to his family.

Suppressing his thoughts, he said: 'Let's try a gin-and-French. That's light enough, although it may go to your head.'

Her grin was mischievous. 'I come from a long line of the strongest heads you ever saw, even if they were a bit short on much else. Don't you worry about that.'

She tasted her cocktail eagerly, then turned to the fairly basic menu with equal enthusiasm. 'Imagine having all this stuff on hand every day,' she said. 'What do happen if nobody comes to buy it?'

'Good question, Lily. Bear it in mind if you're inclined to order anything cooked in sauce. The chances are it will be yesterday's roast mutton resurrected.'

'Ooh, I wouldn't dream of it, not with steak on the menu. And potted shrimps! I've had the fresh ones off the stalls down the Bay, but never potted. What are they like?'

'Delicious. All hot and peppery and buttery, with good brown bread and butter to help them down. Just the thing to go with a little Chablis, I think . . .'

He had not expected to enjoy his food. Something of a trencherman, he had learned to despise commercial hotels and the fare they offered. But this was fresh, at least, and Lily's enthusiasm was contagious. She watched him carefully to make sure she knew how to deal with each course, then sailed through potted shrimps, steak with a mound of vegetables, and a dish of ice-cream. She had been right about her strong head too, he reflected. He had expected to be the one who consumed most of the claret he ordered with their steaks, for she had already done full justice to the Chablis. But she drank plenty of red wine too, with evident pleasure and not the faintest sign of intoxication.

As she set aside her empty ice-cream dish, he gazed at her wonderingly. 'You really are an amazing girl. You've just eaten enough food to keep a navvy going and drunk sufficient to put a country solicitor under the table, but you're still shapely and sober. I don't know how you do it.'

'Simple. I've never eaten a meal like that before and I shouldn't think I'm likely to again. You don't get fat on beef stew and toast and tea. And like I told you, the drink is in the blood.' Her smile faded slightly then, as she went on: 'The bad side from our Dad – strong head, weak will – the good from Uncle Rhys, who always said drunken women looked like trollops.'

'A view I've heard widely expressed. It doesn't appear to have made him discourage you.'

'Good God, no! Uncle Rhys liked everyone to have a good time. No, he just made sure we knew how to hold it, so we wouldn't look sloppy. A different thing entirely.'

'And not one your sainted mother would subscribe to, I think.'

That brought back the smile. 'If Mam do hate anyone more than the Devil, it's Uncle Rhys. In fact I think she'd be hard put to it to see them as two different people.'

As she chattered, he opened the long manilla envelope he

18

had brought from the lawyer's office. She looked at the documents he drew out with undisguised curiosity. 'What have you got there, then?'

'Something I hope will make life easier for you. There's no need to plough through all of it. Just look at the single sheet on the top. That summarizes what it's all about.'

He pushed the papers across the white damask tablecloth towards her, then leaned back in his chair and poured more coffee. Intrigued, Lily reached for the single sheet which was folded on top of the sheaf of older documents. As she read, her eyes widened incredulously, then she laid the deed of gift of the lease on the table and stared at him mutely for long seconds.

Eventually Henderson said: 'You're allowed to say something without the whole thing disappearing in a puff of smoke, you know.'

'It's – it's just I don't know what to say. Nobody have ever done anything like this for any of us. Oh, thank you so much. This will change my life; change our Billie's too, for that matter. If ever a man needed a new reason for living, it's that one.'

'Can I assume, then, that the gift will be accepted?'

'I'd be a bloody fool to turn it down, wouldn't I?'

Henderson roared with laughter. 'Oh, Lily, don't change. Don't ever, ever change!'

19

CHAPTER TWO

Billie Walters sat at the kitchen table in his mother's house and pretended to read the morning paper. He would have liked a long, quiet walk up the Gwyddon valley, where he would not see anyone for hours. But that would have meant going out into the street first, bumping against people as they hurried about their business; exchanging trivial pleasantries; explaining why he wasn't getting a job down the pit . . . no, better stay in here. At least, here, only Mam could get at him.

He glanced sidelong at her as she sat in her Windsor chair beside the kitchen range, mending a worn sheet. A stranger might have thought Margaret Ann Walters was relaxed, concentrating on her domestic task. Billie knew better. Her small mouth was pursed into lines of disapproval. The muscles on her jawline clenched involuntarily from time to time, barely holding in the tirade she wanted to pour out over her son.

They had explained to Margaret Ann that the big guns and the suffering and the endless mud of Flanders had broken Billie, as they had thousands of other soldiers. At the county asylum in Abergavenny, where Billie had lived for two years after the war had ended, the superintendent had been at pains to point out that some of the bravest and best had suffered thus. As he spoke, Lily had watched her mother's face and despair had engulfed her, because it was clear that Margaret Ann Walters had no grain of compassion for her son. Perhaps it would have been different if the casualty had been one of the other boys. Billie had aroused Margaret Ann's hatred so long

20

ago that the hurt was beyond healing. Somehow, though, Lily knew it would have been the same whichever of her mother's sons had been ruined.

To Margaret Ann, child of a mining community, a man was born to withstand appalling pressure every day of his working life; to withstand it and live as if it were of no account. She had seen her beloved husband do it for more than thirty years. It had killed him in the end and he had always accepted that it might. Beside such stoicism, four years on the Western Front seemed like a fleabite.

If Billie had come home lacking a leg, or an arm, or with appalling facial scars, or blinded by mustard gas, Margaret Ann would have held up her head, confident the neighbours and her chapel friends could see the sacrifice the Walters family had made for king and country. But Billie looked the same as he always had. He had come through without a scratch. Margaret Ann found it all too easy to imagine what the village was saying: that when other able-bodied ex-soldiers were out looking for work, Billie had been warm and cosy over in Abergavenny with the Government paying his board and lodging for two years. Some people never knew when they were well off . . .

How could he do this to her? Margaret Ann's bitterness was rising as she sewed. Hadn't he caused her enough grief, going off with his father and brother that time and living with his father's fancy piece as if he were her son, not Margaret Ann's? Refusing to come back when the slut had died? No decent woman could forgive that. And now this business. He might almost be behaving like this just to spite her!

Such was her outrage that she quite forgot Billie had been her favourite boy, the sensitive, imaginative one, the one she wanted to save from colliery work. Her resentment, festering, finally bubbled over. 'For heaven's sake, Billie, are you going to sit there all day over that paper? You must have read it three times by now!'

He sighed and shielded his face from her with his hand. 'I can hardly go out and dig the garden, Mam, can I? Not unless they've invented some way of making paving stones send up grass.'

'There's no need to get cheeky with me, neither. I know

21

you'm supposed to be bad, but I can't see that slummocking around the house all day is going to help.'

For the first time, he turned to face her and said, with great deliberation: 'I've told you before, Mam, I can't bear running into people.'

She sniffed and looked down at her work. 'Afraid of what they'll say, I s'pose!'

'No, Mam. You'm the one who's afraid of what they'll say. Where I been the last few years, I don't care any more what anybody do say, as long as they leave me alone – and you ent going to leave me alone, are you?' He stood up, slowly, as if pushing a vast burden with his hunched shoulders, picked up his jacket and walked towards the back door.

Colour flared in Margaret Ann's cheeks. She had managed to do just what Lily had begged her not to, to get him all worked up and drive him out. Not that she cared about that, but she cared about Lily's opinion, and Lily seemed to be under a spell when it came to Billie. To hear her talk you'd think he was some suffering saint instead of a waster. Apart from anything else, he was driving a wedge between her and Lily. Just as they had been settling down together, just as Margaret Ann was getting over the worst of Evan's death and learning to lean on Lily, she was pushed aside and it was all 'We must look after our Billie!' Look after him, indeed! What did he know about real suffering, about loss of pride, about loss of love? He'd escaped all that, and now he was trying to escape the responsibility of helping to look after his family, his widowed mother, his brothers and sister who were still children.

Self-pity drove Margaret Ann and she snapped: 'Aye, that's right, run out, like you always have. Wouldn't surprise me if that's what you done over in France!'

Billie's face, already pale, seemed to drain entirely of colour. He glared at her, a gleam of tears in his eyes, then said, very quietly: 'Well, then, so now I know how you do feel. All I can say is thank God you'll never know what it was really like, or it would have taken more than a bloody asylum to keep you quiet about it.'

The door closed almost quietly behind him. Margaret Ann stood on the hearthrug where she had been pacing as she harangued him, her face twitching with the strain of the scene.

She wanted to cry, but somehow felt that would have given Billie satisfaction. Controlling the impulse, she muttered: 'There, give 'em everything and that's the thanks you get!' Then she resumed her seat and picked up her work once more, her stitches as precise and perfect as though nothing were amiss.

Billie strode up the narrow street with a look of near dementia on his face. To hell with it, he thought, let 'em get their money's worth if they think I'm so damned mad . . . Then, at the corner, he ran full tilt into Lily and Charles Henderson.

'Billie! What's the matter, mun? Anybody'd think there was a fire!'

'Bloody well would have been, and worse, if I hadn't got away from Mam! I'm telling you, Lily, if I have to stay under her roof much longer, I'll be back over Abergavenny for life!'

Lily slipped her arm around him. 'Been getting at you, have she? I used to wonder how she managed it every time with our Dad. She always was a dirty fighter.' As she spoke, she flashed a pleading look at Henderson. He needed no prompting. It was obvious they would have no peace to discuss Billie's prospects at the Ranks.

'Come along, both of you,' he said, and to Billie: 'The car's just round the corner. We'll all go down to the Swan and have a cup of tea. Lily's got something for you that might help things along.'

Too miserable to be curious, Billie allowed them to lead him away. It couldn't be anything more than some cockeyed class or other to keep him occupied. Willow baskets and trays had been all the rage at the asylum. Dully, he hoped the local alternative might make him feel a little less futile.

By the time they got into Dr Henderson's sitting room, he was much calmer. He often thought that if there had been anywhere to go, away from his mother, his recovery might have been faster. But it was useless to daydream. Those of his brothers who had their own homes had wives and families too, and unless he could earn a living – an unlikely prospect in his present state – he was as dependent as any of the younger children.

Lily kept the conversation light until they were settled with

23

cups of tea and the housekeeper had gone about her business. Then she opened her bag and produced the brown envelope Henderson had given her earlier. 'Have a look at that, Billie boy. Perhaps it will make you feel a bit better.'

Now she had succeeded in arousing his interest. It was years since anyone had thought him sufficiently important to hand over documents in official-looking envelopes. He studied the glossy buff paper briefly, then glanced at Lily, eyes questioning.

'Go on – see for yourself. What's in there is all yours, free and clear and nothing to do with our Mam.'

Billie's mind might have been damaged by the war, but there was nothing wrong with his intelligence. As he read the deed of gift, his gloomy expression lightened to half-incredulous jubilation. Finally he let the document fall on the plush tablecloth and gazed wonderingly at Charles Henderson. 'You'd do this . . . for me?' he said.

Henderson fought an irrational desire to weep. 'I know what you've been through, Billie. I was there too, remember? I was lucky enough to escape with less serious injuries than you. I can't help everybody, but I can do it for one – and you're that one. I hope you're not offended.'

'Offended, mun? It's like being reborn!'

'Now, don't get too carried away. The place is in one hell of a state. It will take you years to put it back on its feet.'

Billie shook his head as if preparing to explain something to a slow child. 'Someone like you wouldn't have no idea of how it do feel to have something of your own for the first time. It wouldn't matter if I had to live in a cave up there; it's mine. Nobody in our family have ever owned the roof over their heads before. It's like a miracle.'

Lily said: 'That's the most I've heard you say since you came home.'

'I expect I'll quieten down again soon, kidda, but now I feel as if I'm bubbling. When can we see it?'

Henderson broke in again. 'Oh, yes – I'd thought about that. It's a long way on foot. Dr Cann is taking evening surgery, so I'm free. Lily, I took the liberty of asking Mrs Jones to stand in as surgery receptionist for you this evening so you can join us. We'll drive up there now.'

'B-but won't Mrs Jones object? After all, she is your house-keeper.'

'Of course not! She's been itching to get her hands on some of those patients' records for years. Far be it from me to tell her she'll find neither Cann's handwriting nor mine any more legible than Mandarin Chinese! You just get the relevant files out for her and leave them in the top drawer of the desk, where the patients can't get at them. Then she'll do your duty. Don't worry, she'll be compensated for it, so she won't take it out on you.'

Lily needed no second bidding. She was longing to see the farm, and the bonus of witnessing Billie's reaction at his first sight of his new life was irresistible.

'My God, Doctor, it's just as well you had the exhaust seen to last week. It'd never have stood up to this punishment other-wise.' Lily was fighting to control the car as it bucked and shuddered along the rough track which replaced the metalled road where the houses ran out a little way up the Gwyddon valley.

'Persevere, Lily. It gets smoother a little further up. This lower section is rutted because it gets more use.'

Billie had lapsed into his customary silence, but there was no melancholy in his manner now. He was gazing around, en-tranced, with the air of one who had entered paradise. It was certainly beautiful, Lily reflected, but she could think of plenty of places she would prefer, and they were still only on the edge of it. The Gwyddon valley ran steep and secretive away from the Ebbw at Abercarn, and never had two rivers been more different. The Ebbw carried the scars of mining in its waters and on its banks, the river incapable of supporting life, thanks to pollution from the coal and iron workings. Terraces of mean houses ran down to its edge, backed by vast coal tips, and in places the surrounding hills had been stripped of their timber by the contaminated atmosphere. The Gwyddon had always been too small and inaccessible for mining, especially as it had no high-grade coal seams. It had been left, with its clean stream running through unspoiled oak and beech forest from its source six miles away on an upland plateau inhabited only by sheep and rabbits.

Billie had loved it since his early childhood, and before he was sent to work in the pits had dreamed of a farming job there. Now he approached it with the air of one coming home after a long journey. Lily regarded the dark columns of trees which pressed down close to the track and suppressed a shudder. What a townie I've become, she chided herself. It'd be safer to walk up here after dark than a back street in Cardiff or Abercarn, yet I'd be far more frightened here. Perhaps when we get out into the light . . . They were passing a broad belt of pine trees at the time and she convinced herself that they were responsible for the gloom. The track turned downhill after a long, gentle climb, and she thought they were at their destination. But they were still barely half way there.

'We used to call this Big Trwyn,' Billie explained, 'because there's a little clearing about a mile back along the stream that was little Trwyn, see. Goodness knows why we called it that, because the stream's the Gwyddon.'

Lily looked about her. 'So where's this farm, then?'

'Oh, we're not nearly there yet,' said Charles Henderson. 'Drive across this open section and up there, into the woods, again. See the track? It's not obvious because it's in shadow.'

Lily began to feel real misgivings about the project. 'I don't want to sound ungrateful, Doctor, but isn't it a bit . . . well, remote? What if something went wrong and Billie was on his own up here?'

Before Henderson had time to respond, Billie himself broke in. 'That's the best part of it, don't you see, Lil? The last thing I want is people about all the time, and I think Dr Henderson's the only one that have understood that from the beginning. Don't worry about me; this'll suit me down to the ground.'

At least the trees were more open here, and a brighter green, she thought. But that lasted for little more than a mile, and when the track began to slope steeply upwards again, the conifers closed in around them, giving the late afternoon a distinctly uncomfortable air of having been plucked from Grimm's Fairy Tales.

As the car crawled around the last hairpin bend and they saw the farm, Lily's doubts were momentarily swept away. The house drowsed in the declining sunshine, mutely inviting them to come in and light a fire in its cold hearth and bring it to life

26

again. It was built on a wide rocky platform overlooking the stream hundreds of feet below. The ruinous drystone garden wall ran along the edge of the drop, a dusty notch in the rock beyond it indicating where there had once been a steep path or flight of steps descending to the lower track. The garden, neglected for more than twenty years, still offered up a tangle of beauty, with climbing roses and straggling nasturtiums all woven together, and a splendid variegated ivy advancing determinedly up the side of the house.

Charles Henderson got out of the car and limped round to the rear, where he ceremoniously flung open Billie's door and escorted him out with a little bow. 'Come along, we must have a formal handing-over ceremony – present the keys to the new master of the house and let him pass over the threshold first.'

It was all the best Christmases and birthdays Billie had ever dreamed of rolled into one. The cottage gate creaked open at Henderson's touch and they went up the granite path to a low, wide front door which looked centuries old. The doctor took a vast bunch of keys from his pocket, found the right one, and handed them over. 'You'll have to work out what the rest are for by trial and error,' he said.

Billie inserted the key and it turned silently in the newly oiled lock. The hinges had been oiled too, and the door swung back silently to reveal a broad hall with a slate slab floor. To the rear a wide staircase rose to the first floor. Immediately in front of them more antique doors gave access to the downstairs living rooms. Most impressive of these was a huge kitchen which opened off the right-hand side of the hall. A range of windows showed off the breath-taking view of the valley below, while thick walls and an enormous inglenook fireplace offered protection from winter gales. 'I'd feel safe from anything in here,' murmured Billie, 'anything at all.'

Lily glanced at him, unaccountably disturbed again by the remoteness of the place and by a sense of desolation which had started to creep over her the moment they entered the house. She looked beyond Billie to Charles Henderson. Both he and her brother seemed completely at home. Lily gave herself a little shake. Of all times to get the collywobbles about a place! This was the chance of a lifetime for Billie and nothing should be put in its way. Why, she was acting almost like her mother!

This thought pushed away all her misgivings. Far more important to make sure Billie had every encouragement to make good up here . . .

Her speculation ceased as she realized Henderson was speaking. 'Of course, it would be asking for trouble to expect you to make good here without backing,' he was saying. 'For a start, you'll need transport: horse and trap, I think, given the state of the track back there. Then you'll need some livestock and the wherewithal to finance basic repairs on the outbuildings and house. I've had a word with a couple of farmers and they reckon that with care, you could manage it for £500. I'm only handing over the farm to you if you accept that sum as working capital, otherwise the whole thing is a waste of money.'

Billie, beside himself with gratitude, tried to break in, but Henderson silenced him with a gesture. 'You'll make a thumping loss for a year or two by any commercial standards, but you have your full army disability pension to keep you alive, so anything you earn on the farm can be reinvested to tide you over the first bad patch. How does that strike you?'

'I think I must have died and gone to heaven.' Billie's expression was bemused, his voice soft and dreamy.

'Hmm – does one have to undertake such back-breaking work in heaven, I wonder? I had always rather hoped for a rest. Still, each to his own!' Henderson turned to Lily. 'And what does Miss Walters think of the establishment?'

'It'll certainly put him out of reach of our Mam.' She mustered a bright smile as she said it, but it still sounded a feeble sort of reaction to a cash gift which amounted to five years' wages for some working men. Lily hurried on with: 'It'll be the making of Billie, I'm sure!'

Or the end of him, said a cold, silent voice deep within her.

CHAPTER THREE

'Mam, where are you? You wait till you hear what our Billie have got to tell you!' Lily had come straight home with her brother to break the news of his new life, in case he needed some moral support to deal with Margaret Ann.

But their mother was far more interested in some news of her own. 'Whatever it is, it can wait five minutes,' she said, coming into the kitchen from the front passage, where she had been seeing someone out. 'Our Rose have got a place up the Rhyswg, to move into the minute they'm married. What d'you think of that, then?'

Momentarily Lily was at a loss. 'Albert Watkins can't afford to rent one of them houses, never in a month of Sundays. Where's the money going to come from?'

Margaret Ann could not quite meet Lily's eyes. 'Well, they haven't exactly got the whole house, see . . . you remember that Mrs Fletcher? Her husband's job don't really run to keeping up their house, and she was saying a couple of days back that she was looking around for a respectable tenant. So I mentioned our Rose was after a place, and that was that.'

Puzzlement was rapidly turning to misgiving in Lily's mind. 'But why the Rhyswg, Mam? It's an awful long way for Albert to traipse up the South Celynen and back every day, and why on earth should they take a couple of rooms in someone else's place when they could have a whole house of their own for the same money down the Ranks or Commercial Road? It doesn't make sense.'

29

Margaret Ann was back in command now. She turned on her daughter, eyes flashing scorn. 'And you don't make no sense, neither! What woman in her right mind would swap the Rhyswg for the Ranks? It's so refined up there, it's worth having apartments any day for the chance of getting up out of these nasty common little houses.'

She was excessively conscious that Lily's words bore a strong resemblance to what her dead husband had said to her, more than thirty years earlier, when they were on the point of marriage and she had tried to make him take on her parents' house in Rhyswg Road. She might have been cheated of her dignified house on the hill, but now that her eldest daughter was about to get married, Margaret Ann was determined the girl would enjoy what she had missed, even if it meant Albert walking extra weary miles each day and coming home to a shared house into the bargain.

'It won't always be like that, it's just a start,' she said. 'You know what a good worker that Albert Watkins is. He won't stay a collier for long, and then they'll have their own place up there soon enough.'

Lily's earlier good humour had evaporated. 'Oh, come on, Mam, stop day-dreaming!' she snapped. 'I know Albert's a good worker – but he hasn't got his official's papers, has he? And so far as I can tell he's hard pressed to get through his *Daily Sketch* every day. That don't say much for his prospects of self-improvement.'

'I might have known you'd take against it!' said Margaret Ann with a sniff. 'You always were the image of your father and he was contrary about the Rhyswg. It's as if you don't want this family to better itself.'

'No, Mam. I just don't call living in a fancy house you can't afford and having to get by on tea and biscuits as a result as bettering yourself; and you're right – I bet our Dad would have felt just the same about it.'

'Well, I'm glad to say our Rose do see it my way, and as it's her that's getting married, nobody else's opinion do matter.'

'I'd have thought Albert might want a say in it, too, but maybe I'm wrong.'

'Albert's a good boy. He'll do just what our Rose do tell him, and no messing, so it's settled. It's unfurnished, so I'm going up there with Rose tomorrow to measure for curtains and see what furniture they'll need.' She paused for a moment, then added: 'Now, what was this news you had for me?'

Lily glanced at Billie, whose expression had grown increasingly apprehensive as his mother developed her eulogy to the joys of Rhyswg Road. Instinctively he knew she would take it as a personal affront that his sudden good fortune was so much greater than Rose's. Determined not to quarrel over a triviality, Lily took a deep breath and plunged in with their news. 'Our Billie's setting up on his own account, and the doctor's going to back him. He's going to be a farmer, like he's always wanted. Isn't that lovely?'

Instantly Margaret Ann's face took on the pinched look it invariably assumed when her son was discussed. 'What nonsense is this? A farm? How in heaven's name can he ever do that? He can't even keep himself, let alone set up on the land!'

Billie blushed furiously at her scornful dismissal, but persevered with the news Lily had started to break. 'It's true, Mam. Dr Henderson is backing me with a farm lease and a bit o' capital. Seems he realized I wasn't no good with people around me no more and wanted to help out.'

'The man must have been drinking. I never heard such nonsense. If I was you, my lad, I'd wait and see what he do have to say tomorrow. It'll be a different story by then, you mark my words.'

'He doesn't have to wait until tomorrow, Mam, it's all signed and sealed. Billie could move in overnight if he had a few sticks of furniture. The farm lease is already in his name and there's money in the bank to stock it and run it for a bit.' She attempted a more conciliatory approach. 'I'm sure Dr Henderson would lend me the car for an hour or two between surgeries tomorrow, and I could take you up there and show you. Oh, you wait till you see it, and you'll really appreciate it.'

Margaret Ann was making desperate attempts to subdue her hostility towards Billie, but it was an uphill struggle. Still almost choking with indignation, she managed to say: 'Which farm is it, then?'

'I don't know whether you'll ever have been up there – it's

31

right up the top, and it's been empty for years – Trwyn Farm.'

Abruptly her mother's resentment dissolved into a secret smile. 'Oh, yes. I know Trwyn Farm; knew it well once. Fancy our Billie wanting to go to a place like that.'

Lily began to feel uncomfortable at her mother's sudden change of mood. 'Well, I know it's remote, but what a chance for a fresh start!'

'Aye, it is at the back of beyond, but I was thinking more along the lines of him not minding living where there's been a murder.' As she said the words she turned to face Billie, all wide-eyed innocence. 'I'm sure they told you all about it before you took it on. People around here couldn't talk about nothing else for months after it happened.'

Her smile, poisonous now, indicated her belief that nobody had breathed a word to Billie about the Trwyn Farm murder, and his horrified expression confirmed it.

'Murder? Really, Mam, what are you talking about now?' Lily forced exasperation into her voice, though she was as worried as Billie.

Margaret Anne's voice was little more than a sibilant whisper. 'The Jobs,' she said. 'Jenny Job was my best friend in the early days after I was married. Used to come down here on market days and play with the babies. But her husband wasn't right in the head . . . ' here she paused significantly and stared at Billie ' . . . and the quiet and isolation up there sent him right over the top in the end. He killed poor Jenny, then he wandered off to the sheep dip at the top of the Gwyddon brook and drowned himself. I know all about it because it was me as found him, so don't you act as if I'm talking nonsense.'

'B-but I've never heard a word about any of this . . . have you, Billie?'

Her brother was apparently bereft of the power of speech. He merely shook his head, and continued to gaze fixedly at his mother. Margaret Ann had hit her stride now and had more to say. 'Of course that place did funny things to the whole Job family. The husband's mam went the same way as he did, and nobody could ever be sure if she did it herself or if the father had a hand in it. Found her in the sheep dip, an' all . . . when I ran down there and found Harry Job under the water, for one

32

terrible minute I thought I was seeing ghosts and it was the mother there bobbing under the surface . . . '

'For God's sake, Mam, stop it – it's horrible.' Lily shuddered and covered her face with her hand in dismay as she thought of Billie's prospects in a place with such a history.

Margaret Ann was all prissy respectability. 'Don't take the name of the Lord in vain under *my* roof, thank you very much, Lily! And don't tell me what I can and can't say to my own family. I just thought Billie should know all about this fine place he've taken on so lightly.'

Something in her venomous tone seemed to liberate Billie from the haunted world she had pushed him into. He smiled calmly at his mother and said: 'Just as well the dead don't bother me really, then, ennit, Mam? I always found the living was far harder to handle, myself. P'raps this poor Job character will rest easier, knowing there's somebody else looking after his land and loving it. Anyhow I'll be a damned sight happier up there than down here, so that's that.'

For long moments the atmosphere in the room was charged with the hostility between mother and son. The tension was broken only by Rose's arrival. 'Oh, Lily, you'm back. Have you got time to come up the Rhyswg and see our new place? It's ever so nice – I expect Mam have told you already.'

Lily smiled, relieved at the excuse to descend to less controversial matters. 'Yes, she has, Rose. I'd love to see it, but I've got to go back down the surgery and do some finishing off this evening. Later in the week, maybe . . . '

Rose, full of her new status as soon-to-be-housewife, nodded her assent and drifted away to take yet another look at the embroidered pillowcases, sheets and tablecloths she had accumulated over the years and kept layered with dried lavender in the deal chest in her bedroom.

Lily flashed her brother a questioning look and he gave her a tiny nod to indicate he was now in command of the situation. As she turned to leave for the surgery, she heard him say: 'I'm going next door to talk to our Haydn, I'll be back in time for supper, all right?' The door swung closed behind Lily before she heard a response from Margaret Ann.

The tidying up in the surgery to which Lily had referred was

33

really an invitation to join Charles Henderson for drinks in his private sitting room. When they had parted at the market square in Abercarn, he had suspected Lily would have a difficult time with Margaret Ann about Billie's good fortune, and had offered the invitation as a refuge for the girl. It gave him the added pleasure of enjoying her company a little longer than he could otherwise have hoped.

Now, an hour after Margaret Anne's vindictive outburst in the kitchen at the Ranks, Lily was curled in the corner of the leather chesterfield in Henderson's private quarters, sipping from a well-filled whisky glass.

He grinned at her, seeking to ease her tension. 'Dear me, if the old Fury could see you now, what went on earlier would pale to insignificance in face of fresh wrath!'

Lily nodded and gave him a weary smile. 'I sometimes wonder what on earth I'd ever do without you, even if it hadn't been for this wonderful thing you're doing for Billie,' she said.

'You know sympathy for him was only a small part of it, don't you? I did it primarily for you, to try and free you from all that seething family emotion.'

She nodded again. 'It would be dishonest if I said no. Of course I know. Why can't everyone be as kind and decent as you?'

His laugh sounded hollow in his own ears. 'Oh, dear Lily, there's not much that's very kind and decent about me, I assure you . . . I simply seem to have developed something of an obsession.'

He knew he need not explain further. This girl might be naïve in many ways where he took sophistication for granted, but she was intelligent and utterly straightforward, and so far life had not taught her to dissemble. She knew he was referring to his own feelings about her, and had no wish to embarrass him by pushing him into more open expression. He stood up and went to the sideboard for the decanter, returning to top up her glass. As he poured the golden liquid into the heavy crystal tumbler, she reached up tentatively and drew her finger along the edge of his hand from knuckle to wrist. Her touch tingled like an electric shock. 'Put the bottle down, why don't you?' she said.

He took away her glass with a shaking hand, and replaced it, along with the decanter, on the sideboard, before returning to her. She stood up and moved towards him until they stood only inches apart. His arms came up and around her waist as if acting independently of him. He bent towards her – only slightly, for she was a tall girl – and her wide, warm lips parted to receive his kiss.

Her tongue was fragrant with the warm, woody flavour of whisky. Her hair smelled of fresh air and clean yellow soap, and her flesh of lavender. It was like embracing a perfect summer day, dipping into it, then submerging oneself . . . Henderson kissed her again, and she slid closer, her lithe, long body moulding itself to his. 'Has Mrs Jones gone back to her rooms yet?' she murmured.

'Hmm, yes . . . Cann is dining out tonight . . . she left a cold supper for me and she's at her sister's . . . '

Lily's smile was as old as Eve. 'Well, then, why don't we sit down by here for a bit and relax, eh?'

Throughout his life, that first love-making with her was to remain in his memory as the most perfect he had ever known. Lily had some experience – she had confided to him when she was worried she might be pregnant during her engagement – but he was certain there had been no other lovers since that first one. And yet now she slid into the ways of love as effortlessly as a fish slips through water, guiding his hands over her body, murmuring encouragement and wrapping him in a cloak of loving desire which disarmed him of all reticence. Henderson stopped seeing himself as a middle-aged man with a stiff leg and no obvious attractions, and for the first time since his careless youth felt he could have scaled mountains or plumbed oceans.

The room was illumined only by two table lamps, and in their golden glow he gradually became aware that Lily was half naked. He could never remember whether she had removed her own clothes or whether they had done it together. Not that it was of the least importance now, as he contemplated her broad shoulders and hips, the large round breasts partially concealed by a brief camisole of peach satiny fabric, and the long, long legs still clad in their white cotton stockings. ' . . . The Rose of Sharon, the Lily of the Valleys . . . ' he murmured, in an almost worshipful tone.

Her eyes were dreamy. 'How did you know about that? My father always said it was the only bit of the Bible he could stand. That's how me and Rose got our names . . . '

'I didn't know, my dearest, but your father wasn't the only man with a limited appreciation of the Good Book, and I've always regarded that phrase as singularly appropriate to you. Now, where were we . . . ?'

Soon he was conscious of nothing beyond their bodies, the soft warmth of her flesh against his hard muscles; the spicy animal smell of her, which inflamed him more than the most expensive manufactured scent. Surely, he thought later, there must have been some physical awkwardness? There should have been, with two of them writhing about together on a narrow leather sofa in progressing stages of undress; but if there had been, the memory did not linger. There were too many wonderful sensations to hold and treasure. As he slid inside her, Lily's whole body seemed to leap to clasp him there, and he wanted nothing else, ever.

He heard her voice, from a great distance, calling joyfully: 'Don't stop, my darling, don't stop now!' Her hair, loosened, tumbled against his face. Her strong, capable hands pressed down on his shoulders and she arched her body against him, still crying aloud her pleasure in his lovemaking.

Afterwards, spent, they sat together on the floor, leaning back against the sofa. Lily turned to look up at his face and said: 'Why ever did you wait so long?'

Henderson shrugged. 'I could never make myself believe you wanted me. It seemed impossible somehow.'

'But you said – so long ago, you said . . . ' remembering it had been on the day of her fiancé's funeral, she was silent again.

'Yes, but people change, Lily. Particularly when they're as young as you were then. I hardly dared think you might find it possible to love me.'

'Don't think I've ever thought about it like that . . . ' she pondered for a moment. 'It's just – well – been *there* somehow, a bit in the background, all shy, like, waiting to come forward when we were ready for it. And now here it is!' She smiled and burrowed closer to him. 'I'm ever so glad!'

There was a sombre note in Henderson's voice: 'I think

you've always been honest with me. Don't change that, will you?' She shook her head and he went on, hesitantly now: 'Are you sure you're not simply sorry for me . . . or grateful?'

He was disconcerted by the snort of mirth his probing produced. 'What have you got for anybody to feel sorry for you about? And as for gratitude . . . I s'pose you mean our Billie and the farm.'

'Yes.'

'Don't be bloody daft. If you'd been looking for a bit o' that sort of gratitude from me, you'd have tried setting me up in some way, wouldn't you, not spent it all on my funny brother? You've got some pretty strange ideas inside that clever head, haven' you?'

He smiled. 'I suppose I have. But it . . . it was the idea of you feeling sorry for me that always really held me back.' It was so obvious she had no idea what he was talking about that he added: 'You know, my leg and all . . . '

'Charlie Henderson, you'm madder than our Billie! Have you ever taken a look at the average collier of your age? They got bits missing all over them, or they're half bent over with dust. Nothing much wrong with you, take it from me. I'd have thought you'd be more worried I was after your money.'

He stared at her. 'Do you know, that never crossed my mind?'

'Well it certainly should have. When I come back here from Cardiff, my Uncle Rhys said I shouldn't leave if I was just going back to a collier. All I said was that there was this doctor, and God, he was off! Had me in high society before we got as far as the station. I think that's why I may have been a bit – well – careful with you, if you see what I mean. I was afraid you might think I only saw you as a good prospect. I don't, honestly.'

Her tone was earnest now, almost pleading he should believe her. 'In any case,' she added, beaming, 'you're hardly likely to think that any more, are you? I can't see you holding on to any honourable intentions you might have had after what we just been doing.'

'Now you've lost me.'

'Well,' she said, 'however strong your feelings might be, you're not going to consider making an honest woman of a girl

37

who slept with her fiancé when she'd hardly known him ten minutes, and then leaped at a chance of a bit of slap an' tickle with you the minute we had the house to ourselves.'

Henderson said: 'I'd prefer it if you never referred to yourself in that tone again. Lily, I love you, as I've never loved any other woman. I want you to be my wife, and the only things that have made me hesitate until now are my age and my crippled leg.'

For once she was at a loss. The silence lengthened until eventually he could stand it no longer. 'I take it you're trying to find a kind way of letting me down.'

Lily gazed at him, eyes shining. 'Oh, you are silly sometimes! I just can't believe how lucky I am, that's all.'

'Then you will?'

'Just as soon as you want to name the day.'

CHAPTER FOUR

Cardiff

It had been a long, hard night, the old woman who had been brought in suffering from pneumonia turned out to have been a lot younger than she looked – barely fifty, they said. Sister had seemed quite cross about Bethan's mistake, saying that as a qualified nurse she should know they would never have bothered to admit a really old patient suffering from something like pneumonia. Not enough chance of recovery. They might as well not have bothered with this poor creature, as it turned out. Malnutrition and poverty had ensured she lacked the stamina to fight such a harrowing disease, and she had died during the night.

God protect me from looking like that at fifty! Bethan thought as she pulled up the sheet to cover the dead woman's face. She was only Mam's age, and Mam had borne all those children, most of them still flourishing. This woman had managed two surviving offspring, who now waited outside with the pathetic patience of the downtrodden, to be told what was happening to their mother.

Bethan tried to rally against the wave of depression which threatened to swamp her. Come on, you silly girl – you should be used to it by now! A twelve-hour night shift and a death on the ward were enough to upset anyone. Didn't mean it was the end of the world . . . She tried to turn her mind to some treat she could give herself when she had gone off duty and had a sleep. Tea down at R.E. Jones' in Queen Street, perhaps, with the orchestra playing. That would brush away the cobwebs . . .

For a moment the idea pleased her, then she glanced down at the bed and saw the dead woman's fleshless profile pressing up, blade-sharp, beneath the skimpy sheet, and her plan lost its savour. You don't need a treat, she thought. You need a different job . . .

It had been getting more and more like this lately; ever since she had finished training really. For the hundredth time Bethan wondered why. While she still had her final exams to aim for she had been full of the whole thing. Even the separation from Uncle Rhys and Lexie after their quarrel hadn't been that bad in the end. She had needed the time for study, anyway. But now all the hard work was over there seemed to be nothing to look forward to. She had her posh belt to show her new rank, but she still had to be back in the nurses' home by ten at night as if she was some baby; still had to take orders from the old dragon of a sister and tremble at the very mention of the matron.

Bethan had no one to tell her that she was merely outgrowing the restrictions she had previously accepted, so she assumed it was something to do with herself. Eventually the day shift came on duty and she went off the ward, going to get her cape from the rack in the kitchen before she went out into the cool early morning. For the tenth time that week she paused beside the noticeboard and read the announcement she already practically knew by heart. It said:

ST THOMAS'S HOSPITAL
NOTED LONDON TEACHING HOSPITAL
offers a limited number of vacancies to
well-qualified junior nurses in their
first post-probationary year.
Good wages, including a London Allowance,
and living accommodation in nurses' home.

Candidates were instructed to apply, with references and proof of qualifications, to the matron. Yet again, Bethan began weighing up the possibilities of a move. As she walked across the Infirmary courtyard towards the barrack-like nurses' home, the usual obstacles presented themselves – one in particular. Its name was Margaret Ann Walters.

40

Margaret Ann never lost an opportunity to tell Bethan her real place was back at home, helping to look after her younger brothers and sister. Even her real pride at Bethan's achievements at school, then as a probationer nurse in Cardiff Royal Infirmary, could not dispel her resentment that the girl seemed content to live miles away from her family. Bethan had talked to Lily about it often enough, but still found it hard to understand. Lily had gone home to play the dutiful daughter, and Lily had always been her mother's undisputed favourite. So why should Margaret Ann want Bethan, too, under her feet?

Lily had laughed gently when Bethan said this. 'What she needs haven't got anything to do with it really, kidda. It's what the neighbours do say that counts for Mam. You should know that by now.'

'But I thought she'd be proud of what I've done. After all, I'm the first one in the family to get the matriculation, and the nearest any of the other girls round here have got to nursing is being attendants over the asylum.'

'Don't make no mistake, Bethan, she *is* proud of you. But the way Mam do think, that's in the past now. You should be home with her, looking for a nice husband. Far as she's concerned, the training and everything was just passing the time till you settled down.'

'But I haven't even started courting anybody yet!'

'She's thinking about that one an' all, don't you worry! You wouldn't remember Alun Pritchard – he'd gone away while you were too little. Used to live up Gwyddon Road until his dad was killed. He went up to live with his mam's family in Lancashire and they sent him to one of the new schools of mines.

'He's back here now, twenty-six years old, no female dependants and with his overman's papers! Mam is bursting to fix 'im up with one of us, and as Albert is all ready to screw up his courage and ask Rose to marry him, it's got to be me or you. I think she've got you and your nursing qualifications in mind!'

Bethan was aghast. 'Just like that? Someone I never even set eyes on? Not even Mam could think like that!'

'It's the only way she've ever thought, love, and I can't see her changing, can you?'

41

'Lil, surely you can see it? I don't want to come back to Abercarn. You and I were lucky to get away when we did. You've chosen something different from my way, but I haven't gone through all that studying and training just to come and marry some glorified miner.'

'I was hoping you'd say that. Look, try not to worry. I'm better at bullying Mam than any of the rest of you, because I'm her favourite. When she gets too bad, just keep quiet. Swallow your temper – I know it's hard, but you'll only come off worse if you don't. I'll sort her out and see she doesn't cause you any lasting trouble.'

'Oh, thanks, Lily. Sometimes I don't know how you put up with her'

Her sister smiled wearily. 'To be honest, neither do I. Mam was born to make trouble, and it's beginning to look as if I was born to protect the family from her.'

That had been only one of many such conversations about her mother. Lily was always as good as her word, and acted as a shield for Bethan against Margaret Ann's worst outbursts. But that only made Bethan feel even worse about what might happen if she really tried to spread her wings – with something like a move to London, perhaps. But could she see herself spending much more time shut up like a nun here in Cardiff? Most of her fellow nurses were middle-class girls from the city. On their days off they went home to family circles which introduced them to presentable young men and offered them a way out of their profession when they were ready to go.

Bethan had never entertained ambitions to remain a virginal career woman all her life; she simply had no intention of giving up her new-found freedom to return to the backward-looking mining community. Unfortunately it was beginning to look as if she had no third option. It was either the nurses' home or the Valleys.

Undressing for bed, she sighed as she remembered the fun she used to have during her time off, down at Uncle Rhys's pub in Bute Street. Always friendly faces . . . always something to joke about . . . except that last time a few months ago . . .

It was still vivid in her memory. The front bar at the Anglesey, frozen in garish gaslight. Rhys turning to smile at her as she

42

stepped inside after her afternoon off to prepare for her return to night shift. Then the cold feeling of disorientation as she recognized the man her uncle was talking to, but failed to place him; the growing anger, mixed with anxiety about what she might find out, which came as she remembered where she had last seen him.

Forgetting her normal shyness, Bethan strode forward to stand aggressively in front of the man. 'You – why didn't you stay last night until we were ready to see you?' she demanded.

The man's gaze shifted to the sawdust on the floor. 'What's she to you?' he said gruffly to Rhys.

Rhys glanced rapidly from one to the other of them. 'She's my niece. Why?'

Before the man could say anything else Bethan broke in: 'I think this is the wrong way round, Uncle Rhys. I should be asking what *he* is to *you*, and I'm afraid of what you'll say.'

Now Rhys was looking away too. After a long pause, he said: 'Just a business associate. Nothing that need concern you.'

From that moment Bethan began to see her uncle as a stranger. 'Ask him if your shared interests took him to the Infirmary at about four o'clock this morning.'

'What are you talking about?'

Bethan was almost choking on her fury now. 'I was on casualty intake,' she said, 'and all of a sudden there was this girl, spark out, clammy, hardly any pulse, vomit all over her pretty frock, and *him* carting her as if she was a sack of potatoes. I told him to wait there while we got her in a cubicle. She was dead before we could even have a good look at her. And guess what? When I went back outside your *associate* was gone. And guess what the girl died of? An overdose of cocaine. Now there's a surprise for you, ennit, Uncle Rhys?'

The man was staring at her now. 'You wanna be careful what you says, love. There might be a lorra people wouldn't like to hear about that, and they might come askin' you to shurrup about it. They might come in the dark, and they might not be too gentle, neither.'

'Stow it, Gerry. She's family.' Rhys looked livid as he rounded on the man.

But Gerry was unabashed. 'If she's family, it's about time you let 'er know which side her bread's buttered, ennit?

Always remember, Rhys boy, you invited me in yer. I didn't have to force no locks.' He shrugged, oddly like a prize-fighter loosening up his biceps, than started towards the door. As he passed Bethan he said: 'Remember now. Men don' like girls with big mouths.'

After he had gone there was a long silence. Finally Rhys stood up and began to move over to the bar. Bethan snatched at his arm. 'Uncle Rhys – wait. You can't just leave it like that . . . '

His expression was shut-off. 'Don't see why not. Offhand I can't think of one thing either of us would say to make a damn of difference.'

'But there must be. You must see it's wrong . . . think of the people it hurts, just to give you an easy living.'

'Don't make me laugh!' His tone indicated that amusement was the last thing on his mind. 'I only got an easy living in comparison to men like our Evan. Don't seem too easy when you line it up beside the way some a them fat docksmen has it. Any road, I never heard you complaining when you was getting your share.'

'How dare you! I never took money from anything like that! You kept us from the pub takings, and that was just because you refused money from Dad for our board and lodging. Lily an' I was always willing workers in the bar to make up, and well you know it.'

Rhys shook his head. 'It ent never that easy, Bethan, and it's time you started realizing that. Remember when you was just a bright little girl in school, clever enough for the scholarship but not quite up to the books and uniforms grant? Who paid up then? Me – and it wasn't with no pub takings, neither. Up around the start of the war, if it hadn't been for a bit a fencing and the rich boys and girls getting a taste for snow, you'd a been a full-time barmaid before you was fifteen.'

'I don't believe you! This has always been a good paying pub.'

'Good, yes; paying, no. Not in the way you do mean, anyhow. Look at the other places this size. They get by, but the women ent dressed anything like as good as you three always was. You always had money to go out and enjoy yourselves, didn't you? Until my day, the Anglesey give its landlord

44

enough of a profit to keep himself respectable – just. There was never no money for fancy clothes and outings and sending kids to the Girls High School!'

Their argument had raged on for half an hour or more, partly conducted in ferocious whispers behind the bar, occasionally flaring louder when Rhys went off into the rear quarters for something or other, and Bethan followed him.

Finally he turned on her and shouted: 'Jesus Christ, girl, will you leave it? I never realized till now, but you'm the spitting image of your mam – nag, nag, nag, without a minute's let-up. You listen to me a minute, 'cos I ent going through it again. This girl you seen up the Infirmary last night – d'you think Gerry tied her up and shoved the stuff into her? No, o' course he didn't. She was some spoiled little tart with too much money and time on her hands and not enough sense.

'The rich have been killing our kids for long enough, Bethan, and if they can't be bothered to look after their own, hard luck. I ent gonna do it for 'em. Nobody'd protect my Lexie if some rich bastard seduced her and drove her on the streets. Their daughters can go to the Devil an' all, and if I'm one o' the ones helping them on their way, so be it.'

'If that's the way you feel I'm not staying here any more.'

'Please yourself. I wish you would stay, but I ent pretending to be some holy Joe just to salve your Valleys conscience and keep you.'

'What about Lexie?'

He looked blank. 'What about her?'

'Well, she'll probably feel the same way . . .'

Rhys managed a weary smile. 'If you do think that, try her. I won't bother to come and defend myself, if you don't mind. I got to go on earning our keep, pulling pints and selling drugs and so on.' He turned away from her.

'Y-you don't care if I just go an' tell her?'

He shrugged. 'Of course I care. I'd love to be St George to all the women in my family. But Lex do know me, warts an' all, and she's grown up enough to know it don't matter in the long run.'

'We'll see about that!' Bethan was now so furious at her own helplessness to stop Rhys's criminal activity that all she wanted was to hurt him. She rushed upstairs and found Lexie in the living room, fluffing up the frills round the neck of her blouse before going down to the bar.

'Bethan, what on earth is wrong?' She had never seen the younger girl so agitated. Bethan was usually the calm, quiet one when Lexie and Lily were getting over-excited about something.

'Oh, everything, Lexie! I dunno where to start . . . ' Bethan began to cry, and Lexie sat down beside her on the sofa, comforting and calming her until she could piece together some account of what had happened downstairs.

'A-and then I came back upstairs . . . oh, what are we going to do?' she said, sniffling, as she ended her story.

'You'll have to do what you think is right. I'm not doing nothing.' Lexie's face was as rigid as her father's had been at the start of the confrontation in the bar.

'But surely you can't stay with him now, knowing where the money comes from and that he haven't got any intention of stopping?'

Lexie gave her a pitying look. 'I'd never leave our Dad even if I found him eating babies,' she said. 'He's my father and I love him more than anyone else in the world and that don't change, whatever people do. Any case, even if I did want to go, have you got the faintest idea how I'd stay alive?'

'W-well . . . there's always the hospital . . . not nursing, of course,' she added hastily, 'got to have your school matric for that . . . '

'Ward maid, perhaps?' Lexie's smile had more than a touch of malice, now. 'Or p'raps some fine lady on Park Place would fancy an exotic-looking parlour maid and I could get a position there? Grow up, Bethan. I love Dad and I'm staying put, but even if I wanted to move, I'm the wrong colour to go anywhere but down. Sooner you understand that, the happier you'll make both of us.'

That silenced her cousin. Bethan was ill-equipped to handle a crisis of the magnitude of her quarrel with Rhys, and now she had stirred up Lexie's troubles to complicate matters further. She started to cry again.

Lexie sighed, but this time there was a note of exasperation in her response. 'Listen, Bethan, nobody'll blame you if you just packs up and goes for good – though you're being a bit self-righteous as far as I'm concerned. There ent a pub down the Bay as isn't tangled up with some funny business or other. But don't go off making big promises to yourself that you'll never come back. You might want understanding friends some day, and one thing about us poor sinners – we don't arf forgive easy.

'Come on, now, or you'll be late on duty. You go back there tonight and have a think about what you really want to do. Then, if you still decide you got to go, you can come for your things next week. All right?'

Sniffing and wiping her eyes, Bethan said: 'Yes, all right. And, Lexie . . . I'm ever so sorry about not thinking straight over what you'd do if you left. That was stupid.'

'Aye, it was . . . but we all gotta learn some time. Just you remember. Now, I'm off down the bar before Dad comes looking for me.'

And that was the last time she had seen Lexie. She had not changed her mind about leaving during the subsequent week. Each time she seemed on the point of relenting, she had a memory of the rich girl's dead face and vomit-stained party dress, and her resolution hardened again. On her next afternoon off, she went back to the Anglesey, packed her belongings, and left her front door key on the table along with a note to Rhys explaining that she would not be back. Ever since she had felt utterly alone.

The memory of her breach with the family returned to her that morning and permeated her dreams. Bethan awoke shortly after noon, hardly refreshed, and knew she would not sleep again. She got up and found the writing paper and envelopes Lily had given her as a birthday present, then sat down at her small desk to write to the matron of St Thomas's Hospital in London. It might be only a different location for the same sort of work, but at least she would be beyond the reach of hurtful memories which would continue to trouble her as long as she remained in the old surroundings.

Once the letter was composed she felt better. She went to bath and then dressed carefully before calling at the matron's office to arrange for references to be made available to accompany her job application.

CHAPTER FIVE

Abercarn

'Whatever else you learned in that Infirmary, they didn't teach you much about tact, that's all I can say!' Lily was glaring exasperatedly at Bethan, who had adopted an air of injured innocence.

'Don't you turn against me as well, Lily. It's bad enough knowing that Mam will have forty fits when she finds out.'

'Yes, well don't be too sure I'm not going to join her. Honest, Bethan – why now? You haven't been qualified five minutes.'

'What has that got to do with it? I told you before, I want to spread my wings, not be trapped. This is a big step.'

'Telling me it's a big step – a hundred and fifty miles or so – and every one of them another pace along the road to Babylon as far as Mam's concerned. Wasn't Cardiff big enough, for a year or two more, anyway?'

'It wouldn't have made any difference, Lil, and you know that as well as I do. Mam doesn't know how to let go, only grip harder. I'm going, and that's that. I just thought I'd save telling her till today because with the wedding and everything she wouldn't take it so hard.'

'And I told you, that will make it ten times worse. She'll be able to do the full tragedy queen act about losing two daughters in one day. Oh, Bethan, what am I going to do with you?'

Bethan wanted to yell out that she couldn't care less what Lily was going to do with her; that she was sick of the family governing everything she did; that Lily herself was getting almost as bossy in her way as their tyrannical mother. But she knew she was being unfair and that her sister was only trying to provide the protection that she herself had asked for. Why was nothing ever easy?

Bethan had gone through the process of applying to St Thomas's, and had taken two days' leave to attend an interview in London, staying overnight at the nurses' home before returning to Cardiff. She had said nothing to the family, not even to her colleagues at the Infirmary. Only her ward sister knew what was happening.

Bethan had been surprised to find herself enjoying the secrecy. It gave her life a little spice of mystery that had been lacking before. Within the week she had received the offer of a post on one of the prestigious surgical wards at St Thomas's, and a suggestion that she might care to train as a theatre nurse with a view to future promotion. She had accepted immediately, knowing she must give three months' notice at the Infirmary, but still had failed to tell her mother or sisters. There always seemed to be a good reason for postponement. But now she could delay an announcement no longer. She was due to start work in London in just under two weeks.

She tried to tell herself she had deliberately planned it thus. With Rose's wedding imminent her mother would be distracted by other matters and would not dwell on the news as a major tragedy. But she knew the weakness of this argument. Margaret Ann would already be rehearsing herself as the mother bravely seeing off one daughter to live her own life; she would turn the departure of another into the stuff of melodrama.

Never mind, Lily would think of a way round it . . . Lily always did. Bethan went back to teasing her pretty red-gold hair into a neat bun. Really, this dark blue dress suited her remarkably well . . . She sighed. It would have been nice to be a bridesmaid, but Mam thought it would have been ostentatious to have two. Lily was the closest to Rose in age, so it was to be her. And it wasn't even as if Lily wanted to dress up and go down the aisle as part of a procession . . . even Angharad got a look-in on the act. The youngest girl apparently did not qualify as bridesmaid in her mother's eyes, and was to be a flower girl, satisfying her own yearning for a pretty dress and making Margaret Ann feel decidedly superior in having two bridal attendants without resorting to what she called swank in making it two adult bridesmaids.

Never mind. The blue silk would attract plenty of attention. Pity that Dr Henderson was a bit on the old side. He was really handsome in an intense sort of way and Bethan would have loved to flirt with him had he been even five years younger. Still, as long as she remembered not to give the come-on to any of those *Sioni ois* her mother kept coming up with, she could have quite a good time. It was fun coming home when you knew that in a few weeks you'd be nearly two hundred miles away and safe from them all.

Rose walked down the aisle at the Garn on the arm of her brother Tom. There were two other brothers older than he – John Daniel and Billie – but the feud with his mother kept John Daniel away altogether and Billie had flatly refused to parade in public except as an ordinary wedding guest. Tom, flamboyant and a friend to all the world, immediately volunteered.

Of Margaret Ann's four daughters, Lily and Bethan had stolen an unfair share of good looks. Rose was pretty enough, and Angharad was an engaging child, but neither was as exceptional as the other two. Rose had her father's perfect skin, but her hair was a nondescript mousy brown and the small curly tendrils around her face looked less captivating than they did on Bethan. Her large, myopic eyes were her best feature, but she normally concealed them behind wire-rimmed spectacles and had only left them off today under threat from her mother. Like the others, she had an exceptionally good figure, but she was shy and excessively modest, and tended to choose clothes which minimized her opulent shape. Today, though, she looked lovely. Together, Lily and Margaret Ann had persuaded her into an ankle-length dress of palest rose-pink silk chiffon, with the theme of her name re-echoed by sprays of tuberoses at the waistband and on the brim of the cartwheel hat she wore. Her Louis-heeled kid shoes had been dyed pink to match the gown, and for the first time since her childhood she looked almost beautiful.

Angharad was dressed in the same colour – Margaret Ann, always prudent, had bought sufficient fabric for the bridal gown to cut a child's dress from what was left. Lily wore creamy crêpe-de-chine, with a small cloche hat pulled down almost to eye-level, and carried a sheaf of lily-of-the-valley. Margaret Ann believed in milking every ounce of significance from the associations conjured by her daughters' names. She had also encouraged Rose in her choice of a pink gown with the half-conscious intention of seeing that Lily was the daughter who attracted most attention. When her conscience troubled her momentarily about thus blighting Rose's wedding day, she dismissed it by reasoning that Rose had already caught her man, but Lily must look her best in order to do the same thing.

As they entered the chapel, Lily was silently grateful the autumn morning was so warm and fine. Mam had been determined to put on a wedding breakfast for forty people, and there was no possibility of cramming them into the house, so they had closed off the row of the Ranks behind the back door and laid out trestle tables there. As the neighbours were invited, objections were unlikely. By now, Ethel Smith and Lucy Webb would be setting out plates for the cold meat and salad which Valleys people only ever seemed to eat at weddings and funerals.

Trust Mam to want to show off . . . nobody in the Ranks had ever had this sort of spread. They couldn't afford it and it wasn't expected of them. But that didn't stop Mam. If she could have disguised the house as a villa on Rhyswg Road, she would have done that too. In fact it had taken all Lily's guile to persuade her that it was unseemly to hold the celebration in Rose's new home up the Rhyswg. Only the fact that her daughter was renting just half the house had stopped Margaret Ann from taking it over for the day.

Lily was only vaguely aware of the progress of the marriage service. She was too preoccupied by all sorts of other matters, mainly Bethan and her scheme for going to London. Lily had been nerving herself to announce her own engagement to Charles Henderson, but if she delivered that bombshell on top of Rose's wedding and Bethan's departure, Mam would never come down off the ceiling. She sighed, mouthing the words of The Lord's My Shepherd – always good for weddings and funerals – and dwelling on the other matters which seethed through her mind. There was this Kitty Jacobs for a start.

51

Where was that going to lead? Mam seemed to have a pretty good idea, and didn't like it. Try as she would, Lily felt much the same way.

Kitty was a small girl, raven-dark with olive skin and black-brown eyes that people in the Valleys associated with the old Celtic Welsh. She was staying with relatives in the area although she normally worked a long way off, in the mid-Wales seaside resort of Aberystwyth. Kitty had been introduced to Lily's brother Emrys on a previous visit, and now she was back with a decidedly matrimonial gleam in her eye. Since she returned permanently from Cardiff, Lily had come to regard Emrys as a cross between best friend and social escort. They were thoroughly at ease together, and both loved dancing. Charles Henderson was unable to dance because of his leg injury, and in any case had no interest in the small-town Saturday evening affairs in Abercarn and Newbridge, so Lily invariably went with Emrys. But that week she had been forced to share him with Kitty, and the girl had made it plain within five minutes that she expected to have his undivided attention next time, without the presence of a sister.

Lily tried to dismiss her hostility as jealousy of the new-comer, but remained convinced it was something more than that. There was a predatory air about Kitty which raised Lily's hackles every time they met. She knew Margaret Ann felt the same, and yet her mother's reaction made her determined not to let her own feelings show. All Margaret Ann's children knew the misery of pitting themselves against their mother to get some-thing they wanted. Lily had no wish to add to Emrys's troubles by supporting her in the inevitable discord which lay ahead.

The hymn had finished long ago. The couple had exchanged their vows and now Lily, a witness, followed them into the vestry to sign the register while the congregation sang the other Valleys wedding staple, 'Love Divine.' Then they moved back down the aisle, accompanied by the boisterous notes of Mendelssohn's Wedding March, and Lily was taking gulps of clean sunlit air. She had forgotten how much she loathed the enclosed smell of over-varnished pitch-pine pews, old hymn books and cheap furniture polish.

Margaret Ann had insisted on inviting Charles Henderson to the wedding: 'After all, our Rose wouldn't be here today if it hadn't been for him,' she had said, writing the invitation card, but Lily suspected the courtesy owed more to Henderson's social standing as doctor than to his role as family saviour. Whatever the cause, she was glad he was here now. As she stood in the barren chapel forecourt, posing while one of the Webb boys took hazy pictures with a box Brownie camera, she caught his eye and responded with a contented glow to the mixture of tenderness and amusement in his smile. What an odd do this must all seem to him, with his prosperous family and big house back in the north of England!

Lily felt no shame for her humble origins: she was merely intrigued by the sudden thought that they must be as alien to Henderson as a tribe of Jivaro Indians to the first explorers of the South American rain forests. As the guests rearranged themselves for a bigger picture, she passed close to him and murmured: 'If you think this is bloody funny, wait till you see 'em get at the ham salad . . . ' Henderson was stretching out a hand to pat her perfect buttocks when he saw Margaret Ann staring at him and thought better of it.

'See you later, hussy!' he said, so that only Lily heard him, and moved off to talk to her mother.

After that the day seemed to go on interminably. It was all right for Rose, Lily reflected. Albert was a careful and considerate young man, and had managed to hoard enough money to take them to Weston-super-Mare for the week-end. At two o'clock they left the wedding party to catch a train for Cardiff and the Bristol Channel steamer that would take them there. The rest of the family had to stay with their mother – Lily with the secret knowledge that soon someone must tell Margaret Ann about Bethan's imminent departure for London.

CHAPTER SIX

Lily already had visions of autumn fading into winter without her having nerved herself to mention her planned marriage to Charles Henderson. Now her attempt to ease matters for Bethan brought her own difficulties to a head. Knowing that in spite of her most diplomatic efforts, Margaret Ann would be furious at Bethan's departure for London, Lily had not told her mother the news on Rose's wedding day. But it was no easier on Sunday, the day Bethan planned to go back to Cardiff.

'One of us is going to have to say something before you go,' she told her sister on Sunday morning. 'You won't be home again in the next fortnight and I think Mam would disown you if you went without her seeing you face-to-face first.'

Her anxiety to keep the peace was pointless. Margaret Ann disowned Bethan anyway. 'If you go off there, my girl, forget any ideas of ever coming back here again. I've got along without two of my other children before now, and I can get along without you, an' all!'

'But Mam, why? What's so terrible about it? Look, it's a wonderful chance. In a few years I'll be a theatre sister in one of the best hospitals in the world. It can't be a question of respectability. Lily told you I'll be living in. You can't carry on like this . . .'

'I'll carry on any way I want to!' Margaret Ann was so angry now that she was responding like a child. 'There's different ideas of respectability, and I'm telling you it's not respectable for a girl to traipse off on her own like an orphan when there ent no need. What'll everyone say?' She lowered her voice: 'They'll be sayin' you ran off with some man; nobody will believe me if I tell them the truth.'

Lily was getting angry now too. 'Look, Mam, you may be willing to live your life for the ladies up the chapel, but we're not. Bethan have got to make her own way in life, just like the boys . . . just like me.' She stopped, eyeing Margaret Ann warily but thinking, she can't get much worse than this. Let's get it over with in one swoop.

She had already slowed Margaret Ann's tirade. 'Just like you? What's that mean, then? You haven't said nothing about going off . . . ' Her face crumpled. 'Don't say you'm off back to Cardiff, Lily, oh, please don't say that!'

Lily embraced her with some reluctance. 'No, of course not, Mam. I told you I'd never go back to live with Uncle Rhys again. No, now listen to me . . . What would be the best news someone could give you about me or Bethan – you know, since you don't want her going off to work?'

For a split second Margaret Ann sensed the trap, but then dismissed her unease. 'Why, for either of you to make a good marriage, of course, here in the village. What could be better than that?'

Lily's smile was radiant. 'Well, then, at least you got your wish with one of us! Charles Henderson have asked me to marry him. That's a good enough marriage, ennit, and it should make up for Bethan being away for the time being?'

There was murder in Margaret Ann's eyes. She had been hoodwinked, and she knew it. Lily married was the last thing she wanted, however much she day-dreamed about it. She adored her second daughter, and even though the girl was out at work for most of the day, they saw a great deal of each other. She would have sacrificed Bethan ten times over to hold on to Lily, but now it seemed she had no choice. She stood to lose them both.

'How long have that been going on? Who said he's going to marry you? I'll believe that when I do see the ring and hear him saying it.'

Lily shook her head, pitying this obsessive little woman. 'Oh, Mam, he'll come and tell you himself, any time. The only reason he's kept quiet till now was that I didn't want him to overshadow Rose's fun. Look, I'm giving you what you said you wanted. What's wrong now?l'

'It don't feel right, that's all. Why should a big noise like him marry his receptionist? Don't make sense . . .'

'Maybe he've lost his marbles, Mam. Tell you what – I'll ask him to come up an' explain it to you himself, all right? You might believe it then.' She turned and started staring out of the window, unable to meet her mother's eye and keep her temper.

Bethan stood, ignored, across the room. Finally she said: 'Well, Mam, aren't you going to say anything to me?'

'I said all I wanted to on that score. Lily haven't said nothing to change the way I feel.'

'In that case, you'd better take a good long look at me, because I've had enough. All you know how to do is boss us all about, and you don't really know what you want yourself, except to stop anybody else enjoying themselves. Well, this is the last time you'll do it to me!' She turned to face Lily. 'And if you had any sense, Lil, you'd go too, first chance you got. If that flat up the surgery was still vacant, you ought to move back in. I'm glad for you and the doctor, but if you think she'll let you have a minute's happiness, you're wrong.'

Neither Margaret Ann nor Lily moved as Bethan's foot-steps hurried up the uncarpeted stairs. The women did not look at each other; it was as though in doing so, they would have accepted the truth of Bethan's accusations and any further closeness between them would have been impossible. Instead they remained frozen, one standing at the kitchen window, the other sitting in the Windsor chair by the fire, until Bethan's returning steps galvanized them into life again. Lily went to the door and followed her sister on to the front step.

'Oh, Bethan, I begged you not to lose your temper! We could have sorted something out without it having to end like this . . .'

But now Bethan was almost as angry with Lily as she was with her mother. 'Oh, for God's sake stop being such a doormat!' she said. 'Mam only understands one language – strength. No wonder our Dad had to knock her about. It was probably the only way he had of getting some sense into her.'

'Now *I've* had enough, you cruel little bitch!' Lily was blazing with temper. 'One day you might have some idea of how to go with people instead of against them all the time. You're just like our Mam, underneath, don't you realize that? The reason you don't see her point of view is that you're every bit as selfish as she is. Well, you got your own way now, so bugger off out of it. Just don't come back here again expecting me to fight your battles, all right?' And she slammed the door so hard behind Bethan that the younger girl half expected to see the front of the house collapse.

In the kitchen Margaret Ann eyed Lily as warily as if she were some wild animal on the rampage. She could not pretend she had not heard what was said, and so she sat, almost meekly, waiting for her own tongue-lashing.

'And there's no need for you to sit there as if butter wouldn't melt in your mouth, neither, Mam,' stormed Lily. 'You know bloody well you was to blame for that lot, and don't pretend you weren't . . . and another thing, don't *dare* tell me I mustn't swear in this house – not ever again, d'you understand?'

'Yes, Lily.'

'Right. Well . . . let's get a few more things straight. From now on, you will stop twisting up everybody in this family just because it do suit you. You won't niggle at me over marrying Charlie Henderson. You won't set Rose after Albert all the time, nagging him to get on in life. And above all, you'll give our Billie a bit of peace. Have you got all that? Because if you haven't, I'll repeat it. I'll bloody repeat it all day and night if it takes that for it to sink in. It's about time you stopped blaming us for the sort of life you'm living and started blessing us for it, and don't you ever forget that!

'Now, I'm going down to the Swan to see Charles, and when I come back I'll probably have fixed a date to go up North and meet his parents. When I do, I'll be staying with them for about a week. If you so much as hint that it ent respectable, I'll move straight in with him when I come back, you understand?'

'Yes Lily.'

Glaring at her, Lily gave her a brusque little nod, then she went out through the back door and headed for the peace of Charles Henderson's house.

They went by train to Cardiff to buy Lily's engagement ring, and travelled first class. Lily stroked the lace antimacassar on the seat back and tested the thickness of the carpet pile with the toe of her shoe. 'There's plenty of front parlours in Abercarn with worse furniture than this,' she said. 'Why on earth would anybody want to waste good money doing up a train like a posh house?'

'I think it's less a case of comfort than showing the world one can afford to travel in style,' said Henderson. 'I must confess I always imagine third-class seats as harder, and I don't really think they are. They only seem to be, because they're cheaply upholstered and there's no carpet to cover the floor.'

Lily's pleasure in the novelty of such things as a railway carriage, and her refusal to be impressed by status symbols, were a source of pleasure to Henderson, but he was apprehensive about the effect of these qualities on his parents. For weeks he had been trying to find a tactful way of preparing her for them, but so far he had failed. Her repeated postponement of any public announcement that they were to be married had deadened his sense of urgency. But the next step must be a trip to Northumberland to introduce Lily to his family, and he had to give the poor girl some idea of the ordeal which awaited her.

'What are you expecting when we go to Northumberland?' he asked in the end, as they were having lunch in Cardiff.

'I haven't dared to think about it too much,' said Lily. 'I've been trying to get some of the Valleys out of my language, though. It seemed to creep back, somehow, when I went to live in the Ranks again.'

'Yes, I've noticed. Much as I hate you feeling you have to do it, I think it's quite sensible, with what we have ahead of us.'

She laughed. 'Don't worry too much on my account. As long as *you* know it's no more than show, I don't mind laying it on a bit for them. Nobody has to explain to me how awkward parents can be.'

He was still uneasy. 'I have a feeling that mine might even outclass Margaret Ann Walters. There's one thing I really should have told you long before now, but somehow the time was never right. My father is a baronet.'

'A *what*? Charlie, you're having me on!'

'Oh, very refined! That should disarm them immediately!'

They looked at each other and began to laugh. Then Lily said: 'It's no good, Charlie. You'll never make a silk purse out of a sow's ear, and I come from a long line of sows' ears. But is that the truth? You've never really got a title in the family?'

'Oh, 'tis true, 'tis true . . . I only wish it weren't.'

'But your eldest brother was killed in the war. That makes you . . .'

'Precisely, my dear. That makes me heir to title and ancestral acres, none of which I want. All I've ever wanted is to practise medicine.'

'But there's another brother, younger than you, isn't there? Couldn't he, sort of, step into the breach?'

'It's not that easy. For a start, it's virtually unheard of unless the eldest is mentally incompetent or has been disowned; second, Peter is even worse than I am. Compared to him, I'm a reactionary!'

'Oh . . . so one day you'll have to give up the practice and go back . . .'

He was studying her closely. 'Would you like that, Lily?'

Lily's face was pale and she seemed on the edge of tears. 'I-I don't think I could do it . . . I've never had day-dreams about being the princess in the fairy story. I like to feel the ground under my feet – Valleys ground. Oh, Charlie, why didn't you say something before?'

He smiled at last, his relief evident. 'I can't apologize enough for springing it on you like this. I admit that was because I was frightened you'd reject me out of hand. There was enough going against me as it was. But as to the rest – there's no need for you to worry. I haven't the slightest intention of going home to tend the family acres. If I ever do inherit, I shall put in a manager, renounce the title, and go on living as I do now. But I had to give you the choice too. Your feelings will give me the strength not to fall in with what my parents expect of me. You might have fancied playing the grand lady – might still do when you see the place. It's quite lovely.'

'Fancy you never saying . . . I just can't get over it. What would it be – Lord Henderson?'

He laughed, shaking his head. 'No more than a humble "Sir", I'm afraid. Father is Sir Ambrose Henderson. I would be Sir Charles if I took up the title, and you would be Lady Henderson. Sure it doesn't appeal?'

'Only as a bit of a giggle. I'm ever so sorry I can't sound

more impressed. Oh, but hang on – what do I call your mother?'

'A good question, dear girl. If she's on form, you might have all sorts of names for her by the time we depart, none of them flattering. But Lady Henderson will do. Not Milady or Your Ladyship, for God's sake.'

'And your father?'

'Oh, Sir Ambrose . . . and don't dare to laugh just because he's not called George or Albert! Ambrose is an old family name.'

'Will your revolutionary brother Peter be there when we go?'

'Not unless he's taking a holiday. He's halfway through his training at Bart's. Took a liking to medicine when he saw me at it, and followed in big brother's footsteps. The war delayed him a bit, but he'll soon be practising on his own account.'

'It must have been hard for your parents, three sons of military age, one killed, one wounded . . . '

' . . . and one a conscientious objector. Harder than you might imagine.'

'God Almighty. How did they cope with that?'

'Admirably, as it happened. Mind you, Peter helped them considerably there. Having made his anti-war views quite plain – he's not a pacifist, just thought *this* war was unjustifiable – he volunteered as a stretcher bearer and spent his war in more danger than the average infantryman.'

'And wasn't wounded?'

'Oh, a couple of scratches. Nothing sufficient to keep him away from the front line for more than forty-eight hours.'

'How old was he when all this was going on?'

'Eighteen when the whole shooting match started. Nineteen when *he* got started. He was driving an ambulance for the last year, but that was hardly safer than stretcher-bearing. Of course, it made all the difference in the world to my parents' attitude. I don't think they could have handled a non-participant conchie, who went to jail for the duration. As it was, their boy was every bit as brave as other people's sons, more so in a way. After all, he was going into action unarmed.'

'How does he get on with them now?'

60

'Not terribly well. His politics are very left wing and Father is convinced he's a Bolshevik. Odd, really. My poor parents are true humanitarians. They taught us the principles of equality and free speech, although in practical terms they don't really believe in either themselves. As a result they turned out a trio of sons whose social attitudes shocked them to the core every day of their lives, and they have no one to blame but themselves.'

Lily sighed. 'I feel quite ashamed, really. You told me your family lived right out in the country and your father was a sort of farmer, and I never got round to finding out more about them. If I'd asked you point blank, you'd have told me months ago, wouldn't you?'

'Yes, if somewhat reluctantly. But you're always so bound up with what's going on this minute, all around you, that I can't see you sitting still for long enough to hear out some boring family history. I can't blame you for being unprepared for the Peel.'

'The Peel – what the hell is that, some horrible initiation?'

'No, idiot! It's the name of our house. We assume it derives from the old pele towers they used to have as defensive buildings in the border country.'

'Ah, I see – a bit like the Ranks.'

'Mmm – perhaps it loses a little in the translation.' His eyes became dreamy. 'The Peel is quite unlike any other place. I have no desire to live there, but if I could simply have it as a holiday home for the rest of my life, I'd be a happy man.'

'You say that as if you're still half under its spell. What's so wonderful about it?'

'Well, for a start, the border country. It's wild, and romantic, and empty . . . Mother and Father live in the dower house – it was built early in the sixteenth century. The original castle really has a pele tower. It sits there, half ruined, brooding on the south bank of the Tweed, a mile from the present house. To the north, all you can see is the Scottish Lowlands. South of the dower house, there are real stately home lawns running down to the edge of farmland, and the farmland runs on to another river, a tributary of the Tweed. It's quite a place.'

'You don't sound to me like a man who'd be able to give it

all up and stay in a grubby mining valley running a medical practice for the rest of your life. Not with all that within your reach.'

Henderson shook himself out of his reverie. 'I can't think why I should have been so nostalgic about it today . . . ' He squeezed her hand. 'Perhaps having found my perfect mate is giving me delusions about being a country squire. Never fear, it will pass off soon enough when I take another look at Ron Gilchrist's hernia.'

Lily managed an uneasy laugh, but the conversation had sent a chill through her. She had seen what happened when incompatible people of different origins made their life together but went on dreaming separate dreams. Her parents' marriage had been a nightmare testimony to the madness of such matches – and they had been separated by the narrowest division of white-collar worker and miner. How much greater would the gulf be for a son of the gentry, however unconventional, and a girl from the Ranks?

She had always imagined Henderson's father as a bluff, overweight farmer and his mother as an apple-cheeked woman who hand-reared lambs beside the kitchen range and collected eggs from her own chicken runs. She knew they lived in a big house, but it had never occurred to her that they might live in a *mansion*, staffed by a regiment of servants, with a ruined ancestral castle in the grounds!

Henderson had seen her unease and resolutely steered the conversation to other topics until they had finished lunch. But she was still not herself when they set off for the city's best jeweller's shop, and even attempted to dissuade him from choosing a ring that day.

'Why, Miss Walters,' he said, 'if I didn't know better, I'd think you were trying to put me off!'

'N-no, of course not . . . just got a lot on my mind for the moment and rings don't seem to fit in with the rest.'

'In that case, I shall choose something and you must put up with it. Come along. I refuse to allow my undesirable origins to sidetrack us from today's business!'

In the display cases diamonds and sapphires lay sparkling on black velvet, their facets polished to impossible brilliance. Lily tried to imagine one of these pieces of frozen fire on her hand

and failed. 'Look at the prices, Charlie. It doesn't make sense,' she said.

'Lily, I never suspected you of harbouring a puritan streak. Come on, it's once in a lifetime – well, I hope so, anyway!' He was still trying, unsuccessfully, to lighten her mood.

She looked, and tried on, and looked again, and all she could see was money thrown away to buy something no one in their senses would want. She had never experienced such emotions before. When Henderson had suggested the trip to choose a ring, she had been as excited as any other girl. Now all she could see was long balance sheet columns, with the weekly totals of men's wages for six shifts underground, and it took an unconscionable number of them to mount up to the price of one small diamond ring.

'I – I just can't choose, really. Shall we leave it for today?' Blushing with embarrassment, hot with the terrible working-class fear that she had wasted the jeweller's time by not buying anything, she sought a quick exit from the shop.

'Come on, Lily, don't be so shy about it. There's only one possible choice – that sapphire half-hoop.' He was pointing to the most expensive piece in the case, a Victorian design of five enormous sapphires on a band of white gold. 'Your hands are lovely, but they're quite big and those smaller rings look silly. That's the one for you.'

The jeweller beamed his agreement with Henderson's choice. 'Perfect, if I may say so, sir. Simply perfect,' he murmured.

Oh, aye, thought Lily, for you it is. These bits of rock are the dearest you've shown us yet. She began to protest, intercepted Henderson's pleading look and thought better of it. 'Go on,' he said, 'put it on again. It really does look lovely.'

It did, too. It sat on her third finger, glimmering obscenely at her and whispering to her conscience . . . eighty pounds . . . three months' wages for a top collier . . . enough to keep a family for six months . . . eighty pounds to put on your finger and impress Mam's neighbours. Lily tried not to shudder, painted a smile on to her face, and kissed Henderson lightly on the cheek. 'You're right, my darling. It do look lovely.' Please, she thought, just let's get away, away from that servile man and Charlie's desperate hope he hasn't done everything wrong, although in his heart he do know he have . . .

Eventually, after an eternity, they were back out on St Mary Street. 'There now,' said Henderson, a trifle too heartily, 'that wasn't too painful, was it?' Lily found it impossible to answer him.

They walked along the busy city streets, looking into shop windows, digging for small talk, eventually finding it. 'I'd take you down to meet my Uncle Rhys,' said Lily, 'but with these restricted pub opening hours, he'll have had to close up and I expect he'll have gone out. Never was one for hanging around with nothing to do.'

'Perhaps we could go and look at Butetown anyway,' said Henderson, pathetically eager to slip into her world after his glimpse of how little she wished to emerge into his.

'No, I don't think so. All we'd see is dusty shop windows and a couple of cafés-that-wasn't with good-time girls-who-aren't sitting inside. And carrying a bit of jewellery like that ring, we'd be asking for trouble. To tell you the truth, Charlie, I think I'd rather go home now.'

He stopped and turned to face her. 'As I told you some time ago, I never want you to tell me anything but the truth. Lily, what's gone wrong so suddenly? Everything was perfect when we set out this morning.'

'Nothing, Charlie . . . n-nothing, honest! I just don't seem to be feeling too grand. I'm ever so sorry if I've spoiled our day. If there's anything you'd rather do . . . '

His smile was forced. 'Just one silly thing. I'd like to become engaged to you on the train on the way home. Go on, we have the ring now. It's not as if we have to wait for parental permission. We're both of age.'

She looked at him darkly. 'There's permission and permission. Will either of us ever have it, I wonder?'

'Please, Lily! It would matter so much to me.'

'All right then . . . I only hope you think it's worth it in the end.'

CHAPTER SEVEN

Armistice Day, November 11, was to be the great national catharsis, when the population of Britain turned out to honour its millions of dead with two minutes' silence and a macabre piece of public melodrama which teetered on the edge of profound bad taste.

It was planned long in advance that the King would mark this second anniversary of the end of hostilities by unveiling the new Cenotaph in Whitehall. The memorial, designed by Sir Edwin Lutyens to represent an empty tomb, appealed to King George as a fittingly dignified monument. Others felt a more full-blooded response was required.

In October the Dean of Westminster had written to Buckingham Palace to suggest that the body of a soldier should be dug up, brought back to England and buried in the Abbey. His class, name, rank and age would be unknown. He could be any woman's husband; any man's son. This symbolic Everyman would unite the country again as it had been in the old days. The King recoiled from the idea, but his politicians grasped the promotional possibilities and he reluctantly accepted it.

There was something of the air of an obscene bran tub draw in the selection of a suitable corpse. To guarantee anonymity, six sets of remains were exhumed by the military authorities in France. On the Marne, at Ypres, Cambrai, Arras, the Somme and the Aisne, the rough crosses marked 'Unkown' were pushed aside and the bodies were removed, sealed into coffins and loaded on to motor ambulances. Each corpse was despatched separately to an army hut near Ypres, where an Anglican clergyman received them. All those involved until now in the exhumation and transport withdrew, and an officer who had not been inside the hut before was led in, blindfold, and left at the door. The first coffin his groping hand touched as he stumbled forward was to be the Unknown Warrior, his destiny to be buried with the full panoply of state and the King of England walking humbly behind his coffin in the funeral procession.

The apotheosis began at Boulogne, where *HMS* Verdun, bearing a mighty coffin made of oak cut from the park at Hampton Court Palace, awaited the glorious dead. The original deal coffin, still sealed, was put inside the oak casket, and the whole bound around with wrought iron straps. Where they crossed on the lid, a great seal was placed, bearing an inscription in gothic lettering:

A British Warrior
Who fell in the Great War
1914–1918
For King and Country

By now the King, too, was enthusiastic about the plan. He had selected an antique sword from his private collection, and this was clipped upon the coffin beneath the inscription.

From mid-channel, six destroyers escorted the *Verdun* to Dover, where the illustrious corpse received a field-marshal's nineteen-gun salute from the castle. On the night of November 10 the coffin rested in a temporary chapel at Victoria Station, where it had been taken in a specially fitted railway carriage.

On the morning of November 11, the pallbearers arrived to escort the body on the last stage of its journey: five admirals, four field-marshals, two generals and an air-marshal. So far official vulgarity carried it. Then the reality of public grief welled up and turned the whole affair into an overwhelming expression of sorrow. The pavements of the West End were crammed with silent crowds. Before an Abbey congregation comprised largely of private mourners, the coffin was lowered into a grave which was then filled with bags of earth brought from the main battlefields of France. A large slab of Tournai marble was laid on top and the bereaved, purged of the first miseries of their loss, streamed away behind their King-Emperor, their need for public recognition of their sacrifice at least partly fulfilled.

Abercarn was staging its own more modest commemorative ceremony: a church parade through the village of anyone with a uniform, from ex-soldiers and sailors to the St John Ambulance Brigade and the Boy Scouts.

Lewis Walters had joined the scouts three months earlier and now he was looking forward to his first participation in military pageantry. He had been drilling for weeks with the other scouts in their battered hut behind the Salvation Army Citadel. Most of the boys came from the prosperous houses in the Gywddon and Rhyswg roads, and already boasted full scout uniforms. Baden Powell's hearty call to defend the empire seldom appealed to children who had seen little evidence of its advantages. But Lewis's friend George, son of a mining engineer, was an enthusiast, and Lewis had gone along with him. After that, Margaret Ann, impressed by the general tone of the membership, had encouraged her youngest son to stay. Encouragement was not money, though, and uniforms were expensive. By the eve of Armistice Day, three members of the First Abercarn troupe still had only their everyday knicker-bockers, jumpers, woollen stockings and hobnailed boots for the big day.

'They'll ruin everything,' moaned Harry Prout, the scout captain, to his lieutenant the night before the big parade. 'How can I turn out a smart company with them three rodneys bringing up the rear?' Harry had not fought in the war; his lungs were not up to it. Now he felt obliged to put on a particularly impressive show of military competence to demonstrate that he could have done it if health had permitted. Lewis Walters, Jimmy Webb and John Llewellyn, the three non-uniformed members of the troupe, were about to tarnish his image.

Jack Evans, the scout lieutenant, was less ruffled. 'No need to panic,' he said. 'There's more than one reason for takin' scouts off parade. Doesn't just have to be the uniforms.' Both men knew without needing to discuss it that if they gave the true reason, they would be mobbed by villagers for victimizing the poor.

Prout brightened. 'Such as what?'

'Well, poor marching, for instance. How many eleven-year-old boys have you ever seen who do really march straight?'

'True, but you could say that about the whole company, mun.'

'But nobody's going to come out with it, are they, 'cos all the mams and dads whose kids are on parade will think their boys is perfect. Look, tell you what. You start the church parade off tomorrow morning. I'll get these three drillin' while you form up and move out. Then I'll leave 'em to get on with it, nip round the short cut behind the Citadel, and catch up with you as you come up past the Ranks. How about that?'

'Jack, boy, you could be a military tactician with the brain you got on you!'

Lewis had done his best to assemble some sort of uniform for the parade. George had a spare scout hat, because a well-meaning aunt had brought him one as a surprise after his mother had fully kitted him out. They stood together in George's bedroom on Saturday afternoon, dubiously eyeing the effect of the rather overlarge hat.

George shook his head. 'I dunno. Don't seem quite right, somehow, without the shirt and shorts. Tell you what! One of our Dad's big hankies for underground is the right colour. I could pinch one a them for a neckerchief, and maybe you could just wear a shirt with it.'

'It's November, mun! An ordinary shirt en' gonna keep me warm enough. Them scout shirts is good and thick.'

'Go on – you'll be all right if you wear a vest underneath.'

Lewis accepted that. 'Yes, all right. But the shirt's dark blue. Nobody'd believe it was like them khaki ones.'

'P'raps we could pretend you was a visitor from the sea scouts . . . anyway, I say it looks a lot more like uniform than your jumper. What about the rest?'

'Ah, I'm all right there! Our Edmund bought me a pair of proper khaki socks with the garter flashes. I got them yer.' Proudly he unwrapped a small paper package and shook free a pair of heavy woollen socks.

'Go on then, try it all on,' George instructed.

By the time they had finished, Lewis resembled nothing as much as a charity orphan kitted out in clothes abandoned by an old frontiersman, but childhood automatically bestows rosy spectacles and both boys were impressed by his overall appearance. That was more than could be said for Jack Evans or Harry Prout when their youngest recruit appeared on parade on Armistice morning.

'*Iesu Mawr*, Jack – I was having second thoughts about hiding them away, but seeing that Walters kid have decided me – I'd never hold my head up again if he was marching with us today,' said Prout.

'Thought you'd see it my way. Righto, you get 'em lined up and I'll sort our three black sheep.' He went to direct the three boys to the far end of the piece of rough ground outside the hut.

Once there, Evans gave them a suitably hearty talking-to about co-ordinating arm and leg movements, walking with a swagger instead of a slouch, and generally keeping their minds uplifted with thoughts of the Empire, God and the King.

When they were footslogging with suitable fervour, he said: 'You keep that up, now, while we go on parade, and I'll try to get back during the service to see if you'm up to standard to come an' join in for the march back to the cenotaph. All right, left, right, left, right, left, right . . . and right . . . wheel . . . left, right – keep it up – that's improvin' already!' He was backing away from them as he spoke, eager to be gone and join with the respectably uniformed children who were marching up the High Street behind the scout flag. He had no intention of returning to them before the parade marched back to the new cenotaph in Market Square. Either they'd have got fed up and gone off home by the time it was all over, or they could be told he had no time to come back for them. It would all be forgotten in a day or two, anyhow . . .

Lewis's fervour lasted about ten minutes. The piece of rough ground was extremely narrow and the trio came to the end of it so swiftly that they seemed to be completing more right wheels than ordinary marching steps. He was proud of his makeshift uniform, and he wanted to show it off. At the back of his mind, he knew they had been tricked, but he still had sufficient faith in adults to take their word unless someone else backed up his doubts. Nevertheless, he was enough of an opportunist to realize it would be too late to find such backing when the parade was over. After the thirty-fifth wheeling manoeuvre turned them by the back wall of the Citadel, he stopped.

'Bugger this,' he said. 'You two hang around yer a minute. I'm going up the High Street to ask our Edmund if this is all right. It do seem funny to me.'

'But if we stop now, maybe they won't let us march back with them!' wailed Jimmy Webb.

'I don't think we'll get a chance whatever we do. At least Eddy will know what to do. Don't you go away, mind. Wait for me yer.' He dashed off to the point where the Ranks fronted the Market Square, and where he knew most of his family would be assembled to watch the march-past.

Edmund Walters was a sturdy youth of sixteen, a keen rugby player of great speed and strength. Lewis adored him. Now he was lounging against the railings of the Commercial with his friends, like most boys of his age, unwilling to be seen with his womenfolk at such a public event. He glanced down at Lewis, started to say: 'Why ent you in the parade?' Then stopped short as he took in Lewis's exotic outfit. 'Christ, kidda, you plannin' a route march?' he added.

Panting from his dash up from the scout hut, Lewis stammered an explanation. As he spoke, Edmund's face darkened. 'Just the three of you Ranks boys, you say . . . '

'Aye, an' it wasn't till they'd gone I realized we was the only ones without uniforms. Didn't like to tell the others, but it ent fair, is it, Eddy? Not after we been practisin', and George helped me with this outfit an' all . . . ' He was a courageous little boy, but Edmund could see he was on the edge of tears.

'March? I'll give the buggers march!' He nudged the husky youth next to him. 'Hey, Dai. They've kept Lewis and your Jimmy out o' the scout parade, 'cos they can't afford uniforms. Are we gonna stand for that?'

'Are we, hell!' Dai Webb was built like Eddy, but at least three inches taller. 'Where's our kid, Lewis?'

'Down the scout hut, still drilling with John Llewellyn. I told 'em to wait there.'

'Aye, well you'm a bit puffed, so I tell you what,' said Eddy.

70

'You go up home – round the back so Mam don't see you – take off them clothes and put your usual stuff on, then come back yer to me, all right?'

Lewis nodded, suddenly, with a wave of distaste, seeing his garb through adult eyes. 'I must look like a proper silly sod!' he muttered, glancing down so that Eddy would not see his shamed tears.

But Eddy reached down, put a hand under his chin and raised the boy's head. 'No you don't, kidda. You'm more of a man than that bloody scoutmaster will ever be, and I want you dressed so the bugger can see that before I do murder 'im. Now off you go, and hurry up.'

All in all, Harry Prout told himself, they had conducted themselves pretty well so far. Pity about the fleur-de-lys crest on the flagpole hitting the church door arch like that. He'd warned Willie Griffiths to get the thing lowered before they got so close, but Willie never did have good timing . . . Never mind. George Probert had the flag now. And this was the best bit, the march back from the corrugated-iron church building at West End, up Bridge Street, round into Market Square, stand for the dedication of the cenotaph, then back in full military order to the scout hut. And not a Ranks boy in sight . . .

As the troupe formed up outside the church, he flashed a grateful smile at Jack Evans, who had emerged from the church behind the detachment of scouts. 'Well done, Jack. Everything all right down there, is it?'

Evans laughed. 'Oh, aye. The rate they was going when I left, they'll have worn the ground down level with the canal by the time we get back! Do 'em good, an' all. You don't always get what you want in this life.' Oozing self-satisfaction, he stood back as the uniformed boys filed past.

'I'll lead them off and you bring up the rear, as usual,' Prout instructed. 'Then when we get to the Market Square and do a right wheel to face the memorial, we'll both be lined up sideways on, if you see what I mean.'

The ex-servicemen led the parade, with the St John Ambulance contingent behind them. There was some trouble between Prout and Tommy Leader, commandant of the Church Lads Brigade, who hotly contended his group of

71

muscular young Christians should take precedence over the Scouts. Prout won by saying his movement was inter-denominational, not just Church of England, so there, and the scouts formed up behind the ambulance men, marching off to a brisk rendering of 'Onward Christian Soldiers' from the Salvation Army band.

The parade was uneventful until they were half way up Bridge Street. Near the old Forge Hammer Inn, two young men slid out of a shop doorway, and the next thing Harry Prout knew, he was not marching alone. Furiously he glanced sideways at his unwanted companion. 'What the bloody hell d'you think you'm doin', mun? This is a church parade!' he hissed from the side of his mouth.

'Thought church parades was only for Christians.' The young man's tone sounded equable enough, but the words were ominous.

'Who are you? What the devil d'you think you're up to?' Prout was getting nervous now. This was the part of the route with fewest spectators. Most of the villagers were up closer to the square. But it looked as if the intruder was here to stay . . . In mounting desperation, he looked over his shoulder, hoping Jack Evans would be coming down to help him. But Evans seemed to have acquired a companion too. A young man much like his own new-found shadow, but rather shorter, was marching beside Evans, and they appeared to be deep in conversation. At a loss for an immediate solution, Prout resumed his marching, while behind him the scouts shuffled and giggled, missing their step and generally losing their smart military aspect.

In fact Jack Evans was desperately trying to talk himself out of trouble. 'Of course I didn't mean no harm,' he spluttered. 'Why would I want to pick on a little boy? They just wasn't up to scratch – couldn't march proper, that's all.'

Eddy gestured contemptuously. 'And you think that rabble can? Come off it. The Guards won't be forming a queue to sign any of 'em up. You know them boys coulda marched with this lot without anybody seeing the difference.'

'Oh, yes they would! Why, they weren't . . . ' realizing he had been about to give the game away, Evans abruptly closed his mouth, but Eddy finished the sentence for him. ' . . .

Weren't dressed proper? Was that what you was gonna say, Jackie boy?'

'Well, yes, seeing as you mention it. This is a day to honour our brave dead, not for a march of the urchins. Haven't you got no respect?'

'A bloody sight more than you 'ave, you bastard. Them soldiers died to make a land fit for heroes, remember? D'you call it a land fit for heroes when a little boy have got to stop home 'cos his mam haven't got the money to put him in uniform? Well, here's where we ruffians teaches you lot a lesson.' They had reached the canal bridge now, and Eddy raised his voice. 'All right, lads, fall in!' and from beneath the bridge, a group of young men emerged, their trousers rolled above the knee, bare-legged, shirtsleeved and sporting old trilbies and bowlers knocked out of shape as travesties of scout hats. 'Here we go, then, boys, for King and Country!' carolled Eddy, and to the horror of Evans and Prout, the parody scout troupe fell in behind the existing ranks and began slouching along only inches from the last row of boys.

Prout attempted to stop to call his charges to order, but Dai Webb got a killing grip on his arm and said with surprising sweetness: 'I wouldn't try deserting your post now, Captain, not unless you want your arm broke. Upward and onward, as they do say!' And the motley army briskly rounded the corner to the High Street and Market Square, where the crowds and the local dignitaries waited.

Margaret Ann saw them first. For a moment, Lily thought her mother was going to have a stroke. She herself was standing with Charles Henderson, a little further up the High Street than her mother, who was with Rose and Albert. She was about to slip down to Margaret Ann to ask what was wrong when she saw the scout troupe and dissolved into helpless mirth. Henderson, who had been lost in his own bad war memories, was jerked back to the present by her inappropriate response, and he too looked down towards the advancing marchers. 'Merciful God,' he exploded. 'Is nothing sacred?'

Lily stopped laughing as abruptly as she had started. 'Charlie, what are you on about?'

He gazed at her as if seeing her for the first time. 'Have you any notion why we're here today? We are supposed to be honouring men who gave their lives to preserve our freedom.'

Her mirth was rapidly turning to indignation. 'Charlie, you can't believe that! I thought it was to pay your respects, no more. You know most of them didn't have the least bit of choice in the matter. That ent heroism. It's bad luck.'

He glared at her. 'At this moment, your views are the last things I wish to discuss. I'm far more interested in what those hooligans think they're doing.'

'Joining the scouts, by the look of it,' said Lily, unchastened by his disapproval. 'That's our Eddy up the back, and Dai Webb next to Harry Prout. Neither of them is known for beating up decent citizens. There'll be a reason for it, believe me.'

'Well your mother doesn't seem to think so. In a moment I think she'll be in need of my professional services.'

The rogue scouts were really getting into their stride now. Eddy kept pushing Jack Evans forward, then, as soon as the unfortunate man began marching again, treading hard on his heels, forcing down the backs of his shoes and making him stumble into the rear of the uniformed boys in the last rank.

As the scoutmaster and his tormentor drew level with Margaret Ann, she found her voice again. 'Oh, Albert, do something to stop it, please, before they do disgrace us all!' she wailed. Charles Henderson was already moving to join her son-in-law, and for a moment Lily envisaged an even more disruptive scene as the two encountered Eddy's group.

But Eddy and Dai had planned their raid to perfection. As the scout troupe, now in total disorder, moved up the street end of the Market Square, Dai Webb twisted Harry Prout's arm and murmured something to him. To the astonishment of the crowd, the scouts were marched straight on up the street towards the Tinplaters Hall grounds nearby, effectively leaving the parade altogether. Within minutes they had disappeared from view behind the high garden wall which surrounded the recreation hall.

The local MP and council officials, lined up behind the new war memorial, did not even notice the incident. The Salvation Army band played louder, the other marching groups lined up smartly in the square, and the excitement was over. The villagers resumed their tribute to the dead.

74

Albert Watkins and Charles Henderson glanced at each other questioningly, then Albert shrugged. 'Ent no business of mine,' he said, 'so long as they ent causing trouble out yer. Mrs Walters? Are you all right now?'

Margaret Ann was still as red as a turkeycock, but now all she wanted was to make people forget what had happened. 'Yes, yes. You'm a good boy, Albert. Thank you. But let it rest, it have blown over, I hope.'

'I'm not at all sure of that,' said Henderson. 'They didn't frogmarch that lot off for a woodcraft exercise.'

Margaret Ann flashed hostility at him. 'I don't care what they'm doing, so long as it ent in front of the village,' she snapped. 'I'll sort out our Eddy after. At the moment I want to watch this service.'

Henderson returned to Lily. She met his angry look with an unspoken challenge, then said: 'I'm going to find out what on earth is going on. Come if you want to . . . or perhaps you still want to stay here and – what was it? – honour men who gave their lives to preserve our freedom?' She started up the road towards the Tinplaters Hall.

Henderson limped along beside her, still furious. 'Lily – what on earth has got into you? I've never seen you like this before.'

'No, because I never thought you took the war seriously before. All of a sudden I'm seeing a different man than the one I thought I knew.'

'I don't believe this is happening! Look at my leg. It will never be of any use to me again. D'you think I got that from not taking it seriously? Lily – I volunteered.'

'I know, dammit. But I always thought you joined up to save lives from all that terrible waste. It never occurred to me you believed in the whole thing.'

'The better part of this countty believed in it!'

That stopped her. She turned to him and said: 'Oh, no, Charlie, not the better part. The noisiest part, perhaps; the stupidest part maybe. I'll even give you the *biggest*. But the *better* part? Never? That was international butchery and nobody'll ever convince me it was anything else. You can't see it any other way.'

'But I did – truly.' There was a pleading note in his voice

75

now, underlying the tatters of his rage. 'It may sound stupid and old-fashioned, but I believed all the talk about preserving what we held dear, of saving an admirable way of life . . . '

'After years down here and in the London slums, you thought there was anything worth saving?'

'Yes, God help me, I did. There are some parts of one's background which never change, and I suppose at heart I've always been the worst sort of Little Englander.'

'I can forgive that, Charlie. What I can't forgive you is not seeing through the dishonesty of all this sanctimonious nonsense about the war. I haven't read such a lot, but I *have* read about the Romans giving their slum people bread and circuses to keep 'em quiet. Our politicians have got 'em beat to a standing start, haven't they? They can get away without providing the bread!'

They had reached the Tinplaters Hall gates now, and went in, their quarrel reducing them both to silence. At first there was nothing to see, but soon they caught the sound of heated argument somewhere around the corner.

In the maintenance yard behind the hall the scouts stood in a ragged circle, surrounding Eddy Walters and Harry Prout. Prout's nose was bleeding. He stood half crouched, his hands slack at his sides, staring at Eddy like a sheep awaiting the slaughterman's death-blow. Tears were coursing down his cheeks and mixing with the blood from his nostrils.

'Y-you touch me again and I'll have t-the law on you, Walters – j-just see if I don't!' he blubbered.

Eddy merely laughed and shaped up, boxer-style. 'Be worth a six-months' stretch, Prouty, just for the pleasure of felling you. Come on, now – ent no fun hitting a man who won't hit back!'

'I'm a sick man. You could 'ave me in the hospital after this . . . my lungs . . . couldn't go in the army 'cos of them . . . same now . . . '

Abruptly, Eddy dropped his fists, his smile turning to a grimace of disgust. 'Ach, go on home, you shitbag! It ent worth dirtying my hands on you. Go on, Jack – you an' all. Might a known I could expect this from a pair who picked on little kids. Just choose someone your own weight next time, all right?'

'Eddy – what's all this about? Our Mam'll have your guts for garters when you go home,' Lily broke in.

His good humour returned. 'I'll be ready for 'er an' all, Lil – but she'll put up a better fight of it than Prouty, I bet! Let me get rid a these boys an' I'll tell you all about it.'

The scouts were standing around, gawping in admiration. They showed no signs of objecting to having their parade disrupted. Fleetingly Lily wondered how many of them would turn up at the next meeting with Harry Prout and Jack Evans. Now Eddy told them they could either head for home or go back to the scout hut.

'I reckon if you all formed up and marched back down the Square, smartish like, you could pick up the tail end of the parade as it come back through the village, and arf your mams and dads wouldn't even know you'd gone missing.'

'What about them as do?' piped a boyish voice from the rear.

'Tell 'em old Prouty got took bad, and marched you off up here out of the way until the turn passed . . .' Eddy glanced around and saw Lewis's friend. 'Hey, George! You got more sense than most. Go on, take charge. You'm carrying the flag anyhow. March 'em back and join on the parade.'

And that was what they did. Within minutes all that was left to show there had been trouble was a splash of blood on the cobblestones and one or two of the beaten-up hats which Eddy's mates had worn to guy the scouts.

'There we are,' he said, smiling and rubbing his palms together as though content with the way matters had turned out. 'Our Lewis's honour satisfied, and no real harm done. Pity Prout wasn't a better scrapper, but if he had any guts, none a this would of happened in the first place.'

'You still haven't said just what *did* happen,' said Lily.

Eddy explained about Lewis's lack of uniform, and the shabby trick resorted to by Evans and Prout. 'Wouldn't a been so bad if the poor kid hadn't trusted them,' he finished. 'I think that's why I lost my temper. I bet Lewis will never trust a grown-up again. After all we keep hearing about Baden-Powell and scouts' honour!'

Lily turned to Charles Henderson. 'You see? I told you there'd be a good reason for what went on back there. We may not be a family of patriots, but we don't go round stopping other people being like that.'

But Henderson had barely unbent. Eddy, seeing there was trouble between them, said goodbye and went off to find his friends. The lovers stood staring at each other.

Finally Henderson said: 'I understand why Eddy got so angry, Lily, but I simply cannot condone what he did. I don't quite know how I would have handled it; I realize Lewis had to see that such behaviour would not go unpunished. But Eddy should not have staged that appalling mockery on such a sacred occasion.'

Lily let out a great snort of exasperation. 'This is getting worse and worse every minute! What happened to the lovely kind man I'm engaged to? Where did all that understanding go? Charlie, I don't really know you at all, do I?'

He shook his head. 'Nor I you, it seems.' Abruptly, he clasped her hands between his. 'Oh, Darling, I love you so much – nothing will ever change that. But you must realize I'm not a man you ordered and had tailor-made to suit your own opinions. We're bound to disagree on many things, and this seems to be one.'

'Yes, but . . .' she hesitated, perplexed about why it should matter so much, ' . . . but I think this particular disagreement do run much deeper than it ought to. The way we felt about what was going on out there was about a lot of other things, wasn't it, not just the war?'

He closed his eyes and made a weary, dismissive gesture. 'Lily . . . I feel a thousand years old. This has turned into a horrible day. It stirred memories I'd have preferred to leave for dead and now I feel wretched. Can't we talk about it some other time. All I know is that I love you as much as ever, and I hope you still love me.'

'Of course I do, silly. Something like this don't make no difference to my loving you!'

'Does it not? I wonder . . . ' His expression bleak, he loosened his grip on her hands and started back towards the village street.

78

CHAPTER EIGHT

One way and another, Margaret Ann reflected, life could have been a lot worse. Of course it could never be the same with Evan gone, but there were compensations . . .

The most obvious of those was the tribe of adult and half-grown children who surrounded her, always within reach of her domineering grasp. She had borne fifteen children, thirteen of whom had lived beyond infancy and twelve still strong and healthy. One boy, Gareth, had died in 1917, of what she euphemistically called chest trouble. Tuberculosis was not a word she liked to hear. It was a disease of the poor and disreputable, not of respectable people . . .

There had been ups and downs with her other offspring, it was true. She had not seen her eldest boy, John Daniel, since Evan's funeral, and had not spoken to him since many years before that. Matters were barely better with Billie, although a certain level of contact was necessary now and then. And Bethan . . . well, Bethan had put herself beyond the pale, going off to London like that. Sometimes Margaret Ann pretended to herself that these three black sheep did not exist. She still had an embarrassment of riches. In the house next door lived Haydn, her fourth son, now father of his own family of two boys. Elwyn and Edmund, now a miner like Haydn, were in lodgings with him and Maisie, his wife. It made a bit of a full house, but she herself had crammed in a lot more than that in her time. As it was, she managed to find room for Emrys, who had moved back home when Billie went, Lewis, Angharad and Lily in the original family two-up and two-down.

Not that Lily was too keen on the arrangement. She wanted to move back to that flat over the doctor's garage, but Margaret Ann had told her it wasn't respectable, not now they were engaged. 'What, you mean it was all right for me to be unchaperoned with him when he hadn't asked to marry me, but now he have, it's not nice?' Lily never could seem to understand the need for proper behaviour. But she was a lovely girl . . . better than any of the others, really. More contrary than Rose, who could be a bit of a doormat; cleverer than any of the boys except Billie – but Margaret Ann tried to think of Billie as seldom as possible. What *was* it that made Lily so special?

In her heart Margaret Ann knew very well. The girl was practically a physical reincarnation of her father, in looks and temperament, and if Margaret Ann could no longer have the real man, this was the best substitute available. Lily was her husband's immortality.

Margaret Ann had prospered modestly during her widowhood. All the boys except Haydn, with his own family to care for, contributed to her rent and money for raising Lewis and Angharad. There was a bit of a compensation payment from the colliery following Evan's accident, and one way and another she saw more money these days than ever she had as the wife of a working miner. The days were certainly gone when she'd had to take in washing.

She contemplated the new private girls' school which had recently opened in Abercarn House, Lady Llanover's old mansion, and for the hundredth time day-dreamed about sending Angharad there to give her a bit of polish. She had told no one of her dream, not even Lily. 'Lily's the last one I'd tell!' she muttered to herself as she thought of it. But the idea grew and flourished. Oh, that would show people the Walters were out of the ordinary run of people . . . Show Bethan, too, that there was a right way and a wrong way of proving you were special, and getting high and mighty qualifications and going after a dirty job a long way from home was not the right way. As she had not been in touch with Bethan since the quarrel a fortnight before the girl went to London, she was hazy on how it would show her. But these things had a way of getting back . . .

80

For some reason Lily was more interested in Lewis than Angharad. Kept saying there was a lot more time yet for Angharad, but Lewis was doing his scholarship this year. That was all well and good, but it would cost a lot more to put a boy through grammar school than a girl through Abercarn House. And she had been counting on Lewis being an earner too, by the time Angharad was ready for improvement. Without that extra bit coming in it mightn't be possible; certainly wouldn't be if Lewis was taking money instead of bringing it in . . .

Margaret Ann considered how much she might confide in Lily. She liked a good talk with the girl because she usually respected her opinion, and when it came to something important she did not like to make a secret of it. But private education for Angharad! And the sort of school that wouldn't train her for anything . . . and at the expense of sending Lewis to grammar school . . . No, better keep it quiet. Anyhow, Lily was not herself these days. Never should of got tied up with that doctor. It was all very well to better yourself, but some jumps were too big and Lily was aiming too high. Margaret Ann had always known it would end in tears.

She was startled from her reverie by the click of the back door latch. Lovely – that would be Tom. Tom, the third son, lived in Newbridge now. His third child – Margaret Ann's first granddaughter – was just a month old and Margaret Ann relished his Friday afternoon visits, when he came straight down from the day shift and brought her news of the family along with a few shillings from his pay packet. One of the best was Tom. She had thought the money would stop when he and Sal had their third, but it hadn't. She got up and went to boil a kettle for his tea.

Lily was not at all sure her affair with Charles Henderson would end in anything. She had not been fully at ease with him since the day he told her about his family. It was not his earlier secrecy about them which worried her. Rather, her unease arose from a deep-rooted suspicion that he was too close to them to cast off their attitudes in order to commit himself to her. And Lily knew she would never be happy trying to pretend to be the lady of the manor.

Now it looked as if the whole thing would be brought to a

head. Since their bitter quarrel on Armistice Day Henderson had been particularly loving and attentive. Finally, this week, he had made his ultimate commitment: she was invited to spend Christmas with his parents at the Peel. And Christmas was barely three weeks off.

'Charlie, I don't like to say this, but there are a hundred reasons I can't do it,' she said.

His laugh was dismissive. 'Nerves, pure nerves! Tell me some of them.'

'Well, let's start with clothes. I like to dress well, but I don't think I've ever spent more than ten shillings on a frock in my life. And anyway, I don't own that many; certainly not enough to change a couple of times a day. I don't own any evening gowns at all, let alone the shoes and bags and things to go with them.'

'Oh, none of that will matter.' But she could see it would, merely by looking at his expression. Until she mentioned the clothes, it had clearly never crossed his mind. After years spent working among the poor, Charles Henderson was still sufficiently remote from them to be unaware of the vast divergence between the wardrobes of rich and poor women.

'What are your other reasons?' he asked, as if they had dispensed with this, the most important of them all.

'How about talk?' she said.

Another dismissive laugh. 'I know you keep referring to your Valleys accent coming back, but when you concentrate, you speak beautifully. You'll always have an accent, and I'd never want you to conceal it, but that's merely charming.'

'I didn't mean that sort of talk. I meant conversation.'

'Ah. What difficulties do you anticipate there?'

'Let's say your mother takes me off to the drawing room after dinner, along with the other female guests. I won't have anything to say to them.'

He was hedging again. 'My mother has a lifetime's practice in putting people at ease in circumstances like that. You won't even need to think about it.'

'What if she doesn't want to put me at ease? What if she wants to drum it into me that I'm unsuited to you and the sooner I disappear the better?'

'She'd never do that. All she wants is my happiness.'

82

But Lily could tell she had made her point. Over the next few days she came back with objection after objection, and Henderson tried, usually without success, to counter them all. Lily, meanwhile, was winding herself up ever tighter about the ordeal ahead of her. She slept very little, ate even less, and was irritable with everyone around her. After one particularly snappy morning when she upset at least three of Dr Cann's patients, she borrowed the practice car for the afternoon and drove up to Trwyn Farm to see Billie.

When she arrived he was outside in the crisp cold air, sitting on the low drystone wall with a mug of tea in his hand, gazing down into the valley below. He had heard her car coming a long way off, and she saw the relief reflected on his face as he realized that she was his guest and not some more unwelcome visitor.

'What are you doing there in just your shirtsleeves?' she scolded him fondly. 'You'll catch your death!'

'Not with what's in this tea,' he said, grinning. 'Come on in and I'll give you a drop.'

The farmhouse kitchen already looked as if it had never been abandoned. Plates sparkled on the open shelves of the dresser and there was a pleasant smell of wax polish from the plain wooden chairs and table. A good fire crackled in the huge inglenook fireplace and there were new curtains at the windows.

'You're turning it into a little palace,' she said. 'I can see you're taking to the place.'

'Taking to it? I don't think I could survive anywhere else now. I only hope that doctor of yours have got the first idea how much he've done for me. He's a saint, so far as I'm concerned.'

Lily's smile faltered. 'Aye, well it's the saint I've come to talk about really. I think I need some advice.'

'Gimme a chance, love,' said Billie. 'That do sound like romantic advice. What would someone like me know about that sort of thing?'

'It's not exactly romantic, and you're the one I want to talk to. I think you might know quite a lot about this, don't ask me why.' She explained about their unexpected disagreements, about Henderson's determination, now, that she should visit his family and his certainty that there would be no awkwardness. 'To be quite honest, Billie, I don't see there's any way of it working.'

He looked at her in silence for a long moment, then said: 'What, the visit or the whole thing?'

Lily sighed. 'I suppose the whole thing, in the end. If he can't see now what trouble it will be for me up with them for a week, he'll never understand me when we're married, will he?'

'Whatever made you think he would, Lil?'

'Well, you know me, I'm all here and now. Never thought of him having a family or nothing like that – or if I did they were a more prosperous version of us. And Charlie . . . he'd settled in so well here, loved the people so much. He was so good with his patients and he never seemed the slightest bit snobbish. I just didn't think his ideas were different from mine.'

'But now you do.'

She nodded. 'I don't really believe he'll be able to turn down this title and the estate when he inherits them. He thinks he wants to, but I'm not even sure that's genuine. He've got this funny streak, like – like a missionary without a God to follow. He wants to make people's lives better, but he doesn't really want to join in with the common herd at all. He only thinks he does.'

'I think you may be jumpin' the gun a bit,' said Billie. 'Let's get this visit sorted out first. Now if you had all the clothes and everything, and if you'd swotted up a few things to talk about with his mam, how would you feel about it then?'

'Terrified.'

'All right, let's try it the other way round. If he said there was no need to go up there; if he wrote and told them he was marrying you, and then arranged a meeting down here – asked them to stay with him, p'raps. How would you feel then, not about the visit, about spending your life with Henderson?'

She pondered the question, then said: 'That's what really scares me, I suppose. I'm not at all sure I want to.'

'But last time I was down the village, just after you announced the engagement, you seemed so fond of him.'

'Oh, I am; always will be. P'raps that's what makes it so difficult. I'm in love with him, no doubt at all about that. I don't think that would be enough though . . . '

'What d'you want to do with your life, Lil? I've never heard you come out with any big ambitions like Bethan, and you certainly ent the life-long housewife like our Rose. There must be something you want.'

'That's the trouble. I'm beginning to think there is, but it's hard to say. I been reading a lot lately, in the papers, and keeping my ears open in the surgery. It don't arf make me angry.'

'About what?'

'The way they'm treating the miners, now the war's over and the coal isn't so important. Billie, they're going to put the Valleys on the scrap heap if we give them half a chance.'

'Oh, Christ, Lil, not politics! Our Mam would crucify you!'

She grinned. 'Not the way you mean. Look, I'm not so sure I even know myself yet – you're the only one I've mentioned it to. All I know is, I don't want to go away. I want to stay here and be part of things. There's a fight coming. I'm part of a mining family and proud of it. That's my future, not being sneered at on some big estate because I don't come out of the top drawer. I don't need no in-laws to tell me that!'

Billie was smiling gently at her. 'You'm just like our Dad,' he said, 'so much I can never work out how you'm so womanly an' he was so manly.'

'I never heard our Dad talking about standing up for our rights.'

'No, because he lived it. Wasn't much of a one for talking, really, except to Ellen Rourke. But he knew he was rooted in the coal dust, same as you do, and he was ready to argue it out with his fists and boots. Boiled down to the same thing in the end, except maybe your weapons will work better.'

'I hope so . . . Oh, *Duw*, Billie, what a daft conversation to have when I come asking advice about my engagement! All these airy fairy thoughts are nothing to do with everyday life. I should be thinking out what's wrong between us, not building a new world.'

'Maybe that's the real heart of the trouble. You want to build a new world; he do just want to shore up the old one.'

'I'm not sure I understand.'

'You look at what he've done for me – don't get me wrong, I'll thank him with my dying breath – but I do often ponder on it up here by myself. You know why I think he done it, apart from being interested in you? I think he really believed he could bring back a little bit of the world we lost with the war . . . you know, restore the yeoman to his soil and all that rubbish, mend the broken spirit . . . '

Lily was regarding her brother with wonder. She had never heard him speak at such length or to such effect.

Now he went on: 'Trouble is, that's an awful tangled dream. I was no dispossessed yeoman, was I? The farmers from England who marched off to war come back to the same as they'd left, even if prices went through the floor straight after. What the generals took away from me couldn't be put back with land, nor jobs, nor nothing like that, and that's what's wrong with your Charlie Henderson. He can't get to grips with that. He do love his country and he don't believe it could do so much wrong to so many people in the name of glory.

'But the world he's harking back to never existed for our sort, Lil. He's just too far from it ever to know that, and his brushes with the poor haven't made him understand. He do just feel ever so sorry for us. Give me a choice between sympathy and revolution, an' I'll take the revolution every time.'

Billie fell silent and sat back in his chair, as if tired by a great physical effort. He groped for a pipe, filled it and made much of getting it lit. All the while Lily went on staring at him.

'I think maybe you know what I should do better than me,' she said softly.

'You won't like the answer, I shouldn't think.'

'Tell me anyway.'

'Marry a miner and start really stirring it up for the bosses!'

'I can't get married to order, just like that!'

'Well you ent going to do it as a single woman, not in these parts, and without no proper education . . . Lily, my love, I happen to think you could do practically anything if you set your mind to it, and a little thing like sorting yourself out a husband isn't going to delay you more than five minutes.'

'And tell me what brought you to this great conclusion.'

'You're the only one in this world or the next as can handle our Mam, and anybody who can do that could destroy capitalism, given the right backing!'

86

CHAPTER NINE

Lily had not seen Charles Henderson all day. He had departed early that morning on the Newport train, saying she was to meet him with the car at the station at four-thirty. He arrived, accompanied by a mound of shopping, which a porter was trundling along on a trolley behind him. She was bursting with curiosity, but he refused to say what he had been doing until they got back to the Swan.

Instead he asked questions about how she had spent her afternoon, and, embarrassed, she was thrown back on detailed descriptions of Billie's initial improvements at Trwyn Farm because she could not tell Henderson the nature of their conversation.

When they arrived at the Swan and she saw the contents of the parcels, it became even more difficult. He had purchased a complete country-house wardrobe for her, down to shoes, bags and gloves.

'All the clothes are ready-made, I'm afraid, because there simply wouldn't have been time to get them done to order,' he said. 'And as I had only that old pair of shoes you keep in your office as a guide to your size, you may find the footwear less than perfect. But at least you'll be confident you *look* right, and it will be one thing less to worry about.'

Oh, God, she thought, how do I tell him I can't go through with it? Aloud, she said: 'But it's all so beautiful, Charlie. I can't begin to thank you . . .'

'Then don't. You never asked me to have the sort of stupid family who expect people to dress for dinner and all the rest of it, so you must regard these bits and pieces as the legitimate price I pay for taking the most beautiful girl in South Wales to meet my parents.'

She sighed. 'D'you think it will work, even with all these lovely clothes?'

'Of course it will – as long as you want it to . . . You *do* want it to, don't you?'

Now – tell him now, said her conscience. But she looked into his eyes and saw the naked love there, vulnerable to the slightest pain she might cause him, and failed.

'Of course. I'd better start to practise calling you Charles. Somehow I think your mother would take a dim view of Charlie.' She hoped he would tell her not to talk nonsense. He did not; he simply flashed her a grateful smile.

At first Margaret Ann was seething about Lily's planned visit to Northumberland. Given half a chance, she began ranting about the impropriety of a single girl going away with her fiancé. Lily finally silenced her by bringing home an out-of-date glossy magazine from the surgery waiting room, and pointing out with the help of its social column that half of England's polite society appeared to embark on a vast un-chaperoned house-hop every Friday afternoon. She knew she had won that particular battle when she entered the butcher's shop behind her mother a few days later, to overhear her boasting to Mrs Parfitt about Lily's plans for a country-house Christmas with her fiancé.

Lily wished her own anxieties could be so easily stilled. She paid Billie another visit a couple of days before her departure to the North of England.

'You must be bloody mad, after all you said to me,' he told her, although there was sympathy, not anger in his tone. 'You'm not helping yourself nor him by doing it this way, and you know you'll have a hell of a time.'

'Oh, Billie, if it hadn't been for all them clothes I'd have had the nerve to tell him. But it seemed so . . . so ungrateful, somehow.'

'Ungrateful, be buggered! In his way he's as bad as our Mam, only he's more of a danger to you because you do always see Mam coming when she tries one on. This un creeps up on you. He wants you to do as he says, no arguments, and when you stand up to him he wheedles you into it, like with them clothes. You be careful, Lil. He's craftier than either of us have given him credit for.'

She denied the truth of what Billie had said, but later she was unable to fault his argument. When she got into the car to drive back to the village, he bent beside the open window and said: 'Here, take this. Just in case, like . . . ' and slipped something into her hand. It was a five pound note.

She laughed, somewhat shakily, and said: 'Our Dad did that when he saw me off to Cardiff on the train in 1911. Escape money, he called it.'

'That's what I'm calling it an' all. I want you to take that to Northumberland with you, and the minute you feel you don't want to go on no longer, you come straight back. If you don't need to use the cash, you can give it me back. If you do, remember that's what it's for. Don't you forget, now, not a minute more than you feel comfortable.'

He kissed her cheek and stood back as she drove off down the mountain.

Penelope Henderson was a few months short of her sixtieth birthday and looked closer to forty-five. Her hair, black like Charles's and with a similar slash of silver at the brow, was pulled into a sleek chignon. An afternoon frock of finest sapphire blue woollen jersey skimmed the curves of her slender body and her shoes and stockings echoed the shade of the dress fabric. No one would have regarded Lady Henderson as a country bumpkin.

At the moment she was standing at the library window, re-reading Charles's latest letter: ' . . . she may appear a little gauche by your exacting standards, but I know you and Father will offer her every consideration. She is quite an exceptional young woman and has it in her to achieve anything she sets her mind to. I know that once you have spent some time with her, you will love her almost as much as I do.'

'That, my dear Charles, is extremely unlikely,' said his mother. She dropped the letter on a side table and gazed, un-seeing, across the frosty parkland outside the window. Really, this was too much! She had tried to humour all her sons when they began believing in the brotherhood of man. It had never occurred to her that none of them would outgrow the notion. Poor Teddy had not survived the war to change his views, but judging by the way the other two had turned out, he would probably have been just as bad. Of course she sympathized with their humane dislike of social inequality – but as Papa had always said, it was easier to call a bricklayer brother than brother-in-law . . .

Still, a week was a long time. On balance she approved of Charles's decision to bring the young woman up here for Christmas. It would enable him truly to see her, his vision unclouded by the inverted romanticism bestowed by her background. Penelope found it very hard to believe that such a girl could stand up to the social pressures of Christmas week at a lively country house, particularly when her upbringing would have qualified her admirably to be on the other side of the green baize door rather than this one. Her face, until now rigid with disapproval, relaxed into a smile. It might prove to be an entertaining week.

She heard wheels crunching on gravel. That must be them now! Perhaps she should have invited a few of the guests a day early. Then Miss Walters would have been met by a battery of strangers instead of merely two . . . Now, now, she told herself, let's not be too greedy for victory. A baronet and his lady will be sufficient to be going on with . . . She smoothed her already perfect hair, straightened her unwrinkled skirt and departed elegantly from the library to greet her guests, having first tucked away Charles's letter.

'Dear God, it's a bloody sight worse than I expected, and that's saying something!' Lily told her reflection in the dressing-table mirror. She stood up and walked round her room, which in her eyes had the proportions of a ballroom. The casement windows looked down on a paved rose garden with a fountain at the centre, and the gentle splash of running water made the air musical. Lily walked across the acres of carpet and opened what she took to be a walk-in cupboard. It was her own private bathroom. She let out a little 'Oh!' of surprise and hastily closed the door.

Her suitcase – a respectably battered pigskin lent to her by Henderson in preference to her cardboard luggage – had been unpacked while she was downstairs taking tea with Sir Ambrose and Lady Henderson. For the first time she felt grateful to Charles for providing the expensive clothing and accessories. It had never crossed her mind until now that someone else would deal with her unpacking. What if that case had been filled with her plain woollen jumpers and carefully repaired walking shoes? She shuddered at the thought. As it was, her modest collection of cosmetics looked quite impoverished ranged on the vast mahogany lake of a dressing table.

As Lily looked at the three evening dresses Henderson had provided, she was overwhelmed by a wave of misery. What was she doing here? Why on earth had she been weak enough to come? Billie was right. She should have rejected the blackmail of all those unwanted new clothes and told Charlie then. And instead, here she was, desperately trying to remember to call him Charles, so scared of doing something wrong that she had experienced an absurd reactive desire to crook her little finger as she held her teacup, and knowing, as surely as if she had been told, that Lady Henderson only awaited the arrival of an audience before declaring war on her prospective daughter-in-law.

There was a tap on the door. Oh, hell, not a maid! How would she handle it?

'Come in!' she called, her voice ringing with all the confidence she could muster.

It was Henderson. 'Hullo, my dearest. You were absolutely marvellous. Just thought I'd come and see how you were getting along.'

She smiled shakily. 'Terribly, if you really want to know! Oh, Charlie, I know there's a disaster out there just waiting to happen.'

'Don't be silly – they love you. And remember, while we're here, Charles. All right?'

His last remark caught her on the raw. 'How about Milord?' she asked.

Henderson looked startled. 'Lily, that wasn't worthy of you.'

'Well, what d'you expect? I've just been through the most terrifying half-hour of my life, and you tick me off for not calling you Charles in private!'

'You know I didn't mean it like that. I was trying to help . . .'

'If you were trying to help, you wouldn't have brought me here in the first place . . .' She blinked back tears. '. . . Oh, hell – how am I going to get through this evening?'

'Fortunately, Father and Mother have taken to the cocktail habit with some enthusiasm. I recommend a couple of gins before dinner. With a head like yours, it'll do no harm and boost your confidence enough for a more comfortable evening. Believe me, once you've gone through the first dinner party, you'll never look back.'

'At the moment I'd rather not look forward, either. Now shoo, go away. I must get dressed . . . Oh, God! I don't know what to wear!'

'Try the royal blue chiffon. It's your perfect colour. Please stop worrying. They'll all love you just as Mother and Father did.'

'In that case, I've had my chips!' she said under her breath, as the door closed behind him.

'You look charming, my dear – absolutely charming,' said Penelope Henderson, rising to greet Lily as she joined the family in the library. Lady Henderson was wearing Lanvin and the family emeralds. Lily would have been unable to identify the designer, but when she saw the workmanship of the gown against her own ready-made clothing, she recognized it as couture. She fought the impulse to stick out her foot and trip her hostess, and instead managed to hold a fixed smile until Sir Ambrose offered a cocktail. Once she held a well-iced gin-and-French in her hand, she was minutely more at ease.

But then the other guests started arriving. With mounting horror, she realized there would be around twenty for dinner. My God, she thought, the only time I ever sat down with that many was at a street party! She was further disconcerted by the discovery that eight of the twenty, excluding herself and Charles, were to be house guests throughout the holidays. This was their first general gathering, as most of them had arrived late that afternoon. Within moments there was a general babble about the fun they would have riding, hunting, attending Christmas midnight service at the beautiful medieval parish church, and playing charades and vingt-et-un after dinner.

Lily had never been inside a medieval church; her chapel up-bringing had left her utterly ignorant of Anglican liturgy; she had never been on a horse; cribbage and rummy were the only card games she knew; and the idea of charades, which she had read about once or twice, seemed unspeakably puerile. It promised to be a more dangerous social minefield than even she had anticipated.

By the time her second cocktail was sliding down, she had gained control of herself again. Why on earth was she so terrified? She had survived worse than this before now. It was only her sense of isolation that had paralysed her so far. Right, if they wanted to play like this, she'd show them she knew how. She started some private strategic planning.

Not everything was against her. It was a great help to discover that Penelope Henderson was easily the best-dressed woman in the room. One of the elderly females looked as if she had flung a faded brocade curtain around her as a wrap. A younger woman, a year or two older than Lily, was trying hard to make the most of a faded silk gown whose outmoded shape proclaimed it as a veteran of the war years. At least, thought Lily, my clothes are smart and new. I'd pass muster with them all if only Lady Muck wasn't all dressed up like a fourpenny rabbit . . . She studied the men. Yes, same there . . . among a scattering of newish evening clothes there were elderly jackets beginning to discolour greenly. It seemed the miners weren't the only ones who'd come out of the last decade poorer than when they went in. Slowly, slowly, Lily relaxed.

At dinner she had been seated between a neighbouring land-owner with estates even bigger than the Hendersons', and a young blade whose mind seemed never to stray beyond the hunting field. She was also very close to Lady Henderson, and wished with all her heart she had been placed out of the woman's eavesdropping range. Never mind; take it as a challenge, she told herself. Don't give her the satisfaction of seeing you go under . . .

'Walters, Walters . . . let me see . . . family in steel, I seem to remember,' her landowner neighbour was saying. It startled Lily out of her reverie with a sensation like going over the top on the Barry Island fairground big dipper, scattering her nervousness.

She smiled brilliantly at him and said: 'No, Lord Ancombe, a different branch. We're in coal.'

'Hmm, you must be having a rough time then, with the price slump . . . ' Then he broke into an answering smile. 'Still, a pretty young thing like you won't be wanting to bother her head with such serious stuff. I expect you're always chasing off to parties and so forth. Never sit still a moment, these days, the young. I remember when I was your age . . . '

And he was off, solving her problems instantly by embarking on a reminiscent monologue to which she was required to contribute only the occasional 'Oh, how dreadful for you!' and 'you must have enjoyed that so much . . . '

But Lady Henderson was not going to let Lily's background slip offstage that easily. During a lull in Ancombe's memoirs, she fixed a poisonous smile on Lily and said: 'My dear, you never did tell me where you were at school. My sister's girl was in the same class as one of the Walters' children, at Manstone. Would that be you, or perhaps one of your sisters?'

Lily shook her head. 'Not one of us, Lady Henderson. You see, one of my sisters was so ill when I was thirteen that I was sent to school locally – ' Church Street Junior, Butetown, sprang to mind and she improvised – 'A church school in Cardiff, decent enough in its way, but hardly the best choice for a good education.' *Iesu mawr*, she thought, I'm even beginning to sound right! She subsided into her seat, feeling the sweat burst out in her armpits and behind her knees.

Lady Henderson had not finished. 'And what did you do after you left?'

'Oh, I'm the same as most girls of my age, I suppose. The war was my finishing school.' Get around that one, *your ladyship* her eyes shouted at Penelope Henderson.

Her hostess's huge brown eyes opened even wider in mock admiration: 'Surely you don't mean you were at the Front?' Touché.

'Hardly; I still couldn't leave the family . . . my sister's health . . . but I did the best I could. Took a man's job to relieve another soldier for the trenches. I trained as a driver and drove the local brewery's delivery trucks for the duration.'

94

Lady Henderson was not defeated yet. 'But after? You must have been at such a loose end since hostilities ended . . .'

'Hardly, Mother. I commandeered her from the brewery and she's been aiding the poor ever since by driving me to and from my medical calls. The reception work is simply a favour she does for me and James Cann in her free time.'

Oh, bless you, Charlie, you rescued me! Lily glowed at him in his place at the far end of the table, whence he had belatedly noticed his mother's attack. After that the pressure eased. The guest on Penelope's right demanded her attention. The young man next to Lily turned to her in open admiration and said: 'I say, do you weally dwive twucks? I always found ordinary cars pwetty impossible. Give me a horse any day.' Then he embarked on half an hour of breathless tales of derring-do on horseback. For the first time ever, Lily found it entrancing. It kept Lady Henderson at bay.

She would have managed perfectly well for the rest of the evening had they remained at the dinner table. But once dessert was finished Lady Henderson rose and led the ladies from the room. Lily's relaxation vanished and for a moment she considered feigning a dead faint. At least it would have put her out of reach until the morning. But that would have been rather like running from battle. Even if it killed her she had to see it through. She rose and followed the elderly woman in the brocade curtain as they processed into the drawing room.

There it was worse than Lily could have imagined. Apart from two young women who were visiting for the first time, respectively with fiancé and new husband, Lily was the only stranger in the room. At first she endured the ignominy of being ignored as old friends exchanged the latest gossip about mutual acquaintances; then, far worse, she was subjected to the undivided, less than friendly, attention of the female half of the house party.

For an hour she fended off prying questions, took care not to antagonize those who provoked her, and generally fought for her life. By the time the men rejoined them she was on the edge of exhausted tears. Charles came straight over, sat on the love seat next to her, and murmured: 'You look rather done up. Was it bad?'

'I don't think you'll ever know what I did for you this evening. Don't ask me to do it again – I'd never survive.'

He squeezed her hand and gave her a secret smile. 'Stop worrying. Now they've tested you, and you've come through with flying colours, there'll be no more trouble. I must confess, though, Mother was particularly red in tooth and claw tonight.'

His tone made Lily tremble. He sounded quite proud of his mother's savage behaviour. But before she could comment, there was something else to worry about. 'Come along, everyone!' It was Lady Henderson's closest woman friend, Baba Wilmington. 'Take your partners: we're going to play backgammon – can't remember when I played it last!'

Lily glanced at Henderson in dismay. 'Can't remember when I *played* it!' she whispered. Again the chances of getting away with a dead faint flitted through her head. But she had nothing to worry about. Felicity Longman, the new fiancée, and Hermione Hampton-French, the bride, protested as one.

'I've never played backgammon in my life, and I don't intend to start now,' declared Hermione. She was seated a few feet from Lily. 'What about you, Miss Walters? I bet you feel the same, but you're too polite to say!'

Lily smiled hugely. 'I never could get the hang of it! Maybe we could make one of the older guests teach us before we leave.'

'Nonsense!' said Hermione. 'You come riding with us instead. Far more fun, and it's good for you. We'll go out for a gallop tomorrow afternoon, if you like.'

'I look forward to it,' Lily said faintly. Then, her mind numb with a combination of strain from the evening and terror about tomorrow's riding, she said her goodnights and went off to bed.

In his boyhood, home from school for the holidays, it had been Charles Henderson's great bedtime treat to join his mother for half an hour's gossip while she prepared for bed. Her hair had been very long in those days, and sometimes she had permitted him to brush it for her. He had never forgotten the vitality of the great silken mane, almost as if it had a life of its own. Later, a young doctor reading about the darker side of the human psyche, he had skipped the sections of Freud which spoke of mother fixations. In any case, by the time he had been to medical school, then into practice, then to the army, the memory of his intense feelings had faded. But he still remembered with great affection those intimate late-evening chats. Nowadays, on his rare visits to the Peel, they maintained their tradition. Penelope wore her hair shorter these days, so the ambiguous ritual of brushing it never arose.

Tonight Henderson sat sideways on a chair a few feet from his mother's dressing table, while she removed the make-up from her face with a pot of cream and a cotton towel. Only a woman of her striking looks would have possessed the confidence to perform such an operation in front of a male, even if he was her son.

Almost teasingly Henderson said: 'You really were rather naughty to poor Lily this evening, Mother. You know all about her background – I explained in my letter. You might have helped her along a little, instead of making it even harder.'

'Nonsense, darling! I had nothing but her interests at heart. This week she'll be on trial, and she must know how to handle anything. I was testing her mettle, that's all.'

'Hmm, it sounded to me as if you were attempting to bury her, but still . . . if you could just try to be a little easier on her, it would help.'

'Charles, have you really considered what you're taking on? I think the young woman has done so, and all credit to her for showing such intelligence. She knows she's confronting a wall which she will never climb.'

'Now you're talking nonsense! There's no such barrier. I brought her here to meet you. She isn't being tested – except by you and Father – and I'm not asking either of you to marry her.'

'No? Then what happens when you inherit the Peel? That requires only your father's death, not mine too, in case you'd forgotten. I might still be here, you know. I refuse to become a social outcast, simply because of your injudicious choice of a wife.'

'Perhaps – perhaps I should choose not to live at the Peel.'

'Not live here? Where else would you live? It's inconceivable that a baronet should practise medicine in some benighted Welsh valley!'

He still lacked the courage to admit he had considered renouncing the title. Anyway, now he was here, the Peel and his mother were exercising their old magic and he was less keen on such a renunciation. He realized the situation had changed subtly. He was no longer postponing telling his mother; instead he was postponing a decision on what he would do with the rest of his life. Suddenly Lily's behaviour for the rest of the week took on new significance.

'Mother, I know it's been an ordeal for you too – receiving Lily, I mean. I don't expect it to be all roses at first; just that you look at what she is, not what she comes from, and like or dislike her on her own merits.'

'Oh, Charles, none of us is afforded such a privilege! We're all judged on matters which have little to do with our own virtue or lack of it. Why should your Miss Walters be any different?'

'Can't you see already why she's so different? Tonight she managed to survive the gentry in full cry, and I thought she managed admirably. She's never been waited on by servants before; never been introduced to a score of people with whom she has nothing in common and expected to make polite conversation with them. Come to that, I doubt whether she's ever even needed to make polite conversation!

'I don't know of any other woman who could rise so successfully to such a challenge . . . Oh, I know they didn't believe she was a sprig of the aristocracy; but they were certainly prepared to believe she was some rich industrialist's not quite fully polished daughter. When you consider that she left school at fourteen and never attended a dinner party before, I think that's magnificent.'

'Yes, dear, so do I – if she were being groomed to marry a bank manager. Being the mistress of a substantial estate is another matter.'

Henderson brushed a weary hand across his face, at a loss to find fresh arguments in Lily's favour. 'Father was very remote,' he said eventually. 'It was impossible to tell how he felt.'

'That is because you've shocked him rigid, you silly boy! Ambrose has no idea of how to be anything but exquisitely polite to a female, be she lady or kitchen maid. All that's changed is that he never expected to have the kitchen maid in his library drinking his gin, with his heir's full approval.'

'I think I'd better go to bed. Any more of this and I shall be tempted to go away again. Please promise me you'll be kinder to her from now on, and help her through bashes like tonight.'

'I shall consider it. You know I was always putty in your hands.'

He gazed at her, affection and exasperation warring in his mind, and realized that with money and breeding, Lily's mother would have been just like this. What an awful thought! Perhaps that was why he felt such instinctive antipathy towards Mrs Walters. She reflected all the worse excesses of his own mother's personality.

At first, nervous exhaustion got the better of Lily. She undressed, took a warm bath, then got into bed and instantly fell asleep. Unfortunately she awoke at two in the morning, and after that there was no more thought of rest. She switched on the bedside lamp after staring into the darkness for half an hour, inconsequentially reflecting that they must switch off the fountain at night. There was no musical sound of water now.

She glanced through the small stack of books which had been left on her bedside table, and tried to read one, a lightweight detective story. By page thirty she decided that not only had she no idea whodunnit, but did not care, and shut it. Instead, she started going over the previous day in her mind.

It did not take long to reach several conclusions, most notably that she could not endure another day like yesterday. After that she got down to practicalities. First, she opened the writing case which had been left for her use on the table beside the window, and sat down to write a note to Charles. That done, she opened the wardrobe and took a long look at the clothes inside.

She found her borrowed suitcase and carefully packed into it all the clothes Henderson had bought for her, then closed the case and put it out on the small folding stand provided for the maid who did the unpacking. She left out a woollen blouse and pullover, a tweed skirt, woollen stockings and her one good pair of walking shoes, the only clothes of her own which she had brought along with Henderson's purchases. She had also

99

worn her own thick winter coat to travel to Northumberland.
Now that, too, was hanging in the wardrobe.

When she and the other two young female guests had
departed for bed, Lady Henderson had told them they might
breakfast in their rooms if they preferred it to the communal
affair in the dining room. Cook would be in the kitchen at any
time after six forty-five if they cared to ring for a tray. At ten
minutes to seven, Lily rang down, and by seven fifteen she was
eating a large breakfast. She was going to need it, with what lay
ahead of her.

When the maid came to collect her tray, Lily was already
dressed. 'Is the chauffeur on duty yet, Mary?' she asked.

'Yes, Miss.'

'Then will you ask him if he's free for the next hour or so?
I've just realized I need to go into Berwick. I won't keep him
longer than it takes to drive in.'

Curiosity leaped in the girl's eyes. 'If it's convenient for you
to come down to the hall, Miss, I'll ask him to come round to
the front door for you in a few minutes.'

Lily fought the impulse to say she would leave by a side
entrance. That would really arouse the maid's suspicions and
she'd be asking the cook or Lady Henderson's maid if it was all
right for the young lady to go off in the car. But what if people
had already started going down to breakfast? It was after seven
thirty. They might see her as she crossed the hall . . .

Couldn't be helped. She must get away, and it looked as if
the front door and the Daimler were the only escape route. Lily
took a deep breath, fastened the belt of her coat, tugged on her
little felt cloche hat, picked up her bag and walked out of the
room.

It worked better than she had thought possible. As she
passed through the hall, she put down the note she had written
to Charles on the post tray just inside the front door. Harker,
the chauffeur, was just mounting the stone steps to the front
door.

'You wanted the car, Miss?'

'Yes. Have you time for a quick trip into Berwick?'

'Of course, Miss. How long will we be, so I can leave word?'

'Oh, only the time it takes you to get there and back. I shan't
be staying.'

'Very good, Miss. In that case I shan't bother to leave a message.'

It was as easy as that, she thought minutes later, sitting in the rear of the limousine and watching the wintry landscape flash by. She felt as if she had come through some vast and terrible experience. I suppose in a way I have, she mused, but what a shame it was caused by such a petty bunch of people!

At Berwick she thanked Harker and told him she would not need to be taken back. He gave her a doubtful look. 'You might have difficulty in getting a taxi to drive you all the way to the Peel, Miss,' he said. 'You may have to look out one of them private car hire firms.'

'Don't worry about that. I have to catch a train. I shan't be back at the Peel today.'

'All right, Miss, if that's all, I'll be getting back.'

She slipped a ten-shilling note into his hand, wondering if he would ever guess it meant as much to her as it did to him, possibly more, then she walked briskly into the station.

There was a train to Birmingham within the hour, and from there she could easily get a connection to Cardiff. Thanks to Billie's escape money, Uncle Rhys was due for an unexpected Christmas visitor.

CHAPTER TEN

The Bay had seen better times, but it had never seemed more colourful to Lily. As the taxi pulled away from the kerb outside the Anglesey she stood quite still and took a deep breath. Yes, it was still there – drains, mud, breweries, coal dust and oriental spices. The soul of Butetown always smelled the same. Congealed smoke and dirt on the windows of the pub filtered the light from inside and made the front bar look like an orange-tinted cavern. A ragged crêpe paperchain with a sprig of mistletoe perched coyly half way along its length were Rhys's idea of Christmas window-dressing. Lily hefted the large shoulder bag which comprised her only luggage, and pushed open the door back to her childhood world.

Time had always dealt kindly with Rhys Walters. At sixty-two, the only signs he showed of a mis-spent life were a high colour and thirty pounds or so of excess weight. As always, he was immaculately dressed. As Lily pushed open the door he glanced up from the pumps where he was dispensing beer to a customer, and momentarily froze as he saw his niece. Oh, *Duw*, she thought, heart lurching, I've come at the wrong time! But then his rugged face cracked into the biggest smile she had seen for weeks, and he was round the bar, embracing and kissing her, bellowing an introduction to all the customers who did not know her, announcing her return to all who did.

'What a Christmas present!' he said. 'I hope you'm staying, now you're here. No Margaret Ann tapping her feet by the back door and waiting for you to get off the last train, is there?'

102

'If you'll have me, I'm here till at least the day after Boxing Day,' she replied. 'How do that suit you?'

'Triffic, kidda, bloody triffic! Now, how about a nice drop a whisky to warm you up after your travels?'

She had been almost ten hours on the journey from Northumberland, but now felt so refreshed she never wanted to sleep again. While Rhys bustled off to get her drink, she went into the cubby-hole office, hung up her coat, dumped her bag and brushed her hair. Then she came out behind the bar, ready to serve.

'Where d'you put the price list, now, Uncle Rhys? I'll be a bit behind the times, I expect.'

'Don't be daft. You'm not serving tonight. Be a lady of leisure for once.'

'I've had enough of being a lady of leisure the past couple of days to last me a lifetime. If you want a bit of help, I'll work down here the rest of the evening. The price is a nice beef sandwich to keep me going now, and supper after, all right?'

'You got yourself a bargain.' He began to turn back to another customer, then said: 'Hey, how are you placed for a bitta shopping up the market tomorrow?' He dropped his voice to a stage whisper. 'I'm between aunties at the moment, and I hadn't bothered with nothin' for Christmas Day, but now that you'm here, we can make a party of it.' The aunties were his daughter Lexie's joking name for the succession of mistresses Rhys periodically installed upstairs in the living quarters.

'Done. I'll be up the market first thing. Still plenty of time to get a nice bitta poultry . . . I know – we could have a goose, couldn't we? I haven't had one since my last Christmas down here. Mam do always want capon.'

'Trust her to want something that 'ave been castrated!' He winked at her and went back to work.

Lily felt like singing with joy as she bent to get bottled beer from under the bar counter, reaching out for the neatly ranged glasses that went with it, checking prices for the first ten minutes and afterwards falling easily back into the rhythm of her old part-time job.

'Never be out of work, you, Lil,' carolled one of the customers from the old days. 'You always set up the fastest round down the Bay.'

She glanced up. 'Bet, Black Bet! Large as life and lovelier than ever! How've you been keeping?'

Black Betty O'Donnell, an Irish tart with a predilection for exotic underwear and hair dye which had given rise to her nickname, said: 'I decided I was gettin' a bit mature for the old beat and I've gone into management now. Got meself a nice tidy house around Loudoun Square. Bit noisy on match nights, but I never did mind high jinks. Doing lovely, thanks love. What about you?'

Lily shrugged. 'Put it this way. I'm glad to be down yer, not in either of the other places I could be.'

'Say no more.' Bet studied her for a few seconds over her large gin and orange, then said: ''Course, if you ever thought you wasn't earning enough behind the bar, I could get a fortune for you in my line. There's a big future for girls like you.'

Lily smiled. 'Thanks, Bet, but I'd never stand the pace.'

The older woman winked lewdly. 'You know what they do say. Practice makes perfect. And you got just the right build for it – and the right sort of walk . . . what do Jake call it, now? Aye, that's it, Circassian slave girl. You got a Circassian slave girl's walk, Lil. The men'll follow it for miles!'

'Oy, Bet, stop corrupting my niece. She ent used to that sorta talk!' yelled Rhys from the other end of the bar.

Bet's glance told him what she thought of that. 'Didn't know you was running a mission hall, Rhys. What am I drinking, communion wine?'

'Bloody fire an' brimstone, more like!' he said, laughing.

At that moment the Peel seemed to be on another planet. Lily sighed with contentment. What on earth had ever persuaded her to leave her own world?

Lily might find it easy, temporarily at least, to dismiss the Hendersons from her mind, but they had thought of little else but her all day.

Penelope Henderson had spent an uneasy night, and in the morning had felt thoroughly ashamed of her behaviour the previous day. She might disapprove of Charles's choice of wife; she might be genuinely convinced the girl was unsuitable. But her son was right; there had been no justification for her to

104

behave so disgracefully to someone who had shown courage and spirit in circumstances which would have daunted far more accomplished girls.

Penelope decided it was time to bury the hatchet. If only it had not been her beloved Charles . . . somehow that had been the last straw. She could have endured Peter throwing himself away, but not her favourite son . . . No matter; now she must make amends, to Charles himself and, especially, to Miss Walters. From now on she would ensure that the girl's visit ran on oiled wheels.

She remembered her own malicious pleasure last night when she heard Hermione offer Lily an escape from embarrassment which was to prove an even worse fate. She had caught the fleeting look of horror on Lily's face and realized the girl had never been on a horse in her life. Well, that would provide no problems. She would whisk her off to do something harmless and keep her out of Hermione's way until early evening. After that, she had full confidence in her own ability to shield Lily from any further difficulties.

Perhaps it would be tactful to find Lily now, and set the girl's mind at rest. She must have passed an even worse night than me, thought Lady Henderson. She glanced at herself in the mirror. Yes, nothing too forbidding there. She was dressed simply in country tweeds. The Lanvin had been pure bravura. She had worn the gown only once previously – to an extremely formal ball in London. Last night had been intended to extinguish Lily, and her failure to do so gave her more faith in her prospective daughter-in-law than almost anything else. Yes, the more she thought about it, the more possible it became that some day they might even be friends . . .

As she reached her bedroom door, someone rapped forcefully and then rushed in so abruptly he almost knocked her over. It was Charles, in a state of high agitation. 'Mother – look – look what you've done! I told you not to be so rough on her! Oh, dear God, I can't even go and look for her. She won't tell me where she is! She'll never forgive me for this . . . I'm as much to blame as you . . . ' He thrust the letter he was holding into her hand, and paced distractedly across the room, turning and padding back towards Lady Henderson before she had time to respond.

'Go on, read it! I hope it makes you feel as ashamed as I do.'

She looked down at the two sheets of writing paper. Lily had written:

Dear Charlie

I know, I should not call you that. But it does not matter now, because I am not staying and nobody else will know. I only came up to the Peel because I did not know how to tell you I could not, after you got me all those lovely clothes. I thought as it meant so much to you I could put up with it, although I knew it would be awfully hard. I did try, but I know it will not work, and your mother does not like me at all. I will never win her around, and perhaps she is right.

I expect she and your father will be angry that I am going off in their lovely car. But it is only as far as Berwick and there was not a bus as far as I know and I really could not stay any longer. Please tell them I am sorry if it inconveniences them. The Peel is very beautiful. You may think now you could give it all up but when the time comes you will have to take it, I can see that.

I know that by going off like this, I will make your mother think she was right to look down on me and treat me like a common little fool. I expect that is what I am to her. There is an awful saying in the Valleys about girls who do not fit in. They say 'she's neither useful nor ornamental'. Well that is how I felt last night. Today will be worse, if I stay, because it will be like yesterday with the extra bit of fun for everybody of seeing me fall off a horse. I am not afraid of horses, but if they want a good laugh they can go to the music hall. I expect there is one in Berwick-on-Tweed.

I have left all the clothes you bought in my room. Only the blue dress and the travel costume have been worn, so perhaps the shop will take the other things back.

I have kept my ring for now, because I must work out a way of breaking the news to Mam when I go back, and she will notice too soon if I am not wearing it. Here I must ask you for a favour. Please do not go looking for me back in Abercarn. I am going somewhere else for Christmas, to friends who will not ask me what the matter is. I will tele-

106

phone in a few days and tell you where I am, then, if it is not too much trouble, you could meet me on your way back home and we could go to Abercarn together. Then I can just tell Mam we are going our separate ways later on, without her ever having to know what happened this week. If she found out she would make my life misery.

I am very sorry if I have embarrassed you in front of your friends and family, but they embarrassed me more than you will ever know, especially your mother. She would never let us be happy together and I was foolish to think she would. I love you very much, but we can never be married.

Lily

Penelope Henderson carried on staring at the paper after she had finished, because she could think of nothing to say to her son. It was one thing to wish he had never become involved with the girl; quite another to be shown such direct evidence of the suffering she had caused to one who had done nothing to deserve it except fall in love with Charles.

Finally, his patience exhausted, he snapped: 'Well, what have you got to say for yourself? Some glib justification of your abominable behaviour, no doubt!'

She shook her head. 'No. All I have to say for myself is that I am profoundly ashamed. I had already realized I was doing the child an injustice, and today I intended to make amends . . . I know you won't believe that, but it's true. However, I think it's worth pointing out that you could have treated her with more understanding too.'

'How dare you? You're just trying to shift the blame on to me.'

'No, not that. I understand why you wanted to bring her here. But darling, you have a dreadful streak of obstinacy which leads you to believe you can make anything happen if you will it to do so. Your Lily knew this visit would not work. I most certainly did. Before you brought her here I was convinced the entire relationship was a mistake. Now I'm less sure of that. She *is* an exceptional young woman. But a little forethought would have shown you this visit was doomed before it started. It would have been better to risk our rejection and marry her quietly, then present her as your wife without giving us any say in the matter. I can assure you I should never have tried to frighten her off in those circumstances.'

'But if you had just shown her some basic courtesy and friendship, none of this would have happened.'

'I realize that, Charles, but please try to understand what I'm saying. I don't like myself very much today, but I *do* see myself clearly. I am a snob. Lily is the last young woman I would have chosen for you. You knew both these things, and yet you were so determined to have your way that you insisted on her coming here. Knowing me as well as you do, you must have realized I would behave badly. I am not attempting to excuse myself, merely pointing out a home truth.'

He had turned away from her as she spoke and now stood, head down, by the window. He said: 'I suppose you're right. But what can I do now? I don't know where she is, and if I leave to look for her I'll miss her when she telephones. I don't know what to do . . .'

'Stop being so feeble! You simply have to accept the situation. If you really want another opinion, I'd say it's all over between you. Forgive me for being brutal, but it seems obvious. If you do still have any chance at all, it lies in going to her when she makes contact, doing as she wishes to keep matters from her mother, and then agreeing unconditionally to live as and where she wants when you are married – no changing your mind later or any trickery like that. I don't believe you're strong enough to do it, and I am convinced Miss Walters won't think so.'

'Oh, it's Miss Walters again, is it? Back on the high horse!'

'Now you're being childish rather than feeble. I know you're dreadfully upset, but there's nothing for you to do except come to terms with it. I am most deeply sorry for my part in the affair. If I could undo it, I would, but it's gone beyond that.'

She left him in the bedroom and went downstairs. She could not walk away from herself, but at least she could escape from everyone else for as long as it took to compose herself again.

The next day was Christmas Eve. Lily was up at the crack of dawn, preparing to go up to Cardiff's big covered market and buy food for the holiday week-end.

Rhys came into the kitchen as she was finishing her breakfast. 'I still don't know where you was running from, Lil, but you weren't arf travelling light. I think I'd better give you a few quid for Christmas so you can get some togs, don't you?'

'I-I think I left a couple of bits and pieces here when I went back to Abercarn,' she said lamely.

'Aye, I know you did.' He chuckled. 'As I recall, they was the sort of items that would have straightened your mam's pretty curls and turned 'em white into the bargain if she'd seen 'em. They'm well over a year old, now girl. You get yourself a couple of blouses and skirts and a nice frock – maybe two. I've had quite a season so far – backing a new jump jockey. He could win a race on a donkey.' Two large white five-pound notes appeared on the table as if by magic. 'And then get all the food you think we'll need – assume there ent nothing yer – and leave me to look after the booze, all right?'

She flung her arms around him. 'Why did I ever imagine I might belong anywhere else?' she said. 'Here and Abercarn, that's where I belong.'

'The only thing I find hard to believe is that you ever thought any different,' he said.

CHAPTER ELEVEN

Several times over the holiday Lily paused to reflect that she could not have chosen a better refuge than the Anglesey. It offered a combination of work and fun, as well as the companionship of Rhys. Inevitably she experienced pangs of misery about what had happened between herself and Charles Henderson, but the incident was somehow remote, entrenched in her past. The present and future seemed to be pointing her somewhere else entirely.

Rhys knew when not to ask questions, and for the first two days he said nothing about the reasons for Lily's abrupt appearance in Butetown. Over breakfast on Boxing Day, she was ready to tell him. He listened with sympathy and interest, but said nothing until she ended her story with the trip to Berwick station in the Daimler.

'You've got an instinct for doing things in style, I'll give you that,' he said then.

'But I'm wondering now if I did the right thing,' Lily replied. 'It must have been so embarrassing for Charlie after I'd gone.'

'Serve the bugger right! If he was daft enough to think some jaunt like that would work in the first place, he do deserve all the embarrassment he gets.'

'Yes, but I went with him, didn't I? I should have said no right at the beginning.'

''Course you should have, but I wish I had a pound for every time I missed doing the right thing when I was your age.' He

110

started to laugh. 'Honest, flower, I'd love to 'ave seen you at it! The coal Walters, not the steel ones, indeed! I suppose I'm in the shipping branch of the family?'

She was finally beginning to see the funny side of it. 'If I could have just watched instead of having to take part, I suppose I'd have been quite pleased with my performance, an' all. But there wasn't much to laugh about at the time.'

Rhys became serious again. 'So what are you going to do now, Lil? You can't just hide here for ever, much as I'd like to have you back.'

'I wish I knew. Of course, I'll have to go back to Abercarn, and if Charlie don't kick up about it, I'll go on working for him. I've brought the telephone number of the Peel, and I'll get on to them from here later on, and arrange to meet him.'

'No need to meet him. He can come down here and get you.'

'Oh, no – I want to choose the territory this time. He've had it all his way for too long. I'm going to phone this afternoon, because he told me he always goes off walking between two and four when he's up there. If I do that, I can leave a message and all he'll have is a time and place to meet me. I got all the train times when I was hanging around waiting for a connection in Birmingham.'

'This do sound worthy of Machiavelli.'

'It's fairly straightforward. I'll leave a message saying I'll meet the six-ten into Newport from Newcastle. He'll have plenty of time to catch it at Berwick in the morning – in fact I expect it's the train we'd have caught anyway to come back.'

'And then you'll go back to Abercarn with him as if nothing has happened.'

'As far as our Mam is concerned, yes. God knows how he and I'll sort it out.'

'Don't you think you'm asking a bit too much of him to discuss things in a twenty-minute train journey up the valley? He'll barely have time to say hello before you're home.'

'Thought of that. I think it might be best. I'll just make sure he realizes I do still mean to break off with him, and tell him we'll talk it over the next day when I go back to work at the surgery. If he wants me to stop working for him an' all, we can settle it then.' For the first time since they had started discussing her reunion with Henderson, Lily met her uncle's eyes. 'I

111

know what you'm gonna say, Uncle Rhys, but I've taken enough this week already. I can't face a big scene with him and then a grilling from Mam the minute I walk back into the Ranks. At least this way I only have to cope with Mam's questions about the Peel.'

'Aye, and make up stories about a whole imaginary week. That'll be quite a trick.'

She managed a smile. 'Not for the brain that gave the Walters family a fortune in coal stocks!'

She made the telephone call that afternoon as planned. She heard the butler say: 'Sir Ambrose Henderson's residence,' took a deep breath and responded: 'I'd like to leave a message for Mr Charles Henderson, please. He is expecting it.'

For an agonized second she expected the manservant to say he would fetch Charles, but instead he answered: 'Very well, Miss. Mr Charles is out at present. I have a pen and paper if you would care to tell me the message.'

'This is Lily Walters. Please say I shall meet him from the Newcastle train that gets into Newport in South Wales just after six in the evening tomorrow.'

'Very good, Miss. Is there a number where he can reach you if he needs to?'

'N-no, I'm afraid not . . . I shall be spending the night with people who are not on the telephone.'

'I shall see he gets your message, Miss. Thank you for calling. Goodbye.' He replaced the receiver and she was safe again, at least until the following evening.

It turned out to be far easier than she had expected, at first. Charles Henderson had been tormenting himself ever since her abrupt departure from the Peel, and by the time he got off the train at Newport, he was ready to abase himself if there was any chance of retaining her affections. He dropped his ebony cane and flung his arms around her, kissing her as if he had thought he would never see her again. Probably had his doubts about me being here at all, she thought.

Eventually he managed to find his voice. 'Lily, my darling, darling Lily. I have missed you so much . . . ' He bent and embraced her again.

After a few seconds she disengaged herself. She reached up

and stroked his cheek, then said gently: 'It's no use, Charlie. I love you as much as ever, but I'm not going to marry you.'

'We can't talk here. Look, there are trains every hour until ten-thirty. Let's find a quiet pub, at least, and talk things over.'

'I don't think there's much talking-over to do.'

'Now you're being silly. Even if I accept what you've just said – and I haven't, by any means – there would still be the question of what we say to your mother, what we do about your job and God knows what else. Now come along, be sensible. I'm not going to get angry about your leaving, far from it. I just need to talk to you.'

He told the porter to put the bags in the left luggage office and she noticed with relief that he had brought back the pigskin case she had borrowed. She had been worried Margaret Ann might notice she was returning without it. After that they walked down Cambrian Road and round to the Westgate Hotel.

Henderson sighed as they went in. 'I wish this was the summer again, and we were walking in as happily as we did that day when we had lunch here.'

Lily felt a pang of guilt as she remembered that had been the day he presented Billie with a farm, but said nothing. Henderson steered her into the quiet lounge bar and they sat in a corner over drinks.

For the first half-hour he pleaded with her to forgive him. He still showed no anger at her abrupt departure from Northumberland, and even offered her his mother's apologies for having behaved badly.

After that he began to repeat himself, and Lily felt it was time she stopped him. 'If I'd known you were just going to keep on like this, I'd have insisted on getting that first train home,' she said. 'Listen, love, you got to accept that you and me will never be happy if we get married. I should of stopped this a long time ago, as soon as I found out how rich and important your parents were. I knew then it wouldn't work.'

'Of course it will! All we have to do is make our life here. I promise I shall never even think of the Peel again. If you felt able to come and visit my parents a couple of times a year, that would be wonderful – I assure you you'd never be treated again

113

as you were last week – but if not, we could see them in London now and then. You know, neutral territory.'

She shook her head. 'Please, Charlie. It's not only them. It just wouldn't work. You think now it would be easy to do what you're saying, but it would get harder for you with every year that passed and in the end you'd be bound to blame me for having cut you off from your home. No, I could never live with that – and neither could you.'

He finally seemed to believe her, and slumped back against the upholstered bench seat with a look of deepest despair. Lily watched him for a while and then said: 'I'm sorry to be such a nuisance, but you were right about us having to agree what we tell Mam, and whether you want me back at the surgery to work.'

He brightened immediately. 'You mean you'll consider staying?'

'Of course I will! I said I wouldn't marry you. That didn't mean I wouldn't be your receptionist or your friend any more, silly!'

'In that case . . . '

'No, don't go building up your hopes. I'll never change my mind.' But she could see the idea gave him a crumb of comfort, and did not press the point. After that, he listened to what she proposed to tell her mother, and agreed to back her. 'I don't really think Mam will be that interested in how we spent the holiday, apart from wanting to know about the nice china and glass and things. She don't really think outside the village. Sometimes I do wonder if that's why she took against Bethan going to London so badly. Maybe she just can't imagine a world outside the Valleys.'

But Henderson was uninterested in Margaret Ann Walters's world. Now he was all eagerness to get back to his practice and work out a strategy to pursue Lily and win her all over again. Lily shrugged mentally. If he thought he could, good luck to him. It would at least stop any unpleasantness developing the minute they were back . . . with a start, she realized he was speaking again and that she had missed what he had said.

'I said, what are you going to tell your mother about our engagement?' he repeated.

'Oh . . . yes, well – I thought we'd let that lie, for a couple of

114

weeks at any rate. She'd go potty if I said now that it was broken off. Probably try to persuade my brothers to come and threaten you for having ruined her daughter's reputation.'

He was beaming now. 'So we're to stay engaged?'

'Now wait a minute, Charlie . . . that's just for public purposes, remember, and even that strictly temporary. After what you and your mother did to me over Christmas, I reckon you owe me that. But beyond that, it's friends from now on, and no more, all right?'

'All right, Lily, anything you say!' But he still looked a lot happier than he had moments before, and Lily realized she had not won the war by any means.

CHAPTER TWELVE

Margaret Ann welcomed Lily home with a mixture of joy and suspicion: joy at seeing her favourite daughter again; suspicion that she might marry immediately and, in spite of what she had said about staying in Abercarn, disappear to some mansion in the North of England. But Lily was right about her mother's concerns being overwhelmingly local. By the day after her return, Margaret Ann was acting as if she had never been away, and regaling her with news of family doings at such a rate that Lily need not have experienced a moment's misgiving about padding her account of the visit to the Peel.

In fact everything returned to normal so quickly that she sometimes had difficulty in believing that the dramatic events of the Christmas holiday had ever taken place. Henderson's partner, Dr Cann, preferred to take New Year off rather than Christmas to visit his sister in Scotland, so he departed as soon as Henderson returned and they were very busy for the next few days.

At first she was anxious and guarded when she was alone with him, but she need not have worried. He seemed to have decided that if he was to have any chance at all of persuading her to reconsider, he must let her come to him. It saddened her because she still loved him enough to want to spare him unnecessary hurt, and she knew that she had broken with him irrevocably, whatever hopes he might still nurture.

The Valleys were on the edge of turbulent times, and soon Lily was distracted from small personal concerns by the prospect of the violent confrontation which was building up between miners, Government and coal owners.

Her first hint that there was trouble ahead came from Emrys, her favourite brother. He was lodge secretary for the South Wales Miners' Federation at the Celynen South Colliery, and one Friday evening when they planned to go dancing together, he came home full of apologies, saying he had to go to a special union meeting instead.

'Why? I thought everything was running all right at the South,' said Lily.

He shook his head. 'Where've you been this long time, Lil? It ent just the South, it's every pit in South Wales – in the whole country come to that. They'm gonna turn us into slaves if we don't do summat about it straight away.'

'But our Haydn said this Commission . . . what you call it, some man's name?'

'Sankey. Aye, what did Haydn say about Sankey?'

'Said it would solve all the miners' problems because for once they was going to get a fair crack of the whip. He was talking about this Sankey as if he was God. Said he'd told the Government they had to hand over the pits to the people . . . '

'Nothing wrong with Sankey. He acted fairer by us than I would have believed, but there's a fly in the ointment – or rather, a spider – by the name of Lloyd bloody George.'

Their mother was firmly of the opinion that miners' womenfolk did not involve themselves in coalfield politics, and in spite of her erratic enthusiasm for the newspapers, Lily was relatively ill-informed as a result. Now she was hungry for information.

'I thought Lloyd George was a champion of the poor.'

'Aye, an' when I was a kid I used to think Father Christmas and all his bloody reindeer climbed down the chimney with presents on Christmas Eve. He's a crook, and the coal owners is crooked enough on their own account, without getting help from the politicians an' all. Lloyd George have shelved the Sankey Report and he's handing the pits back to the owners.'

'Well, that might be hard to take, after the promise, but it's not as if you're losing something you had before, is it?'

'Oh, that ent all they'm doing. There's a little matter of wage cuts – between forty an' fifty per cent, to be precise.'

117

'But everybody'll starve!'

'Not quite everybody. The cuts mean the owners will maintain profits at the old level. We're the only ones as will suffer.'

'You'm never gonna let them get away with that!'

'Right, we're not. That's why there can't be no dances for a bit, Lil.'

'To hell with dancing, and I'm sorry I looked disappointed. I want to help you with this. Will there be anything I can do?'

'Too much, before it do end, kidda. They'll smash us all over the coal house door if they get arf a chance, and it'll be every bit as hard on the women as the men. I gorra feeling we'll 'ave more soup kitchens than hot dinners along the valley by the summer. Now, let's 'ave a cuppa tea an' I'm off to this meeting.'

As winter turned to spring in 1921 the battle lines hardened between miners and coal owners. It was hard for the miners to escape the belief that they had been tricked into giving the owners time to prepare themselves for a long strike. Faced with an industry and a Government which refused to honour the report that had recommended favourable terms for them, the miners in their turn refused to work in the punitive conditions the owners now demanded. On April 1, 1921 the coal owners locked the miners out of every pit in South Wales.

It was a deceptively sunny morning, typically, treacherously April. The sky was bright blue; wild flowers peeped shyly from the roadside verges, and at the same time a mean-spirited wind picked at the bare legs and necks of the women who had come out to support their men at the South Celynen pit entrance. The lock-out had been in force for ten days and tension was running high because management safety men were still working underground. That morning the miners of the area had decided to do something to demonstrate their massive disapproval. From first light they had been converging on Newbridge from the North Celynen, from Oakdale, Crumlin, Cwmcarn and Abercarn, forming three vast processions to march on the South Celynen behind their colliery bands. Their women and children lined the roads to the colliery, cheering

118

them on. The marchers wore red rosettes and had red ribbons in their caps.

By the time they reached the Celynen colliery office, the army of demonstrators had swollen to some five thousand men, and as their representatives negotiated with management, the marchers massed outside, singing 'The Red Flag' with considerable gusto. The night safety men ended their shift a short while after the procession arrived, and the mounted police who had escorted the demonstrators edged forward, belligerently swinging truncheons, to warn the colliers against attacking the safety men.

Nothing had been further from the miners' minds. They still hoped to sway the deputies, the lowest management level and normally in full charge of safety, into joining them voluntarily. With persuasion in mind, a small group of colliers' pickets moved forward to talk to the safety men. As they did so, the mounted police surged up between the two groups, and the flying hoof of a nervous horse caught the leg of one picket, knocking him down. The man was Haydn Walters, and his sister Lily, seeing him fall, ducked beneath the next horse and rushed to help him up. The second horse, doubly frightened by its fellow's skittishness and by her presence, reared over her, almost unseating its rider and staggering out of control.

For interminable seconds it seemed that Lily would be trampled beneath the huge hooves. She gave a little shriek and flung up her arms ineffectually. The horse began to plunge back towards her and Haydn, helpless to get to her in time, shuddered at the prospect of disaster. Then another body rocketed between woman and horse, hurling himself and Lily clear of the beast's hooves and bowling Haydn over again. The trio collapsed in a breathless heap a couple of feet from disaster.

'What the bloody hell was that?' yelled an indignant female voice from the bottom of the heap.

'Sorry, love,' said her saviour. 'Couldn't think o' nothing else that'd work.'

As they disentangled themselves, she peered at him and discovered he was one of the deputies who had just come off shift. 'Oh, shit,' she muttered, 'trust me to get rescued by a blackleg!'

119

'You wanna watch your language,' he said. 'I ent scabbing. We haven't been called out yet, mind.'

Haydn, sweating with relief at his sister's narrow escape, was grinning broadly now. 'He's right, Lil. That's why we're yer today, remember.'

The man glared at him. 'Don't talk bloody wet. You'm yer for a show of strength against the owners. Let's 'ave a bit of honesty on both sides. No need to be coy, anyhow. If these buggers is bringing in the coppers to protect miner from miner, I don't wanna know about keeping the pit safe.'

He stood up and, with an oddly old-maidenish gesture, brushed off the dust from his already blackened colliery clothes. Turning to the straggling line of twelve safety men, who had been gawping at his lightning move, he called out: 'What are we, boys, our own men or the bosses' lapdogs? I do know where I belong – how about the rest of you?'

Seven of the twelve eyed each other and the army of demonstrators, talked briefly among themselves and then moved away from the other five, more senior, officials. A vast cheer broke out from the marchers. Haydn lunged forward and embraced the deputy who had started it all. 'Christ, mun, a life-saving tackle and a bitta rabble-rousing, all after a full shift. What d'you do when you'm rested?' Then he and Lily led him to join the negotiators outside the pit offices.

The management representatives had seen the defection of the safety men and accepted defeat, promptly agreeing to withdraw thirty-six officials from safety work across the three daily shifts. The miners' bands struck up 'Men of Harlech', the pickets formed up four abreast once more, and they marched in triumph back to their villages, deputies from the safety detachment now walking at the head of each column.

The man who had saved Lily marched between her and Haydn, back towards Abercarn. 'You ent a local man, are you?' said Haydn. 'Why ent you marching back with your own village group?'

The deputy grinned sheepishly and gestured at Lily. 'She wasn't going with them, was she?'

'Oh, I get it – if it had been a collier or somebody's mam under that 'orse, you wouldn't 'ave been so quick off the mark.'

'Well, you got to admit she do give a man an incentive . . . '

Haydn pulled an artificially deprecating face. 'You wouldn't say that if you 'ad to live with 'er!'

Scandalized, Lily said: 'Haydn! What will he think?' Turning to the man she said: 'Don't you take no notice. He's my brother.'

The man relaxed visibly. 'I'm relieved to yer it,' he said. 'Look, when this lot do get back, I'll have to get off home. I'm dead beat. But I don't wanna lose touch . . . '

'Don't worry, no chance of that. We need fellows like you,' said Haydn.

'I don't think he's so interested in you, somehow,' said Lily with a twinkle. 'It's all right, you won't lose touch with me, either. I'm Lily – Lily Walters. And I haven't even thanked you properly yet, Mr . . . '

'Richards . . . David Richards. I already know who you are.'

'Well, thank you very much, Mr Richards – though that do seem a bit inadequate for you saving my life.'

'Call me David, everybody do. And I didn't save your life . . . you might have got a nasty cut, that's all.'

Haydn laughed at that. 'You obviously didn't 'ave time to notice the size o' that 'orse, mun. If it had landed on our Lily it'd have made mincemeat out of her . . . I reckon we owe 'im a supper tonight, don't you, Lil?'

'Just what I was going to say. Apart from anything else, I can't recognize you with all that coaldust on. I got to see you clean before I'll know who to thank.'

'I'd like that. Thank you very much . . . but supper? You sure you can manage it, you know, on strike, an' all?'

Lily grinned. 'You're talking to a woman of independent means,' she said. 'I'm working full time – I'll have to hurry in a minute or I'll be late – so we're a bit better off than lots of others. Anyway, our Mam do lay in supplies like a squirrel, so there's always a tin o' corned beef or something if all else fails.'

She told him where they lived and he promised to be at the house at seven that evening, then turned away up the main road to Newbridge, where he lived. Lily glanced up at the clock in the market square and said: 'Hell's teeth, I'm late! Thank God it's Charlie this morning and not Dr Cann!' She stood on tiptoe to kiss Haydn's cheek, then dashed off down the road towards the Swan.

He was a widower, he told them that evening. His wife had died in the big influenza epidemic at the end of the war. There were no children. As they talked over supper, Lily was conscious of her mother oozing charm at David Richards. And when Mam wanted to, she could make a man feel like the only pebble on the beach . . . At the end of the evening Richards was clearly determined to come back as soon as possible.

'Where's your manners, girl? Ent you going to see David out?' demanded Margaret Ann. Lily's brother Emrys made a funny face at her across the table. Normally Mam regarded seeing people out as her personal matriarchal duty. As Lily rose to take him out, Margaret Ann added: 'And front door, mind. I blush to think what he'd say if he could see the state of the back row!'

Richards was a big, gentle man with a splendid physique and a completely unremarkable face. He had confided shyly to Emrys that yes, he was the David Richards who had played rugby for Newbridge until last season. 'Knees is getting a bit stiff now, though,' he said. 'When you get over thirty you should leave it to the youngsters.'

'You'm never over thirty, David! I don't believe it,' said Margaret Ann, in a kittenish tone that made Lily blush.

But it seemed to delight David. 'Oh, aye, I'm thirty-three this summer. Real old man in rugger terms, now!'

'Thirty-three, Lily. That ent old, not a fine man like that,' said Margaret Ann after he had left. 'He can give your Dr Henderson a good five years.'

Lily looked at her sharply. Did she suspect something? She replied rather snappishly: 'I don't know why you should think I'd find that interesting, Mam.'

'Because he's a lovely man, that's why. Steady . . . dependable – and brave, an' all. T'ent every man who'd dive under a horse like that to rescue some strange girl who had no business to be there in the first place.'

Emrys, blissfully unaware that Lily's engagement was no longer any more than a sham, said: 'Hey, Mam, what's all this? You'm normally the one who do want everything respect-

122

able. Our Lily's engaged to Charles Henderson. What d'you want to go waving some other fellow at her for?'

Margaret Ann's mouth pursed like a little button. 'Because chalk an' cheese don't mix, that's why. I said at the beginning, and I'll say it now, Lily's aiming too high there. Better have somebody from her own level – and he've got his own house, an' all!'

Her abrupt change of tack made Emrys snort with laughter as he swallowed a mouthful of tea, and she turned on him, demanding that he mend his manners or go outside.

'Well good grief, Mam, what d'you expect? There you are, one second, going on about what a nice man he is, and next thing you're telling Lily to go for the 'ouse!'

Lily was fighting the desire to giggle now. Margaret Ann caught sight of her face and her temper rose another notch.

'Why won't none o' my children take no notice of respectable standards?' she said, apparently addressing the fireplace. 'You do bring 'em up proper, teach 'em to behave nicely, and then they laugh when you try to guide 'em . . .'

Lily got up and went to hug her mother. 'It's only because we love you,' she said. 'At least we always know what to expect.'

David Richards seemed to have ambitions along the same lines as Margaret Ann. Now he had joined the locked-out miners, he had time on his hands. At first he came often to the house to see if Lily wanted to go walkng, or to see a film at Abercarn Hall. Then he took to meeting her from work and accompanying her back to the house. In the beginning this embarrassed her, but eventually she thought it might be a gentle way of introducing Charles Henderson to the acceptance that their romance really was over.

Meanwhile the lock-out absorbed the energy of everyone in the village. A shoe repair club was set up; the women organized soup kitchens; groups were sent off to collect funds from industrial areas outside the coalfield. The activity kept them in good heart and as the action entered its second month there was no sign of surrender.

The men's resolution was strengthened by the punitive terms of work they were being offered. Skilled colliers who had earned an average of £5. 1s. 3d. for a six-shift week before the dispute were now being offered £3. Labourers, previously on the lower average earnings of £4. 8s. 9d. were subject to even worse cuts, with a new wage offering of £2. 3s. 7d. To a man, they were certain they could not survive on such pay.

But as the dispute went into its third month, they suffered a series of setbacks. All of them knew that the good summer weather would enable the owners to stockpile, and that if they were to have a chance of winning, they must hold out until winter. The obvious solution was joint action by the other big manual unions, the railwaymen and the transport workers. Neither group supported them, and by June the whole coal-field was looking starvation in the face. Donations were drying up, children were going hungry and savings had disappeared long ago.

Throughout the struggle Charles Henderson was curiously remote. He shied away from any discussion of the lock-out, and had long ago stopped trying to persuade Lily to stay on for drinks or supper after surgery ended. More than once she was on the verge of asking him to explain his behaviour, but never quite nerved herself to do so. Then he prompted a discussion himself.

He had just seen out his last patient from evening surgery, a delicate little girl who had cried weakly in her mother's arms. Afterwards he closed his eyes and heaved a deep sigh, then said: 'How can any mother put her children through that?'

Lily glanced up sharply. 'What's wrong with her?'

'Scurvy. It's 1921, this is one of the most prosperous countries in the world, and we are still producing children with the diseases of poverty – scurvy, rickets – how can a man stay out of work deliberately and watch his child suffer like that?'

She stared at him. 'You can't really blame the fathers, surely? You know what's behind this lock-out.'

'Yes. Thousands of men who won't confront reality.'

'Could you confront it if someone came along and halved your pay for the same work?'

'If the alternative to a halved income was no income at all, yes. Better to have a few shillings than empty pockets.'

'Only a man who'd never been short of pounds, let alone shillings, would say that! If your monthly earnings were halved, how much more would it still amount to than the top money any of these miners ever got?'

'I can't help it if I've been fortunate. My comparative comfort has no bearing on the economic realities which affect these men. They'll have to accept it eventually, and the longer they hold out, the poorer they'll be in the end.'

'You must understand human pride! It's not just the gentry who have that, you know.'

'Oh, don't worry, I'm aware of that!' It's the reason for my anger. Pride is the cause of that baby's scurvy, pride and pig-headedness.'

'You should be ashamed of yourself! It's greed that's doing it, and not the miners' greed, either. D'you think they'd stand back and see their families starving to death if there was another way? 'Course not! They're being carved up to keep money in the pockets of people like your family, who have meat twice a day and change their clothes three times to eat it!'

Unable to trust herself further she jumped up and hurried outside, striding off across the main road to the canal bank. She found a quiet spot and sat down for a few minutes until she felt calmer, then went back. She had walked out without finishing her day's work, and even in a rage was too conscientious to leave the records disordered and new prescriptions unrecorded.

There was no sign of Henderson when she returned. Lily filed the records of the last two patients and checked on the list of house calls for the following morning. She noticed her hand was trembling as she wrote out the patients' names on the sheet. How little I knew him! she thought . . . and if I was so wrong about Charlie, maybe it will be the same with anyone. I wasn't that brilliant with poor George Griffiths when we got engaged, either . . .

Well, there was a way round that. It was time she started ignoring sexual attraction and looking for something else. It was true that Charles Henderson had first attracted her because he seemed kind and understanding, but it would never have amounted to anything more than friendship if she had not discovered that he could arouse and satisfy her sensually. Obviously that was the wrong way to choose. Twice, now, she had come within an ace of making a permanent mistake with her life. She did not want to risk a third. Next time it might stick . . .

Lily took off the ostentatious sapphire engagement ring and

was looking about for a suitable container in which she could leave it for Henderson, when he came back into the room. His eyes seemed drawn irresistibly to the ring.

'Oh, Lily, no . . . not for some remote ideal, please . . . ' he said.

'That's dishonest, Charlie,' she told him, forcing her voice to remain gentle in consideration of her real feeling for him. 'You know very well it's been over since Christmas.'

'I - I was beginning to think you'd had second thoughts. That was why I hadn't been pushing you to spend time with me lately.'

'You know that ent true. It didn't stop you until April. Then, all of a sudden, when I got tied up with the colliers and the lock-out, you went all distant. You couldn't cope with me having strong opinions that were the exact opposite from the way you saw the world . . . It must have looked as if I was spitting on all you thought was important.'

He could not meet her eyes, and did not answer her directly. 'You know I've always cared deeply about relieving distress. Why d'you think I worked in the slums - and down here - when I could have been in Harley Street? God knows I'm sufficiently well qualified.'

'Oh, Charlie, you don't arf get things wrong now and then! You care, all right. But you don't care because you think those people deserve to be as well off as you; you care because you'm sorry for them. What you've done with your life is a bit like what the lady of the manor does with her bowls of soup and bags of old clothes - it's charity. It's your little bit of ''there but for the grace of God go I . . . '' You can't expect me to live like that. I'm *one* of these people.'

He was still gazing woodenly down at the linoleum. Lily crossed the room to him, placed the ring carefully on the desk beside him, kissed his cheek and then walked out of the surgery. He did not follow her.

On the last day of June a conference of all the pits in the coal-field narrowly voted to return to work on the owners' terms. Two weeks later Lily Walters married David Richards.

126

PART TWO

I will rise now, and go about the city
in the streets, and in the broad ways I
will seek him whom my soul loveth

Song of Songs
Ch.III v.2

CHAPTER THIRTEEN

London 1924

'Nurse Walters, Mrs Norland is asking for you. Are you busy at present?'

Unless extra nurses have appeared out of nowhere, yes, thought Bethan. But she managed a serene smile and told the ward sister she would be along in a moment. Mrs Norland was a reasonable patient, and had taken a particular liking to Bethan during her long stay on the surgical ward. She was also very rich.

She was in a single-bedded side ward so full of flowers that the usual hospital smells were banished. A bowl of exotic fruit on her bedside locker and a stack of the latest novels were further proof of Mrs Norland's comfortable circumstances. As Bethan arrived she beamed and said: 'Oh, come in, my dear, I'm so glad you weren't too busy. I do need an alcohol rub . . .'

Of course she does, Bethan thought as she went to get the alcohol. Anyone who had spent the best part of six weeks in bed, mostly lying on her back, must be so uncomfortable they would never want to lie down again. But there were plenty of other patients out in the main ward in a similar position, and it would never have occurred to Sister to summon the most senior staff nurse on the ward to administer a rub half way through the busiest part of the morning.

The difference between them and Mrs Norland lay not in the degree of their need but in the level of their resources. Mrs Norland enjoyed the income from a fortune of something over twenty million pounds, the proceeds of her dead husband's motor-car company, now being successfully expanded by her son. She had made it clear that St Thomas's would benefit from her will if she went on being happy about her treatment here. No one intended jeopardizing the hospital's legacy by making her take her turn in getting an alcohol rub.

Still, that was hardly Mrs Norland's fault. She had no idea the others were treated differently – apart from anything else, she never saw them, tucked away in her little private domain here. The only reason she was at St Thomas's and not in some luxurious clinic in Marylebone or St John's Wood was the seriousness of her illness. She had been awaiting a straight-forward gallstone operation when her gall bladder had punctured and she had been rushed in on the edge of death. Emergency surgery and constant care had saved her life, but it had been a long, hard struggle. Only now was she beginning to look normal again.

She lay back with a contented sigh as Bethan finished the rub. 'Oh, that makes me feel so much better! You have true healing hands, my dear . . . Oh, I'm seeing Mr Farrar this afternoon. Do you think he might finally give me a discharge date?'

'I wouldn't like to say, Mrs Norland. You were very ill, you know, and although the wound has healed so well, you'll need a lot of attention for weeks yet. Don't get your hopes up too much, will you?'

'No, perhaps not. It's just that one begins to feel so isolated, tucked away in hospital, and the outside world seems like paradise.'

Bethan uttered a hollow laugh. 'A quick stroll along West-minster Bridge Road would soon cure you of that, Mrs N. It's like a mudbath at present!'

'Oh, dear, it can't be much of a life for you here . . . you're so young and lively, and it's such a grim old area south of the river. What on earth do you find to do?'

'I often ask myself that,' said Bethan. 'It seemed like heaven when I'd just finished my training down in Cardiff, and I suppose it has been in a way.' She gave Mrs Norland a wicked grin. 'It's a good place for collecting male admirers, I'll give you that! All those young doctors at the Medical and Surgical School, you know . . . At least I get taken to plenty of plays and concerts in the West End.'

'I'm sure you do. But I expect you still have to get back to some grim nurses' home in the end. That can't be very much fun for a grown woman.'

'No, that's true. I was twenty-three a fortnight ago, and it seemed a bit much that I had to be home by 10.30 on my birthday evening.'

'Do the restrictions ever make you think about giving it up?'

'Every day, at least ten times! There aren't many vacancies at something else for ex-nurses though. My only way out is to work for promotion to sister. Then I'll either be free to come and go as I please at the home, and have my own self-contained place there, or I shall be earning enough to find a little flat outside.' She chuckled again. 'Trouble is, by the time you're old enough for the promotion, you're too old to enjoy the freedom any more! Now, if you're feeling better, I'll have to get about my business.'

'Of course, nurse. Go along, and thank you again.' After she had left, Margot Norland gazed after her, a speculative expression on her face.

'When I sit down to a plate of slop like this, I wonder why I've spent so many years working for qualifications!' said Bethan, slamming down her fork in disgust. She had just collected her lunch at the nurses' canteen.

Melinda Carter, her friend from Women's Medical, merely said: 'You'd better try to get some of it down, all the same. You can't go through a full shift on a cup of tea and a bit of bread-and-butter.'

'You're right. Oh, well, here we go – through the lips and round the gums, look out stomach, here it comes!'

'Oh, Bethan, don't be so coarse!' said Melinda, giggling.

Bethan smiled back. 'That's what I always say to get my old biddies to open up and swallow their sleeping draughts on the ward. It makes them laugh enough to relax for a minute or so.'

'You're a very good nurse, Bethan. I wish something nice would happen to you as a reward for all your work.'

'I was born in the wrong street for that, I'm afraid. I never realized when I got my references from Cardiff that the old cow of a matron would put something in about me "having overcome the disadvantages of a deprived background". My mother would have killed her if she'd ever known, and it seems to have set me back years with the powers-that-be here. I sometimes think they believe that people from mining families paint themselves with woad and dance naked on the mountainsides at the full moon.'

'It will all come to you eventually, really, darling. You're too good to be held back by a little thing like that.'

Bethan shook her head. 'I'd be more willing to believe that if Venetia Eldon hadn't been promoted to sister last week at the same age as me and with qualifications not quite as good as mine.'

'That was frightful, I agree. It was so blatant . . . me and my daddy the consultant rheumatologist!'

'Hmm, well that sort of family influence counts in the Valleys the same as here. I just have this feeling that if Papa had been a bank manager or a lawyer it would have been just as easy for her. It's only we peasants who can't be trusted with responsibility, you see!'

Melinda blushed. Her father was a professor of Greek at King's College. 'Why *will* they be so patronizing? You know what I'm like – just enough brains to pass my probationer exams. After that, here I stay. But I've already noticed some people treat me better than they treat you, with all your seniority and extra certificates.'

'I don't know what I'd do without you, Melly. You're the only one who treats me the same as everyone else. I'd feel a real freak without that.'

'What about all the students? I haven't noticed them looking down on you.'

'Oh, them! They're men – that's different.'

'Can't see how. After all, most of them are the sons of other doctors or your terrible bank managers and lawyers.'

'Yes, but I'm twenty-three and they are anything from twenty-five to twenty-eight. If ever there was a time when class barriers disappear, it's then. I'm no false blushing violet. I know red hair and blue eyes have a hell of a lot to do with it. Haven't noticed any of them queuing up to propose marriage, though, have you?'

'Would you *want* to marry any of them?'

'That's beside the point, isn't it? If there was anywhere to go, I'd be thinking of moving on . . . '

Melinda pressed her hand. 'Please don't, Bethan. I think perhaps it's even worse outside nursing.'

'I know. Why d'you think I'm still here?'

Returning to the surgical ward, Bethan was more depressed than ever. More than three years of practical and theoretical work, and in a sense she was no better off than she had been as a Cardiff probationer. When she arrived at St Thomas's, the theatre nurses' course was over-subscribed. Her sister tutor had suggested that she add an extra string to her bow by studying midwifery while she waited.

At first Bethan had been unenthusiastic. There had been too many children at home. Pregnancy and labour did not interest her. But in her first days at St Thomas's she had been lonely and had registered for the course to keep solitude at bay. Within a month she was captivated by her studies. There really was a sense of wonder about the inevitable course of pregnancy and the glorious or sometimes terrible result, something inspiring about the effort and courage put in by the mothers-to-be. She spent a year as a student midwife, while working normal shifts on the women's surgical ward, then took her diploma, coming top of the class.

After that she registered as a student theatre nurse, and completed that course too with almost maximum grades. Venetia Eldon had been her contemporary, taking the courses in reverse order. She had managed bare passes in both midwifery and theatre nursing. Nevertheless she had been promoted sister at the youngest age yet known, allegedly on the strength of having qualified in two difficult specialities within two years. Bethan, her excellent grades unremarked, received not even a commendation for her achievement.

Most of the time she did not think about it. She knew that if she did, she would soon be too bitter for her own good. So she concentrated on the job in hand, spent every penny of her wages as she received them, and flirted with every attractive postgraduate medical student who crossed her path. To strangers she seemed to be an exceptionally pretty, empty-headed and slightly mercenary young woman. As long as they did not suspect her of being unworthy of the company she kept, she could not have cared less.

Her lunch break had coincided with Sir Henry Farrar's ward round. Mrs Norland firmly called him Mr Farrar to indicate that she understood the difference between a physician and a surgeon. The knighthood had been awarded for conspicuous services during the war, when he had been responsible for the survival of several young men whose intestinal wounds would normally have ensured death within forty-eight hours. He tended to regard civilian patients as spoiled hypochondriacs unless they were at death's door. As he was almost as rich as Mrs Norland, there was no question of his treating her with deference on that account. She really had been close to death; and for a woman of her age her recovery had been remarkable.

Now she was pressing him for a discharge date, and he was reluctant to let her go. 'You are still in a very delicate state, Mrs Norland,' he told her that day. 'I have insufficient faith in agency nurses to rely on home-care for you for at least the next three weeks.'

'Three weeks! I shall lose my sanity if I have to stare through that window for the next three weeks,' she said. 'What if one of your nurses were attending me?'

He looked puzzled. 'I don't understand you, madam.'

'Come along, Sir Henry!' So she's interested enough to drop the Mr Farrar nonsense, he thought. 'That lovely little Welsh nurse who looks after me – she's so unhappy that she is on the point of leaving. If I offered her a job she'd come like a shot, and if she intends deserting you anyway, I shan't be harming the medical profession.'

'Little Welsh nurse? Who would that be?' He already knew. One of his more promising junior surgeons had mentioned the girl's misery when Eldon's simpering daughter had been made a sister. Chap had pointed out that the girl who was passed over was the quick one he had noticed in theatre, with fingers that scarcely seemed to exert a butterfly's pressure, but were always in the right place at the right time. Shame she hadn't got what she deserved, but without a little influence, who did? Now it looked as though Old Mother Norland might be prepared to give the child a leg up. Well, why not? If it was true they'd lose her otherwise . . .

'If you can guarantee that Nurse Walters will be coming to

134

work for you on a permanent basis, I shall let you go home this time next week. And if you are that eager, Mrs Norland, I shall make sure she is released early from her period of notice to coincide with your discharge.' He began to move away from her bed, then a thought struck him and he turned back. 'I take it you have obtained the young woman's consent to this new arrangement.'

'Oh, of course! She's most enthusiastic.' Margot made a mental note to seize Bethan the moment she reappeared on the ward. An unguarded word from the girl to Sister now would undo all her plans.

Bethan leaped at the opportunity of leaving St Thomas's. Misery at having been passed over for promotion was the chief reason, but close on its heels came dissatisfaction with an on-off romance, and the general drabness of living in London on an income which was insufficient to finance the myriad temptations which the capital offered to a pretty young woman. Margot Norland lured her with a salary as high as any miner's top earnings, all her living expenses, and her own flat in a beautiful country house. In addition she was to be taught to drive as soon as she took up her post, and would have use of a car during her time off. When Mrs Norland made the offer Bethan could scarcely believe it.

She said yes, and went through the first couple of weeks of her truncated notice period feeling as if she were walking on air. Then the ward sister, an ex-theatre nurse like herself, invited her to stay on for a cup of tea in the canteen after duty.

'Are you sure you're doing the right thing, Walters? There'll be no seniority for you if you decide to return to nursing. I know you feel ill-used now, but what will it be like if you have to start again at this point in three or four years? There's still time to reconsider,' she said.

'Thanks, Sister, but no. I lay awake all night thinking it over, after Mrs Norland offered me the job. It will be strange at first – I've lived in hospitals since I was sixteen – but nice-strange. I need to spread my wings . . . ' That expression. It had slipped out so naturally. Why did she dislike the sound of it? Then she remembered. It was what she had told Lily, centuries ago, it seemed, when her sister had begged her to delay her departure from South Wales. Four more years, and she was still not airborne. Maybe this time . . .

She pushed aside the thought because Sister Dean was talking again. 'I know you'd set your heart on theatre nursing, but I always thought your greatest strength was obstetrics. You received the most brilliant reports, you know.'

'I didn't know. Thank you for telling me. Didn't do me much good, though, did it?'

'Oh, my dear – please believe that I understand your misery at being passed over so unjustly. But there will be another time. And if you move back to midwifery I think you'll find it happens much faster than you might expect.'

'I'd have to go out into the community, though, wouldn't I? I need at least a year as a district midwife before I could be put in charge of a maternity ward.'

'Yes, of course. But surely you cannot expect to be promoted to theatre sister or sister on a surgical ward in less than that?'

'Venetia Eldon hasn't had to wait even as long as now, has she?'

'I'm afraid circumstances alter cases – and I hardly need tell you about her circumstances!'

'No – and I'll still be a collier's daughter a year or ten years from now, won't I? And still a staff nurse perhaps? I don't think so, Sister. Thanks for making the effort – but no. The price is too high.'

Louise Dean sighed. 'If only there was something I could say to make you stay. You'll be such a loss to the profession . . .'

'Aye, I can see that by the way they're trying to make me hang around!' She said it in pure Valleys patois and Sister Dean's jaw dropped as suddenly as Bethan's normal refined accent. Bethan grinned at her, resuming her normal tones. 'You see, Sister? What would our patients think if my mask slipped and they ever heard the real me? They might refuse to be treated by a guttersnipe.'

'Oh, Walters, I'm so very sorry. I never really understood.'

'No one from your side of the fence ever does. But thanks for trying, anyway.'

Nevertheless, she suffered a pang when they left the hospital a few days later. Bethan had gone into the ward to supervise Mrs

Norland's discharge. She helped her new employer to the lift and in the vestibule downstairs a porter with a wheelchair met them. Mrs Norland's car and chauffeur awaited them outside. The size of the vehicle and the grandeur of the driver's uniform almost made Bethan lose her composure. The chauffeur wore a pearl grey uniform of some velvet-smooth woollen material, with brilliantly polished black leather gaiters and a grey peaked cap.

'We don't often use the Rolls-Royce,' Mrs Norland explained. 'We like to be seen in our own marque. But James insisted because this one gives me the most room to stretch out.'

Great God Almighty, thought Bethan, she's right there. You could get a ward full of patients into a bus like this . . .

She made Mrs Norland comfortable, then moved to sit in front beside the chauffeur. 'No, no, my dear – come and sit back here with me! I feel like a chat. You must tell me all about yourself.'

I'm going to like this, Bethan told herself, relaxing in the deep upholstery and feeling like a foreign princess, and revelling in the walnut inlay of the car's interior. But she still fought back tears as the car turned into Lambeth Road and she caught her last glimpse of St Thomas's.

CHAPTER FOURTEEN

The house was a place beyond Bethan's wildest fantasies. James Norland senior, founder of the family engineering business, had built Foxhall shortly after making his first million, on several acres of riverside land at Shillingford, which gave him quick access to his huge car factory in Oxford. It was faced in white stucco, with a multitude of sharply-pointed gables and a roof of Welsh slate, the dark blue-grey relieved around the eaves with gingerbread-patterns of ornate woodwork. Tall windows looked out across immaculate lawns and gardens which led down to the Thames and extended a couple of hundred yards along the east bank. At several points, mature weeping willows screened the lawns from the river, so the family were able to choose between seclusion from curious water-borne trippers and an open view.

Around the house was a wide terrace of York stone slabs, edged by stone balustrades. In warm weather it was delightful to eat breakfast or take tea there.

'No wonder you were so anxious to come home!' said Bethan. 'I don't think anyone would ever drag me away if it was mine.'

'A burst gall bladder tends to adjust one's priorities,' replied Mrs Norland. 'But yes, you are right. It made the view from that wretched little window all the more bleak in comparison.'

She had stood up well to the long car journey, but Bethan realized now she was exhausted. 'I think we'd better get you straight to bed,' she said. 'Are you up to managing the stairs?'

Margot Norland shook her head and said faintly: 'I think not, but fortunately it doesn't matter. We had a lift installed when Jimmy had his stroke. I shall use that.'

'I think you'd better sit in the wheelchair to go inside,' said Bethan.

Mrs Norland drew herself up straight with visible difficulty. 'I shall walk through my own front door, thank you. That wheelchair is for emergencies only, as far as I am concerned.'

Bethan signalled frantically to the chauffeur behind her back, indicating that he should nevertheless bring the chair the moment Mrs Norland was out of sight. Only willpower appeared to be holding her employer up at present, and she had no wish to lose a patient on her first day of private care.

But determination got Margot Norland as far as the lift. Once inside she was grateful for the chair, which Patterson, the chauffeur, unfolded so that she could sit down. The lift opened on to the landing outside the master bedroom suite, and Bethan pushed her along to her room, relieved they had finally arrived.

Once Mrs Norland was in bed and had drunk a cup of tea, the colour started coming back to her cheeks and she relaxed. Eventually she managed a shaky smile. 'I'm sorry, my dear. That was rather naughty of me, but you will find I'm frightfully obstinate at times . . . Used to getting my own way all the time, you see . . . Oh, dear! I had planned to introduce you to James when he came home from the plant. But I have a feeling I shall be fast asleep by then!' She slipped down between the fine linen sheets with a sigh of satisfaction. 'There is nothing, *nothing* more comforting than getting into one's own bed in one's own home . . . ' her eyelids were already fluttering closed. ' . . . Find Polly, Bethan. She's my maid. She will show you around and help you make yourself at home . . . ' Then the sedative Bethan had administered took a firm hold on her and she drifted off to sleep.

Hazy and on the edge of slumber, Mrs Norland had given Bethan the impression the house was deserted, but when she went downstairs she encountered enough people to inhabit a small village.

Although the Norland family now comprised only the mother and her grown-up son and daughter, James and

Jessica, and Jessica was shortly to move out on her marriage, the mansion appeared to be fully staffed. There were the lady's maids, Polly for Mrs Norland, Nanette for Jessica; James Norland's manservant, Armstrong; the butler, Fowler; Mrs Fanshaw, the housekeeper; a head housemaid, a parlourmaid and three girls who doubled up as general servants upstairs and kitchenmaids downstairs; Mrs Sampson, the cook; the chauffeur, Patterson; the head gardener, Cheviot, his assistant, who was his son, and seemingly countless garden labourers. Bethan wondered if she would ever remember all the names.

Now they welcomed her cheerfully. She encountered Polly first. The maid was on her way upstairs to see if she was required there. She took Bethan back down to the kitchen, where most of the staff were relaxing over a tea of such sumptuous proportions that Bethan wondered what even greater splendour was offered to the family above stairs.

Eating wafer-thin bread-and-butter with thick rhubarb and ginger jam, she speculated about it, and the cook chuckled. 'They'd drop dead up there if I offered 'em a spread like this!' she said. 'Mrs Norland have always been a small eater. Miss Jessica starts getting fretful if her waist measurement goes over – what is it, Nanette? 'Twenty-one and an' 'alf,' said Nanette in her pretty French-English. '– Aye, that's it.' Mrs Sampson made a half-mocking, half-incredulous gesture, touching her beefy fingers together to describe a handspan waist. 'I'll tell you somefing. One a my thighs is that big! I can enjoy a bitta fruit cake, though, which is more'n you can say for Miss Jessica.'

'And James Norland?' interjected Bethan, unable quite to bring herself to enunciate the service 'Mr James'.

'Oh, he's got a good enough appetite, but never for tea. He's always over Oxford in the factory until about six, and come the weekend he's dashing off to some house party or other.' She smiled fatly at her tea table. 'No, I always looks on this as reasonable servants' perks. We does all right by them, and so it's only fair to see they does right by us. Mrs Norland's generous to a fault, anyway.'

Nanette sniffed. 'That eez more than you can say for the daughter. She counts every penny.' Bethan was eager to hear

140

more, but Nanette abruptly decided she had work to do, and left the kitchen.

Polly and Mrs Sampson exchanged significant glances, and Bethan's curiosity rose another notch. As a source of fascinating gossip, this promised to be infinitely more entertaining than a session in the nurses' canteen at St Thomas's . . .

Polly had obviously received instructions about settling Bethan in her new home. 'You'll be very comfortable, I'm sure, Nurse Walters. There's not a full staff here any more, so we all have plenty of room. Mrs Norland has had the nursery suite opened up for you because it's right over her rooms and you can get to her quickly if she needs you.'

Bethan was astonished at the maid's comment on the staffing. 'But there are dozens of people working here! How many more would make up a full staff?'

'Oh, you should have seen it when Mr Norland was alive! An extra manservant, of course, for him. Another chauffeur – can't run a family of four and their guests around with just one, can you?' Her eyes held a twinkle of malice against her employers. 'Then there were two full-time footmen, and twice the number of general maids that we have now. Mrs Norland has run it down a lot since he's been gone. 'Course, when the children were little there was Nanny, a nursery maid and a governess as well. Even now there's still one you haven't met. Miss Bateman. Started off as Miss Jessica's governess and stayed on as secretary to Mrs Norland after Miss Jessica went away to school. Goes on and on, doesn't it?'

Bethan grappled with the idea of a family of four needing so many people to keep them going in comfort. She had never given much thought to people with servants before. Now she began to wonder how they were able to bear the constant lack of privacy. She had found the presence of her numerous brothers and sisters intrusive, but at least they were family. What must it be like to spend your life among a colony of strangers, some of whom must dislike you for having so much more than they? Bethan had always wanted material wealth and to live in comfortable circumstances, but she promptly decided that if she ever achieved her ambition, she would not be spending the money on live-in servants.

'I thought that since the war all that sort of thing had been toned right down because no one was rich enough to afford it any more,' she said.

'Don't you believe it. Some of the old gentry have come down in the world, because so much of their money was in land, but not this lot. Mr Norland started out in life as a metal-basher up in Brum, but he'd made his first fortune by the time he was twenty-five and another one before his fiftieth birthday. The son is good at business too, so there's no question of this generation spending what the first lot made. They've never been richer, take my word for it.'

Abruptly Polly decided she might have said too much. Her gossip cut off and she was all briskness. 'Come on, I'll keep you hanging about down here all day if you let me . . . Your rooms are up this way.'

On the second floor, approaching the nursery suite along a broad landing, she was her talkative self again. 'Sorry about getting funny down there just now, but if ever it was true that walls had ears, it was here.'

'But who would be listening?'

'Miss – bloody – Bateman, that's who!' Polly enunciated the three words slowly and with considerable venom, her carefully cultivated accent momentarily discarded. 'Honestly, you be careful around her. She'll probably be very friendly towards you at first, but she's pure poison. Seems to think the Nor-lands are in her personal charge and she's got to protect them from the likes of us. God knows why, when you consider what they've got and what we've got. P'raps she thinks we'll hold our own little revolution if she doesn't keep her eyes and ears open.'

Her warning was cut off at that point because they had arrived at the nursery suite. Bethan gave a gasp of surprise. Polly smiled at her. 'Thought you'd get a bit of a shock,' she said. 'Madam obviously thinks highly of you, because she was on the phone for about half an hour to Mrs Fanshaw last week, saying what bits of furniture were to be moved in, what had to be bought new and so on . . . '

'I half expected not to get my own flat, although she said I would,' said Bethan.

'Madam likes to look after the people who look after *her*, if you know what I mean,' the maid replied. 'I get all sorts of

142

little treats the others don't come in for, and she's right, of course. I appreciate it and I work all the better for it. That's why Nanette got so cross downstairs at teatime. That Jessica is a right spoiled little brat and as tight-fisted as a miser. It must be a bit off-putting for Nanette to see me getting extra little holidays and nice clothes as presents, and then only to get Miss Jessica's cast-offs. I don't expect I'd feel too happy about it.'

'Why does she stay on, then? I'd have thought a girl like her would have other opportunities.'

'Not as many as you might think these days. There are so many people out of work now that they're queuing up to get good places in domestic service. Even when the money's terrible, at least they get bed and board provided. Anyway Miss Jessica doesn't work Nanette very hard. She just doesn't treat her very well. Nanette's got her head screwed on the right way. She may not be happy now, but she knows she wouldn't be better off anywhere else.'

'Is she moving with Miss Norland when she marries?'

'Miss Jessica seems to think so, but Nanette insists she hasn't made up her mind. She'll go in the end, though. Miss Jessica's going to live in London and Nanette fancies that, even at the price of going on with Miss Jessica.'

Interested as she was in the maid's stories, Bethan was itching to be alone and explore her new domain. She had never in her life enjoyed so much space . . . so much privacy. Briefly, the vision of the Norlands re-entered her mind. Why, I'm better off than any of them! she thought. Once I close this door behind me, I have complete privacy . . . At last it was beginning to look as if she was finding what she had left Cardiff to seek out.

Polly retreated to the door. 'I'll leave you to get settled, then. There's one bell push in your bedroom and another beside the fireplace in your sitting room, both with speaking tubes, so you can order food for yourself up here or anything you need to go to Mrs Norland's quarters. And Mr James has had a new pair of bells installed from Madam's room to yours – bedroom and sitting room again – so she can call you if she needs you and you're not downstairs. They're over there, see?' She pointed to a small ivory button set in a brass surround with the speaking tube hooked up beside it, and high on the wall near the door, a bell on a spring, to be operated from Mrs Norland's room.

'Thank you, Polly. I'm not at all sure what I do about meals and so on. Have you any idea?'

'Yes. Miss Bateman said . . . let me see now . . . when you're on duty, a meal will be brought up to you in Mrs Norland's suite at the same time as hers is served, and you can eat it in the little dressing room next to her bedroom. I think they've rearranged it like a sort of office and rest room for you. Off duty, you get your food up here. There's still a dumb waiter over in the corner there, from when it was the day nursery, and if you ring when you're ready, the kitchen maid will put your meal on it and send it straight up.

'Of course, you must always come down and have tea in the kitchen, because otherwise you'll not keep abreast of the gossip – and there's usually something going on worth hearing! You won't see dear Miss Bateman down there, though. Thinks she's too good for the common run and has everything in her own room. Mrs Fanshaw thought you might be just as stand-offish, but I new the minute I saw you there was none a that nonsense about you. You're really the only other member of staff who's in that sort of half-superior position along with her, you see.' She dropped her voice and grinned. 'But after that, any resemblance ends, thank God!'

'Why "thank God?" What's wrong with her?'

'You won't need to ask that after you've been here a few days. I'd better leave you to find out for yourself in case my feelings turn you against her. But personally I think she's quite capable of doing that without my help. Anyway I really must go. I'll sit in with Mrs Norland until she wakes, unless you think you should be down there.'

'Oh, no, no need for that. She's resting comfortably because I gave her something. She should wake up by about six. She's not so much ill now as terribly weak. Once she's rested, I can take over from you and then she and I must sort out when she wants me on duty. It will help if you ask Cook when it's easiest for me to have my off-duty meals too. I don't want to be ringing down for my tray when she's putting the finishing touches on a dinner party.'

Polly beamed at her. 'Oh, they're going to like you down-stairs! They're not used to getting that sort of consideration from anyone, let alone the half-way-ups.'

'Half-way-ups? What are they?'

'Don't be offended. It's what Patterson calls people like Miss Bateman and yourself. Governesses, tutors – you know, the skilled people who are refined but still really servants. Neither fish, fowl or good red herring, as my mother used to say. The poor things are so cowed by wanting to be better than they are, that they always treat the proper servants like dirt. We all understand why, but we still don't like it. You seem to have more sense. Go on, now, you take a look round up here. I'll see you later.' And, with a brief wave, she was gone.

With mounting pleasure Bethan discovered she had acquired a self-contained flat. The original suite had comprised day and night nurseries, bedrooms for the nanny and the nursery maid, a nursery kitchen – really just a pantry-sized room with a small gas cooker and butler's sink, sufficient for warming drinks and washing small items – and a bathroom with an enormous claw-footed cast-iron bath, a walk-in airing cupboard, a washbasin almost big enough to bathe in, and a WC in yet another small room.

The nanny's and maid's bedrooms had been left dust-sheeted and closed, but the day and night nurseries were now her bedroom and sitting room. She marvelled at the speed with which wealth could achieve things. It was scarcely more than a week since she had accepted Mrs Norland's offer of a job, yet the rooms had been fully refurbished in that time, with delicate primrose paint in the sitting room and a soft shade of blue in the bedroom. Pretty curtains of sprigged cotton framed the spectacular river views from her windows, and the picture of comfort was completed with a selection of good furniture, nothing new but all chosen to blend well with the light, cheerful atmosphere of the redecoration. Bethan loved it all and momentarily was swamped by gratitude. Somewhere deep inside, a voice was warning her that no one invested so much time and effort without wanting a great deal in return, but for the moment she cast aside the doubt as an unworthy response to such generosity.

Now she set about her unpacking, still feeling like a child let loose in a toyshop with instructions to take whatever caught her fancy.

What caught her fancy turned out to have a price tag all of its own, and it proved very expensive. It was James Norland.

When Bethan had finished unpacking she changed into the smart dove grey button-through dress which Mrs Norland had chosen as her uniform, and went down to her employer's room. Polly was just leaving as she got there.

The maid smiled at her and said: 'Perfect timing. She's going to ring for you in a minute, but I might as well tell her you're here now. Mr James is in there.' She knocked, reopened the door and said: 'Nurse Walters, Madam. Are you ready for her?' then stood aside to let Bethan in.

'Hello, my dear. Whatever you gave me to drink earlier on did wonders for me. I feel better than before I was ill. James, here's the young woman who was responsible for my early return home.'

Bethan looked at him and found it difficult to look away. He was the most elegant man she had ever seen. He wore a casual but immaculately cut suit of herringbone tweed in subdued shades of brown, handmade leather brogues, a plain shirt with a soft collar, and a brown silk tie. His honey-gold hair was slightly longer than fashion dictated, and a lock of it fell forward across his forehead with an untidy grace which might almost have been contrived. He was very slim and consequently seemed even taller than his six feet, one inch. His face was broad, with a generous mouth and a cleft in the chin which made her want to press her fingertip there. What on earth am I thinking about? she chided herself. I'm here to work, not drool over my boss's son!

'We seem to have a lot to thank you for, Miss Walters,' he said. God, his voice is even better than the rest of him, thought Bethan. 'A fortnight ago I thought Mama wouldn't be back with us for months.'

Bethan dragged her attention back to the matter in hand, and managed a shaky smile. 'As Mrs Norland told me herself, she's a very obstinate woman. When she decided to come home, I don't think anything was likely to stand in her way.'

He turned back towards the bed. 'For shame, Mama! And

you told me they were anxious to be rid of you . . . We shall have to keep an eye on her, shan't we, Miss Walters?'

Hmm, that's not quite so attractive, thought Bethan, feeling the patronizing tone as keenly as a slap. She answered mono-syllabically, and was saved from more of his heavy-handed banter by Mrs Norland.

'May I get up, now?' she asked. 'I always feel so much better if I've spent most of the day up and about.'

'Of course you can, if you feel strong enough. It will be good for you.' Bethan moved to help her, glad of the diversion.

'James,' said Mrs Norland, 'you go into the dressing room and wait until I'm respectable. You can ring for drinks, if you like.' She glanced hopefully at Bethan. 'Would I be permitted a small one?'

'I don't know what the doctors would say, but yes, as long as it's just one. You only had a mild sedative and that was four hours ago.'

'I suppose the pretty nurse isn't allowed to drink on duty?' said James, the teasing note back in his voice.

Before Bethan could utter the stock refusal, Mrs Norland cut in icily: 'Really, James – you should know better than to ask!' Norland gave an exaggerated 'oh dear, these old fogies' grimace, and went to order drinks for himself and his mother.

Again, Bethan felt as if she had been slapped. At the hospital she had been a nurse, a free agent, at least as far as Mrs Norland was concerned. Now, instantaneously, she had become a servant, and her employer had just reminded James Norland that one did not drink with the servants.

She firmly put the matter out of her mind, helped Mrs Norland to get up and dress in a loose gown which required her to put on little beneath it, and seated her in a comfortable chair. 'I don't recommend that you go down to dinner tonight, Madam,' she said, reluctantly adopting the servants' standard term of address for the first time in her life. 'Give it a few more hours, at least.'

'Yes, I believe you're right. Come and sit with me and we'll discuss what my routine is to be.'

They established a schedule which permitted Mrs Norland plenty of rest and allowed for either Bethan or Polly to be on hand most of the time. 'Within a month you'll wonder why you

147

needed so much help,' said Bethan, 'but at the beginning it will be terribly tiring for you.'

During their conversation she became aware that James Norland had been gone a long time. Presumably he felt more embarrassed than his mother about sitting with someone in an apparently companionable group, and sipping drinks without inviting them to do so. He came back, carrying a tray with two glasses of gin and tonic, just as Bethan was about to leave.

'I don't think I shall need you again this evening, my dear,' said Mrs Norland, her former easy familiarity restored now there was no danger of its being taken seriously. 'Polly can help me to get ready for bed. You go off to your rooms and settle in.'

'Oh, I must come back and see that everything is in order before you go to sleep tonight, Mrs Norland. Unless you ring for me earlier on, I'll look in at ten-thirty. You shouldn't really stay up longer than that for the first few nights.'

'Very well. Have a pleasant evening.' She turned back to James, taking her drink from the tray and presumably erasing Bethan from her mind.

A couple of hours later the new flat was beginning to lose some of its appeal. Although it had been a hectic day, Bethan was accustomed to working twelve-hour shifts and going out afterwards, surviving on minimal sleep. Now, having finished an excellent dinner, she was relaxing in the armchair in her sitting room, wondering what on earth to do for the rest of the evening.

Abruptly, the problem solved itself. Someone knocked the door and when she went to answer it she found Polly Johnson's arch enemy standing outside.

'Good evening. I don't know whether you noticed me downstairs this afternoon . . . I'm Moira Bateman, Mrs Norland's secretary,' said the woman.

'Oh . . . yes. Do come in . . . I was just about to make some tea. Would you care to join me?'

The other woman's eyes were devouring the decor and furnishings. 'Yes, thank you. I imagine we shall get to know each other quite well over the next few weeks . . .'

Bethan chose not to follow that one through, knowing instinctively that if she did, she would be treated to Miss Bateman's side of the 'half-way-ups' question. Instead, she said: 'Of course . . . Do sit down over there and I'll boil a kettle.'

'Oh, please let me explore your quarters! I'll come through with you . . . '

Bethan led the way to the pantry-kitchen, registering Miss Bateman's sharp sidelong glance through the open bedroom door as they went to the kitchen. While they were waiting for the tea to brew, she said: 'I assume you have a bathroom too, since they always had one for the nursery.'

'Oh, yes – through there, the door beyond the bedroom,' said Bethan. It was impossible to ignore the note of hard resentment in Moira Bateman's voice.

When they returned to the sitting room with the tea it was not long before the woman explained her discontent. She gave a small, brittle laugh, then said: 'It really is quite exasperating! I suggested this set-up to Mrs Norland more than a year ago – pointed out that no one would be using the nursery for years yet – and she flatly refused to let me move in. Now, bring in a new face and give her the earth . . . '

'It's not quite like that.' Bethan retained an even, friendly tone with some difficulty. Why *was* this woman so abrasive? 'Mrs Norland is going to be ill for some months yet. She needs a trained helper close at hand, and I gather this was the handiest place, being directly over her rooms.'

Miss Bateman gave a sceptical sniff. 'I thought they'd say something like that! There's actually a place downstairs, just across the landing from Mrs Norland's suite. It was a bachelor guest room which they fitted up as a nurse's room when Mr Norland had his stroke. It was a male nurse, of course, and I dare say they'd maintain now that it was too basic for a woman. However, one is forced to certain conclusions . . . '

'I can't see why.' Bethan's tone was still friendly, but her smile was taking on a fixed quality. 'I have no idea what conditions of employment you established with the Norlands when you came here, but mine included the type of accommodation which Mrs Norland would provide. I've lived in nurses' homes all my working life and I wasn't prepared to move unless I got something better. If I may say so, Miss Bateman, you should have done the same thing since it was so important to you.'

149

'Oh, talk is cheap! There was no question of choice when I came here . . . ' She appeared to be sliding into a well-rehearsed routine which brought an emotional lump to her own throat, if not to anyone else's. 'I came here as a girl, barely eighteen, with no choice. My father died suddenly and there was nothing left for my mother and me to live on. She went to her sister and I had to come here.'

'But if you were a secretary, surely there were other possibilities?' In her efforts to control her irritation with the woman, Bethan had quite forgotten Polly's reference to an earlier job.

'Secretary! That's what I am now. I came as a governess. Such a waste of a fine education. My father was an Oxford don. He educated me himself. English literature, Latin, Greek, mathematics . . . I was brilliant. If I'd been a boy there would have been no question – I should have been sent to the university.'

Bethan forbore to point out that had she been a boy it would have made no difference to the date of her father's death, and at eighteen she would have found it equally necessary to get a job and not a higher education.

Miss Bateman was continuing her rancorous story. 'When I first came here I was happy enough to take anything. A roof over my head and a few pounds a year seemed like salvation.'

'I can understand that – and in such a lovely house!' Bethan was determined to lighten the conversation, but it was an impossible task.

'A lovely house, perhaps,' said Moira Bateman, 'but who would want to live in it and be obliged to teach that appalling child Jessica? She made my life misery for years until she went away to school.'

'But what about the Norlands' son? Was he just as bad?'

'Oh, I was given no chance to teach him! Here, as everywhere, the boys get favoured treatment. He was already at boarding school when I came to teach Jessica.'

Bethan ploughed on with her diplomatic responses. 'And did Jessica go away to school when the time came?'

'Yes, at fourteen. Roedean. Wasted on her, of course. She never had an intellectual thought in her head! That was when Mr Norland realized my abilities were being wasted and gave me the opportunity for something better. I took on the role of secretary.'

'I'm surprised you didn't move out then to somewhere of your own. Isn't it a little – er – unusual, for a secretary to live in the same house as her employer?'

Miss Bateman uttered a superior laugh. 'No, no – you don't understand! He didn't waste me at the factory. I was his assistant here at the house, fixing all his social engagements, arranging the big receptions and dinners he laid on for senior employees and visiting businessmen from abroad. Terribly responsible job. More like a sort of social director, if you see what I mean.'

'I do . . . I thought it was usual for the wives of men in his position to do that sort of thing.' Bethan got a sharp glance from Miss Bateman for that.

'Elsewhere, perhaps. But Mr Norland's interests were far too complex for a – a mere social butterfly to organize. Mrs Norland would never have coped with it.'

'Oh. She seems very astute, even now, when she's ill.'

'Your standards are hardly those of international commerce, Nurse Walters. I assure you that one needs a trained mind for that sort of work. I did it for ten years.'

Something was nagging at the back of Bethan's mind, something which did not tie in with the story Moira Bateman was telling. That was it – Polly had said the woman was *Mrs* Norland's secretary, not her husband's . . . 'What happened after he died?' she asked.

'Oh, well, of course the world just ended for me . . . At first, I naturally assumed that with Mr James taking over, I should simply go on doing the same job. No one else could have handled it.'

'But it didn't work out like that?'

'It most certainly did not. Our Mr James had his own ideas. Thought that bringing oily commercial types back to what he insists on calling "the old ancestral pile" was too vulgar for words. He entertains them in Oxford or up in Town. He even had an executive entertainment suite built on at the factory, and they have a full-time chef with all the back-up staff to wine and dine people on the premises.'

'That seems to make more sense than dragging people all the

way out here when what they want to see is the car-making. Surely he must have offered to move you there in your old job?'

Moira Bateman had been gazing fixedly at Bethan as she told her story, with the zeal of a missionary confident of making a conversion. Now her eyes slid away. 'N-no . . . some nonsense about requiring someone who knew the industrial end of the business, not just the social side . . . ' She rallied and looked up again, eyes fierce. 'Of course, now he has a battery of young blond women in silk stockings and short skirts, running to do his slightest bidding. Industrial knowledge, my foot! The only sort of knowledge those girls have has been around since Salome's time!'

By now, Bethan was fighting the desire to burst out laughing. It was all to easy to imagine a sharp young girl, deprived of her original function of nursery governess, bullying her way into a position she had created for herself and over the years becoming a petty tyrant. In school holidays, and later when he started to take over while his father was ill, James Norland must have come to detest her – she could hardly be described as an attractive personality – and he had undoubtedly got shot of her at the earliest opportunity. Bethan wondered how pleased his mother had been to acquire a social secretary after years of seeing the same woman usurp her own function at the mansion. She also wondered how on earth Moira Bateman had survived here so long.

The woman had suddenly changed tack. 'This must sound frightfully sour grapes to you,' she said, 'but I confess I felt ill-used when I came in this evening. I'm actually devoted to the family. And of course they are so generous financially that the servants would ride roughshod over them if I were not there constantly with the family interests at heart.'

Bethan remembered her exclusion when the gin and tonic was dispensed, and decided that this family was capable of holding its own against a bunch of servants, however generous they might be in small matters.

Nevertheless Miss Bateman seemed convinced that it was her mission to watch over them. 'I double check every step of the way,' she said, 'and ensure that Mrs Norland knows *precisely* what is going on. There is no cheating in this household.'

152

'The servants seem to do reasonably well, just the same.'

The other woman's face was positively sour now. 'Far too well, in my view! But Mrs Norland was always too generous for her own good . . . you have only to look at your own conditions of employment to see that!'

Bethan sighed. It was no good: this might be her first day; Moira Bateman was undoubtedly a bad woman to have as an enemy; there might be some justice in her complaints about the way she had been treated. But there was also something wildly wrong with a woman who visited the latest arrival in an apparently well-run country house and set up a barrage of accusations about incompetence, victimization and dishonesty.

She said: 'Really, Miss Bateman, I'm sure that having been here so long, you know better than me about many of the problems that come up. But I have to tell you that so far I've experienced nothing but kindness and courtesy from the servants or the Norlands themselves,' – her mind quickly rejected the drinks incident – 'and I feel it would be unfair for me to start gossiping about any of them when I really know nothing about them. Now, would you like me to make a fresh pot of tea?'

For a moment she thought Moira Bateman was going to launch into a stream of personal abuse. There really must be something wrong with her, she thought fleetingly. But then the secretary visibly got herself under control and said, smiling: 'No – perhaps I've stayed too long.' She stood up. 'I must apologize if I've bored you.'

'Quite the reverse, I assure you. And please come to see me again.' Best not to refer to what had just been said.

Miss Bateman took her cue from Bethan's attitude. 'No – you must come to me next time. Of course, you'll have to wait while someone prepares tea in the kitchen. I'm afraid I don't live in the lap of luxury. Now, if you'll forgive me . . . ' She moved towards the door.

Bethan saw her out, then flopped down in the fireside chair, already only half believing that she had gone through such a conversation. And she had been getting bored!

CHAPTER FIFTEEN

It seemed the secretary had been there for hours, but when Bethan looked at her watch it was only a little after nine. She decided to go down to the servants' hall and get to know some of the senior staff. After the brush with Moira Bateman, she was doubly determined not to be classed as one of the half-way-ups. But it seemed Miss Bateman was not to be her only visitor that evening. As she opened her sitting-room door to go out, she came face to face with James Norland, who had been trying to find a way of knocking on the door without dropping the bottles of whisky, gin, and tonic water and the ice bucket he was carrying.

'Ah, telepathic as well as beautiful! That's what I like to see in a woman,' he said, grinning. 'May I come in?'

'You don't look as if you expect me to say no.' She gestured at the drinks.

'Wouldn't be at all surprised if you did, though. This is largely by way of an apology for the nasty little scene down in Mama's room over my bit of *lèse majesté* in asking you if you fancied a drink. Sometime's Mama's snobbery shows in rather an unfortunate light.'

'I'd noticed.' She stood aside to let him in. 'In fact, I might as well tell you, if I'd seen signs of it at St Thomas's, I shouldn't have been here now. I'm a nurse, not a servant.'

He had put down his bottles and bucket and now half-turned back to her, clapping his hands lightly. 'Bravo the Bolshevik candidate for the Thames Valley! My dear, some things never

154

change, and one of them is the attitude of the rich to the less rich.'

Embarrassed at her own uncharacteristic heated outburst, Bethan said she would get some glasses. Moments later they were seated at the fireside, where she and Moira Bateman had been only minutes before. Bethan had a feeling she would enjoy this visit considerably more.

'I owe you a personal apology too, I believe,' said Norland. 'By the look on your face at the time, I believe you thought I was patronizing you down there. I wasn't, you know. Mama has this odd appetite for being treated like a naughty but endearing little girl. It keeps her happy so I go along with it, but I assure you I wasn't trying to make you feel like an idiot.'

'Apology accepted. You're right. I did feel awkward. It's very strange . . . I never saw any of this side of Mrs Norland at the hospital. She seemed so – so strong and determined about everything.'

'Mmm. One way and another, she's had a mixed time of it. Shows in the oddest ways. Enough of that, though. I've come for a little convivial chatter about our new member of staff, not her employer. How d'you like your hideaway?'

'It's marvellous. Much better than I ever expected. How was it all done so quickly?'

He shrugged. 'Most of the furniture already on the premises. Estate carpenter and labourers available at the drop of a hat to paint and remodel. It only took a couple of days.'

'Well, I love it. I shall be spoiled for anywhere else after this.'

His face clouded slightly. 'After this? That sounds awfully temporary.'

'Much as I'd like to think of this job as permanent, Mrs Norland is hardly likely to be ill for that long. I didn't think I would be required for more than a year.'

'If you are interested in staying, I should be much happier about it,' he said. 'Mama likes you enormously, in spite of the icy little display down there this evening. She needs a companion as much as she does a nurse, you know; and we all realize she's never going to be completely all right after the illness she's just been through.'

'Oh – surely Miss Bateman is as much companion as

155

secretary to your mother? I imagine she would be most put out if I took over.'

He stared at her incredulously for a moment, then shouted with laughter. 'Moira Bateman? Mama would rather be a victim of suttee than be companionable with that one! I assure you, their relationship is purely business, and if Mama could persuade Jessica to take the woman with her to London, she'd do it like a shot. No, forget about Moira Bateman in all this, and concentrate on yourself. Mama gave me the impression that once you left the hospital, it was a permanent move.'

'Well, yes, in terms of not gaining any further seniority while I'm away. I'd find it hard to go back at the old level, but they'd certainly take me if I wanted to. There's a permanent shortage of people with my qualifications.'

'That doesn't sound like a testimony to unbridled enthusiasm.'

'It isn't. I left because I was already discontented with it. That would be just the same if I ever went back, perhaps worse.' She smiled at him. 'No, if you are sure this is a permanent offer, I shall be happy to stay for good. It's far better than I would have had at St Thomas's.'

'Good. I'm pleased about that.' He drained his glass and stood up. 'I'll be off now. I imagine you'll be going down to settle Mama for the night in half an hour or so. By the way, don't think this is a touch of the young master slinking up on the pretty nurse with evil intent. In normal circumstances I should expect you to dine with me downstairs and to have drinks with me in the library now and then. All that upstairs, downstairs nonsense begins and ends with my mother.

'She's a darling at times, but unfortunately she convinced my poor father that sort of behaviour was the only way to act soon after they married and in due course Jessica swallowed the same line without any trouble. I have another view entirely. I hope you'll invite me here next time. I'll leave the drinks with you, just in case, and then I shall only be encumbered by an ice bucket. I'll go now. Welcome to Foxhall. I hope you'll be happy here.'

If this goes on I shall have to bar the door to get any privacy, thought Bethan, rinsing glasses and putting away the bottles. But she was smiling as she went over Norland's visit. At the moment she could think of few people whose company she would prefer to his in off-duty moments, and only wished he had stayed longer. So much for her planned visit to the servants' hall . . .

Her life at Foxhall quickly settled into an easy routine. Mrs Norland, initially irritated by the slowness of her recovery, eventually accepted that she would never attain her full strength again. On good days she was able to stroll in the grounds with Bethan or Polly. More often, it was a wheelchair trip, and occasionally she was not even capable of leaving her room. As her world shrank she began to turn to Bethan as confidante and friend rather than nurse. Within a few weeks she thought nothing of offering Bethan an evening aperitif when she ordered her own, and James invariably joined them when he was at home.

To Bethan's disappointment, that happened less frequently than she had hoped. He stayed late at the factory most evenings; frequently hosted business dinners in Oxford, after which he stayed at a city hotel; and disappeared from Friday until Monday for weekend house parties. Oh, well, she reflected, there was hardly any future in it, beyond it being a pleasure to look at him.

Once or twice when he was home for the evening Norland invited her for drinks in the library, although he never followed up his earlier suggestion that they might dine together. His contacts with her were courteous, friendly and mildly flirtatious, but he never made any physical approach. One evening, after three dry martinis had warmed her towards him even more than usual, she decided that this must be his response to any attractive woman, and that he had no special interest in her. Nevertheless she remained powerless to prevent her heart skipping with excitement when she saw him approaching or heard his voice.

As Bethan grew accustomed to Foxhall and its inhabitants she found out more of its past, and got an explanation of sorts for Moira Bateman's odd position in the household. Bethan had become a fast friend of Polly Anderson. At forty-five Polly was much older than she, but there was an effortlessly youthful quality in the woman which held enormous appeal for Bethan.

One afternoon, when Bethan had been working at Foxhall for three months or so, Mrs Norland declared she was fit enough to go visiting friends without either her nurse or lady's maid in tow. 'I'm only going on an eight or ten mile trip, and Patterson can always telephone if I feel unwell while we are calling on anyone,' she said irritably. 'I think it's time everyone stopped making so much fuss. I'm convalescing, not dying!'

After she had gone Polly and Bethan retired to the nursery flat together to drink tea and talk. Polly was standing in the little kitchen, chattering away as Bethan lit the gas stove, when she spotted the gin and whisky bottles. 'Naughty girl – getting tiddly up here all on your own, eh?' she said.

Bethan giggled. 'I'm not that far gone yet! You don't know about the company I keep . . . ' She told Polly about James Norland's visit, squashing any possible speculation about it having been the first of many by saying: 'You can tell how long he stayed by how much is gone from each bottle.' Both were still virtually full.

Nevertheless Polly was wide-eyed and impressed. There was also a certain smugness in her expression. 'I shan't tell a soul unless you don't care,' she said, 'but my God, it tickles me to hear about it! That must have really put Bateman's nose out of joint!'

'Bateman?' Bethan was puzzled. 'What on earth could Moira Bateman possibly have to do with James Norland coming up here for a drink?'

'Plenty, if she knew about it. I think she'd probably try to kill you, which is a pretty good reason for me shutting up about it – you're my friend.'

'This is silly. I know she resents me for having this flat, but she dislikes James Norland too, so she can hardly care if we share the odd bottle.'

Polly gave a gurgling laugh. 'Who on earth gave you the idea she didn't like Mr James? Like the song says, she's mad about the boy!'

Suddenly all sorts of previously unexplained relationships began to fall into place. Bethan stood, dumbstruck, for a minute or two, staring at Polly. Then she said: 'To hell with tea. Let's have some whisky and a good gossip!'

It was a story worthy of the most lurid woman's romantic paper. Moira Bateman had not been altogether honest when she said Jessica's departure for Roedean had ended her work as a governess. According to Polly, Jessica had gone to boarding school in order to release the governess for other work.

'Of course some of us wouldn't call it work, if you know what I mean,' said Polly. 'You mustn't think of her the way she is now. She's changed beyond recognition since the old boy went. It did for 'er, really. She used to be a real stunner, much as I hate to admit it.

'She must have been in her mid-twenties then. Mr James was about twenty and studying up at the university. Not Oxford, Birmingham. He wanted an engineering degree so he could do full justice to the business, and Oxford didn't admit such things existed in those days. Miss Jessica was thirteen, going on fourteen, with no mention of any plans for her going away to school.

'Then all of a sudden Bateman was looking all starry-eyed, and she and Mr Norland always seemed to be coming away from the same bit of the grounds, or out of the same room in the house – usually the one furthest away from where Madam was at the time. You can't hide that sort of thing from servants. There are eyes everywhere in a big house. I think Mr Norland realized that a bit sharpish, and decided to do something to make it easier for them. He only got away with it for so long because he was twice her age.

'That was when he decided he needed a social secretary at home. The way he put it, Mrs Norland could do with someone to set up the big dinner parties an' things. Said it needed a strategist, not a hostess, to do the table plans, and that was only for their friends . . . well, of course Madam said all right – didn't have the choice, did she? – and before we knew where we were, bossy-boots Bateman was a fully-fledged secretary in a black frock and white lace jabot, Miss Jessica was doing her sums and compositions all alone up here in the schoolroom, and there was an atmosphere you could cut with a knife.'

'What happened then?'

'None of us ever found out. One night there was a lot of screaming and shouting from the master suite, and the next thing we knew Moira Bateman was officially the social

159

secretary to Mr *and* Mrs Norland, and Miss Jessica was off to boarding school practically the next day. Caused quite a stir, I can tell you. After that there was no holding Moira Bateman. She acted as if she were the lady of the house and Mrs Norland was some sort of privileged visitor. She went to all the business parties she organized for Norland Motors at the house, and that meant Madam never attended, unless he forced her. Bateman never got to the private dinners, though . . . '

'How long did this go on?'

'Oh, right up until Mr Norland had his stroke – six, seven years, maybe. The stroke was bad, but not a killer – not straight away, anyhow. I'll give Bateman her due, she was red-hot with the work, getting things smoothed out between here and Oxford – all the time the old boy was ill. He was paralysed, but he could speak and his mind was all right so of course he insisted on running the business. It was unnecessary too, 'cos by now Mr James was working at the factory and doing wonders. Mr Norland could have handed over without a qualm, but that had to be over his dead body . . . and in the end it was, too.'

'When he died Mrs Norland must have taken her revenge. How did Moira survive?'

'That's what none of us really understood. We thought she'd be out the minute he breathed his last. I still don't know whether the old devil had put something in his will or what, forcing Madam to keep the cow under her roof, but stay she did. Never mind, though – she got her come-uppance!'

'You mean, when James Norland said he didn't want her as his personal assistant?'

Polly chuckled again. 'So that's what they're calling it these days! Let me tell you, that woman has no idea of her own limitations. By the time Mr Norland died, she must have been thirty-three or four. Mr James would be in his late twenties. She still looked pretty good, mind you, but she didn't look like a young girl. That didn't stop her. She set her cap at him too – more or less threw herself at his feet and said there was no reason why the son couldn't enjoy what the father had been having for so long. She was so blatant about it that Mrs Fanshaw overheard the whole thing. She was out in the hall and they were in the library.'

'What did he say?'

'Laughed in her face. He told her he could never understand what his father saw in her, and if it was left to him she'd have been out on her ear the minute the old boy had breathed his last. He said he hoped she understood the irony of it being his mother who was letting her stay on, and otherwise she'd be dropped like a hot brick. Mrs Fanshaw said she came out of that library looking like the walking dead. Her face was a funny yellowish colour and she was twitching around the mouth.'

'And yet she stayed.'

'She didn't have much choice. Had a sort of nervous break-down a couple of days later. Mrs Norland paid for the best medical treatment and put it about that it was the strain of doing too much in the business during Dear Jimmy's last illness. After that she kept her on almost as a pet charity. They used to lead a very active social life, but it's been so much quieter since Mr Norland died that Madam could have organized everything herself with no trouble.

'That's why she's Miss Jessica's social secretary too. It looks better, and it gives her at least something to do. Miss Jessica is a lot more sociable than Madam these days. The only real reason Bateman is still here is that I think Mrs Norland knew her husband better than he knew himself, and in a funny sort of way she felt sorry for Bateman.'

'Miss Bateman clearly doesn't think that. She appears to believe she's the only thing standing between the Norlands and destruction.'

'She'd have to, I suppose. There's nobody for her to boss about any more, is there, except us servants, and as she hasn't got any real authority over us we just don't take any notice.' Polly broke off and glanced darkly at the drinks bottles. 'You be careful with that Mr James. I know he's not married, but their sort are all the same and he'll follow in his father's foot-steps. If he tries anything on with you, just remember, married or single, they never have honourable intentions with the likes of us.'

'Don't you worry about me. I'm old enough to look after myself.'

'I daresay poor old Bateman thought that once, and look at her now. Four years ago she was monarch of all she surveyed,

161

and now she's just an embittered old bag penned up in a drab little room in somebody's country house, with no family or friends or nothing.' She reached over and squeezed Bethan's hand. 'Don't think I'm interfering, but you're too nice for the likes of him to spoil you, and that's all they do. They don't play for keeps, love.'

Bethan tossed her head and managed what she hoped was a light laugh. 'You're reading too much into a couple of drinks, Polly. I admit I like James Norland, but he doesn't know I'm alive, except as Mrs Norland's nurse.'

'I'm sure you're right. Just don't you forget what I've told you. I'd better be going now. Madam is convinced she'll be fit to dine downstairs tonight, and she wants her gold chiffon pressed. Thanks for the whisky. See you later.'

Margot Norland suffered her first heart attack as Polly was helping her into the gold chiffon dinner gown that evening. She had returned pale and tired from her afternoon calls, but when Bethan tried to persuade her into bed she was scornful.

'I told you earlier, I'm convalescing, not dying. If I continue taking things slowly, I shall never improve. No, tonight I dine downstairs and in a couple of days I think we shall have guests for dinner. Time I got back into the social swim before I'm too old.'

Polly had already run her bath, and Mrs Norland went off to relax in it for twenty minutes. When she returned, the maid noticed her slowness at getting into her underwear and made her sit down. When Bethan returned to make sure she felt fit to go downstairs Polly was helping her into the dinner gown. She raised her arms above her head and wriggled into the cloud of golden silk, then, before it had slipped down over her body, uttered a grunt and staggered back into her chair. She writhed there for seconds before the two women managed to remove the tangle of fabric. By then her lips were turning blue and her face had taken on a sallow tinge. She was shuddering from the pain and incapable of saying anything except that her left arm was hurting.

'Go and telephone the doctor, quick,' whispered Bethan. 'Tell him Mrs Norland is having a heart attack and I need him as soon as he can get here.'

She turned down the bed and then crouched beside Mrs Norland, supporting her until the initial attack subsided. The older woman vomited twice, and then the spasms seemed to die down.

'It's hard to say if she will recover.' The doctor was outside the bedroom with Bethan and James Norland, who had arrived home just as the doctor reached the house. 'It was a severe attack – result of a thrombosis by the look of it. She must be kept completely quiet, and as soon as she has a little more strength I think we should admit her to hospital. I don't like the look of this at all, so soon after major surgery. I think you'd better hire an agency nurse to relieve Miss Walters, Mr Norland. Your mother will need twenty-four hour attention until further notice.'

'How about Polly? She's Mrs Norland's maid and they've been together for years,' said Bethan. 'I'd prefer not to alarm the patient if we can avoid it.'

'Hmm, if she's sensible and will follow your instructions, yes. You're probably right, Miss Walters.' He wrote out a prescription which Patterson was to fetch from a late-opening pharmacy in Oxford, then left.

Margot Norland died at three o'clock in the morning. Both Polly and Bethan were in the room, Bethan sitting with her patient and Polly snatching a few minutes sleep in a chair at the fireside. She had preferred to stay up throughout this first night in case there was another crisis. There was nothing so dramatic. Mrs Norland merely gave a long shudder, sighed and stopped breathing.

Bethan swiftly checked pulse and then shook Polly awake. 'Go and get Mr Norland. She's gone.'

Rubbing her eyes and still half asleep, Polly went off to fetch James Norland from the former nurse's room across the landing, then called the doctor again. Bethan was a model of quiet efficiency for the next hour, then, when all the formalities were completed, excused herself and went off to her flat. She felt impossibly remote, as if she had just watched a woman die in the last act of a slightly boring stage play. Walking dully up the stairs to the nursery landing, she wondered vaguely if this was what shock felt like, and why she felt no real emotion at the passing of a woman whose constant companion she had been for almost four months. Somehow the answers scarcely mattered.

For four days she remained cocooned from reality, unable fully to grasp the changes which lay ahead of her. She had given up her career and left London for four months and a dead end. The nurses' home at St Thomas's had seemed bad enough when she had nothing with which to compare it. How much worse would it be after Foxhall, its grounds, the glorious countryside and her own flat? Mrs Norland had kept her promise about driving lessons, and Bethan had taken instructions from Patterson within a month of starting her new job. For more than eight weeks she had been free to use the small Norland saloon which was kept as a general estate runabout.

All that would stop now and, even with luck, she would find herself back on the wards at St Thomas's, a humble staff nurse with yet another round of newly qualified probationers pushing up behind her. At worst, St Thomas's might not take her, and she could end up in some poky East End district hospital with poor facilities and even poorer patients . . . All Bethan's resilience was used up. She was unable to contemplate an alternative to living at Foxhall and unwilling to try.

Mrs Norland had left instructions that she was to be buried in the local parish church next to her husband. The small medieval building was packed with family and business friends and with the household staff. Afterwards, a professional catering company served a buffet lunch back at Foxhall, then the mourners dispersed. Once they were gone, James Norland called together the staff in the hall to tell them of his plans.

'Most of you need have no worries about your jobs,' he told them. 'I shall continue to live at Foxhall, and my sister will continue to spend a lot of time here after her marriage. There will be some changes, but I am arranging that you will all receive personal letters to inform you of future arrangements.

'My mother left legacies to all members of staff who had served here for more than five years, and details of these, too, will be given to individuals in writing. It only remains to thank you all for your loyal and devoted service, and for the sympathy that you all offered in my sister's and my bereavement. I'll let you get back to your quarters now, but I should like to see Miss Bateman immediately, Polly Latham in fifteen minutes and Nurse Walters in half-an-hour. I shall be in the library.'

Bethan, still in a daze, drifted away to the housekeeper's room for a cup of tea while she awaited her session with James Norland. Presumably he wished to see her to give notice of dismissal. No one here needed a nurse now. Naturally she would not have been mentioned in Mrs Norland's will. Her employer had not expected to die and the document must have been drafted and signed before she ever met Bethan. No hope of a nest egg there . . .

Downstairs Polly and Mrs Fanshaw were opening their envelopes. Each was duly impressed by the size of the cheque she received. Polly had cried herself out immediately after her mistress died, and now was quite cheerful again – the more so now she had some money. 'Just as generous in death as in life, I'll give her that!' she told Bethan. 'She's left me enough to start up the teashop I've always fancied running. It's more than I ever hoped for . . .'

Mrs Fanshaw, who was much older than Polly, had been left an annuity to be taken up when she wished to retire, and £100. 'I think she was just as kind to everyone,' she said in awed tones. 'Mind you, we all knew Polly would do best because she was her personal maid, but still . . .'

Bethan tried to feel happy for them, but their security only deepened her own misery. Mrs Fanshaw and Polly exchanged looks and the housekeeper unobtrusively left the room. Polly said: 'I know you must be feeling terrible, Bethan, and how you must be dreading that hospital again. I – I've been wondering whether you'd consider something else . . .'

Bethan shrugged. 'What is there for me to consider? I'm only qualified for one thing.'

'I wouldn't say that. What would you say if I asked you . . . don't be offended, will you? If I asked you to come in with me. It would really need two to run a place like what I have in mind. You can certainly do all the things you'd need to run a teashop, you'd be a real asset to the business, and we do get on well. What d'you think?'

165

Bethan was so touched she almost cried. 'You'd do that for me? You are such a good friend . . . but I couldn't. I'd have to chip in hundreds of pounds, and I only have fifty in the bank. Even that's more than I've ever had before.'

'Silly, Mrs N. left me enough to cover it. We could work something out – maybe you take a smaller share of the profits. But it would be a proper legal partnership, nothing to make you feel insecure.'

'Oh, Polly, I really don't know how to thank you – or what to say. Look, I don't know how to say this, but I'd feel a bit as though I were sponging if I took you up on it.' She broke off and smiled shakily, then added: 'If you don't mind letting me think it over for a day or two, I'll be grateful for ever.'

'Of course. It'd be a big step. And if I was a qualified nurse, I'm not sure how keen I'd be, either. You just take your time. I shan't ask anyone else if you say no. I'd better go up and see Mr James. He'll be giving me my marching orders. No one wants a lady's maid when the lady has gone, do they?' She said it flippantly, but Bethan knew she was close to tears. Legacy or no legacy, it would be a big change for Polly.

Eventually it was Bethan's own turn to go and hear what James Norland had to say. As she crossed the hall Polly burst out through the library door, beaming with pleasure. 'Well, then, how about that?' she said. 'I'm still off to start up my business, but it *is* nice to know you don't have to go unless you want to!'

Bethan was puzzled. 'What did he say?'

'He said Madam knew about my teashop plan, and that was what the legacy was for, but if I didn't want to leave the family, Miss Jessica would be delighted to offer me the post of house-keeper at her place in Mayfair once she's married. How about that then?'

'Oh, well done! Nobody deserves it more. Why not consider it?'

Polly made a little face and said: 'Two reasons – I don't want to be a servant all my life, and I can't stand that Jessica. Apart from that, it would be perfect!'

'Oh, Pol, you are the limit! Go on down and tell Mrs Fanshaw your news. I wish I could look forward to some sort of offer.'

Polly gave her an odd look. 'You never can tell . . . ' she said, and moved off back to the servants' quarters.

Bethan was about to tap on the library door when she heard a small noise on the staircase above her. She glanced up to see Moira Bateman on her way down. Miss Bateman was carrying an overnight bag. She looked terrible. Now she saw Bethan in the hall and quickened her pace, arriving at her side almost at a run.

'Got you at his beck and call now, has he?' It was a sibilant whisper. 'Well, dear, don't think you'll be any different from me or any of the others. This family sucks you dry and throws you out in the end, and don't you ever forget it. You're all right as long as you're useful, but after that they scrap you like their damned cars.'

She turned away and before Bethan could think of anything to say, had marched out of the front door, leaving it wide open to the chilly autumn afternoon.

CHAPTER SIXTEEN

'This really has been a most unfortunate business for you, Bethan,' said James Norland, waving her to a chair as she entered the library.

Surprised out of her earlier apathy by the encounter with Moira Bateman, she said: 'I imagine it's been far more unfortunate for you, Mr Norland. After all, my mother hasn't just died.'

'No, quite . . . but you know what I mean. It was so kind of you to come down from London with her, and now for this to happen out of the blue . . . I know you were fond of my mother too, but it's perfectly understandable that you should be concerned about your personal future.'

'Well, yes, I am. It looks as if I shall have to reapply to St Thomas's and start all over again. I hope I shan't be in the way if I stay in the nursery flat until I fix something.'

He gestured dismissively. 'Good heavens, no – stay as long as you like! Actually I called you in now because that might not be necessary. There's a project coming up which might interest you . . .'

Hope flared inside her and immediately died. He was going to suggest a servant's job for her, either here or with his sister at her Mayfair house. Even going back to St Thomas's with her tail between her legs would be better than that . . .

'I'm setting up a medical centre at the motor plant. It will be quite a big operation – we employ a couple of thousand men on each of two sites and we're expanding all the time – and I've already engaged a doctor. What we need now is a first class nurse, and I was wondering, since you're free . . . '

She had to struggle to prevent herself from goggling at him. 'You really mean it? You're not just making up a job because you feel sorry for me being left high and dry?' Bateman's voice still rang in her ears.

He laughed. 'Hardly. My humanitarian instincts don't amount to handing out charitable jobs in my factory. It's a responsible post. You'd have a company car – need to, if you're to be properly mobile between the two plants – and your salary would match what you've been getting here.'

'It seems almost too good to be true. But at the risk of sounding ungrateful, I should have to enquire about the price of lodgings or a flat in Oxford. My flat here was an important part of my wage.'

'No need to worry about that. You have a choice: either you can keep the flat here, rent-free – after all, I commute from here to the city every day – or I'll raise your wages by enough for you to rent a place in Oxford. The decision is yours. One other thing: you will, no doubt, realize you were left out of Mama's will because she made it before you came to work for her. She would never have wanted to overlook someone who had helped her so much. Jessica and I have decided, therefore, that you should receive some token of our, and her gratitude.' He slipped a cheque across the table. She fought the impulse to look at it, and continued to stare at him.

'Well,' he said eventually, 'what d'you think? I imagined you'd feel a lot better after that.'

She longed to say, I would have thought so, too, but something is holding me back . . . Instead she smiled and replied: 'It's a very generous offer, Mr Norland. If I may, I'll think about it overnight and give you a decision in the morning.'

'Naturally you'll want a little time. But does it sound reasonable?'

'Yes, very. It isn't the offer . . . I've simply never considered myself in that sort of job. Now, if you'll excuse me?'

'Yes, of course.' He jumped to his feet and went over to open the door for her. As she passed him, he murmured: 'I do hope we can work together. I think we could be quite a team.'

Heart thumping, she hurried away up the stairs to her

quarters. When he gave her that look and smiled that irresistible smile of his, she began getting all sorts of ideas . . . maybe that was the reason she had been so reluctant down there. She had an unaccountable feeling that she was walking into a velvet-lined trap.

There was no real dilemma. Time and time again in later years, Bethan would line up the possibilities she might have considered. There was Polly Latham's offer of a partnership, even more attainable now because she had a cheque for a hundred pounds to add to her fifty pounds savings. It was true there was humiliation in the prospect of reapplying to St Thomas's, but she was ignoring the alternative of applying as a midwife. That would have been altogether different.

Instead she chose to continue working for the Norlands, this time directly for the man she had admired for months. And she quickly discarded the idea of finding a flat in Oxford, telling herself she loved her existing quarters too much to want anything else. It was not as though there was anything disreputable about living under the same roof as her employer – not in a house of this size anyway . . .

What finally swayed Bethan, as she lay awake the night after the funeral, thinking about the future, was that this was the only chance she would ever have to *be* somebody. She did not define for herself how that would come about. There was only one obvious way: after all she had been offered a job as a factory nurse, not a board director. That way had everything to do with the mutual attraction that existed between her and James Norland, and she intended to make full use of it. She was not going to play second fiddle to people like Venetia Eldon for the rest of her life, and James Norland had more money than the entire Eldon family would ever dream of.

Just as well her mother had disowned her when she moved to London. She would certainly have refused to countenance Bethan's proposed new way of life. Well, Mam had never done much for her anyway. No point in regretting what was past and gone. The Walterses, even her adored Lily, were all stuck in the mud of that rotten old-fashioned valley. Ahead of her, Bethan saw a golden opportunity to shake off the last ties of that world. She intended to take it.

* * *

It took her four months – months of flattery, flirtation and application to the art of coquetry. The job at the Norland car plant was quite genuine, and reasonably interesting, but it suffered the drawback of keeping her isolated from James. Just as well I decided to stay at Foxhall and not move to Oxford, she thought at the end of her first week. Otherwise I might only ever have seen him at works' Christmas parties . . .

At first she scarcely saw him more often anyway, for he continued to live the hectic, business-orientated life he had always preferred. The atmosphere at Foxhall was infinitely improved without Moira Bateman, who had, as Bethan had assumed, been dismissed on the day of Mrs Norland's funeral. Polly soon left too, disappointed that Bethan would not go with her but otherwise delighted to slough off her life of domestic service. It was some time before Bethan realized how much she had relied on the older woman for companionship at Foxhall, and during the first weeks when James Norland was hardly at home to focus her attention, she began to feel isolated and bored.

The watershed was Jessica Norland's wedding. It was postponed when Mrs Norland died, but Jessica had no love of country life and wanted to be gone from Foxhall as soon as possible. The wedding was fixed for New Year's Day 1925, with the reception at the house.

Bethan had been dreading Christmas. Every year since leaving South Wales she had worked on the wards and had enjoyed every minute. Now, for the first time, she faced the prospect of a solitary holiday without friends or family.

Polly Latham came to the rescue, writing in November to invite her to spend Christmas at Chipping Campden, where she had set up her little teashop. That left the problem of New Year's Eve and of the wedding day itself.

Bethan's main problem now was that she did not really belong anywhere. The servants were still friendly, because she had always got on well with them, but she was no longer part of the household as she had been in Mrs Norland's day. Nor was she the social equal of the people who would attend the wedding. It was inconceivable that a company nurse, who spent her days bandaging up workmen injured in production-line accidents, should expect to hob-nob with the rich at a

171

society wedding. For the first time Bethan envied the position Moira Bateman had occupied in the old days. As social secretary, she had been expected to go to such events, where business contacts inevitably mingled with the Norlands' social circle. No such privilege went with her own job. She resigned herself to an unpleasant couple of days in which her lowly status would, yet again, be emphasized.

At least she would not feel hard done by on New Year itself. The servants had agreed to forego their usual party to concentrate on the final preparations for the wedding reception. Even with the help of outside caterers, they faced a mammoth task, and for two or three days beforehand the entire kitchen area was a place of controlled bedlam. They were to be given their own party the week-end after the wedding, to make up for missing their New Year holiday. James Norland's generous gesture helped to ensure they would do their utmost to see that the wedding went well.

New Year's Day was different though. It fell on a Saturday, so Bethan did not even have the escape of a day at the factory. It promised to be a miserable week-end.

She was moping over a skimpy breakfast up in the flat early on January 1, when someone knocked on her door. When she opened it she found James Norland outside. 'Thought I'd better come and make a couple of plans for Cinderella to go to the ball,' he said, 'or rather, a ball, not necessarily the bean-feast downstairs.'

'I-I don't understand you.'

He slid past her into the sitting room, as casually as if he were always calling on her there. 'I'd be made of marble if I failed to understand your position, dear girl. You must feel wretched, being shut out of all the junketing. You wouldn't have been, either, but Jessica is even more of a snob than poor Mama was, and I knew better than to suggest she should invite one of my employees. Never mind, I think you've earned yourself something in the way of a Christmas bonus. I wondered if you would care to dine with me tonight at a rather lovely little inn I happen to know. Please say you will – I shall need a breath of fresh air after all the old crocks I have to butter up today.'

'I didn't think it was possible to butter up an old crock . . .'

'Stop changing the subject, you stubborn girl. Will you have dinner with me tonight?'

'Oh, yes, please! It's very kind of you to think of me when you're so busy, Mr Norland.'

'If we're dining *à deux*, don't you think you should call me James – at least, away from the factory?'

'All right . . . James . . . I'll be ready by seven-thirty, if that suits you.'

'I can't wait. Now if I were you, I'd get into my little car and roar off somewhere to buy a pretty frock. That will take you away from all the junketing, won't it? See you at seven-thirty.'

After that night her fate was sealed. The whole thing unfolded with the inevitability of a medieval morality play. The inn was awash with Tudor half-timbering, made even more romantic by the addition of traditional decorations as imagined by the landlord – mistletoe and holly boughs, real pomanders, made from dried oranges stuck with cloves, gilded pine cones and sprays of fir wreathed around bowls of Christmas roses. They drank champagne and Bethan tasted caviare for the first time in her life.

'Now I *know* your intentions are dishonourable!' she told Norland, laughing, as she spooned the pearls of fish roe out of their icebound glass bowl.

'They always have been. I simply couldn't work out an approach until now that wouldn't have sent you rushing back to London on the first train, never to return.'

'I'm not sure I like that. It sounds . . . well, calculated somehow.'

He laughed, but it was an easy, friendly sound, meant to include her and not directed at her. 'Of course it was calculated, you little idiot. You should be flattered. Some women I know have been following me about for years, trying to make me calculate their surrender.'

Bethan wanted to pinch herself. After months of idle daydreams, the discovery that he had been thinking along the same lines was almost unbelievable . . . in fact it *was* unbelievable, her efficient nurse's voice told her. But she wanted to be convinced, and so she was. The dinner progressed from course to delectable course. The logs in the great inglenook fireplace crackled and blazed and eventually settled to a soft, dying glow.

By now they were sitting near the fire on a big squashy sofa, drinking large brandies. They were alone in the dining room. Norland's arm was draped casually about Bethan's shoulders and she felt intoxicated with food, wine and the triumph of an ambition achieved. When he suggested gently that they move upstairs it hardly caused a ripple in her warm contentment.

She questioned him drowsily and he said: 'I don't think we should drive home along those icy lanes after all that brandy, so I . . . arranged matters. Come and see.'

Bethan was not quite a virgin. There had been a short, embarrassing, blundering liaison with a young post-graduate medical student who had been as lonely as she during her first year in London. All she remembered were his bony wrists and the coldness of his Pimlico flat. All memory of his caresses had gone within months of the end of the brief affair. Nothing in the relationship had frightened her, but neither had it tempted her to repeat the experience with more sophisticated admirers. Generally speaking, they had been content with her high-spirited company and the occasional kiss, and Bethan had experienced no hunger to encourage them further.

Now she waited for her respectable upbringing to surge forward, outraged, and put James Norland in his place. This was bare-faced seduction, it would tell her. This is precisely what your chapel and your mother warned you would happen if you went off after dark with handsome, wicked young men and drank alcohol . . . But nothing of the sort happened. She merely continued to sit, smiling through the cloud of brandy fumes in her head, and experiencing only satisfaction that this biggest, most elusive of fish was finally within reach of her tickling fingers. She was not quite sure she knew what she was going to do that night, but she certainly knew what she wanted.

Presumably she got some of it right, at least. They stayed at the ridiculously romantic Thames-side inn until early on Sunday evening. A week later they went there again, and after that it was a regular rendezvous. If Bethan had found her position awkward before, now it became all but impossible. Not that anyone at the car plant suspected what was going on. Bethan continued to run the medical centre at the main factory, to deal with minor accidents and refer major ones to the local hospital.

She drove back and forth between the centre and the other plant, to make sure the emergency medical supplies were kept up to date and to do the rounds of the volunteer first-aid men in every department. None of this entailed any contact with James Norland, and had she herself not been conscious of a change in her status, all would have been normal.

At Foxhall it was different. Although James Norland continued to appear only erratically at the mansion, when he did he spent a great deal of time in the nursery flat. It amused him to preserve an air of mystery and he never made love to Bethan there, nor did he come there late at night. But the servants noticed almost immediately that he never came home without calling there to see her.

They could hardly have failed to notice the other change. Now that Jessica was living in London, James invited Bethan to join him for dinner at least twice a week when he was home. Abruptly the attitude of the domestic staff changed. Where before she had known only friendliness, now she encountered reserve and coldness. Nowadays they watched her like wary civilians eyeing a member of a foreign army of occupation.

It made Bethan unsettled and miserable. She tried to ignore it because she should have been happy, but it became oppressive. Finally she raised the matter with James on one of their visits to their inn.

'I think I must move into Oxford,' she told him. 'Everyone at Foxhall knows what's going on, and it's getting to be a bit of a bore. If you don't mind stumping up the extra salary to make up the rent, I'll start looking next week.'

He was unsurprised. 'I was wondering how long it would take them,' he said. 'Only a matter of time, really. One needs a hide like Moira Batemans's to stand that sort of pressure. Sheer jealousy, you know, but there's no way of fighting it.'

'Well, will you help?'

He smiled at her like a father offering a wonderful present to his favourite child. 'I shall do better than that, my sweet. I've been doing a lot of thinking lately. I'm over thirty, and I've spent all my adult life slaving away making cars. That's all very well for a man who needs the money, but I'd be the first to admit that wasn't true. It's time I had some fun.'

He's going to propose, she thought, exulting. I've won, I've won!

But marriage was a long way from James Norland's mind. 'I think a nice cosy establishment in London is what we want,' he told her. 'Somewhere with room for you to breathe . . . somewhere I could spend as much time as I liked, and just pop down to Oxford once a week or so. We could really have fun. I know so many people I only see once in a blue moon – exciting people, people who do entertaining things – and it would be marvellous if we got to know them together, don't you think?'

'B-but my job . . . ' Say anything to cover your confusion, she told herself, and for God's sake get those wedding bells out of your mind . . .

'Oh, pooh to the job! I'll give you a monthly allowance a lot better than your salary. And of course you'll still have a car, one of our new models, I think. Oh, do say yes, Bethan! It would get round all that holier-than-thou nonsense with the servants at Foxhall, and we'd have a whale of a time . . .'

Faintly she heard herself agreeing, almost as if another person were saying yes. And all the time, behind the acceptance, something half-smothered was clamouring, this isn't what I was trained to do . . . where am I going? What happens when he tires of me . . . ? But nothing in her young life had prepared her to answer such questions, so she smiled confidently and prepared to abandon, perhaps for ever, the last vestiges of the career for which she had worked so hard.

176

CHAPTER SEVENTEEN

Abercarn 1925

Why does a sunny day make grief so much harder to bear, thought Lily, hurrying down Abercarn High Street towards the top of the Ranks. Her youngest brother Lewis had arrived, breathless, at her house in Newbridge half an hour ago to tell her she must come. Emrys was dying.

Oh, Emrys, love, not you – it's too soon, there's too much living still for you to do . . . She bit back the lament, her teeth snapping together as if she was cutting off spoken words, not thoughts. She had known it was inevitable for weeks now. Why did it remain so hard to take?

Because he's your favourite . . . because you remember him dancing better than anyone you've ever known . . . because he was good-looking and brave and funny . . . and oh, dear God, because he was only just coming up to thirty!

Margaret Ann was in the kitchen. 'Oh, love, thank goodness you'm here. I been up all night with him . . . thought he was going a couple of times. He rallied a while back, though. Don' know where he's getting the strength from.'

Lily put a comforting arm around her mother's shoulders. 'You should have sent for me last night. I'd have come straight away. You shouldn't be up with him all on your own.'

Margaret Ann stifled a sob. 'It's a privilege, kidda. I've never seen nobody so brave. He must feel as if he's drowning . . . ' she began to cry in earnest now.

'Hush, hush . . . ' Lily patted and rocked her mother like a suffering child. There were no words of comfort she could give

177

because they both knew Emrys was beyond saving. 'Have the doctor seen him?' she asked eventually.

'Oh, aye . . . you know I was never a great one for your Henderson, but he's a marvellous doctor, I'll give him that. He was up here like a shot, ten o'clock last night, when the first bad attack come on. Cann would have made us wait till this morning. Couldn't do nothing much, though. Nothing anybody can do now except pray for him.'

'Who's with him now?'

'Kitty. She's carrying on terrible, an' all. I don't think she's helping.'

'You mean she's up there whining in front of our Emrys while he's dying? I'll bloody kill 'er . . . ' Lily was half way to the staircase before Margaret Ann caught her sleeve. 'Steady now, Lily. You know you never liked her. The girl can't help it. She do love our Em too.'

'And I'm the Pope of Rome! Emrys was going to be her ticket out of that pub, and don't you ever forget it.'

'Not pub, Lily, hotel. You know she've always been particular about that.'

'Mam, she's a barmaid in a seafront pub in Aberystwyth. If you believe the airs and graces she do put on, you'm a lot dafter than I ever thought. Now out of the way – I'm going up to him.'

Lily had never been entirely rational about Kitty Jacobs' engagement to Emrys. She tried not to look too closely at her own motives because they did not stand up to scrutiny. Kitty was the child of a dirt-poor family of smallholders from the agricultural area of eastern Monmouthshire where labouring families still lived in conditions that made miners look privileged. She had grown up scrawny, barefoot, dirty and hungry, pre-destined to work as a scullery maid or something equally lowly. Lily would have considered none of this relevant, had it mattered less to Kitty herself. Kitty had escaped her background when she turned into a remarkably pretty young girl at about fourteen. By then her mother was dead and she had been lodging for some time with her older sister, a collier's wife living in Abercarn.

The sister decided Kitty might have a better chance of advancement outside the county where they had all suffered poverty and distress, and had sent her off to a distant kins-woman in central Wales, where there were more grand houses, more gentry families and therefore better opportunities of self-improvement in domestic service.

Kitty had learned the rudiments of domesticity in one of several mansions within travelling distance of Aberystwyth, but every time she went to the seaside town on her afternoon off, she felt freedom calling more insistently. Cardiganshire had a strong temperance tradition and it was difficult for local pub landlords to recruit presentable barmaids because their mothers saw pubs as the abode of the Devil. When Kitty pointed out to the landlord of a big seafront establishment that she was trained by ladies in a big house, and now offered all the social skills associated with such a job, he gave her employ-ment at higher wages than she had ever seen, with more free time and a pleasant bedroom of her own thrown in.

Since then she had never looked back, but she was a bright girl and she knew her living in the licensed trade was a pre-carious one. When she took holidays she always visited her sister Maud in Abercarn, and took care to give everyone there the impression she had a refined job as a receptionist in a top-flight hotel. It was no more reputable to be a barmaid in the South Wales Valleys than it was in Cardiganshire. She was twenty-three years old and tired of the never-ending stream of beery faces which confronted her at work every evening, when, on holiday at Maud's, she met Emrys Walters at the Saturday night dance in Newbridge. He was with his sister, a tall big-boned girl whom Kitty disliked on sight. The moment she set eyes on Emrys Kitty decided this was to be her husband.

She had flirted, flattered and eventually won him. They had been engaged for more than six months when he suffered the first of a series of attacks of emphysema which were to kill him eventually. She was unable to grasp the gravity of his illness, telling herself all miners got a little bronchitis now and then and it would soon be gone. Kitty Jacobs had been too long a friendless orphan lightly to contemplate the loss of her future emotional security so soon after she had found it.

But there was no question now of his survival. Kitty sat at the bedside, choking back tears of fear and disappointment and periodically begging Emrys to rally. As Lily entered the room, the younger woman was wailing: 'Just breathe deeper, that's all, and you'll be all right . . . you got to be all right – what will I do if you'm gone?'

'You'll bloody find out in a minute,' Lily gritted out at her. 'If you can't do better than that, get on downstairs and have a cuppa tea with our Mam. I'll sit with Emrys a minute.'

Kitty looked as though she might stand and fight, but Lily's unwavering, silver-grey gaze daunted her and she departed, sniffling self-pity at herself as her high heels clomped down the oilcloth-covered stairs.

'And how's Fred Astaire this morning?' Lily reached out and stroked back the lock of hair which had fallen across his eyes in his last bout of wheezing.

'Lily, is it?' He managed a ghastly parody of a smile, his face bluish, his lips almost purple. 'Don't be too hard on Kitty, love. You know she's all on her own.'

'So are we all, flower. Why should she be any different? Anyhow, it's not her I come about. Mam said you might need a bit of help up here.'

This time the smile was genuine. 'I never thought the Walters women would understand the power of understatement,' he said. 'Aye, Lil. I need someone to help me die. Don't think God will, somehow.'

Lily smiled back at him, forcing herself to speak steadily. 'He never did have a lot to do with the Walterses, did He, in spite of our Mam? Must be somebody else can give a hand.'

His grip tightened on her wrist. 'Christ, Lily, I do love you – you'm the most honest person I ever met.' The effort and intensity of the little speech exhausted him momentarily and he slumped back on the pillow.

Lily sighed. 'Thank you. I always think, just because something is hard, that ent no excuse for not doing it. And we both know this is hard, don't we?'

Emrys nodded, eyes still closed. Then he managed to find more energy from somewhere and said. 'I always thought, if there was just somewhere people could sing hymns, you know, just to enjoy them, no more – no religious nonsense, that might feel a bit like heaven. All that letting yourself go . . . all that lovely noise. Some writer said "and bands of angels speed thee

180

to thy rest" . . . You can work miracles sometimes, Lil. Met any bands of angels lately, could sing me to *my* rest?'

'I know one. Best singer either of us will ever know. And he come off nights an hour ago. He's down in the kitchen now.'

Emrys's eyes had recaptured some of their old sparkle. 'Elwyn . . . d'you think he would? I mean, it's a bit like Victorian melodrama, ennit?'

But Lily was already at the top of the stairs, calling down to the kitchen: 'Elwyn, come up yer a minute, will you? Something Emrys do want.'

Elwyn, who worked in the tinplate processing plant in Abercarn, used every spare moment to practise singing. He had a rich baritone voice and he dreamed about finding fame with it one day. Now he came hesitantly into the bedroom, suddenly shy as he confronted death stalking his elder brother.

'Will you sing for me, kidda?' croaked out Emrys, his few minutes of clear speech with Lily having taxed his voice beyond endurance.

'As long as you want, mun. What d'you fancy?'

'Anything you like, except – except . . . How about that Darkie song you do? I do love that . . . ' His whisper was cut off by a choking cough.

Elwyn smiled. 'Right you are. Start with that, then.' And in the corner of the cramped bedroom, chilly even in the early sunlight, Elwyn, still marked by the dirt of his night's work, let loose his glorious voice to ease his brother's end. Emrys lay, eyes closed, apparently relaxed now, as the honey-smooth words calmed him, in spite of their lugubrious message:

> 'I gets weary,
> And sick o' trying,
> I'm tired of living,
> And scared o' dying,
> But Old Man River,
> He just keeps rolling along.'

Elwyn needed no encouragement to embark on the rest of his repertory, largely the old Welsh non-conformist hymns which had always been a sort of pagan chant for South Wales men, little to do with the chapels and more closely connected with rugby fields and saloon bars. Throughout the morning he went on, showing no sign of weariness, as Lily sat holding Emrys's limp hand with fierce intensity and their brother slipped closer to death.

It was the apotheosis of all these anthems, 'Bread of Heaven', which eventually formed his farewell. Elwyn had just finished the first verse and started the second, when Emrys's eyes snapped open and he managed to say: 'Choking, Lil, I'm choking!' He plucked at her hand as though it were his lifeline. She knelt on the floor beside him, face against the convulsively grasping fingers, pressing every atom of her own warmth and vibrant life out to him. And still Elwyn sang on, the last verse, his talent and the love he and Lily shared for Emrys the only comfort they could give to a man dying without hope of heaven.

> 'When I tread the verge of Jordan,
> Bid my anxious fears subside;
> Death of death, and Hell's destruction,
> Land me safe on Canaan's side:
> Songs and praises, songs and praises
> I will ever give to thee,
> I will ever give to thee.'

A huge, eternal silence descended on the bedroom at the end of the last verse. Moments later it was punctuated by the last saturated breath to rattle from Emrys's swamped lungs, and it was all over. Elwyn crossed the narrow room and bent to ease Lily upright. 'Come on, love. You can't do nothing else for him now.' He moved her gently aside and reached down to close Emrys's eyelids, still open from the last convulsion which had left him gazing unseeingly at the far wall.

Abruptly Lily recovered herself. 'I can do something for Mam, though. Get down them stairs and in to Edith Smith. She and I will lay him out before Mam do come and look at him.'

'Don't be bloody daft – you ent fit to do it. Arf dead with grief yourself. Edith will be glad to do it herself, after.'

'I know that, but I don't want Mam seeing him like this.

Look, his eyelids is going back already. And the smell! *Iesu, mawr*, she'll think she's in a slaughterhouse. Go on, now, tell Edith. And tell Mam I'm sitting up with him for half an hour, and watch Kitty don't come back up yer. I don't want her nowhere near me.'

Edith Smith was with Lily in minutes, and between them they cleaned, straightened and redressed Emrys's body, setting the features into something less distressing than the death-grimace it had assumed such a short time ago. They worked with the window wide open to disperse the thick stench of sickness and death. On her way in, Edith had sent Lewis down the road to the greengrocer to buy up his whole stock of narcissi. 'They got the strongest scent, I think, Lil. Keep everything else down, see,' she explained, dispersing the flowers in vases around the room.

Lily nodded, temporarily taking refuge from grief in the work she was doing. This was her real farewell to Emrys. Only this would convince her he had gone for ever and enable her to accept his departure.

Charles Henderson arrived when they were completing the ritual. He examined the body cursorily. He had seen enough the previous night to be satisfied of the cause of death. He signed a death certificate which he gave to Edith for safe-keeping, then turned his attention to Lily. 'How are you managing?'

She made a small, helpless gesture. 'Bad. I keep telling myself it's blind chance, but I do feel like killing somebody just the same.'

'I know. We all feel like that when it's someone close, and there's nothing to be done but work it out . . . this helps, I take it?' He indicated the bowl of water and the bundle of discarded nightclothes, evidence of her laying-out activity.

'Of course it does. If I wasn't doing this, I'd be outside screaming. How are they downstairs?'

'Your mother is like a little piece of granite. I've never liked her, but my God, she's learned self-control since the first time I ever helped this family through a crisis.'

'Aye. Surprising how much it calms you down to see your husband brought home in pieces in a box . . . Oh, Charlie, I'll miss him so much!' She collapsed sobbing against his shoulder and Edith Smith tiptoed from the room to give Lily a chance to exorcize the pain through tears.

Downstairs, face as calm as a Sphinx, Margaret Ann dispensed tea from the best Delft teapot into bone china cups. Only the twitching muscle in her jaw indicated the iron control required to do so.

Kitty Jacobs had been well on her way to hysterics when Elwyn came into the room, but by the time Edith rejoined them the girl was behaving quite differently. Her face was partly concealed by a scrap of white handkerchief, but to Edith's experienced eye the small sniffles and sobs which occasionally escaped sounded more like proficient acting than misery. Kitty's performance certainly seemed to have charmed Elwyn.

'What am I going to do without him? He was my whole world. I got nobody now – nobody . . . ' Kitty said, pathos dripping from every word.

Elwyn wrapped a big, comforting arm around her diminutive shoulders and said: 'Hush, now. We won't let you down. I'll look after you for our Emrys, how about that?'

The big dark eyes which appeared abruptly over the lace handkerchief held no trace of tears. Their sparkle came from quite another source. 'Really, Elwyn? Will you really help me get over it?'

Margaret Ann, lost in her own tragedy, seemed oblivious to what was going on. But someone else was immediately aware of it. Lily stood in the doorway, watching Kitty with a mixture of rage and contempt. 'Oh, you bloody bet ten pound he will, you callous bitch!' she said, then turned and stalked out into the back street.

Ease off, for God's sake, she told herself, as she walked along the canal bank, slapping the clenched fist of one hand into the palm of the other. She's a conniving little girl from no-where, but both your brothers have been grown men this long time. Em died believing she was in love with him. Now Elwyn's going the same way, but if he wants to it's none of your business. You never let anybody stop you making your own mistakes . . .

That brought Lily uncomfortably close to what was really

184

wrong with her now. Grief for Emrys was tearing her to pieces. Hatred of Kitty was intensifying her suffering. But she had a good husband who adored her and a son who was the light of her life. Why, then, was she so bereft at the death of a brother? There had never been anything unnatural about their affection for each other. She should be sad, now, certainly, but not heartbroken.

Except that you haven't got anyone else to love that much, have you? whispered a mocking interior voice. That's why you loathe Kitty, isn't it? That's why you can't bear to let go of Emrys. Who will you put in his place? How will you pretend David is your whole world now that Emrys isn't going to be there any longer as a dancing partner and best friend?

The canal was all but derelict nowadays, and the stagnant water lay sullen even beneath today's sunny sky. She shivered, remembering another time she had gone to brood beside the water after losing someone close to her. Lily glanced up instinctively. On that occasion, Charles Henderson had appeared out of nowhere to offer her his friendship, his support and the promise of his love. He had saved her from herself that day by a little gentle bullying and a great deal of understanding. But today there was no sign of Henderson. The only other people along the canal bank were two scruffy children kicking a tin under the old stone bridge.

Stop thinking someone will save you, she told herself. It's time you faced this one yourself and started being fair to David . . . Wearily Lily turned for home. Mam would understand if she didn't come back until tomorrow. She had done all she could for Emrys. Now it was time to go and start being a proper wife to her husband.

David Richards was sitting in his armchair with Tommy on his knee when Lily got back. Her face told him all he needed to know about the events of the morning. 'Gone, is he?' he said.

She nodded mutely, and looked round the room. Everything was impossibly normal after what she had just been through. Speech seemed to present an insurmountable obstacle, and she realized she had said nothing aloud since rushing away from the Ranks in a rage at Kitty. She fought for some sense of normality. 'Didn't Mrs Andrews give you any dinner, then?' Mrs Andrews, their next-door neighbour, had stayed with Tommy while Lily was away.

'I told her to leave it till you come back. Thought you'd probably need something, whether you felt like it or not. It's all ready. She've left it in the pan ready to dish up. The potatoes is in it and the plates are in the oven warming.'

'Stew. Iss stew, Mammy. Mrs Andrews gimme some . . . ' Tommy was blissfully normal. At two, he was chattering like a magpie about everything that caught his attention. Everyone loved him and he loved them. Now he raised his arms for his mother's embrace and she wrapped him gratefully in her arms. At least this was perfect . . .

Lily went to the kitchen range and swung the big iron stew kettle off the banked-down fire. A good rich mutton broth bubbled inside, crammed with diced root vegetables and smelling heavenly. She took the plates out of the little oven and began dishing up the food. Her stomach rumbled and she remembered she had not eaten since yesterday afternoon. Thank heaven for small mercies! At least she felt hungry and thirsty. Perhaps her other senses would return to normal in the end too. She might even find she had a heart . . .

David watched her, unable to predict her reactions, as always, wondering how long he had before she tired of him. He was not an introspective man, but he had known from the out-set that his wife did not love him as intensely as he loved her. At first he had hoped that would change with time. In a way, it had. When Tommy was born he seemed to draw them together, somehow, and for most of the time at least David thought he was the luckiest man alive. It was only at times of extreme stress, like now, that he dimly saw the strains in their relationship. And when he did, he was always terrified that Lily would disappear from his life.

Now the fear crowded him so horribly that he said aloud, without realizing it, 'You wouldn't, would you?'

Lily looked up from the table. 'Wouldn't what, love?'

He felt able to go on now he had blurted the first words. 'Leave me. Y-you wouldn't ever leave me . . . would you?'

She hoped her laugh did not sound forced. 'What a silly thing to say! Why ever would I leave you, and where would I go?' The minute that last part was out she wished she had not

186

spoken. That almost made it sound as if she stayed only because there was no escape. 'This is my home,' she blundered on. 'You and Tom are my family. I – I love you both better than anything else.'

'Anything – and anyone?'

There, it was out. She looked him in the eyes now for the first time since he started speaking, and said: 'And anyone, David. I married you to love and to cherish, didn't I? Well, I meant it then and I mean it now.' Even to her own doubting ears, it sounded confident and committed. What was that she had said to her dying brother about always telling the truth?

David's face was suffused with relief. 'Oh, Lil, I do love you so much!' Again, it was an echo of the deathbed conversation with Emrys. It was one of the hardest things Lily ever did to keep the smile on her face while she turned back to the fireplace and made a pot of tea. If David saw her expression now he would never believe anything she said again, and she *did* love him – in her fashion.

Lily found the summer of 1925 very hard to endure. The spring ended almost before it had begun, with Emrys's death wiping all sense of time from her mind. But when she emerged from the first shock, more tribulation awaited her. Kitty Jacobs had already taken a firm hold on her brother Elwyn.

'Mam, I'm gonna kill that girl, I swear, if I do come down here again at tea-time and find her hanging on our Elwyn's every word. It's not as if he was the greatest talker since Lloyd George, is it? When the devil is she going back to Aberystwyth?'

Margaret Ann sighed. 'I don' like it, neither, love. Shifty little piece, she is. But somehow I haven't got the heart to do nothing about it. Elwyn was so cut up about Em, and she *do* seem to comfort him.'

'Oh, aye, for five minutes. Just as long as it takes to get another engagement ring on her finger and set herself up for the future after the first false start. I wouldn't mind if I really thought she loved Elwyn . . .'

'I'm your mam, Lily, remember?' Margaret Ann said softly.

187

Lily glanced up at her sharply. 'I don't know what you'm getting at.'

'I think you do. And I *know* you do mind. There's no need to pretend to me.'

Lily shook her head angrily, as if trying to clear it of the buzzing of insects. 'Oh, I dunno what have got into me. I never used to be like this. Talk about sour grapes . . . ' She fought to prevent herself from crying.

Margaret Ann came and sat beside her at the kitchen table. 'I know it ent easy for you to talk to me, but p'raps I'll understand more than you think.'

'I wouldn't know where to start.' It was almost a sob.

Margaret Ann touched her hand. 'Let me try, then. You'm disappointed in David, and Tommy ent enough to keep your mind off it. So you'm grieving too much for Emrys and getting het up about Kitty going off with his brother. Do that say it all?'

Lily was aghast. 'I didn't know it showed!'

'Only to me, *cariad*, so stop worrying. I felt the same once, only sort of the other way round. I wasn't disappointed in what Evan *was* – he was everything I wanted and more – but oh, *Duw*, I was disappointed in what he *did*! It nearly finished everything for me. No matter how hard I tried, you children never made up for it. And mind you, I had a houseful where you only got the one. If that sort of thing is wrong with your marriage it do sour you for everybody.'

She managed a rueful smile. 'I know you kids think I'm a terrible old fusspot, interfering with your lives, but I wouldn't dream o' carrying on the way you are over Elwyn. He's twenty-seven, Lil, and it's time he was married. Neither of us two is going to like whoever he do choose – he've been around us too long. So let him make his own mistake, all right? I think p'raps if I'd let you make *your* own over your Dr Henderson, instead of pushing David at you, things may have been different for you.'

Lily had momentarily forgotten her grief and anger. She was staring at her mother in astonishment. Eventually she said: 'I never thought I'd live to see the day when you'd talk like that.'

'Nobody knows everything, and don't you forget it.' Margaret Ann's face was beginning to resume its normal prissy expression. 'I do know I'm wrong now an' again, and far be it from me to deny it. But don't you tell none of the others, mind.'

That made Lily laugh for the first time since the long days before Emrys's death.

Margaret Ann's sudden understanding and compassion brought mother and daughter closer than they had ever been, but it would have taken more than that to heal Lily's hurt quickly. As the weeks wore on she grew increasingly conscious of David watching her nervously, as if afraid she would vanish. Then, three months and a couple of days after Emrys's death, Kitty and Elwyn walked into her mother's house one Saturday afternoon to announce they were engaged.

Lily, with Tommy on her lap, was sitting in the kitchen talking to Margaret Ann when the pair arrived. Kitty was carrying a huge bunch of flowers. Unable to contain herself, Lily snapped: 'Going up the cemetery at last, are you?'

Kitty merely coloured prettily and said: 'Oh, no – I hate them places – no, this was a little celebration present from Elwyn.'

The alarm bells were ringing in Lily's head and she felt a surge of rage. Before she could start a quarrel, Margaret Ann stood up and moved between the two women. 'Ooh, they'm lovely,' she said. 'What are you celebrating, though?'

Kitty flapped her left hand. 'Three guesses! Isn't it lovely?' A small emerald cluster sparkled on her third finger. 'We just been down Crouch's in Newport to choose the ring. Antique, of course. It seemed romantic to have a lovely old ring.'

'And cheaper, an' all,' Lily could not resist saying. 'Get more to impress people with for the same money second-hand, eh Kitty?' She would have welcomed a fight now, to burn off all her misery, but Kitty merely smiled, catlike, and said nothing, turning back to Elwyn with an overwhelmed-little-woman expression on her face.

Margaret Ann said: 'Lily was just saying she've got to be getting back to get David's tea, wasn't you, Lil? Don't make yourself late, now.' Her back to the engaged couple, she fixed Lily with a look that brooked no refusal.

Lily picked up Tommy, muttered a surly farewell and fled. Outside she forced a smile on to her lips and said: 'Come on, then, Tom, I'll give you a piggy-back.' She hiked him up on her back and went striding off along the Newbridge road, throwing herself forward in an attempt to exorcize her ill-feeling.

Eventually it passed, but it took a long time. She realized the first flood of pain had ended one October afternoon as she squatted in the grass at Abercarn cemetery and arranged flowers in a little glass pot on Emrys's grave. She was no haunter of graveyards, but today was his birthday, and spending a little while this close to his last physical remains gave her a grain of comfort, at least. Abruptly she knew that now she could go on with her life. Since Easter week, every movement had seemed to drag her down. Every decision required too much effort. Her mother, normally so acid-tongued, had treated her with special gentleness since their talk, but somehow even that had not seemed to matter . . .

But when the sluggish air of late summer changed and the mornings took on a crisp bite of autumn, everything started to improve. Cautiously at first, then with growing eagerness, Lily began taking an interest in the world again. It was all there, unaltered. No mountains had fallen because Em had gone and she was bereft. In a way that alone was some comfort. She still loved David, just as she had before. The fact that he was not her life's passion did not turn him into a monster. And Tommy . . . perhaps in the end Tommy would make up for all that unspent passion. She could not imagine ever bearing a child she would love more – and half of him was David, after all.

The alteration in Lily's outlook did not spring solely from acceptance of the realities of her own life. Other issues were crowding in, and soon they were likely to affect her every bit as much as the love of a son or respect for a husband. Since 1921 the mining community had won a reprieve from the privation imposed by that defeat. Coal was highly profitable again and the colliers' wages reflected the fact. But it was a false dawn. The shortage had arisen from the idleness of the vast German coalfield in the Ruhr valley, paralysed by Allied occupation after the war. Once that started returning to normal things changed. By the summer of 1925 the picture was black, and after a couple of years' prosperity, the miners were back to staring povery in the face.

Since her marriage Lily had become an avid newspaper reader, and followed the fortunes of Britain in the *Daily Herald* and the *British Worker*. Neither presented anything approaching a capitalist point of view, and her innate distrust for bosses had grown along with her grasp of current affairs. When Emrys lapsed into his final illness she had dropped her participation in local politics, but at last she could feel the enthusiasm developing again. The way to stop tragedy descending on the Emryses of the future was to change the world, and she wanted a hand in turning over the old ways.

She stood up, brushed a few grass stalks from her skirt, and caressed the headstone on Emrys's grave, much as she had once pushed back the cow-lick of hair from his forehead. 'So long, kidda,' she said. 'See you Christmas.' As she left the hillside cemetery, she felt lighter and more free than she could remember. There was plenty to do, and she was looking forward to doing it. Perhaps this autumn would turn into a sort of spring for her.

CHAPTER EIGHTEEN

London

Lexie Walters glanced around the room with disfavour. One day she would accept that every night was the same in dumps like this. Why look here for Prince Charming, or Daddy Warbucks, or whoever? They'd never find their way into the Love Apple. It was one of Ma Meyrick's less chic clubs, and Lexie wondered now why she had gone there this evening. No prizes for guessing the answer to that one, silly cow, she thought. Never know when a film producer might pop up here, do you?

A few years ago – although sometimes it seemed like centuries – when she had just arrived from Cardiff with the agent-lover who was supposed to be shaping her future as a movie star, Lexie had come to the Love Apple and met a few of the right people. Be nice to them, darling, Gerry had said. That's the only way you'll get on . . . So she'd been nice, particularly to the big sweaty one who smoked the foulest cigars she'd ever smelled.

And it had got her a part in a film. She had appeared for all of thirty seconds as a cavorting member of a gypsy dancing troupe in an opus called *Flamenco Princess*. It had played briefly at the few suburban cinemas with nothing better to show before the next American smash hit arrived. After that, the sweaty producer had still been interested, but his suggestions for advancing Lexie's career in pictures seemed to revolve around her taking off her clothes and lying on a vast leopard-skin-covered bed with another girl and a man in a black mask. She had told him she had other ideas, ground out his latest cigar on the Turkey carpet at his feet, turned and left.

Gerry had started off calling her a bloody half-wit, then he'd had a bit more to drink and said she was a stuck-up nigger who'd got ideas above her station. Blinded by fury, Lexie had lunged at him, only to be given the worst beating of her life. After that there had seemed little point in pursuing the dream of a movie career. After all, a full year after coming to London, Gerry and the fat man were her only two contacts in pictures, and neither of them would be doing her any favours from now on.

But she had had to do something, and she still wanted it to be connected with show business. Otherwise, what would she tell Dad? She was writing to him infrequently, padding out the letters with mythical accounts of auditions and location trips. Unless she switched to a less highly visible area of the profession, pretty soon he would know she had failed.

So she had tried the smaller nightclubs which gave floor shows. She had good legs and could manage the vague attempts at dance routines offered by most of the amateurish chorus lines. All the managers were interested in was pretty girls with good figures, at whom the customers could leer while they were overcharged for watered drinks. Lexie didn't like it, but it paid the bills.

Then, briefly, she had thought her luck was changing. Lexie was an excellent ballroom dancer, and one afternoon when she went to a tea-dance to escape her fly-blown world, she had run across an equally talented male dancer named Joe Machin. After several similar meetings, he suggested that they form a partnership and dance together as a demonstration team around the clubs. 'Better paid and a lot more fun than what you've been up to lately,' he had told her.

So they got together, and he was right, it *was* fun; they *did* earn more money – until he broke his leg. By that time they were living together, and without a partner a girl found it hard to give demonstration dances. The pittance she had earned in third-rate chorus line-ups would not have covered rent and food for two, let alone Joe's medical bills and decent clothes for her to attend auditions. There seemed only one way of earning that sort of money, and Lexie had taken it. She went to work as a hostess in a couple of the more expensive, discreet clubs, drinking hock-and-seltzers disguised as champagne with rich male clients. She got a tiny basic wage, passable commission on each phoney bottle of champagne she sold, and could keep anything she made from the man when he took her home afterwards.

At first she had thought she would hate it, but it turned out to be less repugnant than that first film producer. At least this was an open business transaction, with no false promises attached. And while they were at it, she could always switch her mind away and day-dream about what great times she and Joe Machin would have dancing together when his leg was better.

The trouble was that the leg never seemed to improve much. He told her the doctor suspected a badly healed break, and said he was to use a stick for a long time yet, because undue pressure or an early return to dancing would probably ruin him for future work. Sympathetically Lexie ploughed on with her evenings of ersatz champagne and imitation love. Joe would vacate their flat while she was at the club, and return the next morning, leaving the place free for Lexie and her men. He had never been forthcoming about where he spent the night, simply saying an old mate owed him a favour.

After a few months Lexie decided his leg might never heal sufficiently for him to dance again, and started making plans of her own to save enough money for them to open a small dance studio some day. It would mean spending a lot more time on her back than she already did, but after the first, who was counting?

She had all but committed herself to going to work in a house run by one of the most efficient madames in the West End, when she discovered the secret of Joe's slow recovery. She was emerging from a perfume shop in Curzon Street, when a familiar figure swung out from beneath the archway ahead of her which led from Shepherd Market. He walked away, fifty feet or so in front of her, and for a few seconds she was tantalized by the mixture of intense familiarity and complete incongruity of his appearance. When the truth dawned on her, she wondered if she had deliberately tried to blank out identifying him. It was Joe; but Joe walking fast and jauntily and without any sign of the stick he had been using for five months.

Lexie had swallowed her first impulse – to go and claw his eyes out – and forced herself to turn away in the direction she had intended to go, back to the flat, back to an hour spent forcing herself to be calm, appear normal, and make a plan. Eventually Joe had arrived, complete with ebony cane and heavy limp. They had supper, she made brittle small talk about her day, asked about his, which he said had been uneventful, and then she got herself ready for the club.

But that night she did not go to work. She crossed Rupert Street to the little coffee shop whose net half-curtains made it an ideal vantage point from which to see without being seen. Forty minutes after her own departure from the flat, Joe emerged, complete with cane but minus the limping walk. He stopped at the newsagent's shop two doors from the flat, spoke to someone inside and then emerged, having left the cane behind the counter. As he sauntered off, unencumbered, into the bustling Soho evening, Lexie hurriedly paid for her coffee and went after him. She had dressed less flamboyantly than usual to cut down the risk of his noticing her.

If his leg was still troubling him, Joe gave no sign of it that night. He covered the distance between Rupert Street and Shepherd Market in little more than fifteen minutes. It was almost dark as he disappeared under the arched entrance to the warren of courtyards, and Lexie was able to slip in behind him almost immediately. He walked directly to the other side of the main court, took out a key and opened a red-painted front door.

The moment it closed behind him, Lexie sped across, knowing already what she would find. Sure enough, the slots alongside the individual doorbells all bore identification of the 'Mlle Nana, French and discipline under private instruction' variety. For five months she had been supporting Joe and some tart of his . . . 'And the bastard never even so much as pimped for his keep!' she muttered.

At first all sorts of vengeful fantasies had crowded Lexie's head. Then she had had second thoughts. He was simply not worth it. She knew the strength of her own temper, and that once it got going she could not control it. She might end up in a police court, charged with wounding him or something . . .

worse still, he could turn on her and beat her the way Gerry once had. No man was worth that. Sod the lot of 'em. She left Shepherd Market, treated herself to a taxi back to Rupert Street, then packed and cleared out, leaving the place empty of everything but what belonged to the landlord. 'Let the bugger sort himself out of that one!' she said with a grim chuckle, surveying the barren tidiness of the living room just before she closed the door for the last time.

After that it was all downhill. The humiliations of a brothel, even one of the best, were too great to justify working there when there was no great dream like the dance studio to justify the misery. Lexie knew she could earn a hand-to-mouth living without resorting to such measures. But what was she doing it for? A few weeks after leaving Joe, back again in one of the countless faceless clubs of Soho, she wondered for the hundredth time. Once she had entertained extravagant dreams of a Hollywood career with accompanying Spanish villa and swimming-pool. Realistically she must now accept she had missed the boat. She was still quite young – twenty-five – but not young enough to start again at the bottom of that particular ladder. Her accomplishments hardly recommended her, either to potential employer or potential spouse. Her employability as a club hostess was strictly short term. It had never been a vocation which went well with wrinkles and greying hair. There had been no obvious answer. Lexie had gone back to the clubs as a temporary measure, and resolved to keep an eye open for a foolproof escape route.

And now here she was, a year later, with nothing changed. She still took the occasional man home, strictly for cash of course, when she needed a new coat or a pair of shoes. But the big dreams were all gone.

This was sheer self-indulgence! The Love Apple had never been much of a place, even with the inducement of the imminent arrival of movie men. She decided to try Uncle's, in Albemarle Street. It was far glossier than this dump, and tonight she'd probably need to take someone home. There were a lot of bills waiting to be paid . . .

The someone she found proved a lot nastier than she had anticipated. When he finally left, dawn was breaking. She thanked Providence that she had her own bathroom attached to the tiny flat, because now she shut herself into it and scrubbed herself from top to toe. Lying in the fragrant water, eyes closed, she shuddered as she remembered what he had done to her, and gradually the realization dawned within her that she was unable to face such a possibility again. Well, at least not tomorrow, not next week or next month . . . who thought further ahead than that?

Towelling herself dry, she pondered the possibilities. God knew, they were thin enough. Back in her father's dockland pub in Cardiff, she had been a first-rate barmaid. But how many pubs within walking distance of here would pay her the sort of wages she needed to keep her flat? That was a dead duck before she started. Time enough to sort something out when she had enjoyed a good sleep and something to eat. She went back into her bedroom just as the sun peeped in across the rooftops, raised the sash window to let out the last traces of tired scent and old tobacco smoke, then pulled down the roller blind and went to bed.

A couple of weeks later she had not broken her resolve to stay away from the clubs, but she had no job, either. She had been right about barmaid's wages. In desperation she had asked at the pub around the corner. A full week's money would just have covered the rent on the flat. On a side table in the living room were all the newspapers whose pages she had ransacked for suitable job vacancies. There were plenty of positions outlined in red ink, but nothing had come of any of them. Now her rent was overdue, she had nothing left beyond the pound in her purse, and she was still determined to stay away from Uncle's and the Love Apple. One more try, she thought, and went down into the street to buy the evening paper and see what it had to offer.

There was only one advertisement she could conceivably answer. It appeared regularly, and she had been avoiding it ever since she had started looking for a job. It occupied a prominent quarter-page position and announced that young women wishing to train for domestic service could obtain a living allowance, free uniform and accommodation under a government-sponsored scheme. Local labour exchanges would supply further details.

Feeling sick, Lexie went over to the window and stood, eyes

tightly shut, pressing her face against the cool glass. It seemed centuries ago that she had harangued Lily about the only job they'd give a coloured girl in Cardiff would be as a maid, even longer since she had snapped the same information at Bethan. Now she was going to prove it was true of London too . . . Momentarily she reconsidered her present position. Her shimmery dresses were still in the cupboard. Uncle's was only a few minutes away. One night with a swine like the one the other week and her troubles would be over again. Yes, but for how long, though? the unwelcome question followed inevitably. Lexie knew she was not acting in haste. It was just that when your only qualifications were barmaid, ballroom dancer and tart you ran out of alternatives pretty damned quick. She tore out the newspaper advertisement, stuffed it into her handbag, then went to start packing.

It never occurred to her that she could go home to Rhys. Lexie believed that in the battle of life you came home only behind your shield or on it.

CHAPTER NINETEEN

If I read one more article about handkerchief hems and white silk stockings I shall lose my mind, thought Bethan, throwing aside the copy of *Vogue* through which she had been skimming. She was sitting in a room which would have brought envious tears to the eyes of many women of her age, she had a wardrobe full of beautiful clothes, a wallet full of money and a heart full of frustration. For the fiftieth time that week she wondered what had ever made her turn her back on nursing for James Norland.

It had all seemed so glamorous . . . a flat of her own in Mayfair - *Mayfair*! How many girls from her background ever got inside a place there, let alone lived in it? A sporty little car . . . a generous allowance . . . endless jaunts to the races, to nightclubs, abroad on holidays . . . it had looked like Aladdin's cave.

And for a time it had been. Then Bethan - everyone called her Beth now; it was more sophisticated - started noticing they always went about with the same sort of people. With the exception of the odd maverick such as Norland himself, though, she never met the sort of people who had come to Foxhall for house parties. Nor did she hob-nob with the rich, smart city-dwellers whom the *Tatler* and *Vogue* assured her swarmed all over Mayfair through the Season.

She was not taken to the opening of the Royal Academy summer show - James had said she could always pop round there once it got going if she wanted to, no need to go on the first day – and the race meetings never included Royal Ascot or Goodwood. It was always the more raffish meetings, like the Derby at Epsom, and they always seemed to go with a group of bookies, showgirls and mysterious men of affairs whose line she could not identify. Sometimes there was a sprinkling of well-known stage or cinema people, and often some rich American or other, catching up on European café society.

Bethan had minded a lot at first, but soon her inborn practicality took over. If he had meant to take her into more exalted company, he would have courted her, proposed and married her, not seduced her at a pretty country inn and set her up in a smart flat. That soon ceased to be important. Far more destructive was the awful shallowness of the people she mixed with. Bethan read fashion magazines, it was true, but she also went through a couple of novels a week and took an interest in the newspapers. The other women in the group never read anything else but magazines and based most of their conversation on the contents. If it wasn't the latest hemline and heel height, it was the film everyone was talking about this month, or the singer all the chic set were going to hear at that funny little club off New Bond Street.

Bethan liked fashion, and movies, and popular music, and had no desire to spend her time discussing Latin verse and the meaning of life, but she wanted more from it than this. Too late, it began to dawn on her that even the privileged conditions of employment she had enjoyed with Mrs Norland had given her more stimulation than her present flaccid existence, and any attempt to compare it with her work at St Thomas's was laughable.

Nowadays she slept late in the morning, took a leisurely bath and dressed in time for cocktails and lunch at an expensive restaurant. In the afternoons it was shopping or a race meeting, or on warm summer afternoons perhaps a trip to Maidenhead for a picnic on the river. Evenings were spent at some nightclub or other, dancing, eating and drinking, always with the same set of silly, anonymous faces, always without any future in mind beyond this one. It was all right for James. After swamping her with attention for the first two months or so, he resumed an active interest in the Oxford car plant and went there two or three days a week. Now and then he spent the whole time at Foxhall, returning on Friday afternoon to take her off somewhere glamorous for the week-end.

She was never short of company, but it always seemed to be the same giggling blondes. Few of them appeared interested in seeing their lovers during the daytime. They preferred gathering in small flocks, to twitter about their latest acquisitions. Brooding about the shortcomings of her gilded cage, she punched the cover of her magazine and said pettishly: 'It wasn't what I intended at all!'

There must be something she could do to relieve the tedium . . . next week they were off to the South of France for ten days, and that still had power to impress her. But when they came back the whole year would spread barrenly ahead of her with nothing to anticipate except the start of the National Hunt racing season and the autumn fashion collections.

Scowling, Bethan picked up the newspaper she had bought on her way back from lunch. That was slightly less vapid than the magazine, but it went almost too far in the other direction, with every story shrieking doom and gloom . . . Abruptly she stopped flipping pages as a headline caught her eye:

'FREE LOVE' DOCTOR'S BIRTH CONTROL
CLINIC PILLORIED BY
LEAGUE OF CATHOLIC WIVES

It was a story about Dr Marie Stopes, who had finally got into full operation with her Holloway Road consulting rooms for women requiring contraceptive advice. The main body of the report was a rant against Dr Stopes's permissive morality, but downpage was an interview with the woman herself explaining, doubtless for the hundredth time, why such a service was needed.

'This latest attack is a direct result of the libel action brought against me in 1923,' she told the newspaper reporter. 'The clinic really went ahead after that, and now we are well established they are prepared to try anything to stop us. But we are too much of a force for good to be deflected from our course by such petty obstacles. In the end, there will be a network of clinics like Holloway Road, advising married women all over England how to escape the slavery of unwanted motherhood.'

Bethan sat and pondered the story for some time. Now there was a woman who was doing something with her life! She had sharp memories from her days as a trainee midwife of young women exhausted by bearing too many children too soon being refused sterilization by doctors who thought it more ethical for nature to take its course. Not that it had been permitted to take its course with *their* wives, of course. Invariably, those doctors had at most three children. If the poor worn-out women in the hospital beds had been given access to contraception, they would have been equally free to choose. Instead they had to rely on their husbands' self-control, and who would dream of guaranteeing that as long as it wasn't the man who had to carry and bear the child?

A small idea began to take shape at the back of Bethan's mind. There was nothing stopping her from doing voluntary work while James was off about his business, was there? Perhaps if she got in touch with the clinic, they would find a niche for her somewhere . . .

The voice at the other end of the telephone line was wary when she said she had read the *Evening News* story. Then she explained why she was calling and the woman's attitude changed immediately. 'Oh, my dear, I wish there were more like you, even if only as supporting voices!' she said. 'Look, we really can't discuss it on the telephone. Are you free in the morning? Why not come over and see me? My name is Gladstone – Joyce Gladstone.'

James was going to be in Oxford for another two days, so Bethan made an appointment and next morning found herself driving through the drabness of the Holloway Road, conscious that her jaunty little car was drawing curious glances. Poverty had made them unused to anything so chic in this part of London.

Mrs Gladstone was jubilant over Bethan's willingness and the excellence of her qualifications. 'Of course some of our more . . . er . . . conservative clients will look askance at your unmarried status, but I think we can get round that by referring to you as Nurse Walters – that always impresses them like mad!' she said, grinning. 'How much time can you give us?'

'It might be a bit erratic, I'm afraid, but I shall know at least a week in advance what my movements are likely to be, if that gives you enough notice. I can do at least two afternoons a week – perhaps two full days or three afternoons some weeks.'

'That would be splendid! Doesn't matter about the short notice. It will simply cut back the clients' waiting time when you come, because we can run three consultations instead of two. We have one doctor and one nurse normally. The doctor sees everyone first time in, and after that they divide between doctors and nurse. Now we can split it between three of you.'

Bethan stayed for coffee and found herself talking to Joyce Gladstone like a fellow professional. By the time she left she felt more alert and enthusiastic about life than she had for years. As Mrs Gladstone showed her out, she said: 'You have no idea how difficult it is for us to find anyone with your background, and with the will and leisure to do work like this. If you stay the course your price will be above rubies!'

Bethan arranged to start at the clinic two weeks after she returned from Cap Ferrat. Half-way through her trip to France, she was forced to acknowledge something she had been trying to ignore for a month or two. She was pregnant.

'Good God almighty, I'd have thought you, of all people, could keep yourself out of that sort of trouble!' James exploded at her when she told him.

'But why? Why should I be any better at that than any other girl?'

He was sulky. 'Well, you're a nurse, aren't you . . . it's well known nurses are bright about that sort of thing . . . '

'Well this nurse isn't! When I was on the wards they taught us how to care for babies, not stop ourselves having them.' She faltered, gazing at him in sudden apprehension. 'D-don't you want me to have it, then?'

'Why on earth would you want to do that? There'd be no future in it! The brat could hardly inherit the business, could he?'

'James – it never occurred to me . . . I thought you loved me.' She managed not to cry, but it was impossible to keep the hurt out of her voice.

He had the grace to look remorseful. 'Dammit, of course I do. But, Beth, you know marriage was never in the air. I never lied to you about anything like that. Of course I love you. But you and I aren't the sort to be married to each other. How could a child fit in with that?'

'Just as it would fit in for any other couple. You're hardly strapped for cash. Surely there would be enough to bring him up – educate him properly? I'm not asking to have him sent to Eton or anything!'

He was looking grim again. 'No – it's out of the question. I've seen this sort of thing happen before. Always raises dreadful competition with the legitimate children when they come along. Sorry, Beth, it just won't do.'

'What legitimate children, James? I thought you were happy with me.'

He finally gathered her into his arms. 'I am, Beth. You're the loveliest thing I've ever seen. I never get tired of looking at you . . . being with you. Everybody envies me. You're a chap's ideal playmate. But a man in my position is bound to marry and raise a family eventually, isn't he?'

'Is he?'

He laughed. 'But of course – who d'you think I'm slogging away building up my little industrial empire for? Surely you don't imagine I'd ever let Jessica's little monsters have it all? And it will be sooner rather than later, at that. I'm well into my thirties now, remember.'

The tears were bubbling close to the surface again. 'But are you saying you – you'll just drop me, and go off to get married?'

'Of course not, silly! No reason why we can't go on as we have before. I don't think I could do without you now. Why should it make any difference?'

Bethan found it impossible to frame the words which would tell him. She seemed to be seeing him for the first time, handsome, glamorous, generous as ever, and completely without heart or imagination. She felt dazed, as if he had hit her with a piece of wood. He was speaking again and she had difficulty in grasping the sense of what he was saying. She forced herself to concentrate: ' . . . I mean, are you absolutely sure of it? Because if not . . . '

'I could have it confirmed by a doctor when I get back, but yes, I'm sure. It's been wishful thinking that stopped me going for one earlier, that's all – that and the fact that it hasn't happened to me before. Each day I told myself it would be all right tomorrow. But yesterday I started being sick. That just about clinches it. Of course I'll see a doctor anyway when we get home.'

'No need,' he gestured dismissively. 'I dare say your training has prepared you to recognize *that* at least. Far better that you go off somewhere quietly immediately this trip is over, and attend to it.'

'What if I want to keep it?'

'I told you, out of the question. If you insist, you'll be on your own, without a penny from me. I can't say I recommend that – you'd never get a nursing job again.'

'You'd do that to me, just to stop me having your child?'

'I hope you won't make me, darling.' He grasped her hands, gazing at her earnestly. 'Don't you realize, it's at least as much for your sake as for mine? It would never work. Now let's be sensible. If it's still early days, you can enjoy the rest of the holiday and we'll arrange something the minute we get back. Try to put it out of your mind, Beth, darling. Come on, let's go for a swim – it'll wash away the cobwebs.' He stood up and crossed to the table where his swimsuit and towel were folded.

Bethan looked away. 'You go on ahead. I may join you afterwards.'

'Hmm, all right. But don't be a silly girl and stay here brooding. Won't make anything different. In a couple of months you'll wonder why you ever got into such a state.'

I'm wondering why I ever got into such a state right this minute, she thought savagely as the door closed behind him.

CHAPTER TWENTY

No wonder they're giving away the uniform, thought Lexie. There's never been a woman born simple enough to *buy* one of these things. She was wearing a voluminous white pinafore which wrapped around her thin hips and almost overlapped at the back. The starched bib stood out stiffly over her breasts, giving her a strangely matronly look. Not that there was anything worth protecting underneath it. The dress was a shoddy little number in blue checked cotton, with a high-buttoned collar and meanly cut gored skirt. Someone must have imagined they were giving the unfortunate girls an illusion of wearing nurses' uniforms, and had added ruched bands of muslin at the bottoms of the short sleeves, in imitation of nurses' cuffs. The whole uniform was topped by a cap which was a cross between the new style worn by nurses, and the design sported by Nippies in Lyons' Corner Houses.

On her first day at the maids' school in Fulham, Lexie put on her clothes in the dormitory, surveyed the result in the full-length mirror supplied so that they could check the correctness of their dress, and said to one of her room-mates: 'I can't see one of the Vere de Veres taking any of us in this tat, servant shortage or no servant shortage.'

Her companion, dull-eyed and cowed by hunger, merely made some unintelligible sound and shuffled off to get her breakfast. Lexie shrugged. If that was a sample of her fellow-students' mental capacity, she should graduate with honours at the top of the class.

That was where she made her big mistake. She could out-think most of the girls there, knew how to speak properly, to keep herself clean and to carry out the extremely basic tasks they were given within moments. But after that she was her own worst enemy.

The middle-aged women who instructed at the institution were former cooks-general or housekeepers from smaller establishments where they had never been paid quite enough for what was demanded of them. The wages at the training schools were good enough to attract them, but certainly not to lure the better type of servant from the really rich households.

To a woman, they were ill-informed, surly and despotic. They treated the girls at the training school much as they imagined the lowliest kitchenmaids were treated in the houses of the rich, and were able to get away with it because the girls had nowhere else to go and were cowed by the fact that they had given a legal undertaking to enter domestic service in return for uniforms, board and training.

Lexie had no such reservations. The first time one of these basement martinets lined them up and showed them how to hold a long-handled brush and dustpan when moving from the broom cupboard to the front hall, Lexie looked along the parody of a military line-up and whispered, none too quietly, 'Jesus Christ Almighty, Fred Karno's Army rides again!'

'Walters, I have experience of girls like you, and there's a word for your behaviour. Cocky, that's what I call it. And I can tell you now, you won't get nowhere if you're too cocky. For that you can brush up out here after the rest of us have gone through to the hall.'

'Out here,' was the insalubrious backyard of the large Georgian house, once a pub, which now housed the training school. As the instructress wheeled and marched her trainees off to better things inside the house, Lexie glanced around and wondered what the punishment was supposed to be. There was no more or less dust out here than in there. It took her some minutes of sweeping to realize that the instructress had assumed she was delivering a dose of humiliation. As Lexie already held her in contempt it had been wasted.

They continued to be powerless to damage Lexie, although they tried. The other girls treated her with extreme reserve, largely because they were used to being bullied and badly treated and were truly afraid of what the instructresses might do to them. Lexie never understood the fear. Edie King, one of the few trainees who tried to befriend her, attempted to explain one night as they lay down on their hard, narrow beds to sleep.

'It might not seem a lot when they're just teaching you,' she said, 'but I been in service before. Only come 'ere because I couldn't afford me own uniform and this place would gimme one to start off wiv. Cows like them downstairs, they may not be able to do much when you're just learning your trade outside a private house, but you once let them getcha below stairs, and you've 'ad it.'

'Why, because they'll shout at you half the night? Come off it!' retorted Lexie.

'Don't be so clever before you try it. They got you bang to rights down there, haven't they? Give you the odd slap round the ear, what're you gonna do, hit 'em back and get discharged without a reference? Never work again, then. Or maybe complain to the mistress? She'd laugh behind your back and then straighten 'er face and tell you Cook or the housekeeper or whoever it is, is in charge below stairs and she won't do nuffink to interfere. She might even say you must be in the wrong if a sensible employee like Mrs So-and-so chooses to 'ave a go at yer. What you gonna do about that, eh?'

Lexie tried to understand, but failed. The course dragged on for three dismal months, and she began to wonder just how long it took girls of average intelligence to learn how to wield a mop and bucket. It was some time before she realized it had been planned by people who did not understand domestic service from the inside, and entrusted to people whose interest lay in prolonging the training as long as possible, and with students who felt the same way. No wonder it was so long drawn-out.

Eventually, though, graduation day came. Other establishments might celebrate with bestowal of certificates and prizes. The Parsons Green School for Domestic Training organized its own hiring fair. They did not call it that. It was described as a potential employers' open day, but a hiring fair it was for all that. Posses of middle-class housewives and housekeepers from the more exalted establishments arrived at intervals and were shown over the house, where they saw demonstrations of the girls' skill at ironing, sweeping and vegetable preparation. In the ground-floor front room was a display of the trainees' plain sewing, and on completion of the tour the visitors were offered coffee, tea and cakes prepared by the girls.

In fact they would have had to be complete incompetents to fail to be hired. Households everywhere were short of servants, and the problem was most obvious at the bottom of the heap, with former scullery maids now commanding assistant-cook jobs, and kitchenmaids becoming head housemaids. These beginners were snapped up for the lowly jobs left by the newly promoted.

Lexie's exotic looks put off the first few modestly placed women. They took one look at her tall, elegant body and her glowing coffee-coloured skin, and to a woman imagined the effect she would have on their husbands and sons. The bigger establishments suffered no such problems. For a start, the lady of the house was not present to select for herself, and anyway the housekeepers doing the recruiting realized that in an establishment the size of theirs, Lexie would probably never spend enough time above stairs to catch anyone's eye. Early in the afternoon, she was 'asked for' as the principal put it, by the housekeeper from a mansion on the edge of Kensington.

In the Number Fourteen bus on the way back to Queen's Gate, Mrs Antony began indoctrinating Lexie on the responsibilities of being a servant at the Grenvilles' town house.

'For a start, that terrible uniform'll have to go,' she said. 'I s'pose it gives you girls something to wear while you're skivvying at the school, but nobody'd dress a respectable housemaid in that.'

Lexie bridled. 'If you think I can afford to buy different uniforms out of twelve-and-six a week . . . '

'I'll thank you to keep a civil tongue in your head, Walters! Nobody was suggesting any such thing. Mrs Grenville likes to see her staff looking nice and she sees to it they do. You can wear the spare set of Lizzie's until we get new ones for you. Lizzie, the girl you're replacing, was a bit shorter than you, but otherwise you were about the same. And don't look so snotty, Miss, you'll find it much smarter than what you're wearing now.'

209

It was, too – a well-cut dress of fine black alpaca, with a frilly white apron, white lace collar and a flat pancake of a cap, streaming lacy ribbons down the back. Given that it was a good three inches too short for her, Lexie decided with some amusement that she looked like something straight out of a French farce, gave a little flounce to add to the impression, and began the long tramp down from her attic bedroom to the basement servants' hall where she was to meet Mrs Antony.

'Now, as second parlourmaid, you'll be in line for head parlourmaid soon enough if you do well. Amy Carter is planning to get married in six months, and Madam said I should look out particularly for someone who might be smart enough to take over from her.'

'Is that supposed to be an honour, then?' Lexie knew she should keep her sarcasm to herself, but somehow this whole sycophantic world depressed her into automatic misbehaviour.

Mrs Antony glared at her. 'No "supposed to be" about it. For a start, it would mean seven-and-six a week on your wages. I don't think you've got the faintest idea how lucky you are, coming into service as old as you are, and having the opportunity to rise so soon. Took me eight years to get from tweeny to head parlourmaid, and now the servant problem is so bad you look like making the jump in less than a year. You count your blessings.'

'Oh, I am. I just been taking a good look at my bedroom.'

The irony was lost on Mrs Antony. 'Yeah, nice little room, that. Used to be for two girls, when there was more staff. That's why you got so much space.'

'I used to have a whole flat to myself, Mrs Antony.' Oh, Christ, she thought. Why did I say that? She'll know I couldn't have come by that in any respectable work. I'm out . . .

But the housekeeper merely glanced around furtively to make sure no other servants had passed through the room and overheard. 'Less said about that the better,' she whispered. 'Now you listen to me, Walters. I know quality when I see it, even if there is a touch of the old tar brush there. Don't breathe a word of what you been doing before this, all right? I want a nice bright girl and I'm sick of trying out downtrodden little drabs who don't know their left from their right. You're runnin' away from somefink and I don't really care what, or

210

want to know. But if you want to stay here, you'd better learn to keep your lip buttoned about the past, and when you speak about anything else, to keep a civil tongue in your head. There's not so much of a servant shortage that you'd find it easy to get any sorta job if you got slung out of here without a reference. Got that?'

Lexie nodded, stifling an urge to hug the woman in spite of the passing insult about her colour. This was someone she understood. Do what you're paid for, use your head and don't make life hard for me, and I'll see you're all right. Lexie hoped the rest of the household was like Mrs Antony.

A week later she would gladly have consigned Mrs Antony and the entire population of Number Nine Queen's Gate to the deepest pit of Hell. Nothing had prepared her for her experiences in this rich man's house. Once or twice that week she remembered almost fondly her past distress at being called 'blackie' or 'nigger' in the street. That had been favoured treatment compared with the appalling invisibility which had been meted out to her as a servant. No one had ever turned Lexie into an inanimate object before, but Mrs Grenville, her two daughters and their assorted menfolk did just that, effortlessly, every day.

She got her first taste of the process when Mrs Antony took her up to the morning room to introduce her to 'Madam'. Mrs Grenville put down her pen and turned from the writing desk to inspect the new arrival. At first she did not speak directly to Lexie. 'What is her name, Mrs Antony?'

'Walters, madam, Lexie Walters. She's just completed the training programme in that Government centre in Fulham and got very good reports . . . ' an impatient hand movement from Mrs Grenville cut off the flow of chatter.

She turned to Lexie with the barest hint of a smile. 'I hope you will like it here, Lexie. As long as you always remember I like my parlourmaids to be as unobstrusive as possible, I see no reason why you should not settle in admirably. Very well, Mrs Antony. You may put her to work. Oh, and one other thing – ' she was no longer looking at Lexie ' – Please make sure she knows she is supposed to say "yes, madam" or "no, madam", when I speak to her, and not stand glowering at me in that surly fashion.'

They were dismissed. Mrs Antony sailed off in front of Lexie, who was digging her nails into the palms of her hands so hard she could feel the flesh cracking. When she had conquered her first paroxysm of rage, she said: 'What's all this "Lexie", then? I didn't expect her to be so chummy one minute and so hoity-toity the next.'

'You've got a lot to learn,' replied Mrs Antony. 'I get the toff's treatment in that – senior female servant, you see, got to be nice to me and Cook. She's Mrs James and I'm Mrs Antony, but after that, the next step is surname only. You'll know madam approves of you when she starts calling you Walters.'

'I'm a girl, not a bloody man!'

'And girls don't swear, not in this house anyway. If she uses your surname, the way I do, it's a sign of respect. Shows she's dropped the familiarity of your first name, see? You behave well and you get the little courtesies.'

Lexie went off, seething, to start her first day's work. If being called by your surname like a little boy at school was a mark of favour, what did they do when they *really* wanted to humiliate you?

After that, she fought a daily battle to keep her temper. Her day, though long, did not seem particularly hard to her. The tweeny and the under housemaid cleared and laid the fires each morning. She had to take the morning tea up to the bedrooms, it was true, but that hardly ranked with trailing up four flights with buckets of coal and kindling. She helped serve breakfast in the dining room, dusted, swept and polished, tidied the bedrooms once the family were downstairs, assisted with luncheon service, served afternoon tea and opened the front door to callers, announcing them in the drawing room or library before she went back to cleaning silver or refreshing flower vases. In the evening, wearing a more formal uniform, she helped the butler and footmen serve dinner, and cleared away before going back below stairs to finish up any tasks which remained undone from earlier in the day.

She had worked far harder on a dance floor, and for longer hours, when she was practising a new ballroom routine. But she had never been so consistently humiliated, not merely by her employers but by the senior servants. The butler treated her almost as loftily as Mrs Grenville had at their only formal meeting. Mr Grenville's valet was determined from the start to bait her beyond endurance. At first he contented himself with heavy-handed references to suntans being all the rage these days, then he progressed to singing snatches of minstrel songs when Lexie was anywhere near him. Then, on her eighth day at Queen's Gate, he triggered the row which parted Lexie from the Grenvilles and from the world of domestic service.

The day had started badly, with two out-of-town guests of Mr Grenville lingering for ever in the dining room so that Lexie could not get in to clear away and lay up for luncheon. That, in turn, meant that she was not ready with Mrs Grenville's pot of coffee at eleven o'clock. Mrs Grenville snapped at her about being slow and Lexie worked herself into a rage, suppressing the retort which sprang naturally to mind.

Half-an-hour later, when she returned to pick up the coffee tray, the cup was still on Mrs Grenville's desk. As Lexie moved to pick it up, her mistress re-entered the room and hurried over in an angry flurry. 'What are you doing there? That's my private correspondence!' Lexie, taken by surprise, pointed at the cup and saucer and began to explain, but Mrs Grenville cut her off by pushing her aside and hastily slapping down her hand on a letter which commenced: 'My darling Edward'. For once, Lexie was determined to avoid a scene. She simply reached around Mrs Grenville's arm and picked up the cup and saucer. At that moment the woman's hand flew up again, catching the edge of the saucer, which shot out of Lexie's grasp, scattering the last few drops of cold coffee across desk and papers.

'Now see what you've done, you clumsy little fool! Get out – and don't come back in here until I send for you!' yelled Mrs Grenville.

Lexie recovered the cup and saucer and fled, too intrigued by what could have been in the letter to feel as angry as she would otherwise have been.

By the time she got downstairs, though, she was furious at the woman's bad manners. Why should she have thought Lexie was reading her private correspondence? And anyway, if Lexie's presence counted no more than that of a piece of wallpaper or carpet, what would it have mattered if she *had* been doing so? In any case, Mrs Grenville must have been aware that she herself, not Lexie, was responsible for the spilled coffee. Lexie shrugged angrily. Why should she start expecting fair treatment now? She had seen precious little of it so far.

She walked into the kitchen with the tray just as Biggs, the valet, entered from the other direction. 'Well, if it ain't Princess Mazzumboola!' he said. 'How are things down in the jungle today, then, Princess?'

She slammed her tray down on the table, eliciting an agonized cry of 'Walters, that's Madam's favourite china!' from Cook, and strode over to Biggs.

'For your information, *Mister* Biggs, I'm more bloody British than you are. If you wanna find out what it's like in the jungle, just come over here a minute an' I'll bite off your balls and ram 'em down your rotten throat!'

Abruptly total silence fell on the kitchen. A solitary pot clanked against the side of the sink as it slid off the draining board. Cook's arm, arrested in mid-stroke as it whisked egg whites for a lunch-time soufflé, gave a convulsive jerk and she set down the whisk. The tweeny let out a shrill giggle, high on the edge of hysteria.

The hush ended as suddenly as it had descended. 'What happened, cat got all your tongues?' said Mrs Antony, coming in through the back door, oblivious of what had just happened.

Cook's face was turning an impossible turkeycock red, and a few outraged gobbling sounds escaped her lips. Finally she managed to blurt out: 'Eliza, I dunno where you managed to find this filthy-mouthed little cow, but if you don't send her back there, quick, there'll be no cook in this house no more!'

Bewildered, Mrs Antony glanced from Cook to the other servants and then at Lexie, who was already undoing her apron strings. 'Don't waste the energy, Mrs Antony,' she said, tossing the apron over a chair. She reached up and unclipped the saucy maid's cap. 'I resigned a second before I explained my plans for old Biggs, so you won't have to take me anywhere. I'm going of my own accord. And if you don't like the idea of breaking the news to our dear Mrs Grenville, allow me. At this minute I can't think of anything I'd enjoy more.'

The cap came loose from her hair and she dropped it to the

flagged floor, stood on it and ground it firmly underfoot. She grinned at the gaping audience. 'That's just in case you were going to try and make me change my mind!'

There was very little for her to collect upstairs. All her dance frocks were stored safely at a girlfriend's flat, packed carefully between tissue paper and locked in a sturdy theatrical trunk. The only clothes of her own she had with her were a couple of plain frocks, two blouses, a tailored skirt and some underwear.

She changed into street clothes, folded her uniform carefully and put it over the back of a chair. She was just combing her hair when someone rapped at the door. It was Mrs Antony. 'I thought I'd give you a bit of time to cool off before . . . oh, you're ready to go!' said the housekeeper, clearly surprised.

Lexie smiled at her. 'Did you expect me to be sitting up here blubbering and waiting for you to come and give me the sack? Of course I am.'

Mrs Antony glanced down at the floor. 'Well, let's not be too hasty about this. P'raps we can sort somefink out. Cook's calmed down a bit now, and though I must say I've never heard language here like what she told me you'd been saying, Biggs asked for it. If you was to apologize to Cook, I don't think . . .'

'Have you talked to Mrs Grenville yet?'

'Madam? Why, no. There's no need to bring this to her attention . . . I'll see Biggs doesn't bother you again, as long as you set yourself right with Cook.'

Lexie gave her a weary smile. 'No, you don't understand, Mrs Antony. I couldn't really care less about that old bigot Biggs. I'd had a run-in with Mrs Grenville over something that wasn't my fault, and that's why I lost my temper with him.'

Mrs Antony covered her face with her hand and sighed. 'What have you done to upset Madam?' she said in a monotone.

'More like what Madam did to upset me!' Lexie told her of the incident and, to her surprise, Mrs Antony laughed.

'Don't let that worry you! That one's got more fancy men than Nell Gwynn. She's always scared she'll get caught, and forever jumping down some maid's throat for snooping. She'll have forgotten it by tonight.'

'But I bloody well won't! Look, Mrs Antony, you've been

kind to me, but I should have known better than to think I could ever be anybody's skivvy. My Dad brought me up to look anybody in the eye and know I was just as good as them. I ent going to change my mind now for twelve-and-six a week and an alpaca uniform.'

Mrs Antony was regarding her as if she was speaking an incomprehensible language. 'But what will you do, child? If you were down-and-out when you went to the training school, you're even worse off now. Nobody will pay you a week's wages if you walk out today.'

'I never thought they would. But something I learned this week. There ent really more than one way of selling yourself. It may be your body, it may be your soul, but you'm still selling it. Well, if I got to, I know places where I can get a much better price than twelve-and-bloody six!' Impulsively, she put her arm around the housekeeper and kissed her cheek. 'I know you been kind to me, much more than you need have been, and I'm sorry if I've got you in trouble, choosing me and then having me walk out like this. But honest, Mrs Antony, if I stay here a day longer, I'll be shoving a dinner knife between Madam's pretty shoulder blades!'

Mrs Antony was regarding her bemusedly. 'You know,' she said, 'until you got mad down in that kitchen and just now, I never noticed you were Welsh?'

CHAPTER TWENTY-ONE

Lexie had been aboard the bus for ten minutes before she realized this was the first time she had been out since she went to work for the Grenvilles. She was elated and felt a sense of freedom greater than she had ever known before. 'P'raps I should go to work as a skivvy more often,' she said, giggling at the thought. 'It's so much fun when you stop!'

She had a little over four pounds left from the allowance she had been paid during her training course. None of the girls had been anywhere to spend their money, and all had expected each week to hear that the Government had stopped it, or at least reduced the amount. Somehow it had seemed too good to be true. Now, Lexie hoped, it would keep her afloat while she found something else to do. No one was likely to pay her unemployment benefit.

Her first stop was at her friend Molly's room around the corner from her own old flat in Soho. Molly was still in bed when she rang the doorbell – it was still not long after noon and Molly's nightclub job kept her out until three in the morning even when she was not bringing a man home with her afterwards. Lexie had rung several times when her friend's tussled platinum-blond head and kohl-smeared eyes peered around the door. Instantly her expression changed from sleepiness to avidity. 'Lex! Christ, kid, I wouldn't have believed you'd last this long! Bet you've had enough now, though!'

'You can say that again. Can I come in, or are you entertaining?'

Molly laughed and looked down at her old-man's tartan woollen dressing-gown. 'Do I *look* as if I'm entertaining? Come on, then, but you'll have to make the tea. Not sure I can see straight yet.' She turned and shuffled into the room which was so untidy it looked like the site of an explosion. Lexie went to the tiny cubby-hole kitchen beyond it and put the kettle on. Then she filled Molly in about what had been happening.

'Told you it was a daft idea, didn't I?' Molly lit a cigarette, wrinkling her pretty nose at the thought of donning a uniform and waiting on people. 'That's what started me off in this game. I tried two years of skivvyin' and anything woulda been a step up after that.'

'I didn't think so three months ago, but I do now. Still it gave me a bit of breathing space – and I can't arf polish a nice sideboard these days!'

'Mmm, play yer cards right an' one of my Joes might even take you home and make an honest woman of you!'

'God forbid! When you're only a servant at least you can up and leave. Somehow I think it gets a bit harder when you're married to 'em.'

'Yeah – can't say it ever tempted me much, neither. Mind you, we're young yet. Bet we feel different when we're thirty-five.'

'I don't even plan to be *alive* when I'm thirty-five!'

'Bet it'll come round soon enough, though.'

They sat and contemplated the possibility for a few moments, then Molly said: 'How are you gonna manage till you got something lined up?'

Lexie shrugged. 'Haven't the faintest idea. I suppose I'll have to find a cheap hotel until I can earn a bitta money. Nobody's gonna give me a room with just over four quid in my pocket.'

'How would you feel about living in this building? Don't think I'll be offended if you can't stand the idea . . . I know you're used to having a whole flat.'

'No, I'd be quite happy here for a while,' said Lexie. 'I was getting a lotta money when I had that place round in Dean Street after me and Joe split, and I took it as much to thumb my nose at him as anything else. One room would suit me fine, why?'

218

'There's one vacant up on the top floor – bigger than this one and there's a lav on the same floor an' all. Reckon old Kowalski would let you have it without a deposit on my say-so. He's seen you around enough before you went off on that course.'

'Would you ask him, Mol? It'd make such a difference if I had a place to start from. What does it cost you?'

Molly grinned. 'That's nothing to go on. He's got different rates depending on whether or not you're on the game. He judges it different from us – casuals classes as full-timers because he says he charges according to all the extra light an' water that gets used, if you please. Are you gonna be on or off?'

'I suppose I'd better say on. Can't see any other way of earning enough money to keep going, and if I do, I may still want to bring the odd one back as an investment.'

'Right, then. He'll charge you thirty bob a week.' She chuckled. 'Shameful, ennit? It's only five shillings if he thinks yer a good girl.'

'Listen, love, this minute I'd find it harder to earn five shillings a week as a good girl than thirty as a bad one. How long will it be before you can see him?'

'Oh, he only lives round in Old Compton Street. I'll nip down an' see him once I'm up and dressed. In the meantime make yourself at home here. You know I can't give you a bed overnight, but you're welcome in the daytime! Or if you wanna go out somewhere, you can take it for granted he'll rent you the room. He'll be relieved it's someone recommended. Last couple he's had up there have been right flighty pieces. Tell you what – unpack some a your pretty clothes from the trunk an' doll yourself up a bit. I've never seen you dressed so prim an' proper!'

'I think I just might. And then, you know what? I'm going down that tea-dance at Alphonso's. I need a bitta perking up after what I been up to the past few weeks.'

The afternoon was pure heaven. Lexie had learned to dance in Cardiff when she was still a child, and now she was brilliant at it. She looked sensational, as always, so she had a steady stream of partners, many of them interested in other matters than dancing. But she was in single-minded pursuit of pleasure this afternoon, and firmly said goodbye to them after each set

219

of three dances. The afternoon was almost over when a tall, middle-aged man came and escorted her on to the floor. He was faintly Latin-looking, with a fashionable pencil moustache and black hair brilliantined flat against his skull. The minute they started to foxtrot, Lexie realized she was in the arms of a professional.

Her eyes lit up as she got into her stride. 'Hey, this is great – best partner I've had all afternoon! Is your card full for the rest of the session?'

He laughed at her cheek and said: 'I've been watching you for some time. I have a proposition that will last a lot longer than this afternoon.'

'Oh, come on, don't spoil it,' said Lexie. 'Not just when I was enjoying myself. All I'm interested in today is dancing, got it?'

'Loud and clear. That's all I have in mind, strangely enough.'

'I don't get it.'

'You will, soon enough. For the moment, let's just save our breath for the dancing, shall we?'

They went through two sets together, and when he said it really was time they talked before the dance ended, Lexie was quite sorry. It had been a magical interlude. He escorted her to one of the small tables with their rose-shaded lamps, and introduced himself.

'My name's Eddie Romano. I run the Park Lane dancing school. I could use half-a-dozen girls who dance like you as instructors. Are you interested?'

'Are you serious? Tell me about the money and I'll answer.'

'Start you off at four pounds a week. You'll go up to five after a month if you turn out as well with the customers as you looked out there today.'

'When d'you want me to start?'

'Tomorrow afternoon, two o'clock suit you? They tend to crowd in a bit between two-thirty and three, and drift off after five. Turn up at one and I'll show you the ropes, okay?'

She nodded, unable to believe her luck. He added: 'Here's my business card, in case you have second thoughts and start wondering if I'm above-board. Oh, and by the way – it would help if I knew your name.'

220

CHAPTER TWENTY-TWO

Abercarn

David Richards' stature had grown incomparably in Lily's eyes in the troubled months since mid-1925. Always a quiet man, he never waved his courage like a banner, but in crisis it was solid as a rock. Now he unobtrusively began to turn up at all the Miners' Federation lodge meetings at the South Celynen, standing out against most of his fellow deputies to insist they must support the colliers when the inevitable showdown came with the owners. When one of the officials suggested that they should meet informally to discuss setting up a branch of the National Federation of Colliery Officials and Staffs, David made sure he was there. If they were represented separately from the men they could refuse to join in any strike unless their own union was involved – and to date, the officials' union never had been. It had no real presence in the South Wales coalfield, and David was determined it would not get a foothold in Newbridge.

They met in an upstairs room at Nant Pennar Working Men's Club. 'We'll be cutting our own throats if we do go out with that rabble, mun!' said Vaughan Edwards, the overman on David's shift and the man who had suggested this discussion. 'You got as much to lose as us – your own house, good money, full sick pay. Ent us who'll be doing more hours for less money when the cuts come. It's about time we was represented by a union that looked after our interests, not every other bugger's.'

David regarded him steadily for a long while before

answering. 'And you think that do make a difference, do you? How d'you manage when they asks you how you like taking food out a their kids' mouths, Vaughan?'

'Don't be soft – arf a them would do the same to us given the chance. What difference would it make to them if we was out an' all?'

'You don't need me to answer that. Without us safety men down there looking after their interests, the owners wouldn't have no pits fit to open once they got the men on their knees. They couldn't afford to lock the colliers out for months – they'd have to make a fast settlement.'

'Don't you read the papers? They can't make no settlement. The bottom have dropped out of coal and everybody'll be on the scrap heap if there ent big cuts.'

'Depends what papers you'm reading,' said David. 'Anyhow, making the day longer would only raise production and make things worse. Admit it, Vaughan, all you'm really saying is officials should be bosses' men and do what they'm told, right or wrong. Well, not me. I'll go back on the face first.'

Back at home Lily looked at him with the air of one seeing him for the first time. 'Would you really, Davey? Do that out of principle? Some a the colliers would run you ragged.'

He smiled. 'With my own muscles and your brothers to keep 'em off? Don't be soft, Lil. It's always amazin' how people recognize a man of principle when he can punch harder than them. Anyhow, they'm not daft. Most a them would realize exactly why I was doing it. Hope I'd get a couple more deputies to join me. In the meantime, at least I seem to have stopped old Vaughan with his talk of a new union for the officials.'

'D'you think it will come to another lock-out, then?'

'Can't see any way around it. We ent gonna be subsidized much longer, and when that stops, phhtt – down goes the money, up goes the hours.'

The trouble had been bubbling ominously since June 1925, when the coal owners had announced that current wage agreements would end in a month. The miners, galvanized to militancy again for the first time since their defeat in 1921, rejected the notice and called on the other trades unions of

Britain for backing. They got it, and by early July the coal companies were threatened with a nationwide stop on all coal movement. With hours to spare, the Conservative prime minister Stanley Baldwin stepped in. He announced an enquiry into the whole situation and offered to subsidize the miners' wages to current levels until a conclusion had been reached.

But work force and management alike knew it was no more than a postponement. The unions watched with mounting suspicion as the enquiry commission was appointed without any miners' representatives, while the Government formed a body called the Organization for the Maintenance of Supplies, and the right-wing national press launched into an unprecedented anti-union, anti-miner propaganda campaign. While the enquiry was in session striking miners in the West Wales anthracite coalfield were jailed, and Communist Party members arrested for sedition.

Now, in the early spring of 1926, almost everyone involved in the coalfields knew what was coming. Lily sat at the window of the front room in her comfortable house, and watched the paper boy open the front gate, his bag already undone to disgorge the *Daily Herald*. Moments later the paper thudded on the doormat and she went out to collect it.

SAMUEL COMMISSION REJECTS MINERS' CASE

screamed the headline. Lily felt sick. Almost dreamily, she put out her hand and stroked the fat pitch-pine newel post at the bottom of her handsome staircase. Something told her it would not be hers for much longer. There had been no newel post – no banisters, either – in the Walters' house in the Ranks. No need. The staircase was so narrow the walls of the adjoining rooms acted as supports to anyone mounting the stairs. That front hall with its stained-glass door panel and those barley-sugar twisted balusters up the staircase had always been her little secret symbol of the improvement in her standard of living. She was no Margaret Ann or Rose, frankly worshipping any sign of material respectability, but somehow that staircase had reassured her that her son's day would be better than her father's had been. Now she was not so sure.

She called up the stairs: 'Tommy, love, hurry up out of bed, now. We're going down to meet Dada from the pit. There's something in the paper he'll want to know about.'

The news cast a pall of uncertainty over the whole valley, but it did not last long. In less than a month, the coal owners posted their demands. The working day was to be lengthened from seven hours to eight for a six-day week, and wages were to be slashed to 1921 levels. There would no longer be any guaranteed minimum wage level, even after the cuts.

In a sense the coal companies had done the militants' job for them. The conditions were so appalling that the most timid, impoverished colliers swarmed to support the union. Arthur Cook, the charismatic new general secretary of the Miners' Federation of Great Britain, stumped the country in drumming up further support, endlessly repeating the mesmeric slogan, 'Not a penny off the pay, not an hour on the day!'

The miners were listening, but no one else appeared to be paying attention. Frenzied negotiations started in Westminster between the miners' leaders and the coal owners, with the Government as mediator, but they achieved nothing. At midnight on April 30 the owners locked out a million miners, from every pit in the country. From then on only safety men were underground.

The TUC had been in almost continuous session since negotiations had broken down between Government, coal owners and miners on April 29. At noon on Saturday May 1 its executive conference assembled to open the written replies to its call for a General Strike. The first letter pledging full support came from the Asylum Workers' Union. As their decision was read out, Walter Citrine, the TUC General Secretary, turned to his assistant and said: 'My God, and no one laughed . . . '

Speaker after speaker rose to rally the unions to the miners' cause, and the pitch of the meeting rose to fevered heights, finally igniting to the echoes of the brass bands passing outside the meeting hall en route to the traditional Mayday rally in Hyde Park. The delegates rose to their feet and roared out 'The Red Flag'. As they poured out into the street to mingle with the last of the Mayday marchers, one of the railwaymen's delegates murmured to his neighbour: 'We're committing mass suicide.'

But no one was listening to him either. By then the taste of blood was on everyone's tongue and they were on their way to war.

Lily was a founder-member of the wives' support committee. 'Meddling in politics!' grumbled Margaret Ann. 'In my time that was men's work, and we kept away from it. You know what happened last time you got tied up with that sorta thing. Could of got killed under a police horse if your David hadn't shoved you out from under.'

'And no doubt if I had, you'd have sent a message of sympathy to the bloody horse!' Lily was not in a mood to be trifled with. 'Really, Mam, you lost our Dad to these sods just a few years back, nobody have given you a penny compensation, our Emrys went last year; any of the other boys, or my David, could get it tomorrow, and you're trying to tell me it ent women's business? Who do mourn them when they'm gone? Not the coal owners, that's for sure!'

'You can stop practising your rabble-rousing speeches on me an' all. The day I see you on a platform I'll die of shame.' Margaret Ann paused for a moment, as a terrible thought struck her. 'You know they put a woman in jail with them Bolshies they locked up down Ammanford last month? Oh, Lil, promise me you won't get involved!'

'Not a chance, Mam. If I did that, *I'd* be the one who died of shame. It's my husband and my brothers out in the firing line, and I'm buggered if they'm going on their own.'

'Will you watch your language? Honestly, you'll have me in an early grave. You don't see our Rose joining your commit-tees, do you, or Sal or Maisie? And you won't, neither.'

Lily made a disgusted face. 'Oh, I know I'll never get our Rose at it. She'll be too damned busy scrubbing her step and thanking the Lord Albert ent bringing home trails of coaldust any more. But Sal and Maisie's a different kettle of fish. I'm going in to see Maisie in a minute and I'll sort Sal out when I go back up Newbridge.'

Margaret Ann was desperate now. 'No, Lil, I forbid you! Not three women in the family . . . I couldn't stand it . . . '

'All right then – make it four. Join us. You'm our mother, you should be there too.'

Margaret Ann was almost sobbing now. 'I can't stand no more of this. I'm going up our Rose's. At least she do talk a bitta sense.'

'Aye. I bet you'll have a lovely chat about the colour of her new curtains. Or won't she get them now Albert is being inconsiderate enough to get himself locked out of work – him and nine hundred and ninety-nine thousand, nine hundred and ninety-nine others?'

Her mother whirled away from her and slammed out of the house. Lily gazed after her, shaking her head. 'You'll never learn to fight the bosses, will you Mam?' she said.

Tommy, who had been next door playing with Haydn's children, toddled into the room. 'Fight the bosses, fight the bosses!' he echoed jubilantly.

Lily sighed. 'Aye, that's right, kidda, you get a bitta practice in,' she said. 'You'm going to have to remember that every day for the next few weeks.'

Overnight the Western Valley became a place of silence. No five o'clock morning whistle to wake the men; no clatter of hobnails on paving stones in the dark pre-dawn as they set off for the pit. The winding engines were still and the overhead lines no longer trundled trucks of small coal up the mountainside to the new tip. Old miners who had lived all their lives with the steady throb of the industry wrapped round them looked around uneasily from time to time, troubled that something was not quite normal. For many of them nothing would ever be normal again.

David came off his shift as a safety man on Sunday morning, bursting with news of the General Strike. 'All the other unions is going to support us,' he said. 'We'll beat the buggers yet. Day after tomorrow the whole country will be stopped in its tracks.'

At midnight on May 3 Britain ground to a halt.

CHAPTER TWENTY-THREE

London

Neville and Pearl were sprawled across the vast white leather sofa in Bethan's drawing room. James was pouring drinks and talking to Bobby Balfour as he did so. Bobby's girlfriend, Ethel, was looking through the stack of new records beside the radiogram.

'Looks like the races will be off tomorrow, then, Jimmy-boy,' said Neville. 'Waddaya gonna do without your little flutter?'

James looked up, apparently surprised at the notion of any sporting event being cancelled. 'Off? Why on earth should they be?'

Neville laughed. 'You must be joking, old son! The whole country grinding to a sickenin' halt, an' all that rubbish – can't see 'em running special race trains down to Ascot for the likes of us!'

'We could always go by car. Where there's a will . . . I shouldn't think the bookies will be on strike – essential national industry and all that.' He paused momentarily, as if trying to decide whether he would tell them something, then said: 'As a matter of fact, if you *do* go, it'll be without me. I've volunteered to do my bit against this bunch of mindless louts.'

Bethan stiffened. She had managed to avoid thinking about the miners until now, carefully ignoring the probability that it was her brothers who were locked out of their work place, her mother who no longer had any money coming in. It dawned on her that it was going to be harder to look the other way now the whole country was involved.

James was speaking again. 'Talked to a couple of my business pals today and they say the Government will need all the help it can get. If we rally round we can keep the country running until we've taught the workers a lesson. What about you, Neville? Fancy driving a Number Eleven for a few days?'

'Is that what you're going to be doing? said Neville.

'Partly – but they've asked me to play more of an organizing role. I'll be part of a team in Public Transport HQ – deploying resources and all that.'

'Well, well, well.' Neville's tone was admiring. 'That doesn't sound as if it was put together overnight. Sounds to me as if Uncle Stanley an' Uncle Winston an' a couple o' the other old boys in the know have been sounding out chaps they can trust in advance.'

James smiled, a hint of cockiness in his stance as he strode back across the room with the drinks. 'Mum's the word, but yes, we were prepared for something like this.'

We? thought Bethan. He sounds like the bloody king! She tried to subdue the instinctive resentment that bubbled up, but it was hard going. Ethel minced over from the radiogram. 'Oh, Jimmy, it does sound exciting!' she said. 'I don't suppose there's anything useful we little girls can do?'

James's grin broadened as he looked at her snowy hands with their long, red-painted nails. 'Well, there's a canteen going to be set up next to the emergency food distribution depot in Hyde Park. By tomorrow it'll be full of society women, peeling potatoes to feed all our eager lads, but I can't see that appealing to you, old thing . . . '

Her smile faltered, but she was still bound up in the glamour of the moment. 'There must be something else. Why, I can drive, too! Maybe you'd let me have one of those nice red buses all to myself.'

Neville snorted with laughter. 'Christ, Ethel, I've driven along Knightsbridge in an Austin Seven with you at the wheel before now and it scared me rigid. You'd be shedding passengers every time you went round a corner! Stick to something on terra firma, for God's sake!'

They discussed Ethel's talents at length before deciding she would be a suitable candidate to join Lady Diana Cooper's team of volunteers who would sit up all night to hand-fold copies of *The Times* emergency strike issue. Pearl, who had been a telephonist before she met her rich bookmaker, was assigned by James to manning a switchboard at London Transport. Neville and Bobby both declared their intention to drive buses. Almost as one, they turned to Bethan.

'And what's our little Welsh daffodil going to do for the war effort?' said Bobby.

'Obviously Beth will use her skills as a nurse,' said James. 'It wouldn't surprise me if there was serious violence once things start warming up.' He dropped his voice portentously. 'The troops are already standing by, you know. If the Reds start anything the streets will be running with blood. We'll be setting up emergency first-aid posts all over the place. I'll sort something out for you first thing in the morning, Beth.'

After that the talk ranged over what momentous times they were living in, how ridiculous it was for working men to think their employers could pay them high wages when there were no profits coming in, and how fortunate they were to have the British spirit to rely on in such a time of national crisis. Bethan had remained silent until now, but the last remark provoked her to say: 'I suppose the strikers don't count as British?'

Neville looked vaguely surprised. 'Sorry, pet, I don't quite follow . . . '

'Well, this famous British spirit we're going to use to defeat them. They're British too. Perhaps they have enough of it to defeat *us*.'

James's good humour dissolved. 'Really, Beth, you talk through your hat at times! These chaps are all right if you show 'em who's boss, but without a strong lead they just disintegrate. I've seen it time and again down at the plant.'

'. . . Which, no doubt, will be out on strike tomorrow with all the rest, leaderless or not.'

He flushed and glared at her. 'You haven't the faintest idea what you're talking about.' He glanced ostentatiously at his watch, then said in a tone of forced good cheer: 'Well, boys and girls, I know it's early for us by our usual standards, but we'll need to be early birds in the morning. One more drink to our sucess, then off you all go.'

After he had seen them out, he came back, scowling, to

Bethan. 'A fine support you turn out to be!' he said. 'That sort of talk can murder people's morale. If you feel that way over the next few days, I'll thank you to keep your views to yourself!'

'Why? Are you afraid my careless talk will have you arrested as a traitor?'

'I quite fail to understand you, Beth. You have everything a girl could possibly want; you never have to do a stroke of work, just swan off to that tin-pot charity of yours in North London, and then you start talking Bolshie nonsense the first chance you get. I'd like to see one of your precious workers setting you up like this.'

She laughed bitterly. 'A set-up like this would keep a working family for the rest of their lives. But maybe they give each other something better than money.'

'Oh, spare me the violins! What have you ever needed from me that you didn't get?'

Her mind jolted back to the previous summer, and the train journey to Switzerland at the end of her French holiday. He had paid for the abortion in a very expensive clinic, but had hurried home to England and left her to travel to Geneva alone. Pressure of business, he had said . . . She thought of all the times since then, when she had tried to explain to him that her life since living with him had been little more than an empty shell, and of how he had cut her off the moment she referred to any emotion that ran deeper than amusement or sexual excitement. She thought of her inability to share with him the rising sense of fulfilment she got from working at the birth-control clinic in the Holloway Road, because she knew instinctively he would forbid her to continue or dismiss it with a sneer. And she said: 'Happiness, James. Only happiness.'

She stood up and moved away, into the bedroom, stripping off the expensive dinner gown – white like the sofa – and removing the diamond ear clips which had cost him a miner's salary for a year. Slipping on a silk dressing-gown, she went into the bathroom and began to clean off her make-up. What would she say to him when she returned to the bedroom? Why hadn't she seized her self-respect last year or the year before, and told him no luxury was worth the price he extracted?

No wonder she was eternally discontented. There was

nothing in her life to feel contented about. Bethan remembered telling her sister Lily that she could survive only by leaving the Valleys. For the first time in her life she began to wonder if that, too, had been self-deception. When she left them all in their little enclosed community, she had almost pitied Lily. Now she began to wonder if, after all, the older girl was not leading a richer, fuller life. 'Well, I shall never know now, that's for sure,' she told her reflection in the bathroom mirror.

She lingered as long as possible in the bathroom, reluctant to face the inevitable confrontation with James. Something told her that tonight's row would be the last they ever had. But when she finally emerged he was still out in the drawing room. She could hear him moving about, heard the telephone click as he replaced the receiver. Moments later he stuck his head round the door.

'I've decided I shall be more useful if I'm over at the control centre in Regent's Park for start of business in the morning,' he said. 'I'm driving over there now. I've left my direct number on the table by the phone. You must do as you think fit tomorrow, but if you come to your senses and want to do something useful, just give me a call.' He did not kiss her good-bye.

It was hours before Bethan slept, and when she did, she dreamed of her father. He was calling her, in an awful, muffled voice, from behind the wall of dust and rock which had killed him. As his voice grew louder a rising panic filled her sleeping mind. Please don't let the wall fall down, she prayed. I don't want to see his dead face. I don't want to see him ashamed of me . . .

She woke, sweating, and it was a beautiful May morning, with pale sunshine filtering in through the white muslin curtains. She laughed shakily as she made herself coffee, tried to banish the heart-squeezing image of the dark dream as she took a shower. And all the time one thought stayed with her. I wasn't afraid of how he'd look, dead, I was afraid of seeing him ashamed of me . . .

It was shortly after seven. She dressed hurriedly and escaped into the quiet street. Knowing James as she did, she suspected

231

it was only a matter of time before he telephoned her and more or less ordered her to do something in support of the anti-strikers. He would never be content to leave it up to her. If she disappeared for a while, he would be powerless to make her do anything . . .

Bethan began walking without any clear aim in mind except to put a healthy distance between herself and the Mayfair flat. Normally this would have been the beginning of the morning rush hour. But Piccadilly was remarkably quiet, with only a trickle of cars disturbing the unearthly peace. Judging from what James had told the others last night it would be short-lived. He had said every car-owner in the south-east would be heading for central London, offering lifts to the loyal workers who were prepared to try walking to their places of employ-ment. It appeared he had been right. As she moved eastward towards Trafalgar Square and the Strand more and more cars appeared on the streets, all crammed full, many stopping here and there to disgorge a couple of passengers outside a shop or office. Then the lorries started – greengrocers' delivery trucks and builders' supply vehicles, today pressed into service as public transport. In the Strand she watched as about half-a-dozen giggling typists dismounted from the open back of a lorry, flashing an inordinate amount of leg as they clambered to the ground.

Bethan began to wonder how the hospitals would manage. Presumably, as suppliers of an essential service, their workers would be exempt from the general strike call. In any case the nurses were not unionized unless things had changed radically since her day. But how would they get there? Many lived in the adjoining nurses' homes, but plenty did not, and practically all the auxiliary staff lived out. Bethan wondered if she could be of some use at St Thomas's. It would be better than strike-breaking in one of those odious canteens . . . She had half made up her mind to turn back along the Strand towards Westminster Bridge and the hospital, when as if anticipating her idea, a bus trundled into view. A hearty-looking young man clad in a herringbone tweed jacket was at the wheel. Next to him was another in plus-fours.

The normal destination board of the vehicle had been removed – instead, on one side was a sign which read:

232

THIS BUS GOES ANYWHERE YOU LIKE
NO FARES AND KIND TREATMENT
JOYRIDES TO THE EAST END

A matching notice on the other side said:

THE DRIVER OF THIS BUS IS
A STUDENT OF GUY'S HOSPITAL.
THE CONDUCTOR IS A STUDENT OF GUY'S.
ANYONE WHO INTERFERES WITH EITHER IS
LIKELY TO BE A PATIENT OF GUY'S.

As Bethan digested the announcement the driver's companion yelled out: 'As I live and breathe, it's the beautiful Bethan Walters! Bethan, my dear, I haven't seen you for years! How about a ride with us for King and Country?'

She had not changed her mind about the strike-breakers, but she was so relieved to see someone who had no connection with her life as James Norland's personal assistant that she smiled broadly at the speaker.

'Alex – Alex Harrison! What are you doing at Guy's? You were a St Thomas's man when I knew you!'

'Times change, m'dear. Didn't quite complete my little educational programme at the postgrad school and a while later Guy's said they'd let me have a second try at it over there. So here I am . . . What have you been doing with yourself in the meantime?'

'Oh, nothing very important, I – '

There was an angry blast from two cars which were snarled up behind the bus and Harrison jumped down from his seat. 'Come on, up you get between me and George, and you can tell us as we go. You can even be our honorary conductress afterwards, if you like.'

He handed her up into the middle of the long, open front seat, then jumped up beside her and George drove off eastward.

'Are you really doing joy rides to the East End?' she asked, curious about how much of a public service that might be.

Alex laughed. 'Haven't much choice, old girl. I expect it will be different once things get going, but the fact is, there aren't that many people in the centre of London to ferry about at

233

present. I suspect they're all still walking in from Penge or somewhere.'

'Then why don't you take the bus down to Penge and bring them in?'

'Don't be silly – that wouldn't be fun at all! No, we'll kick around up here for a bit and when they start arriving in central London we shall spring into action. In the meantime, milady, how about a quick trip to the Far East? At least we shall learn a little about what's going on.'

'What about the passengers? Won't they object?'

'Shouldn't think so. There are two young women who want to get to a bank in Cheapside, so we're going their way, and a grand chap who wants to know what's going on in the docks and is happy to go anywhere down there. Other than that, we're empty.'

At first they passed a swelling stream of makeshift transport bringing in everyone from stockbrokers' clerks to waitresses. Everywhere young women were swinging their legs over the sides of lorries and pony-carts, and eager young men were driving anything with an engine and some carrying capacity. It all had the atmosphere of a larky daytrip to the seaside.

Alex surveyed the scene with satisfaction and said: 'It heartens a man to see the British in crisis. Only we could turn a Red revolution into a charabanc excursion!'

But by the time they reached the far edge of the City, the atmosphere had changed. The hurrying office workers and chirpy waitresses were long gone. Now they entered the first of the residential streets of the East End. Bethan had never ventured this far, but at least she had seen the fringes of London poverty around the Holloway Road clinic. It quickly became clear that George and Alex had never suspected such places existed.

After a while, George said: 'I never realized there were still so many horses in London. To judge by the amount of dung in these streets, they haven't heard about the internal combustion engine down here yet.' It was said in a tone of forced jollity, but Bethan noticed he was looking considerably less assured than he had half an hour before. After a long pause he added: 'What bothers me a bit is seeing those children running around in it without shoes. Can't do them a lot of good . . .'

'Aren't you going to say anything else, George?' she asked gently.

'What? What should I say?'

'Well, I don't think they *choose* to run about it in barefoot. I think perhaps it's something to do with their parents not having money to buy them shoes. And perhaps *that* has something to do with the miners refusing to work for less money. The entire population doesn't go dancing at the Embassy Club every evening, you know.'

'Yes, but dammit, why do the parents drink like fish in that case? That's what causes this squalor, you know!' He was beginning to bluster and Bethan realized she had better stop baiting him if she wanted to stay aboard the bus. In any case, she reflected darkly, who was she to take a high moral tone? She had spent a couple of years relaxing on a cushion of silk stockings, gin and hand-made chocolates. Hardly a champion of the deprived . . .

Their conversation became more and more sporadic as they drove deeper into the East End. Until now they had only caught glimpses of the real squalor as they glanced down side turnings while driving along Whitechapel High Street. Now they plunged into the heart of dockland, down Leman Street and Cable Street, then in a long loop back to Commercial Road and the West India Dock Road. They were caught in the heart of deprivation such as none of them had ever seen. The two young men were grim-faced and silent. Bethan was fighting off tears.

Finally George said: 'Perhaps this wasn't such a bright thing to do after all, Alex. I confess I feel ever so slightly ashamed of myself. Perhaps we should call it a day and go back to the depot.'

'No,' said Harrison. 'I want to see it through now. Since we've started to wake up to what it's like, let's go on and see what's happening at the docks. I agree on one thing, though. If this gets any worse I shall be joining the poor snipes.'

The Old Jamaica tavern and the Customs House flanked the gates to the West India Dock. On either side of the gates was a tableau worthy of Gilbert and Sullivan. Immediately outside, orderly pickets were parading with placards calling on their fellows to support the miners. The men's clothes were unspeakably shabby, and there were few signs of the big bruising docker popularly portrayed in the press. These were mainly stunted men with gaunt cheeks and sunken chests. In stark contrast to their dress was the mass of Great War medals worn by most of them. Inside the dock gates a troop of well-nourished soldiers in immaculate uniforms were at work unloading flour from a cargo vessel. To encourage them in their work, the military band of the Brigade of Guards was drawn up in perfect formation on the quay, playing 'Poor Little Butterfly'. The trio on the bus ground to a halt and gaped at the scene.

Two sentries outside the Customs House clicked smartly to attention as an officer bustled towards them. 'Come to see if you can be useful?' he asked. 'Good chaps – what we like to see . . . but we have it all under control now . . . must do our bit, you know.'

'May we drive in?' asked Alex. 'I'd like to look around.'

'Mmm, don't think we could run to that . . . outside my orders, you know. It's a high-security operation, this. Best stay here.' He lowered his voice. 'They may look harmless, but I have it on good authority that some of these chaps are Bolshie agitators!' He turned and moved off to deploy another group of men who had appeared from a hut along the dock.

The man who had been travelling inside the bus emerged at this point. He strolled over to a police sergeant who was pacing back and forth between the two sentries. 'Hi, Harry, remember me?' he said.

'Good God – Major Gibbs!' The policeman was half-way to a salute when he realized neither of them was dressed appropriately for such an acknowledgement. 'What're you doing here, Sir?'

'Back with the newspaper now. It's a lot better than the Somme, eh, Harry?'

The sergeant looked gloomy. 'I dunno as them poor devils on that picket line will agree by the time this lot ends, Sir. I gotta feeling this might be a war before we've finished.'

'Well, let's hope not . . . any chance of me and my young friends nipping in for a look round?'

'Don't see why not, seeing as you're an old comrade an' all . . . just don't take the bus, or get in 'is nibs's way. He was

General Staff from '14 to '18, so he throws his weight about a lot, now, to show he's a born leader of men.'

'We'll be souls of discretion, Harry, never fear.' The man turned to the trio in the bus. 'Coming, gentlemen and lady? I don't know whether there'll be anything more to see, but I never could resist going where I'm not welcome.'

Gibbs had heard reports early that morning that strikers around the Hyde Park area had actually helped volunteers who were stacking food crates at the emergency supply depot. 'It seems our old Etonians weren't too clever when it came to manoeuvring heavy objects,' he said, smiling ruefully. 'The pickets took the attitude that as it was food, it was all right to help out. I'm curious to see whether the dockers feel the same.'

He soon got his answer. Further along the wharves, another detachment of steel-helmeted troops were trying to shift a consignment of heavy crates full of margarine. A group of picketing dockers could see them through a locked iron gate, and jeered every time one of the soldiers staggered beneath his burden. 'Sling yer 'ook, Tommy, and thank Christ for King an' country!' yelled one of the pickets. 'You'd never get a job in civvy street, tell yer that for nuffink!' His companions cheered raggedly in agreement.

'I thought TUC policy was to allow food through,' Gibbs said to the docker who had shouted. The man looked at Gibbs as if he were mentally deficient. 'We ain't trying to starve people, but we're not plannin' ter starve ourselves, neither, mate. How long d'yer think we'll keep going if we let the bosses feed theirselves as though nuffink's going on dahn 'ere?'

Nevertheless, given the presence in such strength of the Brigade of Guards, Bethan was left wondering at the peaceful atmosphere. She recalled the inflammatory effect of even a mention of troops on middle-aged miners in Wales in her childhood, and wondered whether they, too, were standing back and letting the soldiers through with essential supplies. This entire scene had an air of unreality: dockers armed with nothing more than placards, held back by armoured cars to protect strike-breaking troops. That was the moment when Bethan decided it was a lost cause. Who could hope to win a war in which no blows were being struck by the side which had started the action?

237

But she had made a few premature assumptions. The mood of the pickets was changing by the minute as news reached them of what was happening elsewhere in London.

When Philip Gibbs had finished his investigation of what was going on, Bethan's companions were ready to leave. 'It's giving me the creeps, rather,' said Alex. 'I expected it to be more – more riotous, somehow. But I've seen more trouble at an ordinary Mayday rally.'

They went back to find the bus, and that was when the trouble started. When they re-emerged through the dock gates, the friendly police sergeant was nowhere to be seen and the sentries had turned ostentatiously to face each other across the entrance. The bus outside had been stripped of its two hand-written notices. Suddenly the dockers did not seem so scrawny and undersized after all.

'Fought yer'd come dahn 'ere for a little joyride, did jer?' said one, ambling lazily forward and brandishing one of the bus notices. 'Gonna give us lot kind treatment, are yer, or are yer gonna put us in Guy's as patients?'

'Oh, shit!' murmured George. 'What a time to discover the spirit of the masses!' He was a tall man, and drew himself up as high as he could manage. He towered over the docker, but the man was built squat and powerful and George half expected to be picked up bodily and tied in a knot.

'It was nothing personal,' George announced, as calmly as he could. 'Just trying to keep things moving for ordinary people. You're free to strike. They're free to go to work if they wish.'

'Oh, 'ow quaint, a yoomanist!' crowed the docker. 'Fair crack a the whip fer all of us, eh lad? Well, since we're talkin' freedom, whaddayer fink a my freedom to screw this sign up and shove it so far up yer arse it comes aht yer eyeballs?'

Bethan had progressed from a spurt of terror when she first saw the pickets around the bus, to a strange calm that now pushed her forward. 'You're mad if you do that!' she said. 'Stop fighting them with their own weapons. You're better than that, surely?'

'Aw, hark at Lady Muck 'ere!' said the picket who had taken down the other notice. 'We got anuvver piece a paper here, lady. If yer like I can do the same wiv it as Don 'ave got planned for yer gentleman friend.'

'Oh, that'd make a lot of sense too, wouldn't it? They're down here because of me, if you must know – me and that man over there.' She gestured at Philip Gibbs. 'He's a journalist. I'm a miner's daughter. Go on, screw up your paper and I'll whip off my drawers while you're doing it, and then you can give me the treatment and send me home to the Valleys to tell them all about dockers' solidarity with the miners.'

She had started out with a desperate desire to shock them away from wreaking vengeance on the men and herself, but half-way through it she was carried away by what she had been saying. 'I'm the same bloody class as you!' she yelled in the leading docker's face. 'Are you going to punish me just because I came aboard a scab bus to see what was going on?'

The docker stepped back a pace. 'Well . . . what sorta way is that ter carry on?' He lurched forward again. 'Tell yer somefink for nuffink. If *my* girl said what you just told me in front of a party a men, I'd beat her senseless.'

Bethan played her trump card. 'Then she's damned lucky to have a father to do it. Mine was killed in a pit accident in 1919.'

Silence descended like a spring shower. George and Alex, as chastened as the dockers, edged forward and got into the cab of the bus. Philip Gibbs handed Bethan up to Alex on the front seat, then turned back to the dockers. 'I'm on no one's side,' he said quietly. 'I simply want to report what happens.' He patted the docker on the shoulder with something close to sympathy. 'Try not to get overheated before you know exactly what they're doing to you . . . you have more chance of winning in the end, then.'

They made no move to stop him as he went to the back of the bus and got on. George got the vehicle going and edged away through the crush of pickets, almost down to stalling in his effort to make sure he did not hit anyone. 'Don't turn back the way we came,' whispered Bethan. 'Maybe some of them have gone to ambush us up there. Try the opposite direction – it's not the way they'll expect us to go, but it's bound to come out somewhere along the main roads we came through.'

George took a circuitous route that kept them away from the strikers but also showed them more of the squalid streets. As he slowed down at the top of North Street to turn westward again along the East India Dock Road, two filthy children, barefoot and ragged and with runny noses in spite of the warm day, peered up at them from the gutter like small, timid animals. George shuddered. 'I'll never make sneering remarks about the Great Unwashed again,' he murmured, adding, with rising anger, 'If I had the guts, I'd round up a crowd of those damned debs and Bentley boys tomorrow and drive them down here to see what we're doing to people. Perhaps they'd feel differently, then!'

Alex agreed gloomily. 'Trouble is, I'm not sure we'd get out alive again. Wasn't such a good idea to come down here, was it? I don't think I shall be volunteering for any amateur heroics after today. They can keep their damned bus.'

'That goes for me too,' said George. 'Let's take the thing back now, shall we? I think we'd both be more useful up at Guy's, filling in for people who can't get there.'

Bethan felt her heart lift slightly. At least here were two who had come to understand there was no great adventure in treading on people who were already oppressed . . . Momentarily she savoured her victory over the pickets, with its incidental bonus of making George and Alex think a little more clearly. But then she began to wonder how much better she was. Abruptly she was overwhelmed by self-disgust. What she had told those men was true. She *was* the daughter of a man who had been killed underground. That had been enough for them, because they could not conceive of the child of such a family betraying it.

She had won her escape under false pretences. If she went back to James now, she would be lost for ever. There must be a way out – and there must be a way she could help the people she had seen today. She turned to George. 'Before you take the bus back, would you mind awfully taking me up to the Holloway Road? There's something terribly important I have to do. And then, if you could drop me somewhere central . . . '

George brightened at the prospect of an errand which might take his mind off what had just happened. 'Pleasure, old girl. What're you doin', running away from home?'

'You never spoke a truer word,' said Bethan.

CHAPTER TWENTY-FOUR

Joyce Gladstone gave a little cry of surprise when she saw Bethan. 'Really, my dear, I know today was your afternoon in, but none of us expected you! The circumstances are hardly – er – normal, are they?'

'I know, Joyce, but I needed to ask you something rather urgently. Remember the full-time job you mentioned at the new clinic? Is it still available?'

Hope leaped in the other woman's eyes. 'Still available? Too much so, I'm afraid. Only one applicant so far, and she was totally unsuitable to run the place. I'm afraid we still carry too much of a stigma for the average trained middle-class woman to touch us.'

'How about me?'

'I was hoping you would say that. I'll have to speak to Dr Andrews and Mrs McColl, of course – you know it's a committee decision – but, Bethan, you also know they'd jump at the offer.'

'In that case I'm all yours.'

'The salary is terribly modest – basic hospital Sister's money and without the live-in privileges.'

'Well, accommodation is hardly expensive in Hackney, is it? Maybe I could get something right next to the clinic. It would save travelling.'

'You sound as if that side of it might be somewhat urgent.'

'You could say that. If you're certain that they'll give me the job, I plan to move out of my present flat today.'

Joyce laughed. 'You're mad! How on earth do you propose to go hunting for lodgings with the strike on? Nothing is functioning properly.'

'Yes . . . you're right. Look, I can't stay where I am, that's all I know. I shall just have to find an hotel for a few days and then see what can be done.'

'If you don't mind mucking in, you can always come to us. It's a bit chaotic, but we have a small spare room.' At that point it occurred to her that Bethan, normally very calm, was in a highly nervous state. 'And if you want a shoulder to cry on, I'll provide one. Otherwise, no one will pry.'

'Oh, Joyce, thank you so much! I don't think I've ever needed friends as I do now – and d'you know, I've only just realized I don't really have any?'

The other woman was indignant. 'I hope you consider me a friend. I've always regarded you as one.'

'I am glad. I thought you just saw me as some silly flapper doing a bit for charity.'

'My dear girl, you're far too good at it for that! I knew you'd realize what you wanted to do eventually. I'm only glad it's happened now.'

Bethan managed a shaky laugh, and said: 'You'll never believe this, but I've got a number eleven bus outside, waiting to take me home! Shall I come back here when I've got my things together? I'll come in the car next time!'

'Yes, do. Don't worry if you're held up, I'll wait for you. And don't give this afternoon's session another thought. I suspect half our ladies won't arrive today anyway.'

Alex and George were becoming more cheerful with every mile they put between themselves and the East End. As they drove down New Bond Street George said: 'My God, I shall be glad to get off this bus! Always was a car chap, meself! After today, I'm staying well out of this strike business and sticking to what I know.'

'Me too,' said Alex. 'I don't think I'll ever look at a healthy child again without seeing those poor little devils in the gutter this morning.' He glanced appraisingly at Bethan. 'Meanwhile, you seem to be planning some prank of your own. What are you doing, joining the dockers?'

'Maybe I am . . . I'm certainly starting afresh. Ah, here we are. Hail and farewell, Brookville Court.'

'That sounds rather final.'

'It is, Alex. And the sooner I finish it, the better. Thanks for the lift, and thanks for the eye-opener. It was exactly what I needed.'

'Hmm, wish I could say the same for its effect on George and me!'

'I think maybe you could. Goodbye, Alex. I hope next time we meet it will be in happier circumstances.' She stood on tip-toe and kissed his cheek, gave a little wave to George in his high driving seat, and hurried into the block of flats.

Now she had decided to go, the place had no hold on her at all. She glanced around it, wondering why she had ever thought it glamorous. But then, she had once thought James Norland was glamorous too, and now she found the notion of even touching him again deeply repellent. She put the thought aside and began to look through the cupboards for the things she wanted to take.

Bethan was not at all like Lily. She had no intention of leaving behind the material fruits of her romance. It was unlikely she would ever be able to afford to buy such clothes and jewellery again, and what she could no longer wear would doubtless fetch some sort of price. If she was to live on a pittance in Hackney, she could at least surround herself with a little luxury.

She opened the roll-top desk in the drawing room. The car registration was in her name. So was the insurance. She had all the receipts for her jewellery. Unromantic, perhaps, but James had a thing about burglars and said one never knew when such things would be needed if any valuables were stolen. She packed car documents, jewellers' receipts and an insurance policy into a large leather vanity case along with her jewels. There couldn't be many women in Hackney with a couple of pairs of diamond earrings . . .

The clothes seemed even odder when she considered them in relation to her new home. She had not realized how many evening gowns she had . . . nor how many were white or en-crusted with elaborate embroidery. Hardly the sort of garments for supper at the fish-and-chip shop after a long session in the clinic!

Bethan sat down abruptly on the bed, clutching a scrap of apricot-coloured silk with a feathered hem and narrow rouleau straps. Oh, the night she'd worn that . . . they had danced until dawn, then James had walked her back through the sleeping streets of the West End and let her into this lovely flat. Until then she had just been a guest in the place he kept off Grosvenor Square. He had got it for her as a surprise – the best surprise she had ever received. That night she had thought she had everything, the man she loved, unlimited wealth and a future. A little sob escaped her. What on earth had gone wrong? Was her judgement so faulty that she had been deceived from the beginning about his feelings for her?

Reluctantly she was forced to admit she had been, and largely because she had wanted to be, rather than because he had misled her. Since the previous summer she had been refusing to confront the fact that whatever he might feel for her, it was not love. No man who loved her could have insisted she should have an abortion when she would have preferred to have the baby, then abandoning her with a bagful of money to go through it all alone.

Bethan realized to her shame that had he not behaved so abominably, she would have continued to deceive herself. 'Better for it to end now,' she said aloud. 'At least you're still young . . . ' Still young, yes, her heart mocked her, but where will you ever find another James Norland? One in a lifetime is unlikely enough for a girl like you. There'll never be another . . . Then she began to cry in earnest.

Fortunately the doorman at Brookville Court had turned up for work today. He made three trips to and from the flat to take away Bethan's luggage, and was clearly sceptical about her light-hearted reference to going to the country until the strike was over. She tipped him over-generously before it dawned on her that he was not thinking in terms of raising the alarm with James, but sympathizing at what he took to be her sensible flight before an imminent Bolshevik revolution.

Finally she was in her sporty little car, surrounded by mounds of expensive suitcases, and heading for the Holloway Road again. She felt deeply embarrassed about all the luggage. What on earth would Joyce Gladstone think of her?

Joyce merely burst out laughing. 'It's just as well I wasn't relying on a lift home from you, isn't it? Oh, Bethan, if you ever *do* tell me your story, I can see I shall be agog. You've obviously scaled the heights!'

Have I? wondered Bethan. If that was it, God help me. There must be something a bit better than that ahead of me . . .

The Gladstone house wrapped itself around her like a warm blanket. Edwin Gladstone, Joyce's husband, was yet another doctor, and Joyce had been his receptionist before she took on the administration of the Holloway Road clinic. He cared about it as passionately as she did – indeed their involvement had arisen from his determination to do something about the tragic cases of botched abortion and malnourished expectant mothers which constantly confronted him in his working-class practice.

They were a loving couple with three attractive children and a lodger, a young music student who lived in the roomy attic of their Georgian house. The children liked music as much as the student, it seemed, because there were instruments discarded here and there about the place. Books on every subject under the sun were spread on every available surface, and to judge by the collection of brushes in a jar on the kitchen window sill, someone fancied themselves as an amateur painter. Everywhere lay evidence of people living rich, happy lives which had nothing to do with the arid existence Bethan had so recently abandoned.

'No wonder you said it would be crowded!' she told Joyce. 'Are you sure you can fit me in? I don't want to make things impossible for you.'

'We don't understand the word impossible,' said Edwin Gladstone. 'If you could see what it is like when the children have friends staying during the holidays, you'd *really* understand overcrowding!' He chatted easily to her for a few more minutes and then went off to start his evening surgery. Joyce, seemingly effortlessly, conjured up the beginnings of an evening meal, set various pans to cook, then poured two sherries and led the way into the drawing room.

'How d'you manage to do so much?' asked Bethan. 'I knew you had children, but I always thought you must have a maid and a cook at the very least. Surely you don't do it all yourself?'

'No, I have help with the cleaning, but nothing else,' said Joyce. 'Edwin and I married under a bit of a cloud, without much cash. I learned to do it then and I never got out of the habit.' She chuckled. 'My dear, I was *so* unsuitable as a wife for a well-bred young medical student!'

'I can't believe that! You look like every mother-in-law's idea of the perfect wife.'

'Oh, I do now, but not then. Indian civil service family, out East for generations, you see . . . ' She lowered her voice to a melodramatic whisper. 'And a Babu great-grandmother back there somewhere . . . tut tut, the scandal! Fortunately for me, Edwin was just over twenty-one and he had a tiny trust income from his grandmother – otherwise he'd never have been able to afford to complete his studies without help from his parents.

'We married in the face of total family disapproval, but by the time he qualified I'd produced two of the children and they looked satisfactorily Anglo-Saxon, as well as being beautiful. So we embarked on a period of armed truce with his mother and father, which endured until they died. I confess I feel much happier now that neither of them is there lurking in the background. Even after they'd accepted me I was never more than a necessary evil. I used to get the most awful urge to speak with my mouth full or say ''pleased to meet you'' instead of ''how do you do?'' just to provoke them – and it would have. They were that bad! I'm far more relaxed nowadays.'

Bethan slid gratefully down into the big, comfortably unfashionable armchair and said: 'Oh, Joyce, I am so glad I found you! I seem to have been away from real people for years and years.'

Joyce Gladstone laughed. 'You're going to meet them again with a bang as soon as we get that clinic going! You would never believe what some of them get up to until you're responsible for the whole show. If I can get the other committee members to confirm you in the job some time tomorrow, you might care to spend the rest of this week shadowing what I do at Holloway Road. At least then you won't quite be thrown in at the deep end.'

PART THREE

His mouth is most sweet: yea, he is
altogether lovely. This is my beloved,
and this is my friend, O daughters
of Jerusalem.

Song of Songs
Ch. V, v. 16

CHAPTER TWENTY-FIVE

The Park Lane Dancing School was empty, except for Lexie Walters and Eddie Romano. Lexie crushed out her cigarette, stood up and smoothed the front of her skimpy-elegant fringed dance dress. 'Well, Eddie,' she said, 'unless you gimme a twirl, I'm in danger of spending the day as a wallflower. How about it?'

He smiled. 'Why not? There's bugger-all else to do, is there?'

She put a record on and they moved into a tango. When it finished a few minutes later she laughed and said: 'I gotta do that again. It's done me a power of good!' and went over to restart the record. 'You know, Eddie, you're the best dancer I ever ran into,' she told him when they finished. 'It's like some sorta poetry whizzing around a floor with you. I don't arf wish you were in the market for demo dancing in the clubs.'

He shook his head. 'I make quite enough here, thanks, Lexie. How's that partner of yours shaping up these days? He looked quite promising.'

'Oh, so-so, I suppose . . . No, to be fair, he's good. He's just not *you*, that's all. You're the best.'

'Coming from you, that's quite a compliment.'

She made a little bow with her head. 'Mutual, I'm sure. What a pity we're not in love with each other, Eddie.'

'On balance it's just as well. For one thing there's the little matter of my missis. For another, there's the fact I'm Jewish.'

'So nobody's perfect! What would that have to do with it?'

249

'I'm supposed to be Orthodox, Lexie. Even a nice *unmarried* Jewish boy would have trouble explaining away a shiksa bride to the rabbi . . . not to mention his momma.'

'Ah. Didn't realize.' She regarded him, perplexed. 'I never knew Romano was a Jewish name.'

'Sometimes, girl, you're as green as grass! Can you imagine Hyman Rabinowitz running a successful dancing school in the West End? No, Well he does. You're talking to him.'

She giggled. 'And to think I believed it was just me . . . everybody's at it.'

'At what?'

'Pretending to be something else. Meet Dolores Herero!'

'You must be kidding!'

Lexie shook her head. 'Wish I was, now. At the time I thought it'd fool everybody. I was fed up of being that pretty little half-caste piece from down the Bay, so when I came to London I thought I'd change my identity. I sound about as much like a Spaniard as the barber's cat, o' course, but I was so potty about getting into movies I forgot that the blokes I'd be seeing about it would be listening to me and hearing the Tiger Bay in my talk from the first minute. All it got me was a bit part underneath a fat producer.'

'I'm sorry, Lexie. That must have hurt.'

'Yeah. Suppose it did, really. Anyway, I'm over it now. I know I'll never be a big star or anything. At least I got outa the Bay.'

'Don't you ever miss it?'

'Sure. But how could I go back now? I'm happy at this job and my demo dancing, but I'm not exactly big-time, am I? I don't wanna go home a failure, that's all.'

'I know how you feel. Come on, let's have a quick drink, then we might as well close this place until the trouble's over. All our customers are too busy getting their kicks as bus drivers and special constables to come dancing this week.'

After she left the school Lexie felt at a loose end. She normally crackled with energy, and it had been two days now since she had done much dancing. She needed to let off steam. There was always the club tonight, but that might be just as bad . . . She wondered if Freddie Hunter, her partner, would make it.

Probably. He was hardly the type to go and stand up to big brawny strikers.

For three or four months Lexie had been supplementing her earnings from Eddie Romano's school by working as an exhibition dancer in Soho and Mayfair nightclubs. Her partner, Freddie Hunter, had worked as a part-time instructor at Harry's for a while, but then had decided he was destined for better things. He had been trying to break into West End stage musicals ever since, and did the exhibition dancing with Lexie to pay the rent while he was waiting. Appearing as Freddie and Alex, they made an attractive couple. Three or four clubs regularly gave them an evening spot for a good fee.

In normal circumstances tonight it would have been the Silvery Moon, an exclusive establishment in a back lane between Berkeley Square and New Bond Street. Lexie decided she might as well go there on the chance that Freddie would turn up. Otherwise she would be crazy with boredom by ten o'clock.

Freddie was there, but most of the usual clientele were not. The barman sighed when Lexie mentioned it. 'All too busy showing off how clever they are at driving trains, I expect!' he said. 'They make me bloody sick – think because it's a doddle for three or four days, there's nothing to doing it all your life. I'd like to see them try!'

Lexie's eyes widened. That wasn't a view one heard too often around these parts. She looked around surreptitiously to see if anyone had overheard. With the wrong customer about, Tony could lose his job for that.

But apart from herself and Freddie, there was only one other person near the bar. She glanced at him briefly, then looked again, and kept on looking. The man was well over six feet tall, and beautifully built. His dinner jacket was cut as though it had been moulded on him. He was the handsomest man Lexie had ever seen, and he was black. She almost choked on her drink. She had never seen a black man in a Mayfair nightclub before.

Before she could avert her eyes, he noticed her and came across. Lexie half expected a stream of abuse. Her astonishment had been all too obvious. But he was grinning. 'Don't act so surprised,' he said. 'I'm part of the entertainment.'

251

'Oh! I-I'm sorry I was so rude. That was unforgivable.'

'Yeah, but understandable too. You don't see many of us front of house. Even less so in the States.'

'I thought you must be American. What d'you do?'

'Singer-pianist. I'm the cabaret.' He looked around the empty room. 'Though if they don't start showing soon, I'll be singing along to the chairs and tables. What do you two do here?'

'We're dancers – exhibition ballroom stuff. It'll be just as bad for us. They usually put us on to encourage the people up on to the dance floor after we finish our turn.'

'I think not tonight, Josephine,' he said.

'No, dammit. And I only came along because I was bored at home.'

'Oh, thanks, Lexie – thanks a lot!' Freddie, who liked to pretend she had a crush on him, flounced.

'Don't tell me you'd have been here either if you hadn't hoped they'd pay us just for showing up.'

He looked stricken. 'Don't you think they will, then? I shan't last out the week if they don't.'

She softened, feeling sorry for him. 'I'm sure they will, Freddie. Stop worrying. It might be an idea to go and have a word with the manager, though. Pointless for us to hang about if they really don't want us.'

'While he's gone, come and listen to a little music,' said the stranger. 'By the way, I'm Larry Hines. I heard that guy call you Lexie. What's the rest?'

'Lexie Walters – Alex to the customers. Yes, I'd love a little music.' She followed him over to the white baby grand on the low stage, and sat beside him on the long piano stool.

Hines had a smooth, easy playing style which was wonderfully soothing. He riffled through a couple of slinky arrangements of current hits that were normally played to a more jazzy beat, then ran off a short intro and began to sing to Lexie:

> 'Show me the way to go home,
> I'm tired and I wanna go to bed.
> I had a little drink about an hour ago
> And it's gone right to my head.

No matter where I roam,
Over land, or sea, or foam,
You'll always hear me singing this song,
Show me the way to go home.'

He smiled at her as he finished. 'Somehow I gotta feeling that number suits you,' he said.

She stiffened. 'What a silly thing to say! I love London.'

'Do you? Do you really? D'you know, when I saw you standing up at that bar, I had you down for a little girl lost. I wonder where I got that impression.'

Abruptly Lexie decided pretence no longer mattered. She let her shoulders slump and leaned slightly against his comforting bulk. 'Who am I kidding? London's all right. I'm not. I've been here too long and got nowhere. I'm feeling old and tired and very far from home. You got it in one, Larry. That *is* my song. What do I do about it?'

'For a start, sit up straight and don't show the bastards they got to you,' he said quietly. Lexie glanced up and saw that a party of six people had just come in.

She stood up and smiled at him. 'You're quite a guy, Larry. If you have time to give a little thought to my problem during the evening, I'd be interested to hear what you think.'

'Here, or at your place?'

'That depends on your thoughts . . . See you later.' And she moved off across the dance floor to find Freddie.

The club filled up somewhat after that. By ten o'clock there were enough people for Freddie and Lexie to do their dance exhibition. By then Harry Lines had already done one session at the piano. The customers seemed to like his smooth, easy voice and his original arrangements of familiar tunes, and applauded warmly each time he finished a number.

'Mmm, I wouldn't mind going home with that myself, you lucky girl!' Freddie told her, staring admiringly at Larry.

'Tough – that one's a woman's man, so buzz off!' said Lexie. 'Did the manager say anything about another spot later this week?'

'Oh, yes. He thinks once the excitement of the first couple of days has worn off, they'll all want to get back to their old haunts to boast about what they've been up to during the strike, so he says he'd like us on Friday as well if we have a free night. How about it?'

'Count me in, darling. My dance card is completely empty.'

Freddie nodded towards Hines. 'I think that might be changing quite soon, dear.'

'I used to day-dream about men like you, when I was a sparky little girl going places,' she told him as they lay together in her attic bedroom in the small hours of the morning.

He smiled, the perfect white teeth flashing against the dark skin under the glow of the bedside lamp. 'What, large as life and twice as black?' he asked.

'Funny, I never thought about it until now, but that didn't come into it. Isn't it queer? I've had this thing about being black myself ever since kids teased me about it, but I never saw my knight in armour as any colour in particular – just perfect.'

'And I'm perfect? Just like that, a guy in a bar who plays piano? We know each other a few hours, you wind up in bed with me, and I'm perfect. How do I live with that?'

Lexie grinned at him. 'No reason why you should. It's my problem, not yours. All you need to do is enjoy it.'

'Now that I like! Speaking of which . . . '

Lexie had always approached sex with relish, but familiarity had bred contempt and for a year or two she had found more satisfaction in dancing with a good partner. Making love with Larry Hines was quite unlike anything else she had ever done, and she knew there would never be another like him again.

'You really are the most beautiful man I've ever seen,' she murmured, sliding a finger from his shoulder, down over the bulging pectorals and stroking his flat stomach.

'Flattery will get you everywhere, baby, and you're pretty special yourself.'

'So glad you think so. How'd you like to prove it?'

His body slid across hers and it felt as if they had always been locked together. Her legs curled around him and he entered her, smoothly, gently, becoming part of her almost imperceptibly. Lexie never wanted it to stop. His lips brushed deliciously across her throat, cheeks and eyelids, and he murmured: 'You only want me for my body . . . '

She giggled, happy as a child with a new toy. 'Well, it's a perfect body too, isn't it?'

It was not just his physical beauty and his imaginative, teasing love-making. He talked to her and he listened to her answers. He came from a world which was unlike anything Lexie knew, and he talked about it vividly and without self-consciousness. After that first night he came back to her room from the Silvery Moon every evening, and spent the days with her. He had been in England for two months, and the Silvery Moon was his last booking. He had intended to return to New York in mid-May, but the strike had drawn a question-mark over all plans and he was sufficiently involved with Lexie not to wish a quick end to the delay. But he never said anything about them sharing a future.

At first Lexie was unaware of anything lacking. Then she found herself hoping that the dispute would go on. Every morning she switched on the small wireless set by her window for the latest news bulletin. And every morning she caught herself sighing with relief that there was no sign of a settlement. That made her realize that she had no hopes that Larry would ask her to go back to America with him – or failing that, would ask her to write with a view to them getting together some time in the future. She knew instinctively that when he went it would be for ever.

Now that the idea was planted in her mind she could not let it rest. For their first few times together she had drifted off into a serene, undisturbed sleep every night after they had made love. But once her own imagination had put a term on their relationship she found it increasingly difficult to rest, instead lying for hours, gazing at his sleeping face as dawn slipped in through her high window.

When the end came it took her by surprise because the previous day's news had made the dispute sound more solid than ever. It was Larry's eighth day with her – she counted everything now in terms of days with and without Larry – and the ninth of the dispute. He had been going to see a fellow-musician who had been playing in a club in Soho since Easter. Lexie planned to meet him for lunch in an Italian restaurant in Greek Street. She swung in through the door of her room, laden with shopping, and realized she had forgotten to switch off the radio when she went out. As she started across to it the announcer was saying: 'First news that the strike was at an end came when the Miners' Federation issued a press release stating that the miners were no party, in any shape or form, to the cessation of the strike. Shortly afterwards, the Government made a statement confirming that the dispute was at an end.'

He went on to outline immediate plans to ease the mass return to work. Lexie did not hear him. She uttered a little moan and sank down on the bed. She was still sitting there, staring out of the window and crying silently, when Larry came looking for her almost two hours later.

He stayed until the end of the week. By then transatlantic sailings were practically back to normal and his original booking held good. He spent much of the time before his departure coaxing Lexie into acceptance of the inevitable.

After her first misery had subsided she was all apologies. 'I know you never promised me anything beyond now,' she told him. 'I know you never said you loved me, never pretended . . . I just kept hoping, that's all . . . '

'Hey, wait a minute. I never said I *didn't* love you, either, did I?' he said.

She glanced up at him and shook her head, too numb to answer. He took her in his arms and cradled her there like a tired child. 'Well, I do love you, so you can stop moping about that. But we'd never work together, Lexie – never in a thousand years.'

Her endless crying had given her hiccups. Now she tried vainly to stifle them as she answered him. 'O-of course n-not . . . n-not if you won't even t-try! Why sh-shouldn't it work?'

'Take it from me, honey, it won't. Look, there's no point discussing it now – it'll get us nowhere. I want you to get yourself together for tonight. You know we'll be busy at the club with all those rich bastards celebrating coming out on top . . . We got until Sunday – my ship sails Monday morning. On Sunday we'll have dinner somewhere special and then we'll talk, I promise. Until then, get this straight. I love you. I always will. And I'll never forget you. But with me you'd be unhappy for the rest of your life.' He put his fingers against her lips to seal off the immediate protest. 'Ssh, now, you better believe it. Now you just let me take care of you until Sunday, then I'll explain. Okay?'

She nodded again. He got up, went to the cupboard and took out the bottle of whisky she kept there. 'I think we'll both need a good solid slug a this to calm us down. Then I want you to lie down and rest until tonight.'

To her surprise, once she had accepted the inevitability of their parting, the remainder of the week passed as smoothly as their first few days together. It helped that both the club and Eddie's dancing school were busy again, and that she was fully occupied day and night. Sunday came almost before she was aware of it.

He made it a perfect day for her, waking her early with fresh bread and coffee from the little Italian shop around the corner, then taking her out on the river. Afterwards they strolled back to Soho and he made love to her for the last time – he was travelling to Southampton on the last train that night. By the time they turned out for dinner that evening, Lexie could have believed she was on her honeymoon had it not been for the underlying bittersweet sorrow of his impending departure.

Finally, as they ate dinner, he explained. 'I knew when I first saw you I should have kept right away – that you'd get hurt, and I would, come to that. But I couldn't, Lexie. You were too damned beautiful. So I got tied up with you . . . fell in love with you. This past week has been every bit as wonderful for me as it was for you, and don't you ever think different. But baby, I'm American. I love the place, even though there's plenty wrong with it. I couldn't live over here – and you certainly couldn't live over there.'

'I could try – I'd go anywhere for you.'

'I know. That's the trouble. It would destroy you. In fact, even being over here, with me, would destroy you. It might take a little longer, that's all.'

She was becoming angry now. 'I don't understand a word you're saying.'

'How long is it since anyone last noticed you were black?'

She recoiled as if he had slapped her, but then said: 'About eight or nine months. An old bastard where I worked . . . '

'And before that?'

She pondered for a moment, then shook her head. 'Must be

257

years. People usually think I'm half Italian, or Spanish. What's that got to do with us?'

'You don't really need to ask, do you?'

'Yes. Tell me. It had better be a good reason if it's going to split us up.'

'I carry my race around with me like a thorny crown, Lexie – everyone can see it. I don't want to hide it – I'm proud of my origins. But I never pretend it's easy, even with a lifetime's practice behind me to prepare me.

'A black kid in America is getting called "nigger" from the day he learns to talk. It don't get any better after that, but you *do* get used to it. Them sly little digs you been getting all your life, the things that made you leave your home town . . . those people were just amateurs. Tied up with me, you'd stop being that beautiful dark girl, the one who might be Italian, and turn into a nigger overnight. And then you'd know you hadn't heard nothing yet!'

She was staring at him, shamed by the intensity of his tone into forgetting, for a moment, her broken heart. 'Dear God,' she whispered eventually, 'is it really that bad?'

'That's only the beginning. Listen, Lexie, I know we're both fighters in our way, but not that sorta fighters. I like a quiet life. I aim to be one a those big, smooth fish who weave about quietly in the backa the aquarium without making waves, just making a good living and staying outa trouble. You think you want to prove yourself, be a big name, show you're nobody's inferior, but really all you want is the same as me – dark comfortable waters without no trouble.

'Sure, we could get together. You'd get so knotted up the first time you met the most casual racism in the States, I'd have to stop being relaxed and quiet and make them eat their words. In five minutes that would put us right up front with the Equal Rights people. I got no ambitions to be there. I only got one life and I'm doing my best with it. I already know black's just as good as white. I'm not wrecking that one life to prove it to the world.'

This time she was silent for so long that he thought she would never speak to him again. In the end he said: 'Do you find what I say so very terrible?'

She nodded, then found her voice. 'Y-yes, but not for the

reason you think. When I look right inside myself, I know you're right. I go off the deep end even now if someone just looks at me the wrong way. I couldn't take all that other stuff.'

Larry let out a long sigh. 'Well, thank God you see it. At least you know I'm not trying to dump you. Believe me, I gave it a lot of thought. I know you'll feel bad for a long time after I'm gone, but at least we've had this time together.'

'Oh, Larry – what am I going to do?' Her voice was rising towards hysteria. 'There's no place for me anywhere, no safety. This will make it worse. I know I couldn't survive in your world, but I'm not even sure I can keep my head above water in my own any more!'

He clasped her hand so hard that the pain drove away her tears. 'You're being melodramatic! Stop it. Remember what I sang to you the night we met? ''Show me the way to go home . . .'' That's what you need, Lexie. You ran from that to escape the one thing you'll never get away from – yourself. Yourself happens to be quite a dame. Why not go home and get to know her better?'

She sat glaring down at the tablecloth for a while. Then disjointed pictures began to form in her mind. Rhys, her father, chuckling conspiratorially with some fence from along Bute Street. The exotically clad tarts down around the Packet Boat pub. The little steamers that took trippers across to Weston-super-Mare for day trips. Bowler-hatted clerks hurrying away from the city's dockland financial district at the end of the office day. With it came the memory of a rich smell – curry spices, estuary mudbanks at low tide, coal dust, and a little sweet trace of opium underlying it all. It was like climbing into the arms of the mother she could not remember.

'All right, Larry,' she said, smiling for the first time since they had sat down to dinner. 'I'll do it. Next week I'll go home to Cardiff. At twenty-eight, it's about time I started growing up!'

CHAPTER TWENTY-SIX

The dockers showed their real mettle almost immediately after Bethan's bus trip to the East End. After Tuesday there were no more joy-rides in wittily signposted vehicles driven by medical students. Pickets were out throughout the dockland boroughs before seven the following morning, stopping buses and lorries which attempted to ferry people or food to the City. Several buses were burned and one was thrown into the Thames. That night rioting and fights between police and the local strikers ended with forty people in Poplar Hospital. The troops were unable to force a re-entry to the docks when they returned for fresh food supplies, and from Wednesday afternoon dockland was effectively closed to the anti-strike forces.

By Friday morning, the Midlands and South-East, the area supplied from London, was suffering severe food shortages, with barely forty-eight hours' supply of flour left in the capital.

On Saturday the Government sent in the Grenadier Guards. A hundred and five lorries packed with troops, escorted by twenty armoured cars crewed by Royal Tank Corps men, lumbered out of the Hyde Park depot, en route for the docks, at four-thirty that morning. Meanwhile teams of volunteers went by river from Westminster Pier to the docks, and at eight o'clock started loading lorries with flour from the ships there. They were protected by Lewis guns and two fully armed Guards battalions.

The column which set out for the City a couple of hours later was two miles long. At first it passed through streets lined with sullen masses of strikers and their families, cowed by the massive military presence into letting the food chain pass. But as the column entered the City, headed by cavalry and armoured cars, huge crowds gathered to cheer it on.

After that the entire dispute took on a different aspect. Thousands of people all over the country rushed to volunteer as special constables, and trouble flared spontaneously as untrained, over-enthusiastic keepers of the peace provoked strikers who were already strained to breaking point. As the strike entered its second week, the streets of Britain were crawling with uniformed, helmeted volunteers intent on suppressing a revolution which had never been intended. Outside the trades unions, it had apparently been forgotten that the strike was a wages and working hours dispute and, for the strikers at least, had no connection with politics. Now every working man from London Docks to the Swansea Valley mines was labelled revolutionary and the comfortable class rose en masse to protect itself.

There was an almost dreamlike quality to the nine days of the General Strike in South Wales. Only elsewhere, it seemed, were there skirmishes between strikers and police or soldiers. Elsewhere orators ranted at meetings, and well-heeled young men zoomed about in Bentleys, delivering Winston Churchill's scurrilous *British Gazette*. Destroyers lay at anchor in Cardiff Docks and protesters rioted in the city's streets. But the Valleys remained peaceful, lying inactive under the warm May sunshine.

Every day Lewis Walters and a group of his friends, all of them young colliery boys, went down to the weir on the River Ebbw a mile below the Celynen South pit. Normally the water was filthy, but after almost a week with every colliery on its banks closed down, it was already running clear again. Once this weir had formed an elegant perspective from the windows of Abercarn House when it was a rich man's mansion. The pleasure grounds were overgrown now and the house had been a girls' school since the end of the war, but the illusion of a rural paradise was almost perfect.

The young miners stripped and plunged into the sparkling

261

water, fighting and playing like happy seals. An onlooker might have mistaken them for schoolboys on holiday – they were all young enough – but these children had all been full-time workers since they had reached the age of thirteen.

Up in the village everything looked normal. The Miners' Federation had taken over running day-to-day supply lines. A communal soup kitchen had opened in the Tinplaters Hall and part of the wash-house at the bottom of the Ranks had been turned over to a boot-repairing co-operative. Lily, at the centre of a group of women preparing food in the kitchen, was happier than she had been for a long time.

'You ent supposed to be pleased about all this, Lil,' said Edith Smith. 'You look like the bloody cat as ate the canary. Just you remember there ent no money coming in to support any of us.'

'I know, but isn't it marvellous? They're all working for each other. Nobody will do anyone down. What if it went on for good like this?'

'Look, I'm bloody amazed it 'ave got this far. Don't get your hopes up, or you'll be disappointed. We'll all be humming a different tune when the shortages begin to bite.'

'With all the other unions behind us, maybe the bosses'll cave in before it do come to that.'

Edith's laugh was cynical. 'You'm still ever so young in some ways, ent you? They won't let us win, kidda. They need to show everybody who's boss, and do it in a way none of us'll forget. And they'll do it, you mark my words.'

'If you think that, why are you here?'

'Oh, I'm a bugger for a lost cause! I may not be your most optimistic supporter, love, but you can count on me still being here at the bitter end, don't worry.'

Lily gave her arm a playful slap. 'You'd be gloomy if someone give you a thousand pound!'

'Listen, Lil, if they give it me, it'd be either forged or stolen, and I'd get put in jail for having it! Now come on, let's get this dinner in.'

For the moment, at least, there was plenty of food. The local farmers had donated whole lambs and bullocks, as well as loads of root vegetables. When Edith commented on their generosity, one of them said morosely: 'I'd rather give it than 'ave your menfolk up my place pinching it, and that's what they'd be doing soon enough.'

Billie came down from Trwyn Farm for the first time since March, intending to buy a few essential supplies and then go for a meal with Lily and David, whom he liked. It was nearly an hour before he nerved himself to ask a shopkeeper in Abercarn why everything was so quiet; to learn what was going on, and to find out about the General Strike.

He found Lily at her soup kitchen, and drew her out into the sunlit street for a talk. 'Why don't you send Tommy back up with me for the summer?' he said.

Lily, still in her utopian day-dream, gazed at him in puzzlement. 'It's nice of you to offer him a holiday, Billie, but why should I want to do that?'

'Have you got any idea what's going to happen down here?'

She smiled at him. 'Oh, aye. For once in a while we're going to show them all that the worm will turn. Think of it, Billie – the whole working class of this country united, not for a revolution, but just to show those important men they can't ride roughshod over us. That'll be a famous victory!'

'It would be if it was going to happen, Lil, but it ent.'

She came to earth with a bump. 'What are you talking about? You been up your mountain too long, Billie Walters! I told you – we've had enough of being told what to do.'

'Maybe the miners have, but not the rest. There's too many little men with savings accounts in the unions, same as anywhere else. After a few days they'll see them savings shrinking and they'll wriggle out of it. Principle do vanish ever so fast when you'm in a corner.'

'No! No, I don't believe you. I *won't* believe you!'

'P'raps it's time I told you a little story, Lily, love. About the war.'

Lily was astonished. 'I didn't think you remembered any of it.'

'Oh, Christ, I wish I didn't! I do remember every second. That's why I can't talk about it. But this bit I can, to you, because it's important for you to understand.

'They put me up trees, sniping, and I used to play an 'orrible little game with myself. Fairground ducks, I called it. See, as long as I was good at fairground ducks, I didn't have to do the things I knew would drive me barmy. But they got me in the end, ducks or no ducks . . .

'I sat up my tree, or on my barn roof, with my lovely rifle, telescopic sights, perfect bit a precision engineering an' all, and them fairground ducks would pop up on the skyline, or out of a dug-out, or crossing a farmyard, and *bam-bam-bam*! Give the boy a coconut an' no more ducks today. Close the fairground stall and send him home for his tea. He've done brillliant. Only these was ducks in uniforms, Lily. They was really called German soldiers, only for me they was ducks. I'm better killing cardboard ducks than flesh-and-blood men. So there we were. Me up my tree, them fighting their war. For a long time I thought I was gonna come out of it okay. Then they remembered me.

' "Sergeant Walters," one a the brass-hats said. "Sergeant Walters – you were a miner in civvy street, I believe." Not for a long time, sir, I said. "No matter," he said. "Like riding a bicycle. Once you learn, you always know how. Mining detail. We need chaps like you in the sappers." I explained to him, Lil. I told him, give me my lines a fairground ducks and I'll kill as many as you like. Win the war for you single-handed, if you give me long enough and keep me supplied with ammunition. But no mining.

'He wasn't having none of it, of course. Kept on, and on, and on. And in the end he said he'd have me court-martialled for failing to obey an order. I wouldn't even eat for a week, but they shoved a tube up my nose in the end. Said it was a trick they'd learned with the suffragettes before the war. By the time they finished with me I'd a done anything to get out a their rotten jail. It was what I'd run away from the mines for, see. They was locking me in. I thought I'd made a deal with the bastard. I'd do the sapping on that one salient, then they'd let me go back to my sharp-shooting.'

'I shoulda known better, o' course. Up goes the Huns. Down comes the trenches. Brilliant, Sergeant Walters! What, Sergeant Walters? Waste the talents of a sapper like you up a tree with a rifle, when you can take out fifty Bosches with one well-judged tunnel! No, you stay where you are. Bargain, what bargain? And they kept me where I was, Lil, under the earth, with the mud crammed with bits a corpses over my head, pressing down on me, for the rest a the war. I used to go crazy every morning in there when we started. A little lance-corporal a mine, fellow from the Durham coalfield, he understood. Used to hold me like a baby till the fear went, then I'd start tunnelling like a demon – anything to be outa there before it all come down on us . . . It got me in the end, though. One of my tunnels collapsed and they didn't dig me out for three hours. Poor little corp – suffocated. I ended up over Abergavenny Asylum. It happened about a week before Armistice, trust my luck. Like I told you, the buggers do always beat you.'

Lily had listened, close to tears, while he told his story. When he finished she said gently: 'But why do you think that has got something to do with the strike, Billie? I don' understand.'

'Then you ent as clever as I always thought,' he said, impatience sharpening his soft voice. 'Don't you understand, Lil? They do always win. They know what they want, and they get it. The blokes who sent me in that tunnel is the same ones that's supporting the coal owners now. They don't know what it feels like to lose, and they ent gonna start finding out now. Send Tommy back with me, girl. It'll be easier on him.'

But her mouth was set much as Margaret Ann's was when she was determined about something. 'No. I don't think you'm right, Billie, but even if I thought you was, he's a miner's son and a miner's grandson. He've got to find out what it's like, and just as well now as later.'

'Lily, he's only three. That's bloody young to starve.'

Her face was suddenly pinched with anxiety. 'D'you really think it will come to that?'

'Aye, I do. Principle is a fine thing, but the entire working population of the country ent going to lose everything just to stop the miners working eight hours underground every day. Only other miners will do that.'

'So you think the miners will stay solid.'

'Oh, aye, 'course I do. But Lil, nobody wants coal at the moment. That's what the cuts is about. It'll suit the owners if the men stay out. Once the other unions cave in you've lost.'

'Enough!' She stood up and squared her shoulders. 'We ent going to lose and the other unions ent going back without us.

Next month you'll feel a real fool for having said all that, Billie. You going to wait till I finish here, and come up Newbridge for your tea?'

He shook his head. 'You got enough to think of at the moment. But you remember what I said. If things get rough, you send your Tommy to me. At least I can feed him proper until it's all over.'

She kissed his cheek, tears in her eyes. 'Thank you, my lovely. And I'm ever so sorry about the war. Thanks for telling me . . . I know what it must have cost you. But this is different. This time we'll win.' She squeezed his arm, then turned away, back towards the soup kitchen.

Watching her proud walk as she moved away from him, Billie said: 'Aye, kidda. They used to tell us that on the Western Front an' all. I still wake up screaming, all the same.'

CHAPTER TWENTY-SEVEN

Somehow the sparkling May sunlight made the worn-out houses around Mare Street look even shabbier than they might have on a damp winter day. Bethan looked about her with misgiving. As her time with James Norland receded to mere memory, it became progressively harder to recall that she had chosen to lead a more useful life, to employ her hard-won professional skills. Looking around this neighbourhood, she longed for a brightly lit shop window or a chic nightclub to cheer things up.

Joyce Gladstone had come with her on two previous flat-hunting expeditions, but now that the Holloway Road clinic was fully reopened after the strike, she had no time to spare. In any case Bethan suspected the other woman was becoming a little impatient with her desired standards for a new home.

The day before, when they had turned away from the fifth two-rooms-and-kitchen set-up, Joyce had said: 'Really, Bethan, I don't think the sort of place you want exists in an area like this. If you're to find somewhere you must set your sights lower.'

'But that one wasn't even clean, Joyce! I'll swear there were bed bugs behind that wallpaper.'

'Nonsense – if you went inside a *real* slum, you'd soon see the difference between shabby and lousy. For one thing, true poverty carries a sour smell with it. Nothing wrong with that last place that a couple of coats of white paint wouldn't cure.'

'But it didn't have its own bathroom . . . the idea of sharing with some of the people I saw there . . . ' Her voice tailed off in genteel horror.

'What did you do as a child in the mining valleys?' snapped Joyce. 'How did you cope with emptying people's slops when you were training as a nurse? I think your years in Mayfair have led to a severe case of loss of memory, my dear!'

Bethan had the grace to blush at that point. But she did not go back to the tall, grimy house and tell the landlady she had changed her mind about the flat.

Now she was out searching on her own. She had already seen two places – for all practical purposes mere duplicates of what she had looked at with Joyce. She began to wonder whether she could, after all, afford to get somewhere in a more salubrious area and drive in each day, instead of carrying out her original intention of living within walking distance of work. The prospect of travelling was looking less daunting by the minute.

She had been standing outside her next prospective home as she pondered the question. It was part of a Georgian terrace, a four-storey house of austere elegance under the dirt and decay built up by later generations. It stood out from its fellows only because the window frames and front door were painted a garish shade of yellow. All the other houses either had brown or green paintwork, or had been redecorated so long ago that it was impossible to distinguish any colour. The throbbing sunshine shade did not reassure her. There was something vaguely anarchic about it, which hinted at an owner who might not know where to draw the line . . . Bethan was very strong on people knowing where to draw the line. She preferred everything clear-cut and comprehensible. The yellow paintwork promised neither.

She was about to turn away when the front door opened and her worst doubts were confirmed. The man who stood there could have been anything from thirty to forty-five. He was stockily built, with nondescript brown hair and a broad, muscular face with the sort of suntan which spoke of being out in all weathers rather than lying on Mediterranean beaches. He wore a pair of baggy canvas trousers and a dark blue tradesman's smock, covered in splashes of paint. Some of it was the same yellow as the window frames and doors. He did not look at Bethan immediately. Instead his eyes went to her smart car, parked directly in front of the house. He smiled and it was as if the entire world lit up. Bethan had to fight an impulse to smile too.

He came down the front steps and hurried past her to the car, still not acknowledging her presence. Then he said: 'What a little beauty – triumph of speed and economy, this design. Bet they're fun to drive!' He turned to her as he spoke, but Bethan's only indication that he was addressing her was that she was the only other person in the street. She was still drawing breath to reply when he added: 'Of course, it wouldn't last five minutes down here. Anything more elaborate than an Austin Seven gets stripped down overnight if you leave it outside in these streets.'

'Who said I had any intention of leaving it in these streets?'

'Well, as it's parked outside my house, and as you're clutching the *Star*, folded open at the "Rooms to Let" pages, I assumed you were coming to look at the flat I advertised. There's no garage attached to this house.'

'Well that isn't likely to make me lose any sleep. I had just decided the place was probably unsuitable anyway.'

'Really? Are we in the presence of a woman who can see through walls, we ask ourselves? What drew you to your conclusion, dear lady?'

Bethan fought a childish impulse to stamp her foot and shout 'your yellow paint and your bossy manner', and instead said: 'It's hardly the best neighbourhood in London, is it?'

'If that was your main criterion you wouldn't be looking anywhere in this borough, so let's stop pretending. Look, the front door is open. You've taken the trouble to drive over here. At least go in and take a look. I promise not to bite if you don't like it.'

She almost refused. This man might not be big or expensively dressed, but he carried an aura of power which made her feel almost cowed. She fought the irrational notion that if she went to live there, she would be taking orders from him within ten minutes. For heaven's sake, she told herself, he's only a damned landlord! Go in and look at his wretched flat and stop being such a coward.

Compared with what she had looked at before, the place

269

was heavenly. The ground-floor, which was raised above pavement level to permit direct window light into the basement, was the floor on which the flat was located. That in itself was surprising. Most owners kept the big, accessible lower rooms for themselves and let off the top of the house. The man caught her look of surprise and murmured something about wanting the extra daylight obtainable higher up the building. As he spoke, he opened the door of the vacant flat and she stopped taking notice of what he was saying.

It had started off as a double-aspect reception room with floor-to-ceiling folding doors half-way across its length so that the size and arrangement could be changed at will. The obvious layout now would be to use one half as bedroom and the other as living room. At the front a lofty bay window looked into the street. At the back french doors opened on to a paved terrace with a short flight of steps leading into the garden. The rooms were distempered in plain, immaculate white and looked brand new.

'Whoever takes the flat will need green fingers,' said the landlord. 'I like the look of a garden, but I haven't time or patience to keep it up. Goes with the flat.'

'Does the flat have sole access to the garden?'

He peered at her intensely, as though seeing her for the first time. 'Sole access? Were you thinking of selling tickets? For God's sake, I'm the only other bloody tenant!'

'Oh! I . . . er . . . that is, it's quite a big house. I thought there would be others . . . '

'Listen, Miss Whatever-your-name-is, perhaps we should define a few terms. I'm Max Grant. I own this shambling wreck of a house. Until three months ago my mother, a singularly unco-operative woman, inhabited the rooms you are examining. She expired at short notice, in hospital, and I have been brooding about what to do with the house ever since. In the end I decided I preferred London-shabby to Dorset-picturesque, and elected to stay put. But this place was rather large, not to say expensive, for a single man, so I decided to relet Mama's chunk.

'I don't ask much of the tenant, beyond solvency, a certain restraint of personal habits, an ability to discipline a modestly sized garden, and a willingness to be sociable on the rare occasions when I emerge from my studio with a bottle of Chateau Talbot and a need for companionship. Do you fulfil those requirements?'

'Only if I don't have to share a bathroom with you.'

'Great God Almighty – you've just conclusively proved the Pythagorean doctrine of the transmigration of souls. That could have been my mother speaking! Of course you don't have to share my bathroom. Bathroom and kitchen in the basement. Go down and look if you're so fussy.'

Beneath the ground-floor rooms, the basement boasted a vast kitchen looking up through a half-submerged bay window into the garden. Behind it, tucked in at the street end of the house, was a modern bathroom. It was the answer to Bethan's wildest dreams, had it not come complete with this fully paid-up eccentric.

When he had guided her around the basement, she said: 'Why wouldn't your own mother share a bathroom with you?'

Grant roared with laughter. 'It's perfectly all right – I'm house-trained! She didn't like me stretching canvases in there all the time, that's all. Said it played havoc with her personal plumbing to have to remove a primed, stretched piece of six-by-four from the lavatory seat before she could have a pee. Very weak bladder, my mother . . . *You* haven't got a weak bladder, have you? No? Didn't think so, somehow. It wouldn't dare . . . ' He began to wander off before she could suppress her outrage and answer him.

In the end her response sounded pathetic, even to her own ears. 'Canvases? Oh – I thought you were the other sort of painter . . . '

He stared at her, nonplussed, then looked down at his smock. Realization dawned. 'Bloody hell, of course – the house and I are both yellow! No, no – I like the colour. Got some chap to paint the house with it. Liked it even more after that, and I've been doing a canvas in the same tones. I shall call it ''Summer Day'' if I don't paint it over and start again . . . Well, what d'you think? Are you interested in moving in?'

'Very. It's the best place I've seen, by far. But it's unfurnished, and I'd have to start from scratch. I don't know if I could possibly afford it . . . '

He inspected her closely. 'Hmm, you're hellish bossy . . .

but you're extremely good-looking too. Make a wonderful model. I was going to charge fifteen bob a week for the flat. If you'll sit for me when I want you, I'll make it ten. How about that?'

'It's very reasonable, but I still have the problem of buying furniture.'

'That's solved in a minute. I told you – the locals will have your car in pieces overnight. Sell it, buy something less conspicuous. You could furnish the place with some nice bits of Sheraton for the cash you'll get. I'll even introduce you to a likely dealer or three if you like . . .'

She looked round again, largely because she knew if she set eyes on his beaming, boyish face without getting herself fully under control, she would burst out laughing. Then she said: 'It's a deal, Mr Grant. When do we start?'

'Painting or furniture buying? Listen, they're both terribly thirsty work. There's a nice pub round the corner. What if we went there, you know, to oil the wheels a bit before we get going? Then we can see my pet dealer for a few essentials after closing time, and the place will be set up ready for you to move in any time after tomorrow. How about that for service with a smile?'

She nodded. 'You're on. Lead the way.'

At the front door he paused. 'Dammit, there was one thing I forgot to ask. Vital, really. Can you cook?'

Bethan bridled. 'As a matter of fact, no. And if you thought just because I'm a woman . . .'

'No, no!' He was flapping his hands as if subduing a large and angry dog. 'Quite the reverse – I do, and I hate women interfering when I'm making a meal for them. If you're incapable of boiling an egg, kindly keep it that way – it gives me the chance to shine!'

With an extravagant bow, he ushered a somewhat bemused Bethan off the premises.

CHAPTER TWENTY-EIGHT

On May 13th the workers of Britain were told they had won their fight and the greatest peaceful dispute in history had been called off. Over the next few days they learned they had surrendered unconditionally without even being aware they had done so. After nine days in which they had come closer to complete victory than any of them had thought possible, the men of the TUC's General Committee lost their nerve and took the severed head of the miners' cause on a platter to Ten Downing Street. Some local union branches, receiving their telegrams calling off the strike, thought they were hoax victims and jammed the TUC's London switchboard asking for the matter to be cleared up.

In South Wales the miners and their families swooped from euphoria to dejection within hours. At least the workers who had supported them, although defeated, were going back into paid employment. They remained locked out of their mines, with no way of supporting their families and no prospect of earning money in the foreseeable future.

Billie descended from his secluded valley again and sought out Lily. 'Now will you let that boy come back with me?' he said. 'All you've proved to him is that the poor get trodden on. Leave it there and don't show him they starve an' all.'

'No. It's bad enough the TUC have sold us out, without me sending my child away. Others haven't got the chance. He stays.'

Billie looked appealingly at David who, he was sure, shared his feelings, but David only shrugged and shook his head. In this house Lily's word was law.

There was something in what she said, thought Billie, as he made his way back up Gwyddon Road. There was no sign here of anyone cracking, just a rock-hard opposition to surrender. They really were prepared to starve rather than give in. And starve they would, by the look of it.

The miners, cut off from the support of the other unions, cast around for some means of feeding their families. Their dependants qualified for Outdoor Relief under the Poor Law. The Nine Mile Point Colliery lodge called on all the villages of the Western Valley to march on the workhouse en masse to claim it. At first there was a luke-warm response. Then the wives got hold of the idea.

'I'm not having any child of mine going for relief cap in hand,' said Lily at the Women's Food Committee meeting at the workmen's institute. 'We go proud, or not at all.'

Myra Roberts looked at her incredulously. 'Go proud to the workhouse? You'm outa your mind!'

'We'll see about that. Edith – go on downstairs to the reading room and see if Idwal Pugh and Gerry Roberts is in there. Bring 'em up if they are.'

The two men were the bandmaster and drum major of the Celynen Colliery Band. When they arrived at the women's meeting room, Lily said: 'How d'you fancy a practice outing with the boys next week, Idwal, full uniforms an' all instruments polished? If you do, you're elected to lead us all to Woollaston House and back.' Woollaston House was the area workhouse in Newport.

'You serious, girl? I'd go tomorrow,' said Idwal. 'I need the sound of a few trombones in my ears to cheer me up a bit.'

'Right. Get 'em together an' start practising. Nothing morbid and plenty of marching songs. And don't forget "The Red Flag", since every other bloody union in the country do seem to have done since May 12th.'

After that the whole valley was involved within hours. What had been sketchily discussed by the men as a doleful procession in search of charity started to turn into a triumphal progress. By the second day Lily had all the children whose shoes were not strong enough to take them to school quartered upstairs at the workmen's institute, making banners for the march.

'I want boots for them kids to put on if we gotta steal them,' she told Haydn. 'They're making the banners and they should have the fun of coming on the march an' all. When are you expectin' another of those Soviet Aid packages?'

He grinned sheepishly. 'One come yesterday, but the boots ent arf funny. They'm like the clogs we used to wear before the war. That's why I was a bit slow giving them out.'

'I don't care if they'm made of felt with turned-up toes. Get the little ones kitted up and then we'll see about finding some more for the ones who are left out.'

The roll of villages planning to send delegations to the workhouse was swelling every day. All were doing the same as Abercarn: those who had colliery or village bands, reactivating them for the march; those who did not, making banners or hastily practising to become comb-and-paper instrumentalists.

On May 21, every healthy woman and child in Abercarn, and most of the men, were lined up in the Market Square, the band at their head. Immediately behind the band was a row of children, holding aloft a banner with the slogan:

GIVE US THIS DAY OUR DAILY BREAD

At the back of the procession was a team of sturdy miners, with one which said:

WORKERS OF THE WORLD UNITE

'Thought that was a bit political for the kids to carry, just in case someone do get ideas about fisticuffs,' Lily explained to Maisie.

Between the two banners were rank after rank of people, all wearing their remaining best clothes, all determined to march without shame or apology. The Walterses were well represented. David was absent, still working underground as a safety man, although he put his wages into the Federation fund every week and took out only the same strike pay as those who were locked out. But Haydn, Tom, Eddy and Lewis were all there, and so were Rose's husband, Albert, and Tom's and Haydn's wives. Haydn's eldest boy and Lily's son Tommy were there too, but they were likely to need carrying before the end of the march so the rest of the children had been left at home.

Lily looked around in satisfaction. 'All I need is our Mam to make my cup runneth over,' she said, 'but I can go on wishing for that until Doomsday.'

'Well Doomsday have come early,' said Haydn. 'Look behind you.'

Lily glanced over her shoulder, to discover Margaret Ann bustling down the road from the Ranks, dressed to kill. 'Mam, what're you up to?' she asked. 'I didn't think you'd be waving us off.'

'I ent, neither.' Margaret Ann was obviously furious. 'But if you'm determined to go on with this madness, I'd better come an' all to make sure you don't get in any more trouble!'

She elbowed her way between Tommy and Evan, Haydn's boy. Haydn bent close to Lily and said: 'Or then again, she may just be coming 'cos she's too bloody nosey to miss it!'

'Ssh, for God's sake! I'm that pleased to see her here I don't want her getting cross an' going home before we start.'

She broke off in time to hear Tommy piping up to his grand-mother: 'No, Nana, it do go like this – "The workers' flag is deepest red, it shrouded oft our martyred dead" . . . '

'Oh, Lily, how could you! Fancy teaching a little boy a wicked song like that!' Margaret Ann broke in dolefully. 'No, Tommy, *bach*, I do know a better song than that: "We're marching to Zion, beautiful, beautiful Zion" . . . '

'Don't worry, Lil,' said Haydn, chuckling. 'Neither of them do understand the other, so they'll be happy.'

As they moved south contingents of villagers swelled the stream of marchers. When they reached Cross Keys they were joined by most of the villagers of Cwmfelinfach in the adjoin-ing Sirhowy valley, as well as all the mining families of Cross Keys itself. They picked up several hundreds more at Pontymister and Risca, where groups also came in from the far west of the county, Bedwas and Machen. By the time they were within three miles of Newport they were thousands strong and singing as if their lives depended on it.

There were more women and children then men, but at the last moment many husbands had decided they did not trust the police to refrain from attacking women and children, so they came along as bodyguards. When they reached the village of Bassaleg, out of the coalfield now and effectively on enemy territory, they swung out of the main street on to the Newport road and encountered a barrier. A squad of mounted police faced them without a break from side to side of the road. In front of them was the chief constable.

The Abercarn marchers led the procession, the other contingents having joined in behind as they advanced down the valley. Now the band stopped its latest tune, with a suitably mocking bleat from one of the brass instruments.

The chief constable waited for complete silence, then said: 'I could class this as a riotous assembly. Where d'you all think you're going?'

'Where do it look like on this road? Newport, of course!' Alf Barnett, one of the miners from the front row immediately behind the band, was feeling testy. He had walked eight miles in tight boots. He was hungry and his corns were giving him trouble. This was no time to burden him with rhetorical questions.

'Purpose of your visit?' The chief constable's tone was brusque and the question might have come from a customs official at some foreign frontier.

'Outdoor relief,' said Alf. 'The women and children is entitled to it. And we do hear,' he added with heavy irony, 'as some a the relieving officers have been refusing to release the money until the husbands do sign receipts. So we'm here in case we have to do that. Satisfied now?'

'Certainly not. If thousands of people cram into the Woollaston House area the whole town will be disrupted. I will give you a choice. Either you disperse to your homes and go singly to apply for relief, or you remain here and split into groups of twenty or less, departing at half-hour intervals, to collect it. The decision is yours.'

Alf turned and surveyed the mass of people behind him. 'But there's upwards of five thousand of us, mun. It'd take till a week Tuesday!'

'Very perceptive. That is why I suggest you take the first alternative and disperse, now, to your homes. This type of demonstration will get you nowhere.'

'Look, some of us has walked eight miles an' more. There's a lot of little kids yer and none of the women have eaten a square meal for weeks. You can't seriously suggest we should go back after we've come so far.'

'I'm not suggesting it.' He stepped forward. 'I am ordering it. And if you do not obey my instructions, I shall tell these mounted officers to ride you down.'

Lily had been coming to the boil while this encounter played itself out. Now she stepped out of line, and said: 'The hell you will! We're going to collect what's ours and you lot ent going to stop us.' She came forward and stood facing the chief constable. 'Thirty seconds from now, I'm bringing a rank of women and young kids through this line to get what's due us. Tell your thugs to charge if you like. By the time that do get in the papers there won't be a copper safe to walk the streets in the whole of South Wales.' Striding back and forth along the ranks of marchers, she yelled out: 'Come on, girls, who'll be first through with me? Bring your kids an' all.'

For a few seconds there was no movement. The chief constable had stood aside, ready to unleash the horsemen on the demonstrators, and the mounted sergeant at the head of the column had been sitting tensely watching Lily. Now, assuming from the lack of instant reaction that her appeal would fail, he began to relax. At that point, she reached forward into the lines beside her and led out a small, blond, angelic-looking boy. 'Come on, Tommy love,' her voice floated up clearly. 'Let's show 'em we prefer to die on our feet.'

Her mother's instinctive cry of 'Lily, no – are you mad, girl?' was swamped by the swelling roar of agreement from thousands of throats. Along the lines at least fifty women stepped out, accompanied by small children, and came forward to join her in front of the Celynen Colliery band. They formed a group about four rows deep. Linking hands with the children, they advanced on the mounted policemen. The children looked exceedingly small against the vast bulk of the horses.

Lily, with a fine disregard for her own atheism, began singing in a high steady voice:

> 'Who is on the Lord's side?
> Who will serve the King?'

and a thousand others joined her:

'Who will be His helper, other hearts to win?
Who will leave the world's side?
Who will face the foe?
Who is on the Lord's side?
Who for Him will go?'

The police column parted like the Red Sea as the miners'
baritones tore into the triumphant chorus:

'By Thy call of mercy,
By Thy grace divine,
We are on the Lord's side,
Saviour, we are Thine!'

'Lily – how dare you? The Lord will punish you for taking
His name in vain!'

Lily had been floating along in an ecstasy of victory and the
furious intervention confused her momentarily. Then she
focused on Margaret Ann, who had caught up with the front
rank of women and was skipping about in her anger. Lily
smiled. 'They say faith do move mountains, don't they, Mam?
Well I still dunno about that, but it's certainly moving them
coppers!'

But Margaret Ann was not to be placated. 'No – it's not
right. The word of God was not meant for the misuse of man.
Stop this blasphemy at once!'

The smile was fading from Lily's lips, but before she had
time to retaliate, her attention was diverted to something more
urgent. The police had been surprised by the women's surge
forward, but had not given up. They had regrouped, trotted
their horses forward a few yards and were now in the process of
reforming, as in their previous line-up, ahead of the advancing
women. 'Shurrup Mam, and take Tommy,' hissed Lily,
thrusting the boy into Margaret Ann's arms. 'And don' you let
'im go for nuthin'!' Then she threw herself forward, yelling,
'Oh no you don't, you buggers!' and lay down in the road
where the horses were about to be repositioned.

Acting as if drilled in advance, the other front-line women
joined her. For long seconds the scene was a confusion of
hooves, skirts and flying hair. Then the horsemen drew off

slightly. Standing in his stirrups, the sergeant bawled: A'll right, you women, I'll only say this once. You have thirty seconds to get yourselves off the highway, and if any of you is there then, we're comin' in with batons!' He turned to the constables behind him. 'All right, men. Dismount, alternate officers each hold two horses. The rest, draw truncheons and advance to my order.'

Most of the women were sitting up now, arms folded, determined not to budge. The policemen looked less formidable now they were no longer mounted. Then the uniformed men were among them and the blows started to fly. 'Dear God, someone'll get killed!' muttered Haydn, and started to dash forward towards his sister.

But he was beaten to it. Lily had already taken a heavy blow across her left shoulder and had curled into a ball to protect herself against the next. It never fell. As the policeman lifted his arm to strike again, a sizeable stone caught him behind the left ear and he crashed to his knees. Haydn stopped in disbelief. The man's assailant, now busy rearming herself with bigger rocks, was Margaret Ann Walters. Tommy, beside her, was enthusiastically stockpiling rocks. To Haydn's right and left, other women were doing the same thing.

'We got to Newport after all, then, Lil,' murmured Haydn, his grin made lopsided by the lump which was swelling along his jaw.

'Aye. Pity they didn't bring us past Woollaston House, wasn't it? We coulda called in for our money on the way.' The general mêlée which had ensued after the stone-throwing started had been quelled only when the troops were called out. The main body of marchers had scattered back northward and the group of women who had lain in the road, along with a scattering of the men who leaped to their defence, had been rounded up and arrested. Margaret Ann and Tommy had been bundled into the police van along with them as it set off for Newport.

'Mam!' Even Haydn was shocked at the sight of his mother in such unlikely surroundings. 'What the hell is going on?' he asked, turning to one of the two soldiers who had jumped into the van to keep order.

The soldier, a Londoner, was uncomfortable. 'Don't blame me, mate – I tried to keep her out, didn't I? Could see she was an old lady . . . '

'I'll give you old lady if I do lay hands on you!' intervened Margaret Ann.

Ignoring her, he went on: 'She said we wasn't going nowhere wiv her boy an' girl and if we was taking you, she was coming an' all. I told her not to be daft and she thumped me round the 'ead. Didn't 'ave no choice after that.'

Haydn passed a hand across his face and wondered if perhaps the men of South Wales had got it wrong all down the years. Maybe they should always have sent in their women-folk to do the fighting. They certainly never seemed to know when they were beaten.

Finally he turned to his mother and said: 'What about Tommy? Why did you bring him?'

Margaret Ann's mouth had pursed into the familiar disapproving button-shape. 'I couldn't see Maisie nor Sal, and I could hardly let the child run the roads, could I?'

Lily sighed. 'S'pose not. Oh, well, if he's gonna grow up with a criminal record, he might as well start young.'

The magistrates in Newport were quite out of sympathy with the miners. This was the town's first direct contact with trouble arising from the lock-out, and they wanted no more of it. Two of the more prominent marchers, county councillors, came in for heavy criticism for what the magistrate termed their criminal indifference to their own exalted position in the community. They were committed to Assizes for a heavier prison sentence than the magistrates were permitted to impose.

Then came the turn of the rank-and-file marchers. The gravity of individual offences did not seem to count overmuch unless they were pillars of the community, so Margaret Ann was, perhaps, treated more leniently than she would otherwise have been. Along with four men who had followed her stone-throwing example, she was fined forty shillings for inflicting grievous bodily harm. Haydn, who had been prevented from more serious involvement when a blow to the jaw from a police truncheon knocked him unconscious, was fined ten shillings for riotous behaviour.

Lily was in a class of her own. 'Lily Richards,' intoned the magistrate, 'you might not have thrown the first stone at a police constable, but I am satisfied that you were the ring-leader who set such a bad example to the women of the district. I find that women have been taking too prominent a part in these disturbances and I must impose a penalty that will be a deterrent to others. You will go to prison for two months.'

Lily tossed back her mane of dark hair and smiled defiantly. 'It'll be a pleasure!' she said, before the prison officer hustled her downstairs to the cells.

Outside the main door of the courtroom Margaret Ann was still stunned. 'Our Lily . . . in prison?' she whispered. 'Oh, dear God, how will she manage?'

For some reason her reaction made Haydn want to cry. Yet again this narrow-minded, tough little woman had taken him by surprise. He had dreaded leaving the court, as much in anticipation of a rant from Margaret Ann about what the Chapel would think of her having a jailbird daughter as any-thing else. And here she was, oblivious to such superficialities, heart-broken about what Lily would suffer.

'Maybe,' she said in a low voice, 'they'd send me with her, you know, if I refused to pay my fine? At least she wouldn't be all on her own then.'

'You can forget about that straight away, Mam,' said a new voice. They turned to confront David, who had not arrived in Newport early enough to see them in the cells before the hearing. 'Your fine is paid and you'm coming back home, now. The matron from Woollaston House is bringing our Tommy down in a coupla minutes, the police told them I was here for him.'

Margaret Ann choked back a sob. 'To think we was marching on the workhouse and in the end he wound up in it!'

Such false sentimentality was wasted on David. He had real matters to grieve about. 'Aye, well let's hope it's the last time he do ever see the inside of it, is it?' he said with some im-patience. 'Once he's back here with us I wanna go an' see our Lily. Find out what they'll be doing with 'er an' all. I can't see them putting a woman in Cardiff jail.'

The thought of Cardiff jail was enough to set Margaret Ann off again, but she took one look at David's face and thought better of it. Eventually Tommy arrived with the prison matron who had fetched him from the workhouse, and David left him in the care of his grandmother while he went down to see Lily alone.

She was shaky but still defiant. David gazed at her for a long moment, then said: 'What's up, kidda? You look ready to attack me. I'm on your side, remember?'

Lily gave herself a little shake. 'Oh, I'm in a real state after that lot up there.' She bit her lip. 'I – I thought you'd be livid with me.'

David began to laugh. 'Me? When 'ave you ever known that happen? Don't be daft!'

'I never been sent to prison before, have I?'

'No, but like you said, *you'm* the one going to prison, not me. Why should I be angry with you over that?'

'Well, you know, not being there to look after you and Tommy . . . making an exhibition of myself, all like that.'

He reached across the bare table and took both her hands in his. 'Let's get one or two things straight. Yesterday you did something that made me so proud of you I want to shout out about it. Oh, Lily, my love, I'm gonna miss you more than you'll ever understand while you'm in prison, and if I could go there for you, I would. But angry with you? You'm one a the best of us.'

A solitary tear trickled down her cheek and she brushed it aside with the back of her hand. 'I bet Mam is calling down hell an' damnation on me!'

'On the magistrate, more like! She's upstairs with Tommy, Lil, and she'll look after him lovely all the time you're away.' A stray thought brought the smile back to his face. 'Tell the truth, I think she's a bit ashamed of having enjoyed herself so much yesterday. From what I hear she got her revenge on the whole male half of the human race up Bassaleg with her little pile a rocks!'

The prison officer over in the corner stood up and came across. 'You'll have to leave now,' he said. 'Van'll be coming for your wife an' the others soon.'

'Oh . . . er . . . righto. How do I find out where she'll be taken, things like that?'

'Outside. Desk sergeant. Come on, now, off you go . . . '

'Just a minute. Look the other way a tick, will you? I won't

283

see 'er again for two months.' And David came around the table, gathered Lily in his arms and kissed her with greater passion than she had ever known from him. 'I love you,' he whispered. 'I love you so much I wanna burst with it, and don't you ever forget that. Now, go an' show the buggers what you'm made of!'

After that he turned away from her and started to walk out of the room. As he reached the door, she said, almost so quietly he missed it, 'There ent another man on earth like you, Davey Richards. I love you, too, more than you'll ever know.'

He turned back for a moment and said: 'Don't you never forget that, Lily, 'cos if I thought you didn't, I wouldn't want to go on living.'

LILY OF THE VALLEYS

Catrin Morgan

Evan Walters did not intend to marry Margaret Ann Jones when they first met in 1887. He knew they were too different. For one thing, her family were slaves to respectability; and besides, his heart belonged to the lovely but wayward Ellen Rourke.

But Evan never could resist small, helpless creatures. The sudden death of Margaret Ann's parents elicited the long-awaited marriage proposal and she became a miner's wife in the rough end of Abercarn – a far cry from the lace-curtained propriety of her dreams.

From this troubled union a vast brood of children would spring. Of the girls, Lily inherited her father's dark good looks, and looked set to inherit her mother's narrow way of life too. Then a family crisis in 1911 swept her and her sister Bethan off to live at Uncle Rhys's pub in Cardiff.

In that rumbustious, vibrantly alive city, with her exotic cousin Lexie at her side, she would experience a freedom undreamed of in the prudish valleys. When the war came, that too would broaden Lily's horizons, even as the men around her were marching away to the trenches . . .

Lily of the Valleys

FUTURA PUBLICATIONS
FICTION
0 7088 4307 7

HER FATHER'S SINS

Josephine Cox

Queenie seemed born to suffer. Her Mam died giving birth to her, her drunken father George Kenney ignored her unless he was cursing her, and only beloved Auntie Biddy provided an anchor for the little girl. Growing up in post-war Blackburn, life could be tough when Biddy had to take in washing to make ends meet – at a time when the washing machine began to gain popularity. After Auntie Biddy's death there was only Queenie to care for the home and to earn money from the dwindling supply of laundry and no one to protect her from the father who blamed his daughter for her mother's death.

But Queenie was resilient. And in spite of hardship, she grew up tall and strikingly beautiful with her deep grey eyes and her abundant honey-coloured hair. Love, in the shape of Rick Marsden, might have released her from the burden of the drink-sodden George. But the sins of the father would not be easily forgotten . . .

HER FATHER'S SINS

a novel of a young girl's courage and endurance, overshadowed by forbidden love, set against a gritty but warm-hearted world of cobbled streets and flaring gaslamps.

FUTURA PUBLICATIONS
FICTION
0 7088 3639 9

THE CORSICAN WOMAN
Madge Swindells

Sybilia Rocca is uncommonly beautiful. Men admire her and women envy her. A warm and generous woman who endures her hardship with dignity and patience, Sybilia is intelligent, cultured and kind. But she is also Corsican and in her blood run the intense passions of her race – the passions that drive her to shoot her father-in-law before stunned witnesses in the village square of a sea-swept town set high on a Corsican cliffside.

What is the terrible secret – the dark act of treachery that took place twenty years previously – that compels Sybilia to carry out her vendetta? Virtually everyone in her village knows, yet the unwritten law of their impassioned culture keeps them silent. Even Father Andrews, the Irish priest whom she called her friend, shares the knowledge, but he too refuses to talk. And now Sybilia is fighting for her life.

Doctor Jock Walters, an American anthropologist, is the only man who can help her. His search for the truth takes us back to the days before World War Two, when Sybilia, a young girl poised on the brink of womanhood, first arrives in the village of Taita. Through the years of her marriage and the black time of Nazi occupation to the fateful afternoon in August 1960, we discover the forbidden love, the heartbreak and the betrayal experienced by this gentle and courageous woman. And thread by thread the web of deceit is unravelled to reveal the scandal that will decide her fate.

THE CORSICAN WOMAN is a gripping saga of intrigue, suspense and romance woven deftly through a portrait of the Corsican people and the passionate and enduring ties that bind and destroy them.

FUTURA PUBLICATIONS
FICTION
0 7088 4211 9

All Futura Books are available at your bookshop or
newsagent, or can be ordered from the following address:
Futura Books, Cash Sales Department,
P.O. Box 11, Falmouth, Cornwall TR10 9EN.

Please send cheque or postal order (no currency), and
allow 60p for postage and packing for the first book
plus 25p for the second book and 15p for each additional
book ordered up to a maximum charge of £1.90 in U.K.

B.F.P.O. customers please allow 60p for
the first book, 25p for the second book plus 15p per
copy for the next 7 books, thereafter 9p per book

Overseas customers, including Eire, please allow £1.25
for postage and packing for the first book, 75p for the
second book and 28p for each subsequent title ordered.